WELCOME TO ARRAKIS

You have arrived on the planet Arrakis. You will embark on a walking tour of epic proportions. Rarely does a visitor on the road to Dune make his or her way without an Imperium guide. Here is a sampling from such a guide...

— from Frank Herbert's
The Road to Dune

PRAISE FOR *EYE*

"Readers will discover Herbert's fascination with ecology, conservation, religion, fanaticism, and people under stress."

— *The Washington Post*

"Well worth reading."

— *Minneapolis Star*

FRANK HERBERT
EYE

MASTERWORKS
OF SCIENCE FICTION
AND FANTASY

ILLUSTRATED BY
JIM BURNS

A BYRON PREISS
VISUAL PUBLICATIONS, INC.
BOOK

ACE BOOKS, NEW YORK

To Theresa

Introduction copyright © 1985 by Frank Herbert. *Frogs and Scientists* copyright © 1985 by Frank Herbert. Text for *The Road to Dune* copyright © 1985 by Frank Herbert. *Rat Race* copyright © 1955 by Conde Nast Publications, Inc. for *Astounding Science Fiction*. *Dragon in the Sea* appeared as *Under Pressure* in three installments copyright © 1955, 1956 by Conde Nast Publications, Inc. for *Astounding Science Fiction*. *Cease Fire* copyright © 1958 by Conde Nast Publications, Inc. for *Astounding Science Fiction*. *A Matter of Traces* copyright © 1958 by *Fantastic Universe*. *Try to Remember* copyright © 1961 by UPD Publishing Company for *Amazing*. *The Tactful Saboteur* copyright © 1964 by World Editions, Inc. for *Galaxy*. *By the Book* copyright © 1966 by Conde Nast Publications, Inc. for *Analog*. *Seed Stock* copyright © 1970 by Conde Nast Publications, Inc. for *Analog*. *Murder Will In* copyright © 1970 by Mercury Press for *The Magazine of Fantasy and Science Fiction*. *Passage for Piano* copyright © 1973 by World Editions, Inc. for *Galaxy*. *Death of a City* appeared in *Future City*, Trident Press, story copyright © 1973 by Frank Herbert.

This Ace book contains the complete text of the original edition.

EYE
Masterworks of Science Fiction and Fantasy
An Ace Book / published by arrangement with
Byron Preiss Visual Publications, Inc.

PRINTING HISTORY
Berkley trade paperback edition / November 1985
Ace edition / November 1987

ISBN: 0-441-22374-5

Contents

FRANK
HERBERT
EYE

I t was a happy time, an educational time and I was utterly fascinated with making a film of my novel, *Dune*.

———   Early in the experience, I reverted to my background as an investigative reporter. What you read here is editorial comment (subjective) and reportage (as objective as I can make it).

When Sterling Lanier bought *Dune* for Chilton in 1963 we had no ideas about a movie. It was enough that the novel would be published and I could make jokes about Chilton, publisher of many how-to manuals, saying: "They'll want to retitle it *How to Repair Your Ornithopter.*"

My first visit to Churubusco Studios in Mexico City put a different stamp on what it means to adapt a novel to the screen.

The snaking lines of electrical cables, the big yellow buses with "DUNE" on the front, the mobs of people in and around the sound stages, the shops turning out props, costumes and special effects, the pulsing sounds of machinery, the glaring lights, the shouted orders—all said "industry."

It was poetic justice that we should be in Mexico, which had given me an inexpensive place to live when I began writing, and now *Dune* was providing well-paid employment for more than a thousand Mexicans.

I was glad to be back in Mexico and worried about it—a worry borne out by the troubles that plagued shooting the film there: the necessity to bribe Mexican officials before you could work or ship your film; shoddy equipment; some of the worst air in the world; and something apparently no one considered when deciding on a location—in at least some of the major cities, Mexican police *are* the criminal syndicate and corruption goes very high in the government.

The problems created by that corruption were no surprise, but the film industry itself? That was full of surprises.

I had heard many warnings about Dino De Laurentiis, yet I found him honorable and trustworthy. He was a creative force, able to hold back and allow others room to work. Daughter Raffaella was a hard-headed business woman and an organizational powerhouse as concerned as a mother would be about those who depended on her.

Director David Lynch and I hit it off because I understood film to be a language different from English. He spoke it and I was a rank beginner.

To make a film, you *translate*, as though from English to German. Each of the world's languages contains linguistic experiences unique to its own history. You can say things in one language you cannot say in another. I was continually brought up short by the process of taking pages from *Dune* and shifting them to quick visual effects.

Example: *Dune* recreates a feudal society. To impress that on you, the film decor echoes Renaissance (and feudal) Italy—a stroke of genius and visually exciting.

Filming *Dune* did something else. I have David to thank for teaching me to write screenplays. During that education, I was able to influence some decisions about the film, but I was unable to influence the ending or how much would be cut for the theater. From the approximately five hours of film in the original footage, only about two-fifths emerged from the cutting room.

What was cut?

Here's a partial list for the aficionados:

The confrontation between Stilgar (Everett McGill) and Duke Leto (Jurgen Prochnow) where Stilgar spits on the table—the gift of his water.

Development of the relationship between Shadout Mapes (Linda Hunt) and Jessica (Francesca Annis).

Most of the love story between Paul Maud'dib (Kyle MacLachlan) and Chani (Sean Young).

The fight where Paul kills a Fremen and cries (giving water to the dead).

Development of Kynes (Max Von Sydow) as the Imperial Planetologist and (most vital) the place of mélange in a space-faring society.

The relationship between Paul and his mentors: Duncan Idaho (Richard Jordan); Thufir Hawat (Freddie Jones); Gurney Halleck (Patrick Stewart), and Dr. Yueh (Dean Stockwell).

The death of Thufir Hawat.

The relationship between Paul and the Fremen widow, Harah (Molly Wryn).

Scenes with Jessica and The Reverend Mother Mohiam (Sian Phillips) that would have made the Bene Gesserit sisterhood more understandable.

That's only a partial list.

Dino and Raffaella have talked about restoring the out-takes and making a miniseries (à la *The Godfather*). This may happen because Dino wanted a longer film all along.

The film of *Dune* is the result of a paradox—product of an industry that pretends to creativity and shies away from risks. Creation takes risks and that's the movie industry's dilemma. It's why so much control over creativity is in the hands of noncreative people. The reasoning behind their decisions is enlightening.

So many films are aimed primarily at early-to-late teens because this age group is more easily seduced by hype. These also are viewers with time and money and the inclination to join a date at the local cineplex—powerful forces in the entertainment business.

Why a film of only about two hours?

Because that length can be shown more frequently on a day-to-day basis, returning the investment quickly.

Don't condemn this out of hand. If investors had not been found to put up about forty million dollars, *Dune* would never have been filmed. And all of the essentials in the book are on film, even though all of it did not get to your screen.

Never forget it's an industry.

There is more here than meets the eye. One of the most important things is corporate politics. Big corporations are bureaucracies that often promote people who are best at covering their asses. Such people run scared, fearful of any suggestion they can make mistakes. And they surround themselves with others who run the same way.

Don't take risks.

Find out what succeeds and copy it.

Some of the most successful practitioners plagiarize and steal without a qualm, knowing they can stall their victims for years with expensive legal maneuvers. Creativity often has little to do with movie-making except when writing promotional copy.

So what happened with the movie of *Dune*, the sixth biggest money-earner of 1984? What happened to the film that, at this writing, is still number two at the box office in Germany, Japan and France? I can only tell you what I saw.

There was scrambling and many false starts around the film's release, a clear signal of nervousness to audiences, including critics.

Critics who were inclined to be sympathetic were not permitted to see advance screenings.

The hype machine grinded into action, telling people to expect the complete Dune. My efforts were enlisted. I joined in wholeheartedly because I enjoyed the film even as cut and I told it as I saw it: What reached the screen is a visual feast that begins as *Dune* begins and you hear my dialogue all through it.

Overseas there were none of these negative signals and *Dune* set box office records. It was up 29 percent the third week in Great Britain. There were some 40,000 viewers each day the first three days in Paris alone, and to quote a French commentator: "Visually magnificent, rich enough for many repeat viewings."

In Europe you did not find critics bragging (as did one closet aristocrat on CBS): "I don't like movies that make me think." (He wants to feed you "bread and circuses" and keep you docile.)

Was it a success or a failure as a movie? I'm the wrong person to ask. Like me, *Dune* movie audiences, fans and newcomers, wanted more. They would have returned many times to see that "more." What they saw was true to my book, even though most of it stayed on the cutting room floor. *Dune* fans could supply the missing scenes in imagination but they still longed for those scenes.

Investors will get back their investment. There will not be large immediate profits as there might have been had they risked a longer film and satisfied the expectations they raised.

Catering to the lowest common denominator is the way you play the no-risk movie game, and David, with agreement from Dino and Raffaella, went against that directive.

I have my quibbles about the film, of course.

Paul was a man *playing* god, not a god who could make it rain.

Dune was aimed at this whole idea of the infallible leader because my view of history says mistakes made by a leader (or made in a leader's name) are amplified by the numbers who follow without question.

That's how 900 people wound up in Guyana drinking poison Kool-Aid.

That's how the U.S. said "Yes, sir, Mister Charismatic John Kennedy!" and found itself embroiled in Vietnam.

That's how Germany said *"Sieg Heil!"* and murdered more than six million of our fellow human beings.

Leadership and our dependence on it (how and why we choose particular leaders) is a much misunderstood historical phenomenon.

You see, we often get noncreative leaders, people most interested in preserving their own positions. They flock around centers of power. Such centers attract people who can be corrupted. That is a more descriptive observation than to say simply that power corrupts and absolute power corrupts absolutely.

If you are corruptible and your imagination is confined to worries about loss of power, you exist in a self-destructive system. Eventually, as all life does, you must encounter something you did not anticipate, and if you have not strengthened your creative resources, you will have no new ways for adapting to change. Adapt or die, that's the first rule of survival.

The limited vision of noncreative people is not difficult to understand. Creativity frightens the unimaginative. They don't know what's happening. Things new and unexpected arise from creativity. This threatens "things as they are." And (terrible thought) it undermines illusions of omnipotence.

Besides, at least in the movie industry, they "know" an audience can be enticed into the theater by the right promotion. It's all a matter of "hype." You buy an audience.

The next time you watch a political campaign, ask yourself if that sounds familiar.

There is more.

David had trouble with the fact that *Star Wars* used up so much of *Dune*. We found sixteen points of identity between my novel and *Star Wars*. That is not to say this was other than coincidence, even though we figured the odds against coincidence and produced a number larger than the number of stars in the universe.

The fact that David was able to translate the written words

into screen language speaks of his visual genius. If you were disappointed or wanted more, chalk it up to "That's show biz" and pray for the miniseries.

So much for the wonderful world of film and corporate decisions. I recommend you read Ed Naha's "The Making of Dune" and Harlan Ellison's two-part essay in the *Magazine of Fantasy and Science Fiction*. Screen them through my comments.

Don't get the idea from any of this that I'm ungrateful. Making that film was a superb education. And don't take this as a swan song. I'm alive and well and intend to stay that way while I continue writing as long as possible.

It's my opinion that David's film of *Dune* will also be alive and well long after people have forgotten the potboilers that come out of corporate boardrooms. This is based partly on the reactions of everyone who worked on the film: They were sad to be parting when it was over and glad they had done it. The wrap party was a rare scene of happy nostalgia.

Francesca labeled it: "Hard work but great work."

Dune is a film addressed to your audio-visual senses in a unique way, forcing you to participate and not just sit there while it is "done to you." A miniseries restoring the out-takes would make this even more apparent.

That's how I wrote the novel, wanting you to participate with the best of your own imagination. I did not aim for the lowest common denominator and "write down" to anyone. You and I have a compact and my responsibility is to entertain you as richly as possible, always giving you as much extra as I can. I assume you are intelligent and will enlist your own imagination. You'll see that when you read the *Dune* excerpt and the other stories in this collection.

Don't ask yourself if I succeeded or if the film succeeded.

The only valid critic is time. Does it endure? We can only guess and give our opinions. No one living today really knows, but people in the next century certainly will.

RAT
RACE

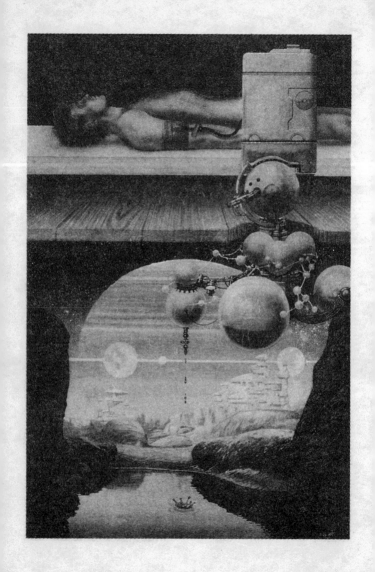

n the nine years it took Welby Lewis to become chief of criminal investigation for Sheriff John Czernak, he came ____ to look on police work as something like solving jigsaw puzzles. It was a routine of putting pieces together into a recognizable picture. He was not prepared to have his cynical police-peopled world transformed into a situation out of H. G. Wells or Charles Fort.

When Lewis said "alien" he meant non-American, not extraterrestrial. Oh, he knew a BEM was a bug-eyed monster; he read some science fiction. But that was just the point—such situations were *fiction*, not to be encountered in police routine. And certainly unexpected at a mortuary. The Johnson-Tule Mortuary, to be exact.

Lewis checked in at his desk in the sheriff's office at five minutes to eight of a Tuesday morning. He was a man of low forehead, thin pinched-in Welsh face, black hair. His eyes were like two pieces of roving green jade glinting beneath bushy brows.

The office, a room of high ceilings and stained plaster walls, was in a first-floor corner of the County Building at Banbury. Beneath one tall window of the room was a cast-iron radiator. Beside the window hung a calendar picture of a girl wearing only a string of pearls. There were two desks facing each other across an aisle which led from the hall door to the radiator. The desk on the left belonged to Joe Welch, the night man. Lewis occupied the one on the right, a cigarette-scarred vintage piece which had stood in this room more than thirty years.

Lewis stopped at the front of his desk, leafed through the papers in the *incoming* basket, looked up as Sheriff Czernak entered. The sheriff, a fat man with wide Slavic features and a complexion like bread crust, grunted as he eased himself into the chair under the calendar. He pushed a brown felt hat to the back of his head, exposing a bald dome.

Lewis said, "Hi, John. How's the wife?" He dropped the papers back into the basket.

17

"Her sciatica's better this week," said the sheriff. "I came in to tell you to skip that burglary report in the basket. A city prowler picked up two punks with the stuff early this moring. We're sending 'em over to juvenile court."

"They'll never learn," said Lewis.

"Got one little chore for you," said the sheriff. "Otherwise everything's quiet. Maybe we'll get a chance to catch up on our paperwork." He hoisted himself out of the chair. "Doc Bellarmine did the autopsy on that Cerino woman, but he left a bottle of stomach washings at the Johnson-Tule Mortuary. Could you pick up the bottle and run it out to the county hospital?"

"Sure," said Lewis. "But I'll bet her death was natural causes. She was a known alcoholic. All those bottles in her shack."

"Prob'ly," said the sheriff. He stopped in front of Lewis's desk, glanced up at the calendar art. "Some dish."

Lewis grinned. "When I find a gal like that, I'm going to get married," he said.

"You do that," said the sheriff. He ambled out of the office.

It was about 8:30 when Lewis cruised past the mortuary in his county car and failed to find a parking place in the block. At the next corner, Cove Street, he turned right and went up the alley, parking on the concrete apron to the mortuary garage.

A southwest wind which had been threatening storm all night kicked up a damp gust as he stepped from the car. Lewis glanced up at the gray sky, but left his raincoat over the back of the seat. He went down the narrow walk beside the garage, found the back door of the mortuary ajar. Inside was a hallway and a row of three metal tanks, the tall kind welders use for oxygen and acetylene gas. Lewis glanced at them, wondered what a mortuary did with that type of equipment, shrugged the question aside. At the other end of the hall the door opened into a carpeted foyer which smelled of musky flowers. A door at the left bore a brass plate labeled OFFICE. Lewis crossed the foyer, entered the room.

Behind a glass-topped desk in the corner sat a tall blond individual type with clear Nordic features. An oak frame on the wall behind him held a colored photograph of Mount Lassen labeled PEACE on an embossed nameplate. An official burial form—partly filled in—was on the desk in front of the man. The left corner of the desk held a brass cup in which sat a metal ball. The ball emitted a hissing noise as Lewis approached and he breathed in the heavy floral scent of the foyer.

The man behind the desk got to his feet, put a pen across the burial form. Lewis recognized him—Johnson, half owner of the mortuary.

"May I help you?" asked the mortician.

Lewis explained his errand.

Johnson brought a small bottle from a desk drawer, passed it across to Lewis, then looked at the deputy with a puzzled frown. "How'd you get in?" asked the mortician. "I didn't hear the front door chimes."

The deputy shoved the bottle into a side pocket of his coat. "I parked in the alley and came in the back way," he said. "The street out front is full of Odd Fellows cars."

"Odd Fellows?" Johnson came around the desk.

"Paper said they were having some kind of rummage sale today," said Lewis. He ducked his head to look under the shade on the front window. "I guess those are Odd Fellows cars. That's the hall across the street."

An ornamental shrub on the mortuary front lawn bent before the wind and a spattering of rain drummed against the window. Lewis straightened. "Left my raincoat in the car," he said. "I'll just duck out the way I came."

Johnson moved to his office door. "Two of our attendants are due back now on a call," he said. "They—"

"I've seen a stiff before," said Lewis. He stepped past Johnson, headed for the door to the rear hall.

Johnson's hand caught the deputy's shoulder. "I must insist you go out the front," said the mortician.

Lewis stopped, his mind setting up a battery of questions. "It's raining out," he said. "I'll get all wet."

"I'm sorry," said Johnson.

Another man might have shrugged and complied with Johnson's request, but Welby Lewis was the son of the late Proctor Lewis, who had been three times president of the Banbury County Sherlock Holmes Round Table. Welby had cut his teeth on *logical deduction* and the logic of this situation escaped him. He reviewed his memory of the hallway. Empty except for those tanks near the back door.

"What do you keep in those metal tanks?" he asked.

The mortician's hand tightened on his shoulder and Lewis

felt himself turned toward the front door. "Just embalming fluid," said Johnson. "That's the way it's delivered."

"Oh." Lewis looked up at Johnson's tightly drawn features, pulled away from the restraining hand and went out the front door. Rain was driving down and he ran around the side of the mortuary to his car, jumping in, slammed the door and sat down to wait. At 9:28 A.M. by his wristwatch an assistant mortician came out, opened the garage doors. Lewis leaned across the front seat, rolled down his right window.

"You'll have to move your car," said the assistant. "We're going out on a call."

"When are the other fellows coming back?" asked Lewis.

The mortician stopped halfway inside the garage. "What other fellows?" he asked.

"The ones who went out on that call this morning."

"Must be some other mortuary," said the assistant. "This is our first call today."

"Thanks," said Lewis. He rolled up his window, started the car and drove to the county hospital. The battery of unanswered questions churned in his mind. Foremost was—*Why did Johnson lie to keep me from going out the back way?*

At the hospital he delivered the bottle to the pathology lab, found a pay booth and called the Banbury Mortuary. An attendant answered and Lewis said, "I want to settle a bet. Could you tell me how embalming fluid is delivered to mortuaries?"

"We buy it by the case in concentrated form," said the mortician. "Twenty-four glass bottles to the case, sixteen ounces to the bottle. It contains red or orange dye to give a lifelike appearance. Our particular brand smells somewhat like strawberry soda. There is nothing offensive about it. We guarantee that the lifelike—"

"I just wanted to know how it came," said Lewis. "You're sure it's never delivered in metal tanks?"

"Good heavens, no!" said the man. "It'd corrode them!"

"Thanks," said Lewis and hung up softly. In his mind was the Holmesian observation: *If a man lies about an apparently inconsequential thing, then that thing is not inconsequential.*

He stepped out of the booth and bumped into Dr. Bellarmine, the autopsy surgeon. The doctor was a tall, knobby character with gray hair, sun-lamp tan and blue eyes as cutting as two scalpels.

"Oh, there you are, Lewis," he said. "They told me you were down this way. We found enough alcohol in that Cerino woman to kill three people. We'll check the stomach washings, too, but I doubt they'll add anything."

"Cerino woman?" asked Lewis.

"The old alcoholic you found in that shack by the round-house," said Bellarmine. "You losing your memory?"

"Oh...oh, certainly," said Lewis. "I was just thinking of something else. Thanks, Doc." He brushed past the surgeon. "Gotta go now," he muttered.

Back at his office Lewis sat on a corner of his desk, pulled the telephone to him and dialed the Johnson-Tule Mortuary. An unfamiliar masculine voice answered. Lewis said, "Do you do cremations at your mortuary?"

"Not *at* our mortuary," said the masculine voice, "but we have an arrangement with Rose Lawn Memorial Crematorium. Would you care to stop by and discuss your problem?"

"Not right now, thank you," said Lewis, and replaced the phone on its hook. He checked off another question in his mind—the possibility that the tanks held gas for a cremato-rium. *What the devil's in those tanks?* he asked himself.

"Somebody die?" The voice came from the doorway, break-ing into Lewis's reverie. The deputy turned, saw Sheriff Czernak.

"No," said Lewis. "I've just got a puzzle." He went around the desk to his chair, sat down.

"Doc Bellarmine say anything about the Cerino dame?" asked the sheriff. He came into the room, eased himself into the chair beneath the calendar art.

"Alcoholism," said Lewis. "Like I said." He leaned back in his chair, put his feet on the desk and stared at a stained spot on the ceiling.

"What's niggling you?" asked the sheriff. "You look like a guy trying to solve a conundrum."

"I am," said Lewis and told him about the incident at the mortuary.

Czernak took off his hat, scratched his bald head. "It don't sound like much to me, Welby. In all probability there's a very simple explanation."

"I don't think so," said Lewis.

"Why not?"

Lewis shook his head. "I don't know. I just don't think so. Something about that mortuary doesn't ring true."

"What you think's in them tanks?" asked the sheriff.

"I don't know," said Lewis.

The sheriff seated his hat firmly on his head. "Anybody else I'd tell 'em forget it," he said. "But you, I dunno. I seen you pull too many rabbits out of the hat. Sometimes I think you're a freak an' see inside people."

"I am a freak," said Lewis. He dropped his feet to the floor, pulled a scratchpad to him and began doodling.

"Yeah, I can see you got six heads," said the sheriff.

"No, really," said Lewis. "My heart's on the right side of my chest."

"I hadn't noticed," said the sheriff. "But now you point it out to me—"

"Freak," said Lewis. "That's what I felt looking at that mortician. Like he was some kind of a creepy freak."

He pushed the scratchpad away from him. It bore a square broken into tiny segments by zigzag lines. Like a jigsaw puzzle.

"Was he a freak?"

Lewis shook his head. "Not that I could see."

Czernak pushed himself out of his chair. "Tell you what," he said. "It's quiet today. Why'ncha nose around a little?"

"Who can I have to help me?" asked Lewis.

"Barney Keeler'll be back in about a half hour," said Czernak. "He's deliverin' a subpoena for Judge Gordon."

"O.K.," said Lewis. "When he gets back, tell him to go over to the Odd Fellows Hall and go in the back way without attracting too much attention. I want him to go up to that tower room and keep watch on the front of the mortuary, note down everybody who enters or leaves and watch for those tanks. If the tanks go out, he's to tail the carrier and find out where they go."

"What're you gonna do?" asked the sheriff.

"Find a place where I can keep my eye on the back entrance. I'll call in when I get set." Lewis hooked a thumb toward the desk across from his. "When Joe Welch comes on, send him over to spell me."

"Right," said Czernak. "I still think maybe you're coon-doggin' it up an empty tree."

"Maybe I am," said Lewis. "But something shady about a mortuary gives my imagination the jumps. I keep thinking of how easy it could be for a mortician to get rid of an inconvenient corpse."

"Stuff it in one of them tanks, maybe?" asked the sheriff.

"No. They weren't big enough." Lewis shook his head. "I just don't like the idea of the guy lying to me."

It was shortly after 10:30 A.M. when Lewis found what he needed—a doctor's office in the rear of a building across the alley and two doors up from the mortuary garage. The doctor had three examining rooms on the third floor, the rear room looking down on the mortuary backyard. Lewis swore the doctor and his nurse to secrecy, set himself up in the back room with a pair of field glasses.

At noon he sent the nurse out for a hamburger and glass of milk for his lunch, had her watch the mortuary yard while he called his office and told the day radio operator where he was.

The doctor came into the back room at five o'clock, gave Lewis an extra set of keys for the office, asked him to be certain the door was locked when he left. Again Lewis warned the doctor against saying anything about the watch on the mortuary, stared the man down when it appeared he was about to ask questions. The doctor turned, left the room. Presently, a door closed solidly. The office was silent.

At about 7:30 it became too dark to distinguish clearly anything that might happen in the mortuary backyard. Lewis considered moving to a position in the alley, but two floodlights above the yard suddenly flashed on and the amber glow of a night light came from the window in the back door.

Joe Welch pounded on the door of the doctor's office at 8:20; Lewis admitted him, hurried back to the window with Welch following. The other deputy was a tall, nervous chain-smoker with a perpetual squint, a voice like a bassoon. He moved to a position beside Lewis at the window, said, "What's doing? Sheriff John said something about some acetylene tanks."

"It may be nothing at all," said Lewis. "But I've a feeling we're onto something big." In a few short sentences he explained about his encounter with the mortician that morning.

"Don't sound exciting to me," said Welch. "What you expecting to find in those tanks?"

"I wish I knew," said Lewis.

Welch went into the corner of the darkened room, lighted a cigarette, returned. "Why don't you just ask this Johnson?"

"That's the point," said Lewis. "I did ask him and he lied to me. That's why I'm suspicious. I've been hoping they'd take those tanks out and we could trail them to wherever they go. Get our answer that way."

"Why're you so sure it's the tanks he didn't want you to see?" asked Welch.

"That was a funny hallway," said Lewis. "Door at each end, none along the sides. Only things in it were those tanks."

"Well, those tanks might already be gone," said Welch. "You didn't get on this end until about ten-thirty, you said, and Keeler wasn't on the front until about eleven. They could've been taken out then if they're so all-fired important."

"I've had the same thought," said Lewis. "But I don't think they have. I'm going out to grab a bite to eat now, then I'm going down in the alley for a closer look."

"You won't get very close with all them lights on the yard," said Welch.

Lewis pointed to the garage. "If you look close you can see a space along the other side; in the shadow there. The light's on in the back hall. I'll try to get close enough for a look through the window in that rear door. They're tall tanks. I should be able to see them."

"And if they've been moved someplace else in the building?" asked Welch.

"Then I'll have to go in and brace Johnson for a showdown," said Lewis. "Maybe I should've done that in the first place, but this is a screwy situation. I just don't like a mystery in a mortuary."

"Sounds like the title of a detective story," said Welch. "'Mystery in a Mortuary.'"

Welch sniffed. "There's already death inside there," he said. "This could be something mighty unpleasant."

Welch lighted a new cigarette from the coal of the one he had been smoking, stubbed out the discard in a dish Lewis had been using for an ash tray. "You may be right," said Welch. "The only thing impresses me about this she-bang, Welby, is like Sheriff John said—I've seen you pull too many rabbits out of the hat."

"That's what he told you?" asked Lewis.

"Yeah, but he thinks maybe you're gonna pull a blank this time." Welch stared down at the mortuary. "If you go inside, do you want me to round up a few of my men and smother the place if you don't come out by some set time?"

"I don't think that'll be necessary," said Lewis. "Don't take any action unless you see something suspicious."

Welch nodded his head. "O.K.," he said. He looked at the glowing tip of his cigarette, glanced down at the yard they were watching. "Mortuaries give me the creeps anyway," he said.

Lewis bolted down a hot beef sandwich at a cafe two blocks from the mortuary, returned along a back street. It was cold and wet in the alley. A perverse wind kept tangling the skirts of his raincoat. He hugged the shadows near the mortuary garage, found the row of boards which had been nailed across the area he was going to use. Lewis clambered over the boards, dropped to soft earth which was out of the wind but under a steady dripping from unguttered eaves. He moved quietly to the end of the shadow area and, as he had expected, could see inside the window on the rear door of the mortuary. The tanks were not visible. Lewis cursed under his breath, shrugged, stepped out of the shadows and crossed the lighted backyard. The door was locked, but he could see through the window that the hallway was empty. He went around to the front door, rang the night bell.

A man in a rumpled black suit which looked as though he had slept in it answered the door. Lewis brushed past him into the warm flower smell of the foyer. "Is Johnson here?" he asked.

"Mr. Johnson is asleep," said the man. "May I be of service?"

"Ask Mr. Johnson to come down, please," said Lewis. "This is official business." He showed his badge.

"Of course," said the man. "If you'll go into the office there and have a seat, I'll tell Mr. Johnson you're here. He sleeps in the quarters upstairs."

"Thanks," said Lewis. He went into the office, looked at the colored photograph of Mount Lassen until the night attendant had disappeared up the stairs at the other end of the foyer. Then Lewis came out of the office, went to the doorway leading into the hall. The door was locked. He tried forcing it, but it wouldn't budge. He moved to the hinge side, found a thin crack which gave a view of the other end of the hall. What he saw made him draw a quick breath. The three metal tanks were right where he had expected them to be. He went back to the office, found a directory and looked up the number of the doctor's office where Welch was waiting, dialed the number. After a long wait Welch's voice came on the line, tones guarded. "Yes?"

"This is Welby," said Lewis. "Anything come in the back?"

"No," said Welch. "You all right?"

"I'm begining to wonder," said Lewis. "Keep your eyes peeled." He hung up, turned to find Johnson's tall figure filling the office doorway.

"Mr. Lewis," said Johnson. "Is something wrong?" He came into the office.

"I want to have a look at those metal tanks," said Lewis.

Johnson stopped. "What metal tanks?"

"The ones in your back hall," said Lewis.

"Oh, the embalming fluid," said Johnson. "What's the interest in embalming fluid?"

"Let's just have a look at it," said Lewis.

"Do you have a warrant?" asked Johnson.

Lewis's chin jerked up and he stared at the man. "I wouldn't have a bit of trouble getting one," he said.

"On what grounds?"

"I could think of something that'd stick," said Lewis. "Are we going to do this the easy way or the hard way?"

Johnson shrugged. "As you wish." He led the way out of the office, unlocked the hall door, preceded Lewis down the hallway to the three tanks.

"I thought embalming fluid came in sixteen-ounce glass bottles," said Lewis.

"This is something new," said Johnson. "These tanks have glass inner liners. The fluid is kept under pressure." He turned a valve and an acrid spray emerged from a fitting at the top.

Lewis took a shot in the dark, said, "That doesn't smell like embalming fluid."

Johnson said, "It's a new type. We add the masking perfumes later."

"You just get these filled?" asked Lewis.

"No, these were delivered last week," said Johnson. "We've left them here because we don't have a better place to store them." He smiled at Lewis, but the eyes remained cold, watchful. "Why this interest?"

"Call it professional curiosity," said Lewis. He went to the rear door, unlatched it and locked the latch in the open position, stepped outside, closed the door. He could see the tanks plainly through the window. He came back into the hallway.

He's still lying to me, thought Lewis. *But it's all so very plausible.* He said, "I'm going to give your place a thorough search."

"But why?" protested Johnson.

"For no good reason at all," said Lewis. "If you want, I'll go out and get a warrant." He started to brush past Johnson, was stopped by a strong hand on his shoulder, something hard pressing into his side. He looked down, saw a flat automatic menacing him.

"I regret this," said Johnson. "Believe me, I do."

"You're going to regret it more," said Lewis. "I have your place watched front and back and the office knows where I am."

For the first time he saw a look of indecision on Johnson's face. "You're lying," said the mortician.

"Come here," said Lewis. He stepped to the back door, looked up to the black window where Welch stood. The glow of the deputy's cigarette was plainly visible, an orange wash against the blackness. Johnson saw it, "Now let's go check the front," said Lewis.

"No need," said Johnson. "I thought you were playing a lone hand." He paused. "You came in the backyard again and had a look in the window, didn't you?"

"What do you think?" asked Lewis.

"I should've anticipated that," said Johnson. "Perhaps I was too anxious to have things appear just as they were. You startled me coming in here at night like this."

"You saw me come in the front?" asked Lewis.

"Let us say that I was aware you were downstairs before the attendant told me," said Johnson. He gestured with his gun. "Let's go back to the office."

Lewis led the way down the hall. At the foyer door he glanced back.

"Turn around!" barked Johnson.

But the one glance had been enough. The tanks were gone.

"What was that humming sound?" asked Lewis.

"Just keep moving," said Johnson.

In the front office the mortician motioned Lewis to a chair. "What were you looking for?" asked Johnson. He slid into the chair behind his desk, rested his gun hand on the desk top.

"I found what I was looking for," said Lewis.

"And that is?"

"Evidence to confirm my belief that this place should be taken apart brick by brick."

Johnson smiled, hooked the telephone to him with his left hand, took off the receiver and rested it on the desk. "What's your office number?"

Lewis told him.

Johnson dialed, picked up the phone, said, "Hello, this is Lewis."

Lewis came half out of the chair. His own voice was issuing from Johnson's mouth. The gun in the mortician's hand waved him back to the chair.

"You got the dope on what I'm doing?" asked Johnson. He waited. "No. Nothing important. I'm just looking." Again he paused. "I'll tell you if I find anything," he said. He replaced the phone in its cradle.

"Well?" said Lewis.

Johnson's lips thinned. "This is incredible," he said. "A mere human—." He broke off, stared at Lewis, said, "My mistake was in telling you a plausible lie after that door was left open. I should have—." He shrugged.

"You couldn't hope to fool us forever," said Lewis.

"I suppose not," said Johnson, "but reasoning tells me that there is still a chance." The gun suddenly came up, its muzzle pointing at Lewis. "It's a chance I have to take," said the mortician. The gun belched flame and Lewis was slammed back in his chair. Through a dimming haze, he saw Johnson put the gun to his own head, pull the trigger, slump across the desk. Then the haze around Lewis thickened, became the black nothing of unconsciousness.

From a somewhere he could not identify Lewis became aware of himself. He was running through a black cave, chased by a monster with blazing eyes and arms like an octopus. The monster kept shouting, "A mere human! A mere human! A mere human!" with a voice that echoed as though projected into a rain barrel. Then, above the voice of the monster, Lewis heard water dripping in a quick even cadence. At the same time he saw the mouth of the cave, a round bright area. The bright area grew larger, larger, became the white wall of a hospital room and a window with sunshine outside. Lewis turned his head, saw a metal tank like the ones in the mortuary.

A voice said, "That brought him around."

Vertigo swept over Lewis and for a moment he fought it. A white-clad figure swam into his field of vision, resolved itself into a county hospital intern whom Lewis recognized. The intern held a black oxygen mask.

The sound of the dripping water was louder now and then he realized that it was a wristwatch. He turned toward the sound, saw Sheriff Czernak straighten from a position close to his head. Czernak's Slavic face broke into a grin. "Boy, you gave us a scare," he said.

Lewis swallowed, found his voice. "What—"

"You know, you are lucky you're a freak," said Czernak. "Your heart being on the right side's the only thing saved you. That and the fact that Joe heard the shots."

The intern came around beside the sheriff. "The bullet nicked an edge of your lung and took a little piece out of a rib at the back," said the intern. "You must've been born lucky."

"Johnson?" said Lewis.

"Deader'n a mackerel," said Czernak. "You feel strong enough to tell us what happened? Joe's story don't make sense. What's with these tanks of embalming fluid?"

Lewis thought about his encounter with the mortician. Nothing about it made sense. He said, "Embalming fluid comes in sixteen-ounce bottles."

"We got those three tanks from the hallway," said Czernak, "but I don't know what we're doing with them."

"From the hall?" Lewis remembered his last look at the empty hall before Johnson had ordered him to turn around. He tried to push himself up, felt pain knife through his chest. The intern pushed him gently back to the pillow. "Here now, none of that," he said. "You just stay flat on your back."

"What was in the tanks?" whispered Lewis.

"The lab here says it's embalming fluid," said the sheriff. "What's so special about it?"

Lewis remembered the acrid odor of the spray Johnson had

released from the tank valve. "Does the lab still have some of that fluid?" he asked. "I'd like to smell it."

"I'll get it," said the intern. "Don't let him sit up. It could start a hemorrhage." He went out the door.

"Where were the tanks when you found them?" asked Lewis.

"Down by the back door," said Czernak. "Where you said they were. Why?"

"I don't really know yet," said Lewis. "But I've something I wish you'd do. Take a—"

The door opened and the intern entered, a test tube in his hand. "This is the stuff," he said. He passed the tube under Lewis's nose. It gave off a musklike sweet aroma. It was not what he had smelled at the tanks. *That explains why the tanks disappeared,* he thought. *Somebody switched them. But what was in the others?* He looked up at the intern, said, "Thanks."

"You were sayin' something," said the sheriff.

"Yes," said Lewis. "Take a crew over to that mortuary, John, and rip out the wall behind where you found those tanks and take up the floor under that spot."

"What're we supposed to find?" asked Czernak.

"Damned if I know," said Lewis, "but it sure should be interesting. Those tanks kept disappearing and reappearing every time I turned my back. I want to know why."

"Look, Welby, we've got to have something solid to go on," said the sheriff. "People are running around that mortuary like crazy, saying it's bad business an' what all."

"I'd say this was good for business," said Lewis, a brief smile forming on his lips. His face sobered. "Don't you think it's enough that somebody tried to kill one of your men and then committed suicide?"

The sheriff scratched his head. "I guess so, Welby. You sure you can't give me anything more'n just your hunch?"

"You know as much about this as I do," said Lewis. "By the way, where's Johnson's body?"

"They're fixin' it up for burial," said Czernak. "Welby, I really should have more'n just your say so. The D.A. will scream if I get too heavy-handed."

"You're still the sheriff," said Lewis.

"Well, can't you even tell me why Johnson killed himself?"

"Say he was mentally unbalanced," said Lewis. "And John, here's something else. Get Doc Bellarmine to do the autopsy on Johnson and tell him to go over that body with a magnifying glass."

"Why?"

"It was something he said about mere humans," said Lewis.

"Askin' me to stick my neck out like this," said Czernak.

"Will you do it?" asked Lewis.

"Sure I'll do it!" exploded Czernak. "But I don't like it!" He jammed his hat onto his head, strode out of the room.

The intern turned to follow.

Lewis said, "What time is it?"

The intern stopped, glanced at his wristwatch. "Almost five." He looked at Lewis. "We've had you under sedatives since you came out of the operating room."

"Five A.M. or five P.M.?" asked Lewis.

"Five P.M.," said the intern.

"Was I a tough job?" asked Lewis.

"It was a clean wound," said the intern. "You take it easy now. It's almost chow time. I'll see that you're served in the first round and then I'll have the nurse bring you a sedative. You need your rest."

"How long am I going to be chained to this bed?" asked Lewis.

"We'll discuss that later," said the intern. "You really shouldn't be talking." He turned away, went out the door.

Lewis turned his head away, saw that someone had left a stack of magazines on his bed stand. The top magazine had slipped down, exposing the cover. It was done in garish colors— a bug-eyed monster chasing a scantily clad female. Lewis was reminded of his nightmare. *A mere human . . . A mere human.* The words kept turning over in his mind. *What was it about Johnson that brought up the idea of a freak?* he wondered.

A student nurse brought in his tray, cranked up his bed and helped him eat. Presently, a nurse came in with a hypo, shot him in the arm. He drifted off to sleep with the mind full of questions still unanswered.

"He's awake now," said a female voice. Lewis heard a door open, looked up to see Czernak followed by Joe Welch. It was daylight outside, raining. The two men wore damp raincoats, which they took off and draped over chairs.

Lewis smiled at Welch. "Thanks for having good ears, Joe," he said.

Welch grinned. "I opened the window when I saw you come out the back door," he said. "I thought maybe you was going to holler something up to me. Then when you went right back inside, I thought that was funny; so I left the window partly open or I'd never've heard a thing."

Czernak pulled a chair up beside Lewis's bed, sat down. Welch took a chair at the foot.

Lewis turned his head toward the sheriff. "Is the D.A. screaming yet?"

"No," said Czernak. "He got caught out in that rainstorm the other day and he's home with the flu. Besides, I'm still sheriff of this county." He patted the bed. "How you feeling, boy?"

"I'm afraid I'm gonna live," said Lewis.

"You better," said Welch. "We got a new relief radio gal who saw your picture in the files an' says she wants to meet you. She's a wow."

"Tell her to wait for me," said Lewis. He looked at the sheriff. "What'd you find?"

"I don't get it, Welby," said Czernak. "Right behind where them tanks was there was this brick wall covered with plaster. We took away the plaster and there's all these wires, see."

"What kind of wires?"

"That's just it, Keeler's old man is a jeweler and Keeler says this wire is silver. It's kind of a screen like, criss-crossed every which way."

"What were they hooked up to?"

"To nothing we could find," said Czernak. He looked at Welch. "Ain't that right?"

"Nothing there but this wire," said Welch.

"What did you do with it?" asked Lewis.

"Nothing," said Czernak. "We just left like it was and took pictures."

"Anything under the floor?"

Czernak's face brightened. "Boy, we sure hit the jackpot there!" He bent his head and peered closely at Lewis. "How'd you know we'd find something under there?"

"I just knew those tanks kept appearing out of nowhere," said Lewis. "What was under there?"

Czernak straightened. "Well, a whole section of the hall floor was an elevator and down below there was this big room. It stretched from under the hall to clear under the embalming room and there was a section of the embalming room floor where a bunch of tiles come up in one piece and there was a trapdoor and a stairway. Hell! It was just like one of them horror movies!"

"What was down there?"

"A buncha machinery," said Czernak.

"What kind?"

"I dunno." Czernak shook his head, glanced at Welch.

"Craziest stuff I ever saw," said Welch. He shrugged.

"Doc Bellarmine came down and had a look at it after the autopsy last night," said Czernak. "He said he'd be in to see you this morning."

"Did he say anything about the autopsy?" asked Lewis.

"Not to me," said Czernak.

Welch hitched his chair closer to the foot of the bed, rested an arm on the rail. "He told me it was something about the autopsy made him come down to have a look at the mortuary," he said. "He didn't say what it was, though."

"What about the mortuary staff?" asked Lewis. "Did they say anything about the secret room?"

"They swear they never even knew it was there," said Czernak. "We took 'em all into custody anyway, all except Tule and his wife."

"Tule?"

"Yeah, the other partner. His wife was a licensed mortician, too. Ain't been seen since the night you were shot. The staff says that Johnson, Tule and the wife was always locking doors around the building for no good reason at all."

"What did this machinery look like?"

"Part of it was just an elevator for that section of floor. The other stuff was hooked up to a bunch of pipes coming down from the embalming table upstairs. There was this big—." Czernak stopped as the door opened.

Dr. Bellarmine's cynical face peered into the room. His eyes swept over the occupants; he entered, closed the door behind him. "The patient's feeling better, I see," he said. "For a while there I thought this would be a job for me in my official capacity."

"This guy'll outlive all of us," said Welch.

"He probably will at that," said the doctor. He glanced down at Lewis. "Feel like a little conversation?"

"Just a minute, Doc," said Lewis. He turned to Czernak. "John, I have one more favor," he said. "Could you get one of those tanks of embalming fluid to a welding shop and have it cut open with a burner. I want to know how it's made inside."

"No, you don't," said Czernak. "I'm not leavin' here without some kind of an explanation."

"And I don't have an explanation," said Lewis. "All the pieces aren't together yet. I'm tied to this bed when I should be out working on this thing. I've ten thousand questions I want answered and no way of answering them."

"Don't excite yourself," said Bellarmine.

"Yeah, Welby, take it easy," said Czernak. "It's just that I'm about ready to pop with frustration. Nothing makes sense here. This guy tries to kill you for no apparent reason and then commits suicide. It seems to be because you wanted to look inside them tanks, but they're just embalming fluid. I don't get it."

"Would you have those tanks cut open for me?" asked Lewis.

"O.K., O.K." Czernak hoisted himself to his feet. Welch also arose. "Come on, Joe," said the sheriff. "We're nothin' but a couple of leg men for Sherlock here. Let's take them—"

"John, I'm sorry," said Lewis. "It's just that I can't—"

"I know you can't do it yourself now," said Czernak. "That's why I'm doing it. You're the best man I got, Welby; so I'm countin' on you to put this together. Me, I gave up when I saw that machinery." He left the room, muttering, followed by Welch, who stopped at the door, winked at Lewis.

Bellarmine waited until the door closed, sat down on the foot of the bed. "How'd you get onto them?" he asked.

Lewis ignored the question. "What'd you find in that autopsy?" he asked.

The surgeon frowned. "I thought you were nuts when the sheriff told me what you wanted," he said. "Any fool could see Johnson died of a gunshot wound in the head. But I guessed you had a reason; so I did my cutting carefully and it was a lucky thing I did."

"Why?"

"Well, this is the kind of case an autopsy surgeon sloughs off sometimes. Visible wound. Obvious cause. I could've missed it. The guy looked to be normal."

"Missed what?"

"His heart, for one thing. It had an extra layer of muscles in the cardiac sheath. I experimented with them and near dropped my knife. They work like that automatic sealing device they put in airplane fuel tanks. Puncture the heart and this muscle layer seals the hole until the heart's healed."

"Damn!" said Lewis.

"This guy was like that all over," said Bellarmine. "For a long time doctors have looked at the human body with the wish they could redesign certain things to better specifications. Johnson looked like our wish had come true. Fewer vertebrae with better articulation. Pigment veins into the pupil of the eye which could only be some kind of filter to—"

"That's it!" Lewis slapped the bed with the palm of his hand. "There was something freakish about him and I couldn't focus on it. The pupils of his eyes changed color. I can remember seeing it and—"

"You didn't see anything," said Bellarmine. "His pelvic floor was broader and distributed the weight more evenly to the legs. The feet had larger bones and more central distribution of weight over the arch. There was an interlaced membranous support for the viscera. His circulatory system had sphincter valves at strategic points to control bleeding. This Johnson may have looked human on the outside, but inside he was superhuman."

"What about the machinery in the mortuary basement?" asked Lewis.

Bellarmine stood up, began to pace the floor, back and forth at the foot of the bed. Presently he stopped, put his hands on the rail, stared at Lewis. "I spent half the night examining that layout," he said. "It was one of the most beautifully designed and executed rigs I've ever seen. Its major purpose was to take cadaver blood and fractionate the protein."

"You mean like for making plasma and stuff like that?" asked Lewis.

"Well, something like that," said Bellarmine.

"I didn't think you could use the blood of a corpse for that," said Lewis.

"We didn't either," said the surgeon. "The Russians have been working on it, however. Our experience has been that it breaks down too quickly. We've tried—"

"You mean this was a Communist set-up?"

Bellarmine shook his head. "No such luck. This rig wasn't just foreign to the U.S.A. It was foreign to Earth. There's one centrifugal pump in there that spins free in an air blast. I shudder every time I think of the force it must generate. We don't have an alloy that'll come anywhere near standing up to those strains. And the Russians don't have it, either."

"How can you be sure?"

"For one thing, there are several research projects that are awaiting this type of rig and the Russians have no more results on those projects than we have."

"Then something was produced from cadaver blood and was stored in those tanks," said Lewis.

Bellarmine nodded. "I checked. A fitting on the tanks matched one on the machinery."

Lewis pushed himself upright, ignoring the pain in his chest. "Then this means an extraterrestrial in—." The pain in his chest became too much and he sagged back to the pillow.

Dr. Bellarmine was suddenly at his side. "You fool!" he barked. "You were told to take it easy." He pushed the emergency button at the head of the bed, began working on the bandages.

"What's matter?" whispered Lewis.

"Hemorrhage," said Bellarmine. "Where's that fool nurse? Why doesn't she answer the bell?" He stripped away a length of adhesive.

The door opened and a nurse entered, stopped as she saw the scene.

"Emergency tray," said Bellarmine. "Get Dr. Edwards here to assist! Bring plasma!"

Lewis heard a drum begin to pound inside his head—louder, louder, louder. Then it began to fade and there was nothing.

He awoke to a rustling sound and footsteps. Then he recognized it. The sound of a nurse's starched uniform as she moved about the room. He opened his eyes and saw by the shadows outside that it was afternoon.

"So you're awake," said the nurse.

Lewis turned his head toward the sound. "You're new," he said. "I don't recognize you."

"Special," she said. "Now you just take it easy and don't try to move." She pushed the call button.

It seemed that almost immediately Dr. Bellarmine was in the

room bending over Lewis. The surgeon felt Lewis's wrist, took a deep breath. "You went into shock," he said. "You have to remain quiet. Don't try to move around."

His voice low and husky, Lewis said, "Could I ask some questions?"

"Yes, but only for a few minutes. You have to avoid any kind of exertion."

"What'd the sheriff find out about the tanks?"

Bellarmine grimaced. "They couldn't open them. Can't cut the metal."

"That confirms it," said Lewis. "Think there are any other rigs like that?"

"There have to be," said Bellarmine. He sat down on a chair at the head of the bed. "I've had another look at that basement layout and took a machinist with me. He agrees. Everything about it cries out mass production. Mostly cast fittings with a minimum of machining. Simple, efficient construction."

"Why? What good's the blood from human cadavers?"

"I've been asking myself that same question," said Bellarmine. "Maybe for a nutrient solution for culture growths. Maybe for the antibodies."

"Would they be any good?"

"That depends on how soon the blood was extracted. The time element varies with temperature, body condition, a whole barrel full of things."

"But why?"

The surgeon ran a hand through his gray hair. "I don't like my answer to that question," he said. "I keep thinking of how we fractionate the blood of guinea pigs, how we recover vaccine from chick embryos, how we use all of our test animals."

Lewis's eyes fell on the dresser across his room. Someone had taken the books from his night stand and put them on the dresser. He could still see the bug-eyed monster cover.

"From what I know of science fiction," said Lewis, "that silver grid in the hall must be some kind of matter transmitter for sending the tanks to wherever they're used. I wonder why they didn't put it downstairs with the machinery."

"Maybe it had to be above ground," said Bellarmine. "You figure it the same way I do."

"You're a hard-headed guy, Doc," said Lewis. "How come you go for this bug-eyed monster theory?"

"It was the combination," said Bellarmine. "That silver grid, the design of the machinery and its purpose, the strange metals, the differences in Johnson. It all spells A-L-I-E-N, alien. But I could say the same holds for you, Lewis. What put you wise?"

"Johnson. He called me a *mere human*. I got to wondering how alien a guy could be to separate himself from the human race."

"It checks," said Bellarmine.

"Buy why guinea pigs?" asked Lewis.

The surgeon frowned, looked at the floor, back at Lewis. "That rig had a secondary stage," he said. "It could have only one function—passing live virus under some kind of bombardment—X-ray or beta ray or whatever—and depositing the mutated strain in a little spray container about as big as your fist. I know from my own research experience that some mutated virus can be deadly."

"Germ warfare," whispered Lewis. "You sure it isn't the Russians?"

"I'm sure. This was a perfect infecting center. Complete. Banbury would've been decimated by now if that's what it was."

"Maybe they weren't ready."

"Germ warfare is ready when one infecting center is set up. No. This rig was for producing slight alterations in common germs or I miss my guess. This little spray container went into a..."

"Rack on Johnson's desk," said Lewis.

"Yeah," said Bellarmine.

"I saw it," said Lewis. "I thought it was one of those deodorant things." He picked a piece of lint off the covers. "So they're infecting us with mutated virus."

"It scares me," said Bellarmine.

Lewis squinted his eyes, looked up at the surgeon. "Doc, what would you do if you found out that one of your white rats was not only intelligent but had found out what you were doing to it?"

"Well—," Bellarmine looked out the window at the gathering dusk. "I'm no monster, Lewis. I'd probably turn it loose. No—." He scratched his chin. "No, maybe I wouldn't at that. But I wouldn't infect it anymore. I think I'd put it through some tests to find out just how smart it was. The rat would no longer be a simple test animal. Its usefulness would be in the psychological field, to tell me things about myself."

"That's about the way I had it figured," said Lewis. "How much longer am I going to be in this bed?"

"Why?"

"I've figured a way for the guinea pigs to tell the researchers the jig's up."

"How? We don't even know their language. We've only seen one specimen and that one's dead. We can't be sure they'd react the same way we would."

"Yes, they would," said Lewis.

"How can you say that? They must already know we're sentient."

"So's a rat sentient—to a degree," said Lewis. "It's all in the way you look at it. Sure. Compared to us, they're vegetables. That's the way it'd be with—"

"We don't have the right to take risks with the rest of humanity," protested Bellarmine. "Man, one of them tried to kill you!"

"But everything points to that one being defective," said Lewis. "He made too many mistakes. That's the only reason we got wise to him."

"They might dump us into the incinerator as no longer useful," said Bellarmine. "They—"

Lewis said, "They'd have to be pretty much pure scientists. Johnson was a field man, a lab technician, a worker. The pure scientists would follow our human pattern. I'm sure of it. To be a pure scientist you have to be able to control yourself. That means you'd understand other persons'—other beings'—problems. No, Doc. Your first answer was the best one. You'd put your rats through psychological tests."

Bellarmine stared at his hands. "What's your idea?"

"Take a white rat in one of those little lab cages. Infect it with some common germ, leave the infecting hypo in the cage, put the whole works—rat and all—in front of that silver grid. Distort—"

"That's a crazy idea," said Bellarmine. "How could you tell a hypothetical something to look at your message when you don't even know the hypothetical language—how to contact them in the first place?"

"Distort the field of that grid by touching the wires with a piece of metal," said Lewis. "Tie the metal to the end of a pole for safety."

"I've never heard a crazier idea," said Bellarmine.

"Get me the white rat, the cage and the hypo and I'll do it myself," said Lewis.

Bellarmine got to his feet, moved toward the door. "You're not doing anything for a couple of weeks," he said. "You're a sick man and I've been talking to you too long already." He opened the door, left the room.

Lewis stared at the ceiling. A shudder passed over his body. *Mutated virus!*

The door opened and an orderly and nurse entered. "You get a little tube feeding of hot gelatin," said the nurse. She helped him eat it, then, over his protests, gave him a sedative.

"Doctor's orders," said the nurse.

Through a descending fog, Lewis murmured, "Which doctor?"

"Dr. Bellarmine," she said.

The fog came lower, darkened. He drifted into a nightmare peopled by thousands of Johnsons, all of them running around with large metal tanks asking, "Are you human?" and collecting blood.

Sheriff Czernak was beside the bed when Lewis awoke. Lewis could see out the window that dawn was breaking. He turned toward the sheriff. "Mornin', John," he whispered. His tongue felt thick and dry.

"'Bout time you woke up," said Czernak. "I've been waiting here a coupla hours. Something fishy's going on."

"Wind my bed up, will you?" asked Lewis. "What's happening?"

Czernak arose, moved to the foot of the bed and turned the crank.

"The big thing is that Doc Bellarmine has disappeared," he said. "We traced him from the lab here to the mortuary. Then he just goes *pffft!*"

Lewis's eyes widened. "Was there a white rat cage?"

"There you go again!" barked Czernak. "You tell me you don't know anything about this, but you sure know all the questions." He bent over Lewis. "Sure, there was a rat cage! You better tell me how you knew it!"

"First tell *me* what happened," said Lewis.

Czernak straightened, frowning. "All right, Welby, but when I get through telling, then you better tell." He wet his lips with his tongue. "I'm told the Doc came in here and talked to you last night. Then he went down to the lab and got one of them white rats with its cage. Then he went over to the mortuary. He had the cage and rat with him. Our night guard let him in. After a while, when the Doc didn't come out, the guard got worried and went inside. There in the back hall is the Doc's black bag. And over where this silver wire stuff was he finds—"

"Was?" Lewis barked the word.

"Yeah," said Czernak wearily. "That's the other thing. Sometime last night somebody ripped out all them wires and didn't leave a single trace."

"What else did the guard find?"

Czernak ran a hand under his collar, stared at the opposite wall.

"Well?"

"Welby, look, I—"

"What happened?"

"Well, the night guard—it was Rasmussen—called me and I went right down. Rasmussen didn't touch a thing. There was the Doc's bag, a long wood pole with a tire iron attached to it and the rat cage. The rat was gone."

"Was there anything in the cage?"

Czernak suddenly leaned forward, blurted, "Look, Welby, about the cage. There's something screwy about it. When I first got there, I swear it wasn't there. Rasmussen doesn't remember it, either. My first idea when I got there was that the Doc'd gone out the back way, but our seal was still on the door. It hadn't been opened. While I was thinking that one over—I was standing about in the middle of the hall—I heard this noise like a cork being pulled out of a bottle. I turned around and there was this little cage on the floor. Out of nowhere."

"And it was empty?"

"Except for some pieces of glass that I'm told belonged to a hypo."

"Broken?"

"Smashed to pieces."

"Was the cage door open?"

Czernak tipped his head to one side, looked at the far wall. "No, I don't believe it was."

"And exactly where was this cage?" Lewis's eyes burned into the sheriff's.

"Like I said, Welby. Right in front of where the wires was."

"And the wires were gone?"

"Well—." Again the sheriff looked uncomfortable. "For just a second there, when I turned around after hearing that noise— for just a second there I thought I saw 'em."

Lewis took a deep breath.

Czernak said, "Now come on and give, will you? Where's the Doc? You must have some idea, the way you been askin' questions."

"He's taking his entrance exams," said Lewis. "And we'd all better pray that he passes."

DRAGON
IN
THE
SEA

Belland's chair rasped on the floor. He got to his feet, went to the side wall at his left, indicated a north-polar projection map. "Ensign Ramsey, we've lost twenty subtugs in these waters over the past twenty weeks," he said. He turned to Ramsey altogether like a schoolteacher about to propound a problem. "You're familiar with our pressing need for oil?"

Familiar? Ramsey restrained a wry smile. Through his mind sped the almost interminable list of regulations on oil conservation: inspections, issuance forms, special classes, awards for innovations. He nodded.

The admiral's bass rumble continued: "For almost two years now we've been getting extra oil from reservoirs under the marginal seas of the Eastern Powers' continental shelf." His left hand made a vague gesture over the map.

Ramsey's eyes widened. *Then the rumors were true: the sub services were pirating enemy oil!*

"We developed an underwater drilling technique working from converted subtugs," said Belland. "A high-speed, low-friction pump and a new type of plastic barge complete the general picture."

The admiral's mouth spread into what he probably imagined as a disarming grin. It succeeded only in making him appear even more piratical. "The boys call the barge a *slug,* and the pump is a *mosquito.*"

Dutiful chuckles sounded through the room. Ramsey smiled at the forced response, noted that Dr. Oberhausen maintained his reputation as Old Stone Face.

Admiral Belland said, "A *slug* will carry almost one hundred million barrels of oil. The EPs know they're losing oil. They know how, but they can't always be sure of where or when. We're outfoxing them." The admiral's voice grew louder. "Our detection system is superior. Our silencer planes—"

Dr. Oberhausen's brittle voice interrupted him. "Everything

we have is superior except our ability to keep them from sinking us."

The admiral scowled.

Ramsey picked up his cue, entered the breach. "What was the casualty percentage on those twenty subtugs we lost, sir?"

An owl-faced captain near Belland said dryly, "Of the last twenty missions, we lost all twenty."

"One hundred percent," said Dr. Oberhausen. The sightless eyes seemed to look across the room at a beet-faced lieutenant commander. "Commander Turner, would you show Mr. Ramsey the gadget your boys found?"

The lieutenant commander pushed a black cylinder about the size of a lead pencil down the table. Hands carried the object along until it reached Ramsey. He studied it.

"Mr. Ramsey's work, of course, involves electronics," said Dr. Oberhausen. "He's a specialist with the instruments used for detecting traumatic memories."

Ramsey caught the cue, also. He was the omniscient BuPsych electronics expert. The Man Who Knows Your Innermost Thoughts. *Ergo:* You don't have Innermost Thoughts in this man's presence. With an ostentatious gesture, Ramsey put his black box onto the table. He placed the cylinder beside it, managing to convey the impression that he had plumbed the mysteries of the device and found them, somehow, inferior.

What the devil is that thing? he wondered.

"You've probably recognized that as a tight-beam broadcaster," said Belland.

Ramsey glanced at the featureless surface of the black cylinder. *What would these people do if I claimed X-ray vision?* he asked himself. *Obe must have hypnotized them.*

Belland transferred his tone of deference-fear to Ramsey. "The EPs have been getting those things aboard our subtugs. We think there's a delayed-action device which turns them on at sea. Unfortunately, we've been unable thus far to dismantle one without exploding the antitamper charge."

Ramsey looked at Dr. Oberhausen, back to Belland, implying without words: "Well, if they'd turn these problems over to BuPsych...."

The admiral rallied some of his Pride of Department, said, "Turner believes he has it solved, however."

Ramsey looked at the beet-faced lieutenant commander. *And*

you'll be a rear-rank swabby if you fail, he thought. The lieutenant commander tried to make himself inconspicuous.

The commodore to Dr. Oberhausen's right said, "Enemy agents aboard the tugs could be turning them on."

Dr. Oberhausen said, "To make a long story short, these devices have been leading the enemy to our secret wells."

"The real trouble," said Belland, "is that we're shot through with sleepers—people the EPs planted years ago—long before the war—with orders to wait for the right moment. People in the damnedest places." He scowled. "Why, my driver—" He fell silent, turned the scowl on Ramsey. "We're reasonably certain you're not a sleeper."

"Reasonably certain?" asked Ramsey.

"I am reasonably certain no one in this room is a sleeper," growled Belland. "But that's all I am." He turned back to the wall map, pointed to a position in the Barents Sea. "This is the island of Novaya Zemlya. Off the west coast is a narrow shelf. The edge is in about one hundred fathoms. It's steep. We've a well into the flank of that shelf tapping one of the richest oil reservoirs we've ever encountered. The EPs don't even know it's there—yet."

Dr. Oberhausen put a bony hand on the table, tapped a finger once. "We must make certain Mr. Ramsey understands the morale factor." He turned toward Ramsey. "You understand that it has been impossible to keep our losses completely secret. As a result, morale in the subtugs has dropped off to almost nothing. We need *good* news."

Belland said, "Turner, take it from there." The admiral returned to his chair, lowered himself into it like a battle-wagon settling into dry dock.

Turner focused watery blue eyes on Ramsey, said, "We've screened, screened and rescreened our subtug crews. We've found one that looks good. They're at Garden Glenn Rest Camp now and will be coming out in five weeks. However, they do not have an electronics officer."

Ramsey thought: *Great Grieving Freud! Am I going to be palmed off as a submariner?*

As though he had read Ramsey's thought, Dr. Oberhausen said, "That's where you come in, Ramsey." He nodded to Turner. "Please forgive me, Commander, but we're taking too much time with this."

Turner shot a glance at Belland, sank back into his chair. "Of course, Doctor."

Dr. Oberhausen arose, again with that air of vast assurance. "This is my field, anyway. You see, Ramsey, the previous electronics officer suffered a psychotic blow-up at the termination of their last mission. It's the same problem you were working on with the men of the *Dolphin*. Amplified. The subtugs are smaller, a complement of only four men. The focal symptoms point to a kind of induced paranoia."

"The captain?" asked Ramsey.

"Precisely," said Dr. Oberhausen.

We are now impressing the natives with our mysterious knowledge, thought Ramsey. He said, "I noticed similar conditions in the battle-fatigue syndrome when I was on the *Dolphin*." He patted the box in front of him. "The captain's emotional variations were reflected in varying degrees all through the ship's personnel."

"Dr. Oberhausen outlined your work with the men of the *Dolphin*," said Turner.

Ramsey nodded. "I'm troubled by one point here. You say this crew rates high. That doesn't check if the captain is a borderline psychotic."

"Again, that's where you come in," said Dr. Oberhausen. "We were about to beach this captain. But now BattleComp tells us he and his crew have far and away the highest chance of success in this mission to Novaya Zemlya. But only if certain other conditions are present." He paused, tugged at an earlobe.

Ramsey caught the signal, thought: *Ah, there's the bite. Somebody important hasn't agreed to this arrangement and it's vital to Obe that I get on that subtug crew. Who are we playing to? The admiral? No, he'd go himself if Obe said the word.* Ramsey's eyes abruptly caught the scowling glare of the commodore on Dr. Oberhausen's left, and at the same moment he noted for the first time the tiny sunburst on the commodore's collar. *A presidential aide! That would be the one.*

"One of the other conditions would be that they have secret psychological monitoring," said Ramsey. "How had you planned to link in my remote-control vampire gauge to his pivotal captain without his knowing?"

"An ingenious solution has been proposed by Admiral Belland," said Dr. Oberhausen. "Security has a new type of detector to combat those spy-beam transmitters. A speaker pellet is surgically imbedded in the neck and tuned to wave scanners which are similarly imbedded beneath the armpits. Micro-instrumentation would permit us to include with the speaker the recorders you need."

Ramsey nodded toward the admiral. "Clever. You'd rig this subtug skipper that way, send me along to keep him in balance."

"Yes," said Dr. Oberhausen. "However, there has been some objection raised." The sightless eyes seemed to peer down at the commodore on his left. "On the grounds that you have no extended deep-tug combat experience. It's a specialized service."

The commodore grunted, glared at Ramsey. "We've been at war sixteen years," he said. "How is it you've escaped combat?"

Old school tie, thought Ramsey. He turned his telemeter box until one flat surface faced the commodore, squinted at the officer over it. *When in doubt, fire a broadside.*

"Every man we preserve for combat brings victory that much nearer," said Ramsey.

The commodore's leathery face grew dark.

"Mr. Ramsey has a special combination of training—psychology and electronics—which have made him too valuable to risk," said Dr. Oberhausen. "He has made only the most essential cruises—such as that with the *Dolphin*—when that was absolutely required."

"If he's so valuable, why're we risking him now?" demanded the commodore. "This all seems highly irregular!"

Admiral Belland sighed, stared at the commodore. "The truth is, Lewis, this new emotional-telemetering equipment which Mr. Ramsey developed can be used by others. However, his inventive talents are the very things which make his services so essential at this time."

"You may think me rude," said the commodore, "but I'd like to know also why this young man—if he's as good as all that—is still—" he flicked a glance at Ramsey's collar bars— "an ensign."

Dr. Oberhausen held up a hand, said, "Permit me, my dear Admiral." He turned to the commodore. "It is because there are people who resent the fact that I have been able to keep myself and my top department heads out of uniform. There

DRAGON IN THE SEA 49

are those who do not see the necessity for this essential separation. It is regrettable, therefore, that those of my people in the lower echelons, who are required to wear uniforms, sometimes find it difficult to gain advancement no matter how talented they may be."

The commodore looked as though he were about to explode.

"By rights," said Dr. Oberhausen, "Mr. Ramsey should be at least a commodore."

Several fits of coughing broke out simultaneously around the table.

Ramsey suddenly wished he were anywhere else but under the eyes of this commodore. The latter said, "Very well, my objection is withdrawn." The tone of voice said: *I will pass sentence in my own court.*

"I have planned," said Dr. Oberhausen, "upon completion of this mission, to have Mr. Ramsey released from the service and installed as head of a new department devoted to problems of submariners."

A harsh smile pulled at the corners of the commodore's mouth. "If he lives through it," he said.

Ramsey swallowed.

As though he had not heard, Dr. Oberhausen said, "The training will be a problem, but we have five weeks plus the full facilities of BuPsych."

Belland heaved his bulk from the chair, stepped to one side. "If there are no more questions, gentlemen, I believe we are all satisfied with Mr. Ramsey." He glanced at his wristwatch. "The medics are waiting for him now, and he's going to need every minute of the next five weeks."

Ramsey got to his feet, took the telemeter box under his arm, a question in his eyes.

"You're also going to be rigged as a walking detection system," said Belland.

Dr. Oberhausen appeared to materialize beside Ramsey. "If you'll come with me, please, John." He took Ramsey's arm. "I've had the essential material about Commander Sparrow— he's the captain of this subtug—and the other two crewmen reduced to absolute minimum. We've set aside a special ward at the bureau for you. You're going to be our prize patient for..."

Ramsey heard Turner speaking behind him. "Dr. Oberhausen called the ensign John. Is he the *Long John* Ramsey who..."

The rest was blurred as Dr. Oberhausen raised his voice. "It's going to be rough on you, John." They stepped into the outer corridor. "Your wife has been notified." Dr. Oberhausen lowered his voice. "You handled yourself very well in there."

Ramsey suddenly realized that he was allowing himself to be guided by a blind man. He laughed, found that he had to explain the laughter. "It was the way you handled that brassy commodore," he said.

"You don't lie at all well," said Dr. Oberhausen. "But I'll let it pass. Now, about the commodore: he's a member of the board which passes upon promotions for BuPsych men."

Ensign Ramsey abruptly found that laughter had left him.

Ramsey often referred to his five weeks' training for the subtug mission as "the time I lost twenty pounds."

They gave him three rooms in the sound wing of Unadilla Naval Hospital: blank white enclosures furnished in rattan and cigarette-scarred mahogany, a functional TV set, equally functional hospital bed on high legs. One room was set up for training: hypnophone, wall diagrams, mock-ups, tapes, films.

His wife, Janet, a blond nurse, received a weekend schedule for visits: Saturday nights and Sundays. Their children, John junior, age two, and Peggy, age four, were not permitted in the hospital, had to be packed off to their grandmother's at Fort Linton, Mississippi.

Janet, wearing a one-piece red dress, came storming into the sitting room of Ramsey's suite on their first Saturday night. She kissed him, said, "I knew it!"

"Knew what?"

"That sooner or later the Navy and that awful Obe would be regulating our sex life."

Ramsey, aware that everything he said and did in the hospital was being monitored, tried to shush her.

"Oh, I know they're listening," she said. She threw herself onto the rattan couch, crossed her legs, lighted a cigarette, which she puffed furiously. "That Obe gives me the creeping creeps," she said.

"That's because you let him," said Ramsey.

"And because that's the effect he wants to give," she countered.

"Well...yes," admitted Ramsey.

Janet jumped to her feet, threw herself into his arms. "Oh, I'm being a fool. They said I wasn't to upset you."

He kissed her, rumpled her hair. "I'm not upset."

"I told them I couldn't upset you if I tried." She pushed away from him. "Darling, what is it this time? Something dangerous? It isn't another one of those horrible submarines?"

"I'm going to be working with some oilmen," he said.

She smiled. "Oh, that doesn't sound bad at all. Will you be drilling a well?"

"The well's already drilled," he said. "We're going to see about increasing production."

Janet kissed his chin. "Old efficiency expert."

"Let's go to dinner," he said. "How're the kids?"

They went out, arm in arm, chatting about the children.

Ramsey's weekday routine began at 0500 when the nurse entered with his wake-up shot to rouse him from the hypnophone drugs. High-protein breakfast. More shots. Blood test.

"This is going to hurt a little."

"Owooooooch! Whatta-y-mean a little? Next time warn me!"

"Don't be a big baby."

Diagrams. Floor plans of Hell Driver Class subtugs.

They turned him over to a large subtug expert from Security. Clinton Reed. Bald as an egg. Thin eyes, thin nose, thin mouth, thick skin. Sense of duty as solid as his neck. Absolutely no sense of humor.

"This is important, Ramsey. You have to be able to go anywhere on this vessel, man any control blindfolded. We'll have a mock-up for you in a couple of days. But first you have to get a picture of it in your mind. Try flashing these plans and then we'll test your memory."

"Okay. I've finished the general layout. Try me."

"Where's the pile room?"

"Ask me something hard."

"Answer the question."

"Oh, all right. It's forward in the bulb nose; first thirty-two feet."

"Why?"

"Because of the teardrop shape of this class, and for balance. The nose gives the most room for shielding."

"How thick is the radiation wall behind the pile room?"

"I missed that."

"Twelve feet. Remember it. Twelve feet."

"Well, I can tell you what it's made of: hafnium, lead, graphite, and poroucene."

"What's on the aft face of the radiation wall?"

"Direct-reading gauges for the reactor. Repeaters are in the control room, forward bulkhead to the right of the first-level catwalk. Then there are lockers for 9BG suits, tool lockers, doors to the tunnels leading into the pile room."

"You're getting it. How many tunnels into the pile room?"

"Four. Two top; two bottom. Not to be entered for more than twelve minutes at a time unless wearing an ABG suit."

"Fine. What's the rated horsepower?"

"Two hundred and seventy-three thousand, reduced to about two hundred and sixty thousand by the silencer planes behind the screw."

"Excellent! How long is the engine room?"

"Uh... nope. That one's gone, too."

"Look, Ramsey, these are important. You have to remember these distances. You have to get a feeling for them. What if you don't have any lights?"

"Okay. Okay. How long is the damned thing?"

"Twenty-two feet. It fills the whole midship section. The four electric engines are set two to a level with the gearbox for the drive below center aft."

"Gotcha. Here, let me take a flash of the aft section. Okay. Now try me."

"How many catwalks in the engine room and where located?"

"Look. I just flashed the *aft* section."

"How many catwalks and—"

"Okaaaa. Let's see: one center of the control desk going forward. One off center into machine stores on the second level below. One called A level into top stores. Same for bottom level: called B level. Short bridging catwalks from A and B levels to the engines and oxy tanks. And one very short to the conning-tower-retracted which lifts into a section of steps when the tower is extended."

"Good. You see, you can do this if you set your mind to it. Now tell me how the four staterooms are placed."

"Staterooms yet."

"Stop dodging the question."

"Wise guy! Let's see: captain is top level starboard behind the electronics shack. First officer portside behind the recreation room-sick bay. Engineering officer starboard below the captain's quarters and behind the machine shop. Electronics officer portside below the first officer and aft of galley stores. That's the place for me. Gonna cut me a private door into galley stores."

"Where's the galley?"

"That one I can answer. It's far port, top level, entered through the wardroom. Selector controls for the prepackaged meals are against the bulkhead separating galley and wardroom. The galley-wardroom unit is between control deck and rec room."

"What's behind the staterooms?"

"Machinery of the Palmer induction drive."

"Why an induction drive?"

"Because at the dive limit for Hell Divers, there can be no weak points in the hull, therefore no shaft through the hull."

"You're getting the drive on the hypnophone tonight. Every man blindfolded. There'll be a model for you to work on day after tomorrow."

"Oh, goody!"

"What's the pressure hull limit for Hell Divers?"

"Three thousand and ten pounds to the square inch or seven thousand feet."

"Stick to your first answer. Pressure varies with different water conditions. You'd be okay at seventy-one hundred feet in one place, dead at sixty-nine hundred another. Learn to depend on your static pressure gauge. Now let's go to the atmosphere composition. What's a vampire gauge?"

"A little device worn on your wrist during deep dives. Needle goes into your vein, tells you if your CO_2 diffusion is fast enough so you won't crock out. It also tattles on nitrogen."

"What's minimum diffusion?"

"When you get below .200 on CO_2 you get the jeebies. If your blood CO_2 count goes to four percent you're in trouble. With nitrogen it's different. The subtug atmosphere is supposed to be entirely cleared of it. A small quantity of helium is substituted."

"How do you get by with the high atmospheric pressure?"

"Aerobic carbonic anhydrase is fed into the atmosphere by

the ventilator system. This speeds up the CO_2 loading and unloading of the blood, prevents gas bubbles forming."

"You're good on that. Did you know it before?"

"My emotional telemeter is just a glorified vampire gauge."

"Oh, sure. Now, why is the electronics officer so important?"

"Contact with the exterior control motors is by coded wave pulse. If the E-system breaks down when a subtug is submerged, it stays submerged."

"Right. Now, let's go through the plans again."

"Not again!"

"Start with the reactor room. In detail."

"Slave driver!"

The nightly hypnophone sessions flooded Ramsey's mind with the new knowledge: pressure hull, resonating hull, tank hull...pressure compensating system...header box...reactor controls...search and sounding...diving plane controls...valve controls...pile check-off...sonoran automatic-navigation board...atmosphere controls...automatic timelog, Mark IX ...gyro controls...tow controls...plastic barge, oil, components of...needle torpedoes, external racking system...torpedo homing systems...scrambler systems...systems... systems...systems....

There were times when Ramsey's head felt filled to the bursting point.

Dr. Oberhausen appeared in Ramsey's quarters on the fourth day of training. The doctor's unpressed clothes gave him the appearance of a bedraggled robin. He came in quietly, sat down beside Ramsey, who was seated in a viewerscope-sequence training hook-up.

Ramsey pulled the fitted faceplate away from his eyes, turned to Dr. Oberhausen. "Ah, the chief of the inquisition."

"You are comfortable, Johnny?" The sightless eyes seemed to stare through him.

"No."

"Good. You are not supposed to be comfortable." The doctor's chair creaked as he shifted his weight. "I have come about the man Garcia who is engineering officer of this crew."

"What's wrong with him?"

Qualifications: navigator—superior; gunnery officer—superior; medical officer (advanced first aid and pressure syndrome)—excellent; general submarine competence—superior.

"Wrong? Have I said anything was wrong?"

Ramsey completely disengaged the viewerscope, sat back. "Come to the point."

"Ah, the impatience of youth." Dr. Oberhausen sighed. "Do you have a file on Garcia?"

"You know I have."

"Get it please, and read me what you have."

Ramsey leaned to his right, took a file folder from the bottom ledge of his coffee table, opened it. Garcia's picture on the inside front cover showed a short man—about five feet seven inches— slim. Latin features—dark. Black curly hair. Sardonic half-smile. The picture managed to impart a sense of devil-may-care. Under the photograph a note in Ramsey's handwriting: "Member Easton championship water-polo team. Likes handball."

"Read to me," said Dr. Oberhausen.

Ramsey turned the page, said, "Age thirty-nine. Came up from ranks. Ex-CPO machinist. Ham radio license. Born Puerto Madryn, Argentina. Father cattle rancher: José Pedro Garcia y Aguinaldo. Mother died at birth of daughter when Garcia age three. Religion: Catholic. Wears rosary around neck. Takes blessing of priest before each mission. Wife: Beatrice, age thirty-one."

"Do you have her picture?" asked Dr. Oberhausen.

"No."

"A pity. I am told she is quite beautiful. Continue, please."

Ramsey said, "Educated at New Oxford. That accounts for his British accent."

"I grieved when the British Isles were destroyed," said Dr. Oberhausen. "Such a lovely culture, really. So basically solid. Immovable. But that is weakness, also. Continue, if you please."

"Plays bagpipes," said Ramsey. He looked at the doctor. "Now there's something: a Latin American playing the bagpipes!"

"I see nothing wrong with that, Johnny. For certain moods, nothing is more soothing."

Ramsey raised his gaze to the ceiling. "Soothing!" He looked back at the BuPsych chief. "Why am I reading this?"

"I wanted to get the full flavor of Garcia in mind before imparting the latest morsel from Security."

"Which is?"

"That Garcia may be one of these *sleepers* who are giving Security so many *sleepless nights*."

Ramsey snorted. "Garcia! That's insane! As well as suspect me!"

"They are still investigating *you*," said Dr. Oberhausen. "As to Garcia—perhaps; perhaps not. Counter-Intelligence has turned up the description of a sleeper supposed to be in the subtugs. The description fits Garcia. Security almost called off the mission. I convinced them to go ahead by suggesting that you be primed to watch Garcia."

Ramsey returned to the color photograph in his file folder, observed the sardonic smile. "I say we're chasing shadows. And that may be what the EEPs really want. If it's carried to its illogical extreme, certain Security-thinking is first cousin to paranoia—dementia praecox type."

Dr. Oberhausen lifted himself from the rattan chair. It gave off a reedy creaking. "Do not say that to the Security gentlemen when they come to brief you on Garcia," he said. "Oh, and one other thing: the commodore is sharpening knives with which to carve you if there is some error on this mission."

"I have you to thank for that," said Ramsey.

"I take care of my own," said Dr. Oberhausen. "Fear not on that score." He waved toward the viewerscope. "Continue with your studies. I have other work."

Ramsey waited for the door to close, threw the file folder back onto the coffee table, took twenty deep breaths to calm his nerves. Presently, he leaned to the right, captured the folders on the other two crew members, scanned them.

Commander Harvey Acton Sparrow. Age forty-one. Picture of a tall, thin man with balding sandy hair, a face of sharp planes, stooped shoulders.

He looks like a small-town college professor, thought Ramsey. *How much of that is conditioned on his early desire to teach mathematics? Does he resent the fact that his hardcrust Navy family forced him to follow in the old man's footsteps?*

Father: Rear Admiral Acton Orwell Sparrow lost with subcruiser *Plunger* in Battle of Irish Sea, 16 October 2018. Mother: Genene Cobe Sparrow. Invalid (heart), lives at Watters Point Government Rest Home. Wife: Rita. Age thirty-six. Blonde? Childless.

Does Sparrow know that his wife is unfaithful? Ramsey asked himself. *Most of their friends are aware of it.*

Ramsey turned to the other folder.

Lieutenant Commander Leslie (none) Bonnett. Age thirty-eight. Picture of a heavy-bodied man (just under six feet) with brown wavy hair (artificial wave?), aquiline nose, overhanging eyebrows, the look of a brooding hawk.

Orphan foundling. Raised at Cape Neston Home for the Unwanted.

For the Unwanted! thought Ramsey.

Married four times. Two children—one by each of first two wives. Maintains marriage relationship with wife number four: Helene Davis Bonnett. Age twenty-nine. Miss Georgia of 2021.

The unwanted, thought Ramsey. *He's carrying out an unconscious revenge pattern against women, getting even with the mother who deserted him.*

Qualifications: navigator—good; supply officer—excellent; gunnery officer—superior (top torpedo officer of subtugs four years running); general submarine competence—excellent plus.

Ramsey looked at the note in the psych record: "Held from advancement to his own command by imperfect adjustment to deep-seated insecurity feelings."

The Unwanted, he thought. *Bonnett probably doesn't want advancement. This way, his commander supplies the father authority lacking in his youth.*

Ramsey tossed the folder back onto the coffee table, leaned back to think.

An association of twisted and tangled threads.

Sparrow and Bonnett were Protestants; Garcia, a Catholic.

No evidence of religious friction.

These men have evolved a tight working arrangement. Witness the fact that their subtug has the highest efficiency rating in the service.

What has been the effect of losing Heppner, the other electronics officer? Will they resent his replacement?

Damn! Heppner was the wrong one to go! A case history with no apparent clues. Quiet childhood. Calm home life. Two sour notes: a broken love affair at age thirty-two. It should have been someone like Bonnett. The Unwanted. Or Captain Sparrow. The frustrated mathematician.

"Sleeping?"

It was Reed, the constant tutor.

"It's three o'clock," he said. "I brought a layout plan of the electronics shack on these Hell Divers." He handed a blueprint to Ramsey, pointed as he spoke. "Bench here. Vise there. Wrench kit. Micro-lathe. Vacuum pumps. Testingboard plugs."

"Okay, I can read."

"You have to be able to plug into that test board in total darkness," said Reed. He sat down squarely in the rattan chair lately occupied by Dr. Oberhausen. "Tomorrow you're going to start training on a mock-up."

"Tomorrow's Saturday, Clint!" Ramsey glared at him.

"You don't get out of here before 1800," said Reed. He bent forward over the plan. "Now, concentrate on that plug layout. This here is emergency lighting. You'll be expected to find it the first time."

"What if it takes me two tries?"

Reed leaned back, turned his flinty gaze on Ramsey. "Mr. Ramsey, there's something you should understand so thoroughly that it's second nature to you."

"Yeah? What's that?"

"There is no such thing as a *minor* accident on a submarine."

Commander Sparrow trotted down the ramp from the tube landing, slowed as he stepped into the cavernous, floodlighted gloom of the underground submarine moorage. A fine mist of condensation from the rock ceiling far away in upper blackness beat against his face. He picked his way through the pattern of scurrying jitneys, darting, intent people. Ahead of him, the bulbous whale mound of his subtug rose above the pier: a 140-foot Wagnerian diva center stage beneath banks of floodlights.

Instructions from the final Security session jangled through his mind.

"Your crew has the top Security rating of the service, but you must remain alert for sleepers."

"In my crew? Hell, man, I've known them all for years. Bonnett's been with me eight years. Joe Garcia and I served together before the war. Heppner and—" His face had crimsoned. "What about the new E-officer?"

"You won't need to worry about him. Now, the inspectors assure us there are no enemy signal devices aboard your boat."

"Then why this gadget in my neck?"

"That's just an added precaution."

"What about this new man? What's his E-rating?"

"He's one of the best in the service. Here, look at his record."

"Limited combat experience in gulf patrol! He's practically a dryback!"

"But look at his E-rating."

"Limited combat!"

A jitney driver shouted at Sparrow, bringing him out of his reverie. He glanced at his wristwatch: 0738—twenty-two minutes until castoff. His stomach tightened. He quickened his steps.

Damn Security's last-minute details!

Across the ebony velvet of the mooring pool he could see the glow tubes outlining the marine tunnel. Down the 160-mile slant of that tunnel, out into the underwater deeps of De Soto Canyon and the Gulf of Mexico—and beyond—ranged the enemy. An enemy grown suddenly, terrifyingly, 100 percent effective against vessels such as his.

It came to Sparrow that the marine tunnel formed a grotesque birth canal. This cavern carved under a Georgia mountain was nestled in the earth like a fantastic womb. When they took their vessel out to do battle they were born into a terrible world that they did not want.

He wondered what BuPsych would think of an idea like that. *They'd probably rate it as an indication of weakness,* he thought. *But why shouldn't I have weakness? Something about fighting a war a mile and a half under the ocean—the unrelenting pressure of water all around—exposes every weakness in a man. It's the pressures. Constant pressures. Four men isolated in pressure, held in a plasteel prison as they are held in the prisons of their souls.*

Another jitney scurried across Sparrow's path. He dodged, looked up at his boat. He was close enough now to make out the nameplate on the retractable conning tower high above him: *Fenian Ram S1881.* The boarding ramp swooped down from the tower in a long graceful curve.

The dock captain, a moon-faced lieutenant commander in fatigues, hurried up to Sparrow, a checklist in his hands.

"Captain Sparrow."

Sparrow turned without stopping. "Yes? Oh, hullo, Myers. Are all the ready crews off?"

Myers fell into step beside him. "Most of them. You've lost weight, Sparrow."

"Touch of dysentery," said Sparrow. "Got some bad fruit up at Garden Glenn. Has my new electronics officer showed up?"

"Haven't seen him. His gear came along earlier. Funny thing. There was a sealed box with his stuff. About so by so." He gestured with his hands. "Cleared by Admiral Belland."

"ComSec?"

"None other."

"Why was it sealed?"

"It's supposed to contain some highly delicate instruments to monitor your new long-range search equipment. It was sealed so no zealous searcher could foul the works."

"Oh. I take it the new long-range gear is installed?"

"Yes. You're battle-checking it."

Sparrow nodded.

A cluster of men at the foot of the boarding ramp snapped to attention as the two officers approached. Sparrow and Myers stopped. Sparrow said, "At ease."

Myers said, "Sixteen minutes, Captain." He held out his hand, shook with Sparrow. "Good luck. Give 'em hell."

"Right," said Sparrow.

Myers headed for the foot of the dock.

Sparrow turned toward a heavy-bodied, hawk-faced man beside the ramp, First Officer Bonnett. "Hi, Les."

"Good to see you, Skipper," said Bonnett. He tucked a clipboard under his left arm, dismissed three ratings who were with him, turned back to Sparrow. "Where'd you and Rita go after the party?"

"Home," said Sparrow.

"So'd we," said Bonnett. He hooked a thumb toward the submarine behind him. "Final safety inspection's completed. Spare gear checked out. But there's a bit of a delay. Heppner's replacement hasn't reported."

Sparrow cursed inwardly, felt a stomach-gripping surge of frustration-anger. "Where is he?"

Bonnett shrugged. "All I know is that Security called and said there might be some delay. I told them—"

"Security?"

"That's right."

"Suffering Jesus!" barked Sparrow. "Do they always have to wait until the last minute? They had me—" He broke off. That was classified.

"They said they'd do their best," said Bonnett.

Sparrow pictured the complicated arrangements which would pass the *Fenian Ram* through their own defense network outward bound.

"It could take another day to set up a new passage time."

Bonnett glanced at his wristwatch, took a deep breath. "I told them 0800 was the latest. They wouldn't answer a damned one of my—" He fell silent as the ramp beside them rattled to descending footsteps.

Both men looked up, saw three figures coming down: two ratings carrying heavy-duty electronics detection gear, followed by a short wiry man with dark Latin features. He wore stained service fatigues, carried a small electronic search box under his right arm.

"Don José Garcia," said Sparrow.

Garcia shifted the search box to his left arm, stepped down to the dockside. "Skipper! Am I glad to see you!"

Sparrow moved back to permit the ratings to pass with their load, looked questioningly at the search box under Garcia's arm.

Garcia shook his head. "For God and Country," he said. "But sometimes I think I overdraw my account with God." He crossed himself. "The Security chaps have had us at this floating sewer pipe half the night. We've been over it from stem to stern four distinct times. Not a blip. Now, I say to you: they want me to make another search after we get underway down tunnel!" He raised his eyebrows. "I ask you!"

"We'll have to do it," said Sparrow. "I've allowed time before our first contact point for total deep-dive inspection."

"I say," said Garcia. He grinned. "You know, I've already gone and rigged for it."

Sparrow answered the grin, felt some of the tensions inside him begin to unknot.

Bonnett glanced significantly at his watch. "Twelve min—"

The whine of a command jitney's electric motor intruded upon him. All three men turned toward the sound. It came down the dark line of mooring slots, its single light casting an erratic Cyclops gleam upon the damp concrete. The jitney swerved up to the ramp, jerked to a stop. A red-headed man with a round, innocent face sat beside the driver, clutching his uniform cap in his hands.

Sparrow saw ensign's bars on the man's collar, thought: *That will be my new E-officer.* Sparrow grinned at the man's obvious relief upon a safe arrival. The recklessness of the base jitney drivers was a standard service joke.

The new man put his cap over his red hair, stepped out of the jitney. The machine rebounded from his weight. The driver whirled the jitney back the way they had come.

The ensign stepped up to Sparrow, saluted, said, "I'm Ramsey."

Sparrow returned the salute, said, "Glad to have you aboard."

Ramsey handed his service record to Sparrow, said, "No time to send these through channels."

Sparrow passed the papers to Bonnett, said, "This is Mr. Bonnett, first officer." He turned to Garcia. "Mr. Garcia, engineer."

"Good to meet you," said Ramsey.

"We'll soon dissuade you of that illusion," said Garcia.

Sparrow smiled, offered his hand to Ramsey, was surprised to feel strong muscle in the new man's grip. The fellow just *looked* soft. Bonnett and Garcia also shook hands.

Ramsey was busy cataloging his first visual impressions of the three men in the flesh. It seemed strange to be meeting these people for the first time when he felt that he already knew them. And that, he knew, would have to be concealed. Odd bits of knowledge about the personal lives of these men— even the names of their wives—could not be in the memory of a new man.

"Security said you might be delayed," said Sparrow.

"What's got Security on its ear?" asked Ramsey. "I thought they were going to dissect me."

"We'll discuss that later," said Sparrow. He rubbed at the thin scar on his neck where the Security surgeons had imbedded the detection-system speaker. "Castoff is 0800. Mr. Garcia will take you aboard. Get into fatigues. You'll be assisting him in a final spy-beam inspection as we get underway."

"Yes, sir," said Ramsey.

"Your gear came along hours ago," said Garcia. He took Ramsey's arm, propelled him toward the ramp. "Let's get with it." They hurried up the ramp.

Ramsey wondered when he could break away to examine his telemeter box. He felt an anxiety—a need to study the first records on Sparrow.

That mannerism of rubbing his neck, thought Ramsey. *Extreme nervous tension well concealed. But it shows in the tight movements.*

On the pier, Sparrow turned to look across the mooring basin at a string of moving lights. "Here comes our tow, Les."

"Do you think we'll make it, Skipper?"

"We always have."

"Yes, but—"

"'For now is our salvation nearer than when we believed,'" said Sparrow. "'The night is far spent, the day is at hand: Let us therefore cast off the works of darkness, and let us put on the armor of light.'" He looked at Bonnett. "Paul wrote that to the Romans two thousand years ago."

"A pretty wise fellow," said Bonnett.

A bos'n's whistle sounded at the head of the dock. A swifty crane came darting up to take away the boarding ramp. Ratings hurried to attach the hooks, looked inquiringly at the two officers.

Men hurried along the pier, a new purposefulness in their movements. Sparrow swept his gaze over the scene. "We're being asked to perform," he said. He gestured for Bonnett to precede him up the ramp. "Like the man said: Let's get with it."

They climbed to the conning tower. Bonnett ducked for the cable rack which mounted the float for their TV periscope. As a matter of routine, he glanced at the housing, saw that it was secured for dive. He grasped the ladder arms, slid down into the subtug.

Sparrow remained topside. Around him, the mooring basin appeared a vast lake. He looked at the rock ceiling's blackness.

There should be stars, he thought. *Men should get one last look at stars before they go under the sea.*

On the pier below, scurrying figures moved to cast off the magnetic grapples. For a moment, Sparrow felt like a useless pawn being thrown into a sacrifice position. There had been a time, he knew, when captains conned their vessels away from the dock, shouting orders through a megaphone. Now, it was all automatic—done by machines and by men who were like machines.

A surface tug swung up to their bow, slapped its tow grapples onto them. White water boiled from beneath the tug's stern. The *Fenian Ram* resisted momentarily, as though reluctant to leave, then began a slow, ponderous movement out into the basin.

They cleared the slot, and another tug slid alongside their stern. The magna-shoe men leaped onto the *Ram's* silencer planes, hitched the tow and guide cables of the long plastic tube which stretched out across the dark water of the basin. Their shouts came up to Sparrow in the tower like the clear noise of children. He tasted a sudden oil-tainted breeze and knew they had crossed the path of a ventilator duct.

No special fanfare, no brass bands, no ceremony for the departure of a raider, he thought. *We are as a reed shaken with the wind. And what go we out into the wilderness to see? No John the Baptist awaits us. But it's a kind of baptism all the same.*

Somewhere in the darkness a klaxon hooted. *Turn and identify the man next to you. Another Security scheme: Show your identification when the horn sounds. Damn Security! Out here I identify myself to my God and none other.*

Sparrow looked astern at the set of the tow. *Oil. War demanded the pure substance born in the sediment of rising continent. Vegetable oil wouldn't do. War was no vegetarian. War was a carnivore.*

The tow tug shifted to the side of the *Ram* and now the sub was being nosed into the traveler rack which would carry it down to the underwater canyon and the gulf.

Sparrow looked at the control console in the conning tower, and the green *clear-away* light. He flashed the standby signal to the tug below him and, with a practiced motion, touched the controls to retract the tower. It slid smoothly into the sub, its plasteel lid twisted into the groove seats.

A chest microphone hung beside the tower console. Sparrow slipped it on, spoke into it: "Rig for dive."

He focused his attention on the dive board in front of him.

Back came Bonnett's voice, robbed of life by the metallic mutes of the intercom: "Pressure in the hull."

One by one, the lights on Sparrow's dive board shifted from red to green. "Green board," he said. "Stand by." Now he could feel the hull pressure and another pressure in his stomach. He closed the signal circuit which told the outside crews that the subtug was ready to go down tunnel.

The *Ram* shifted, lurched. A dull clang resonated through the boat. Across the top of the dive board amber lights flashed: They were in the grip of the tunnel elevator. Twenty hours of free ride.

Sparrow grasped a handhold beside the dive board, swung down and out onto the engine-room catwalk. His feet made a slithering sound on the catwalk padding as he made his way aft, crawled through the control-room door, dogged it behind him. His gaze paused for a moment on the hand-etched brass plate Heppner had attached beside the door—a quotation from some nineteenth-century pundit:

"No one but a crazy man would waste his time inventing a submarine and no one but a lunatic would go down in it if it were invented."

Through the gulf shelf in the Florida elbow, De Soto Canyon slashes the soft peninsula limestone like a railroad cut; fourteen fathoms where it starts in Apalachee Bay, more than two hundred and sixty fathoms where it dives off into the ocean deeps south of Cape San Blas and east of Tampa.

The gulf exit of the marine tunnel opens into the canyon wall at fifty fathoms: a twilight world of waving fan kelp, red fingers of gorgonian coral, flashing sparkles of reef-dwelling fish.

The *Fenian Ram* coasted out of the dark hole of the tunnel like a sea monster emerging from its lair, turned, scattering the fish, and slanted down to a resting place in the burnt-umber mud of the canyon bottom. A sonar pulse swept through the boat. Detectors in the triple hulls responded, registered on control gauges of the navigation deck.

Garcia's clipped accent—oddly squeaking in the oxygen-high atmosphere—repeated the checklist as he watched the Christmas tree lights of the main board. '... no leaks, trim weights balanced, external salvage air clear and pressure holding, atmosphere free of nitrogen, TV eyes clear and seeing, TV periscope surfaced and seeing; periscope gyro checks with—" His laughter echoed through the intercom: "Seagull! It tried to land on the peri-box as I started to reel in. Lit on its fanny in the water."

Bonnett's crisp tones interrupted. "What's it like topside, Joe?"

"Clear. Just daybreak. Going to be a good day for fishing."

Sparrow's voice rasped over the speakers: "Enough of that! Was there anyone up there to spot the gull's flop? They could've seen our box."

"Negative, Skipper."

Sparrow said, "Les, give me the complete atmosphere check. Vampire gauges everyone. Follow the check. Report any deviations."

The patient inspection continued.

Ramsey interrupted. "I'm in the induction-drive chamber. A lot of static here as I entered."

Garcia said, "Did you go back by the lower shaft tunnel?"

"Lower."

"I noticed that myself earlier. We'll rig a ground for the scuff mat. I think that'll fix it."

"I grounded myself before entering."

Sparrow said, "Run that down, Joe. Les where are you?"

"Second-level catwalk in the engine room."

"Relieve Joe on the main board. Ramsey, get into your shack. Contact with base in eleven minutes."

"Aye, Skipper."

Sparrow moved from his position on the control deck below Garcia to a point at the first-level door which was open to permit visual inspection of the big gauges forward on the radiation wall. *That room in the bow,* he thought. *That's what worries me. We can see into it with our TV eyes; gauges tell us what's happening. But we can't touch it with our bare hands. We don't have a real feeling for that place.*

He mopped his forehead with a large red handkerchief. *Something, somewhere is wrong.* He was a subtug skipper who had learned to depend on his feeling for the boat.

A string of Spanish curses in Garcia's voice, rendered metallic by the intercom, interrupted his reverie.

Sparrow barked: "Joe! What's wrong?" He turned toward the stern, as though to peer through the bulkheads.

"Wiper rag in the rotor system. It was rubbing the induction ring every revolution. That's Ramsey's static."

"Does it look deliberate?"

"Did you ever come across a *silk* wiping rag?" The sound of a grunt came over the intercom. "There, by heaven!"

Sparrow said, "Save that rag." Then: "Ramsey, where are you?"

"In the shack warming up the transmitter."

"Did you hear Joe?"

"Yes."

"Tell base about that rag. Tell them—"

"Skipper!" It was Garcia's voice. "There's oil in the atmosphere back here!"

Sparrow said, "A mist of oil plus static spark equals an explosion! Where's that oil coming from?"

"Just a minute." A clanking of metal against metal. "Open pet-cock in the lube system. Just a crack. Enough to squirt a fine spray under full drive."

Sparrow said, "Ramsey, include that in the report to base."

"Aye, Skipper."

"Joe, I'm coming back there," said Sparrow. "We're going over that drive room with a microscope."

"I've already started."

Bonnett said, "Skipper, would you send Ramsey up here after he gets off the contact? I'll need help checking the main board."

"Hear that, Ramsey?" asked Sparrow.

"Aye."

"Comply."

"Will do."

Sparrow went aft, dropped down to the lower level, crawled through the shaft tunnel and into the drive room—a cone-shaped space dominated by the gleaming brass induction ring, the spaced coils. He could smell the oil, a heavy odor. Garcia was leaning into the coil space, examining the induction ring by magnifying glass.

"They're just little things," said Sparrow. "But taken together—boom!"

Garcia turned, his eyes glittering in the harsh work lights. "I don't like the feel of things, Skipper. This is a bad beginning. This is starting like a *dead-man* mission."

Sparrow took a deep breath, exhaled slowly. With an abrupt motion, he thumbed the button of his crest mike. "Ramsey, when you contact base, request permission to return."

"Aye, Skipper."

Ramsey's thoughts leaped. *What will that do to morale? The first raider in months turns back without getting out of the gulf. Bad.* He stared at the wavering fingers of the dial needles. His contact timer hit the red line, buzzed. He rapped out the first pulse with its modulated message: "Able John to Red Hat. Over."

The speaker above his head hissed with background noise like a distant surf. Presently, a voice came out of it, overriding the noise: "This is Red Hat. Over."

"Able John to Red Hat: We've discovered sabotage aboard. A silk rag was put in the motor system of our drive room. A static spark from the rag could've blown us out of the bay. Over."

"Red Hat to Able John. Stand by, please. We are routing your message to Bird George."

"Security!"

Again the speaker came to life. "Bird George to Able John. This is Teacher. What is the situation? Over."

Clint Reed! Ramsey could almost see the humorless face of his Security teacher. *Teacher Reed. Impromptu code.* Ramsey bent over his own mike: "Teacher, this is Student." He repeated the story of sabotage.

"Teacher to Student. What's your suggestion? Over."

"Student to Teacher. Permit us to go on with inspection out here. There's less chance for an unknown factor. Just the four of us aboard. If we check safe, allow us to continue the mission. Bad for morale if we came back. Over."

"Teacher to Student. That's the way we see it. But stand by." Pause. "Permission granted. How much time do you need? Over."

Ramsey turned on his intercom microphone. "Skipper, base suggests we continue the inspection here and not return if we check secure."

"Did you tell him what we'd found?"

"Yes, sir."

"What'd they say?"

"That there's less chance for a security slip out here. Fewer personnel. They suggest we double-check each other, give every—"

"Suffering Jesus!"

"They want to know how much time we'll need."

Silence.

"Skipper, they—"

"I heard you. Tell them we'll need ten hours."

Ramsey turned back to his transmitter. "Student to Teacher. Skipper says give us ten hours. Over."

"Teacher to Student. Continue as ordered. We'll clear new

checkpoints for you. Over and out."

Ramsey sat back, thought: *Now, I've really stuck my neck out. But Obe said this one has to go through.*

Bonnett's voice rasped over the intercom: "Ramsey! If that contact's over, get your ass up here and help me on this board!"

"Coming."

In the drive room, Sparrow hefted a socket wrench, looked at Garcia crouched under the secondary coils. "They want this one to go through, Joe. Very badly."

Garcia put a contact light on two leads. It glowed. "Yes, and they give us a green hand like that Ramsey. A near dryback."

"His service record says limited combat in gulf Security patrols."

"Get the priest and the parish!" He shifted to a new position. "Something odd about the chap!"

Sparrow opened the plate over a condenser. "How so?"

"He strikes me like a ringer, a chap who pretends to be one thing when he's actually something else."

"Where do you get that idea?"

"I really couldn't say, Skipper."

Sparrow shrugged, went on with his work. "I dunno, Joe. We'll go into it later. Hand me that eight-inch flex wrench, please."

Garcia reached up with the wrench, turned back to his own work. Silence came over the little room, broken only by the sound of metal on metal, buzzing of test circuits.

Sparrow ducked through the door into the control room, stood silently as Bonnett and Ramsey reinstalled the final cover plate of the main board.

Bonnet straightened, rubbed the back of his neck. His hand left a grease smear. He spoke to Ramsey: "You're a boy, Junior. We may make a submariner out of you yet. You've just gotta remember that down here you never make the same mistake once."

Ramsey racked a screw driver in his tool kit, closed the kit, turned, saw Sparrow. "All secure, Skipper?"

Sparrow didn't answer at once. He looked around the control room, sniffed the air. Faint smell of ozone. A distant humming of stand-by machinery. The round eyes of the indicator dials like symbiotic extensions of himself. The plucking disquiet remained within him.

"As secure as mortals can make it—I hope," he said. "We'll repair to the wardroom." Sparrow turned, ducked out the way he had entered.

Ramsey put his tool kit into its wall rack. Metal grated against metal. He shivered, turned. Bonnett was going through the door. Ramsey stepped across the control room, ducked through the door, followed Bonnett into the wardroom. Sparrow and Garcia already were there, Garcia seated to the right, Sparrow standing at the opposite end of the table. Ramsey's eyes widened. An open Bible lay on the table before Sparrow.

"We invoke the help of the Almighty upon our mean endeavors," said Sparrow.

Bonnet slipped into a chair at the left.

Sparrow indicated the seat opposite himself. "Will you be seated, please, Mr. Ramsey?"

Ramsey lowered himself into the chair, rested one hand on the green felt of the table cover. Sparrow towered above them at the other end of the table. *The Giver of the Law with hand upon the Book.*

Religious services, thought Ramsey. *Here's one of the binding forces of this crew. Participation Mystique! The consecration of the warriors before the foray.*

"What is your religion, Mr. Ramsey?" asked Sparrow.

Ramsey cleared his throat. "Protestant Episcopal."

"It's not really important down here," said Sparrow. "I was merely curious. We have a saying in the subtugs that the Lord won't permit a *live* atheist to dive below a thousand feet."

Ramsey smiled.

Sparrow bent over the Bible. His voice rumbled as he read: "'Woe unto them that call evil good, and good evil; that put darkness for light, and light for darkness; that put bitter for sweet, and sweet for bitter! Woe unto them that are wise in their own eyes, and prudent in their own sight!'"

He closed the Bible, lifted his head. It was a movement of power, of authority. Ramsey received an impression of deep strength.

"We do our job with what we have at hand," said Sparrow. "We do what we believe to be the *right* thing. Though it grieve us, we do it. We do it that the godless shall perish from the earth. Amen."

Sparrow turned away, placed the Bible in a case against the

bulkhead. With his back still turned to them, he said, "Stations, everyone. Mr. Ramsey, contact base, tell them we are ready to go. Get the time for the first checkpoint."

Ramsey got to his feet. Foremost in his thoughts was the almost physical need to examine the first telemeter record on Sparrow. "Yes, sir," he said. He turned, ducked through the door to the companionway and across into his shack, contacted base.

First checkpoint in four hours.

Ramsey relayed the information to Sparrow.

"Zero the automatic timelog," said Sparrow. "Check in, everyone."

"Garcia here. Drive and tow secure."

"Bonnet here. Main secure."

Ramsey looked at his board in the electronics shack. A queer sensation of belonging here passed over him. A sense of familiarity, of association deeper and longer than the five weeks of training. "E-board secure," he said. "Two atmospheres in the hull." He looked to the vampire gauge on his wrist. "Diffusion normal-plus. No nitrogen."

Back came Sparrow's voice over the intercom: "Les, slide off."

Ramsey felt the subtug lurch, then a faint whispering pulse of power. The deck assumed a slight upward incline, leveled. Presently, it tipped down.

We're headed into the deeps, thought Ramsey. *Physically and mentally. From here on it's up to me.*

"Mr. Ramsey, come to the control deck," Sparrow ordered.

Ramsey closed down his board, went forward. Sparrow stood, hands behind his back, feet braced slightly apart almost precisely in the center of the control deck. He appeared framed in a background maze of pipes, wheels, levers, and dials. To his right, Garcia worked the tow controls; to his left, Bonnett held the high-speed pilot wheel. The big static pressure gauge high in the control bulkhead registered 1,310 pounds, increasing; they were below 3,000 feet.

Without turning, Sparrow asked, "What's in that little box that came aboard with your effects, Mr. Ramsey?"

"Monitoring equipment for the new search system, sir."

Sparrow's head moved to follow the flickering of a tow-control dial; he turned back. "Why was it locked?"

"It's extremely delicate and packed accordingly. They were afraid someone—"

"I'll want to see it at the first opportunity," said Sparrow. He stepped over behind Bonnet. "Les, is that a leak in compartment nine?"

"There's no moisture or pressure variant, Skipper. It has to be condensation."

"Keep an eye on it." Sparrow stepped back beside Ramsey.

I'm going to find out quick if that disguise system in the box satisfies his curiosity, thought Ramsey.

"What's your hobby?" he asked Ramsey.

Ramsey blinked. *"Astronomy."*

Bonnet spoke over his shoulder: "That's a peculiar hobby for a submariner."

Before Ramsey could reply, Sparrow said, "There's nothing wrong with astronomy for a man who goes to sea."

"The basis of navigation," said Ramsey.

Sparrow glanced sidelong at Ramsey, returned his gaze to the board. "I was thinking as we moved out across the mooring basin back at base that we were entitled to a last look at the stars before going under the sea. They give one a sense of orientation. One night before we left Garden Glenn I was struck by the clarity of the sky. The constellation of Hercules was—" He broke off as the *Ram's* nose tipped upward.

A down hands moved over his controls to correct for the deflection.

"Hercules," said Ramsey. "Do you mean the Kneeler?"

"Not many call him that anymore," said Sparrow. "I like to think of him up there all these centuries, guiding mariners. The Phoenicians used to worship him, you know."

Ramsey felt a sudden wave of personal liking for Sparrow. He fought it down. *I must remain clear-headed and objective,* he told himself.

Sparrow moved to the left to get a clearer view of the pilot gauges. He studied them a moment, turned to Ramsey. "Has it ever occurred to you, Mr. Ramsey, that these Hell Diver subtugs are the closest thing to spaceships that mankind has developed? We're completely self-contained." He turned back to the control board. "And what do we do with our spaceships? We use them to hide under the liquid curtain of our planet. We use them to kill one another."

Ramsey thought: *Here's a problem—a morbid imagination vocalized for the benefit of the crew.* He said, "We use them in self-defense."

"Mankind has no defense for himself," said Sparrow.

Ramsey started to speak, stopped, thought: *That's a Jungian concept. No man is proof against himself.* He looked at Sparrow with a new respect.

"Our underground base," said Sparrow. "It's like a womb. And the marine tunnel. A birth canal if I ever saw one."

Ramsey thrust his hands into his pockets, clenched his fists. *What is going on here?* he asked himself. *An idea like that should have originated with BuPsych. This man Sparrow is either teetering on the ragged edge or he's the sanest man I've ever met. He's absolutely right about that base and the tunnel and we've never spotted the analogy before. This bears on our problem. But how?*

Sparrow said, "Joe, secure the tow board on automatic. I want you to go with Mr. Ramsey now and test out the new detection gear. It should be ranged on our first checkpoint." He looked to the big sonoran auto-nav chart on the forward bulkhead and the red dot showing their DR position. "Les, surface the peri-box and get a position reading."

"Right, Skipper."

Garcia closed the final switch on his board, turned to Ramsey. "Let's go, Junior."

Ramsey looked at Sparrow, a wish to be part of this crew uppermost in his mind. He said, "My friends call me Johnny."

Sparrow spoke to Garcia. "Joe, would you also initiate Mr. Ramsey into the idiosyncrasies of our atmospheric system? The carbonic anhydrase phase regulator would be a good place to start."

Ramsey felt the rejection of his first name like a slap, stiffened, ducked through the aft door and into the companionway.

Garcia followed, dogged the door behind them, turned, said, "You'd better know something about the subtug, Ramsey. A new hand is always known by his last name or anything else the crew feels like calling him until after the first combat. Some guys hope they *never* get called by their first name."

Ramsey cursed inwardly. Security had missed that point. It made him appear like a green hand. Then he thought: *But this is a natural thing. A unit compulsive action by the crew. A bit of magic. Don't use the secret name of the new man lest the gods destroy him . . . and his companions.*

In the control room, Bonnett turned to Sparrow, sniffed. He rubbed a hand across the back of his neck, turned back to the control board. "He's green," he said.

"He appears willing, though," said Sparrow. "We can hope for the best."

Bonnett asked, "Aren't you worried about that last minute Security check-up on the guy?"

"Somewhat," said Sparrow.

"I can't help it," said Bonnett. "The guy—something about him—I dunno. He strikes me as a wrongo." Bonnett's shaggy brows drew down in thought.

"It could've been routine," said Sparrow. "You know the going over they gave us."

"I'm still going to keep an eye on him," said Bonnett.

"I've some paperwork," said Sparrow. "Steady as she goes. Call me before the first checkpoint."

"What's the watch schedule?" asked Bonnett.

"That's what I'm going to be working on," said Sparrow. "I want to set it up so I can spend some time with Ramsey while we're still in comparatively safe waters. I don't want him goofing when the chips are down."

Sparrow ducked for the aft door, went down the companionway and into the wardroom. The first thing that struck him as he entered was the color of the wardroom table cover—a cover and a color he had seen thousands of times.

Why is it that Navy wardrooms always have green table covers? he asked himself. *Is it a little of the color of the growing land? Is it to remind us of home?*

In the electronics shack, Garcia and Ramsey closed down the board after testing the detection gear.

"What now?" asked Ramsey.

"You'd better log a little sack time," said Garcia. "It's Les's watch. The skipper's probably setting up the schedule right now. You may be called next. Things are pretty loose the first day or so."

Ramsey nodded, said, "I am tired." He turned aft, said, *"See you later."*

Garcia's "Righto" floated after him.

Ramsey hurried to his room, dogged the door, dragged out the telemeter box, unlocked it, extracted the first record strips, sat back to examine them.

Pituitra and adrenaline high points showed early on the scrolls. Ramsey noted that one was before he arrived and the other coincided with the moment pressure was first bled into the hull.

The first tense moments, he thought. *But that's normal.*

He reeled the scrolls of telemeter tape forward to the moment the sabotage was discovered, double-checked the timed setting, scanned backward and forward across the area.

Nothing!

But that can't be!

Ramsey stared at the pattern of rivets on the bulkhead opposite him. The faint whispering of the drive seemed to grow louder. His hand on the blanket beside him felt every tuft, every thread. His nostrils sorted out the odors of the room: paint, oil, soap, ozone, perspiration, plastic...

Is it possible for a person to go through anxiety without glandular changes? he asked himself. *Yes, under certain pathological circumstances, none of which fit Sparrow.*

Ramsey remembered the sound of the captain's voice over the intercom during the period of stress: higher pitched, tense, clipped.

Again, Ramsey examined the tape. *Could the telemeter be wrong?*

He checked it. Functioning perfectly. Could there be disfunction in the mechanism within Sparrow's flesh? Then the other fluctuations would not have registered.

Ramsey leaned back, put a hand behind his head, thought through the problem. Two major possibilities suggested themselves: *If Sparrow knew about the wiper-rag-oil-spray thing then he wouldn't be anxious. What if he planted the rag and set that lube-system petcock himself? He could've done it to disable the ship and stop the mission because he's lost his nerve or because he's a spy.*

But there would've been other psychomotor indications which the telemeter would have registered.

This led to the other possibility: *In moments of great stress Sparrow's automatic glandular functions are taken over by the higher cortical centers. That could tie in with the known paranoiac tendencies. There could be a systematic breakdown of normal function under stress: such a turning away from fear that the whole being believes there could be no danger.*

Ramsey sat bolt upright: *That would fit the pattern of Sparrow's religious attitude. An utter and complete faith would explain it. There had been religious paranoiacs before. They'd even tried to hang the label on Christ.* Ramsey frowned. *But of course Schweitzer made the ones who tried to look like fools. Tore their arguments to shreds.*

A sharp rap on Ramsey's door interrupted his thoughts. He slipped the tapes into the false bottom of the telemeter box, closed the lid, locked it.

Again the rap. "Ramsey?" Garcia's voice.

"Yes?"

"Ramsey, you'd better take a couple of anti-fatigue pills. You're scheduled for the next watch."

"Right. Thanks." Ramsey slipped the box under his desk, went to the door, opened it. The companionway was empty. He looked at Garcia's door across the companionway, stood there a moment, feeling the ship around him. A drop of moisture condensing from the overhead fell past his eyes. Abruptly, he had to fight off a sense of depression. He could almost feel the terrible pressure of water around him.

Do I know what it is to be truly afraid? he asked himself.

CEASE
FIRE

Snow slanted across the frozen marshland, driven in fitful gusts. It drifted in a low mound against the wooden Observation Post. The antennae of the Life Detector atop the OP swept back and forth in a rhythmic halfcircle like so many frozen sticks brittle with rime ice.

The snow hid all distance, distorted substance into gray shadows without definition. A suggestion of brightness to the north indicated the sun that hung low on the horizon even at midnight in this season.

Out of possible choices of a place for a world-shattering invention to be born, this did not appear in the running.

A rifle bullet spanged against an abandoned tank northeast of the OP, moaned away into the distance. The bullet only emphasized the loneliness, the isolation of the OP set far out ahead of the front lines of the Arctic battlefields of 1972. Behind the post to the south stretched the long reaches of the Canadian barren lands. An arm of the Arctic Ocean below Banks Island lay hidden in the early snow storm to the north.

One operator—drugged to shivering wakefulness—stood watch in the OP. The space around him was barely six feet in diameter, crammed with equipment, gridded screens glowing a pale green with spots that indicated living flesh: a covey of ptarmigan, a possible Arctic fox. Every grid point on the screens held an aiming code for mortar fire.

This site was designated "OP 114" by the Allied command. It was no place for the sensitive man who had found himself pushed, shunted and shamed into this position of terror. The fact that he did occupy OP 114 only testified to the terrible urgencies that governed this war.

Again a rifle bullet probed the abandoned tank. Corporal Larry Hulser—crouched over the OP's screens—tried to get a track on the bullet. It had seemed to come from the life-glow spot he had identified as probably an Arctic fox.

Much too small for a human, he thought. *Or is it?*

The green glow of the screens underlighted Hulser's dark face, swept shadows upward where they merged with his black hair. He chewed his lips, his eyes darting nervously with the fear he could never hide, the fear that made him the butt of every joke back at the barracks.

Hulser did not look like a man who could completely transform his society. He looked merely like an indefinite lump of humanity encased in a Life Detector shield, crouching in weird green shadows.

In the distant days of his youth, one of Hulser's chemistry professors had labeled him during a faculty tea: *"A mystic—sure to fail in the modern world."*

The glow spot Hulser had identified as a fox shifted its position.

Should I call out the artillery? Hulser wondered. *No. This could be the one they'd choose to investigate with a flying detector. And if the pilot identified the glow as a fox*—Hulser cringed with the memory of the hazing he had taken on the wolf he'd reported two months earlier.

"Wolfie Hulser!"

I'm too old for this game, he thought. *Thirty-eight is too old. If there were only some way to end—*

Another rifle bullet spanged against the shattered tank. Hulser tried to crouch lower in the tiny wooden OP. The bullets were like questing fingers reaching out for unrecognized metal—to identify an OP. When the bullets found their mark, a single 200 mm. mortar shell followed, pinpointed by echophones. Or it could be as it had been with Breck Wingate, another observer.

Hulser shivered at the memory.

They had found Wingate hunched forward across his instruments, a neat hole through his chest from side to side just below the armpits. Wind had whistled through the wall of the OP from a single bullet hole beside Wingate. The enemy had found him and never known.

Hulser glanced up nervously at the plywood walls: all that shielded him from the searching bullets—a wood shell designed to absorb the metal seekers and send back the sound of a bullet hitting a snowdrift. A rolled wad of plot paper filled a bullet hole made on some other watch near the top of the dome.

Again Hulser shivered.

And again a bullet spanged against the broken tank. Then the ground rumbled and shook as a mortar shell zeroed the tank.

Discouraging us from using it as an OP, thought Hulser.

He punched the *backtrack* relay to give the mortar's position to his own artillery, but without much hope. The enemy was beginning to use the new "shift" shells that confused *backtrack.*

The phone beside his L-D screens glowed red. Hulser leaned into the cone of silence, answered: "OP 114. Hulser."

The voice was Sergeant Chamberlain's. "What was that mortar shooting at, Wolfie?"

Hulser gritted his teeth, explained about the tank.

Chamberlain's voice barked through the phone: "We shouldn't have to call for an explanation of these things! Are you sure you're awake and alert?"

"Yeah, Sarge."

"O.K. Keep your eyes open, Wolfie."

The red glow of the phone died.

Hulser trembled with rage. *Wolfie!*

He thought of Sergeant Mike Chamberlain: tall, overbearing, the irritating nasal twang in his voice. And he thought of what he'd like to do to Chamberlain's narrow, small-eyed face and its big nose. He considered calling back and asking for "Schnozzle" Chamberlain.

Hulser grinned tightly. *That'd get him! And he'd have to wait another four hours before he could do anything about it.*

But the thought of the certain consequences in arousing Chamberlain's anger wiped the grin from Hulser's face.

Something moved on his central screen. The fox. Or was it a fox? It moved across the frozen terrain toward the shattered tank, stopped halfway.

A fox investigating the strange odors of cordite and burned gas? he wondered. *Or is it the enemy?*

With this thought came near panic. If any living flesh above a certain minimum size—roughly fifty kilos—moved too close to an OP without the proper IFF, the hut and all in it exploded in a blinding flash of thermite: everything incinerated to prevent the enemy from capturing the observer's Life Detector shield.

Hulser studied the grid of his central screen. It reminded him of a game he'd played as a boy: two children across a room from one another, ruled graph paper hidden behind books in their laps. Each player's paper contained secretly marked squares: four in a row—a battleship, three in a row—a destroyer, two in a...

Again the glow on his screen moved toward the tank crater.

He stared at the grid intersection above the glowing spot, and far away in his mind a thought giggled at him: *Call and tell 'em you have a battleship on your screen at O-6-C. That'd get you a Section Eight right out of this man's army!*

Out of the army!

His thoughts swerved abruptly to New Oakland, to Carol Jean. *To think of her having our baby back there and—*

Again the (fox?) moved toward the tank crater.

But his mind was hopelessly caught now in New Oakland. He thought of all the lonely years before Carol: to work five days a week at Planetary Chemicals...the library and endless pages of books (and another channel of his mind commented: *You scattered your interests too widely!*)...the tiny cubbyhole rooms of his apartment...the tasteless—

Now, the (fox?) darted up to the tank crater, skirted it.

Hulser's mind noted the movement, went right on with its reverie: *Then Carol! Why couldn't we have found each other sooner? Just one month together and—*

Another small glowing object came on the screen near the point where he'd seen the first one. It, too, darted toward the tank crater.

Hulser was back in the chill present, a deadly suspicion gnawing him: *The enemy has a new type of shield, not as good as ours. It merely reduces image size!*

Or is it a pair of foxes?

Indecision tore at him.

They could have a new shield, he thought. *We don't have a corner on the scientific brains.*

And a piece of his mind wandered off in the new direction— the war within the war: the struggle for equipment superiority. A new weapon—a new shield—a better weapon—a better shield. It was like a terrible ladder dripping with maimed flesh.

They could have a new shield, his mind repeated.

And another corner of his mind began to think about the

shields, the complex flicker-lattice that made human flesh transparent to—

Abruptly, he froze. In all clarity, every diagram in place, every equation, every formula complete—all spread out in his mind was the instrument he knew could end this war. Uncontrolled shivering took over his body. He swallowed in a dry throat.

His gaze stayed on the screen before him. The two glow spots joined, moved into the tank crater. Hulser bent into the cone of silence at his phone. "This is OP 114. I have two greenies at co-ordinates O-6-C-sub T-R. I think they're setting up an OP!"

"Are you sure?" It was Chamberlain's nasal twang.

"Of course I'm sure!"

"We'll see."

The phone went dead.

Hulser straightened, wet his lips with his tongue. *Will they send a plane for a sky look? They don't really trust me.*

A rending explosion at the tank crater answered him.

Immediately, a rattle of small arms fire sprang up from the enemy lines. Bullets quested through the gray snow.

It was an enemy OP! Now, they know we have an observer out here!

Another bullet found the dome of the OP.

Hulser stared at the hole in terror. *What if they kill me? My idea will die with me! The war will go on and on and—* He jerked toward the phone, screamed into it: "Get me out of here! Get me out of here! Get me out of here!"

When they found him, Hulser was still mumbling the five words.

Chamberlain's lanky form crouched before the OP's crawl hole. The three muffled figures behind him ignored the OP, their heads turning, eyes staring off into the snow, rifles at the ready. The enemy's small arms fire had stopped.

Another one's broke, thought Chamberlain. *I thought shame might make him last a little while longer!*

He dragged Hulser out into the snow, hissed: "What is it, you? Why'd you drag us out into this?"

Hulser swallowed, said, "Sarge, please believe me. I know how to detonate enemy explosives from a distance without even knowing where the explosives are. I can—"

"Detonate explosives from a distance?" Chamberlain's eyes squinted until they looked like twin pieces of flint. *Another one for the head shrinkers unless we can shock him out of it,* he thought. He said, "You've gone off your rocker, you have. Now, you git down at them instruments and—"

Hulser paled. "No, Sarge! I have to get back where—"

"I could shoot your head off right where you—"

Fear, frustration, anger—all of the complex pressure-borne emotions in Hulser—forced the words out of him: "You big-nosed, ignorant lump. I can end this war! You hear?" His voice climbed. "Take me back to the lieutenant! I'm gonna send your kind back under the rocks, you—"

Chamberlain's fist caught Hulser on the side of the head, sent him tumbling into the snow. Even as he fell, Hulser's mind said: *But you told him, man! You finally told him!*

The sergeant glanced back at his companions, thought, *If the enemy heard him, we've had it!* He motioned one of the other men in close. "Mitch, take the watch on this OP. We'll have to get Hulser back."

The other nodded, ducked through the crawl hole.

Chamberlain bent over Hulser. "You stinkin' coward!" he hissed. "I've half a mind to kill you where you sit! But I'm gonna take you in so's I can have the personal pleasure of watchin' you crawl when they turn the heat on you! Now you git on your feet! An' you git to walkin'!"

Major Tony Lipari—"Tony the Lip" to his men—leaned against the canvas-padded wall of his dugout, hands clasped behind his head. He was a thin, oily-looking man with black hair, parted in the middle and slicked to his head like two beetle wings. In civilian life he had sold athletic supplies from a wholesale house. He had once worn a turban to an office party, and it had been like opening a door on his appearance. Somewhere in his ancestry there had been a Moor.

The major was tired (*Casualty reports! Endless casualty reports!*) and irritable, faintly nervous.

We don't have enough men to man the OPs now! he thought. *Do we have to lose another one to the psych boys?*

He said, "The lieuten—" His voice came out in a nervous squeak, and he stopped, cleared his throat. "The lieutenant has told me the entire story, corporal. Frankly, it strikes me as utterly fantastic."

Corporal Hulser stood at attention before the major. "Do I have the major's permission to speak?"

Lipari nodded. "Please do."

"Sir, I was a chemist...I mean as a civilian. I got into this branch because I'd dabbled in electronics and they happened to need L-D observers more than they needed chemists. Now, with our shields from—" He broke off, suddenly overwhelmed by the problem of convincing Major Lipari.

He's telling me we need L-D observers! thought Lipari. He said, "Well, go on, Hulser."

"Sir, do you know anything about chemistry?"

"A little."

"What I mean is, do you understand Redox equations and substitution reactions of—"

"Yes, yes. Go on!"

Hulser swallowed, thought: *He doesn't understand. Why won't he send me back to someone who does?* He said, "Sir, you're aware that the insulation layer of our L-D shield is a special kind of protection for—"

"Certainly! Insulates the wearer from the electrical charge of the suit!"

Hulser goggled at the major. "Insulates...Oh, no, sir. Begging the major's pardon, but—"

"Is this necessary, corporal?" asked Lipari. And he thought: *If he'd only stop this act and get back to work! It's so obvious he's faking! If—*

"Sir, didn't you get the—"

"I had a full quota of L-D shield orientation when they called me back into the service," said Lipari. "Infantry's my specialty, of course. Korea, you know. But I understand how to operate a shield. Go on, corporal." He kicked his chair away from the wall.

"Sir, what that insulation layer protects the wearer from is a kind of pseudo-substitution reaction in the skin. The suit's field can confuse the body into producing nitrogen bubbles at—"

"Yes, Hulser! I know all that! But what's this have to do with your wonderful idea?"

Hulser took a deep breath. "Sir, I can build a projector on the principle of the L-D suits that will produce an artificial substitution reaction in any explosive. I'm sure I can!"

"You're sure?"

"Yes, sir. For example, I could set up such a reaction in Trinox that would produce fluorine and ionized hydrogen—in minute quantities, of course—but sufficient that any nearby field source would detonate—"

"How would you make sure there was such a field in the enemy's storage area?"

"Sir! Everybody wears L-D shields of one kind or another! They're field generators. Or an internal combustion motor... or ... or just anything! If you have an explosive mixture collapsing from one system into another in the presence of fluorine and hydrogen—" He shrugged. "It'd explode if you looked cross-eyed at it!"

Lipari cleared his throat. "I see." Again he leaned back against the wall. The beginning of an eyestrain headache tugged at his temples. *Now, the put-up-or-shut-up,* he thought. He said, "How do we build this wonderful projector, corporal?"

"Sir, I'll have to sit down with some machinists and some E-techs and—"

"Corporal, I'll decide who sits down with whom among my men. Now, I'll tell you what you do. You just draw up the specifications for your projector and leave them with me. I'll see that they get into the proper hands through channels."

"Sir, it's not that simple. I have all the specs in my head now, yes, but in anything like this you have to work out bugs that—"

"We have plenty of technical experts who can do that," said Lipari. And he thought: *Why doesn't he give up? I gave him the chance to duck out gracefully! Scribble something on some paper, give it to me. That's the end of it!*

"But sir—"

"Corporal! My orderly will give you paper and pencil. You just—"

"Sir! It can't be done that way!"

Lipari rubbed his forehead. "Corporal Hulser, I am giving you an order. You will sit down and produce the plans and specifications for your projector. You will do it now."

Hulser tasted a sourness in his mouth. He swallowed. *And that's the last we'd ever hear of Corporal Larry Hulser,* he thought. *Tony the Lip would get the credit.*

He said, "Sir, after you submit my plans, what would you

do if someone asked, for example, how the polar molecules of—"

"You will explain all of these things in your outline. Do I make myself clear, corporal?"

"Sir, it would take me six months to produce plans that could anticipate every—"

"You're stalling, corporal!" Major Lipari pushed himself forward, came to his feet. He lowered his voice. "Let's face it, Hulser. You're faking! I know it. You know it. You just had a bellyful of war and you decided you wanted out."

Hulser shook his head from side to side.

"It's not that simple, corporal. Now. I've shown you in every way I can that I understand this, that I'm willing to—"

"Begging the major's pardon, but—"

"You will do one of two things, Corporal Hulser. You either produce the diagrams, sketches or whatever to prove that you *do* have a worthy idea, or you will go back to your unit. I'm done fooling with you!"

"Sir, don't you under—"

"I could have you shot under the Articles of War!"

And Lipari thought: *That's what he needs—a good shock!*

Bitter frustration almost overwhelmed Hulser. He felt the same kind of anger that had goaded him to attack Sergeant Chamberlain. "Major, enough people know about my idea by now that at least some of them would wonder if you hadn't shot the goose that laid the golden egg!"

Lipari's headache was full-blown now. He pushed his face close to Hulser's. "I have some alternatives to a firing squad, corporal!"

Hulser returned Lipari's angry glare. "It has occurred to me, *sir,* that this project would suddenly become 'our' project, and then 'your' project, and somewhere along the line a mere corporal would get lost."

Lipari's mouth worked wordlessly. Presently, he said, "That did it, Hulser! I'm holding you for a general court! There's one thing I can do without cooking any goose but yours!"

And that ends the matter as far as I'm concerned, thought Lipari. *What a day!*

He turned toward the door of his dugout: "Sergeant!"

The door opened to admit Chamberlain's beanpole figure. He crossed the room, came to attention before Lipari, saluted. "Sir?"

"This man is under arrest, sergeant," said Lipari. "Take him back to area headquarters under guard and have him held for a general court. On your way out send in my orderly."

Chamberlain saluted. "Yes, sir." He turned, took Hulser's arm. "Come along, Hulser."

Lipari turned away, groped on a corner shelf for his aspirin. He heard the door open and close behind him. And it was not until this moment that he asked himself: Could that crackpot actually have had a workable idea? He found the aspirin, shrugged the thought away. *Fantastic!*

Hulser sat on an iron cot with his head in his hands. The cell walls around him were flat, riveted steel. It was a space exactly the length of the cot, twice as wide as the cot. At his left, next to the foot of the bed, was a barred door. To his right, at the other end of the floor space, were a folding washbasin with water closet under. The cell smelled foul despite an overriding stink of disinfectant.

Why don't they get it over with? he asked himself. *Three days of this madhouse! How long are they—*

The cell door rattled.

Hulser looked up. A wizened figure in a colonel's uniform stood on the other side of the bars. He was a tiny man, gray-haired, eyes like a curious bird, a dried parchment skin. In the proper costume he would have looked like a medieval sorcerer.

A youthful MP sergeant stepped into view, unlocked the door, stood aside. The colonel entered the cell.

"Well, well," he said.

Hulser came to his feet, saluted.

"Will you be needing me, sir?" asked the MP sergeant.

"Eh?" The colonel turned. "Oh. No, sergeant. Just leave that door open and—"

"But sir—"

"Nobody could get out of this cell block, could they sergeant?"

"No, sir. But—"

"Then just leave the door open and run along."

"Yes, sir." The sergeant saluted, frowned, turned away. His footsteps echoed down the metal floor of the corridor.

The colonel turned back to Hulser. "So you're the young man with the bright ideas."

Hulser cleared his throat. "Yes, sir."

The colonel glanced once around the cell. "I'm Colonel Page of General Savage's staff. Chemical warfare."

Hulser nodded.

"The general's adjutant suggested that I come over and talk to you," said Page. "He thought a chemist might—"

"Page!" said Hulser. "You're not the Dr. Edmond Page who did the work on pseudo-lithium?"

The colonel's face broke into a pleased smile. "Why ... yes, I am."

"I read everything about your work that I could get my hands on," said Hulser. "It struck me that if you'd just—" His voice trailed off.

"Do go on," said Page.

Hulser swallowed. "Well, if you'd just moved from organic chemistry into inorganic, that—" He shrugged.

"I might have induced direct chemical rather than organic reactions?" asked Page.

"Yes, sir."

"That thought didn't occur to me until I was on my way over here," said Page. He gestured toward the cot. "Do sit down."

Hulser slumped back to the cot.

Page looked around, finally squeezed past Hulser's knees, sat down on the lid of the water closet. "Now, let's find out just what your idea is."

Hulser stared at his hands.

"I've discussed this with the general," said Page. "We feel that you may know what you're talking about. We would deeply appreciate a complete explanation."

"What do I have to lose?" asked Hulser.

"You may have reason for feeling bitter," said Page. "But after reading the charges against you I would say that you've been at least partly responsible for your present situation." He glanced at his wristwatch. "Now, tell me exactly how you propose to detonate munitions at a distance ... this projector you've talked about."

Hulser took a deep breath. *This is a chemist*, he thought. *Maybe I can convince him*. He looked up at Page, began explaining.

Presently, the colonel interrupted. "But it takes enormous amounts of energy to change the atomic—"

"I'm not talking about changing atomic structure in that sense, sir. Don't you see it? I merely set up an artificial condition *as though* a catalyst were present. A pseudo-catalyst. And this brings out of the static mixture substances that are already there: Ionized hydrogen from moisture—fluorine from the actual components in the case of Trinox. White phosphorus from Ditrate, nitric oxide and rhombic sulfur from common gunpowder."

Page wet his lips with his tongue. "But what makes you think that—in a nonorganic system—the presence of the pseudo-catalyst—" He shook his head. "Of course! How stupid of me! You'd first get a polar reaction—just as I did with pseudo-lithium. And that would be the first step into—" His eyes widened and he stared at Hulser. "My dear boy, I believe you've opened an entirely new field in nonorganic chemistry!"

"Do you see it, sir?"

"Of course I see it!" Page got to his feet. "You'd be creating an artificial radical with unstable perimeter. The presence of the slightest bit of moisture in that perimeter would give you your ionized hydrogen and—" He clapped his hands like a small boy in glee. "Kapowie!"

Hulser smiled.

Page looked down at him. "Corporal, I do believe your projector might work. I confess that I don't understand about field lattices and these other electronic matters, but you apparently do."

"Yes, sir."

"How did you ever stumble onto this?" asked Page.

"I was thinking about the lattice effect in our Life Detector systems—when suddenly, there it was: the complete idea!"

Page nodded. "It was one of those things that had to remain dormant until the precisely proper set of circumstances." Page squeezed past Hulser's knees. "No, no. Stay right there. I'm going to set up a meeting with Colonel Allenby of the L-D section, and I'll get in someone with more of a mechanical bent—probably Captain Stevens." He nodded. "Now, corporal, you just stay right here until—" His glance darted around the cell, and he laughed nervously. "Don't you worry, young man. We'll have you out of here in a few hours."

Hulser was to look back on the five weeks of the first phase in "Operation Big Boom" as a time of hectic unreality. Corps ordered the project developed in General Savage's reserve area after a set of preliminary plans had been shipped outside. The thinking was that there'd be less chance of a security leak that close to a combat zone, and that the vast barrens of the reserve area offered better opportunity for a site free of things that could detonate mysteriously and lead to unwanted questions.

But Corps was taking no chances. They ringed the area with special detachments of MPs. Recording specialists moved in on the project, copied everything for shipment stateside.

They chose an open tableland well away from their own munitions for the crucial test. It was a barren, windy place: gray rocks poking up from frozen earth. The long black worm of a power cable stretched away into the distance behind the test shelter.

A weasel delivered Hulser and Page to the test site. The projector box sat on the seat between them. It was housed in a green container two feet square and four feet long. A glass tube protruded from one end. A power connection, sealed and with a red "do not connect" sign, centered the opposite end. A tripod mounting occupied one side at the balance point.

The morning was cold and clear with a brittle snap to the air. The sky had a deep cobalt quality, almost varnished in its intensity.

About fifty people were gathered for the test. They were strung out through the shelter—a long shed open along one side. An empty tripod stood near the open side and almost in the center. On both sides of the tripod technicians sat before recording instruments. Small black wires trailed away ahead of them torward an ebony mound almost a mile from the shed and directly opposite the open side.

General Savage already was on the scene, talking with a stranger who had arrived that morning under an impressive air cover. The stranger had worn civilian clothes. Now, he was encased in an issue parka and snowpants. He didn't look or act like a civilian. And it was noted that General Savage addressed him as "sir."

The general was a brusque, thick-bodied man with the overbearing confidence of someone secure in his own ability. His face held a thick-nosed, square-jawed bulldog look. In fatigues without insignia, he could have been mistaken for a sergeant. He looked the way a hard, old-line sergeant is expected to look. General Savage's men called him "Me Tarzan" mainly because he took snow baths, mother naked, in subzero weather.

A white helmeted security guard ringed the inside of the test shed. Hulser noted that they wore no sidearms, carried no weapons except hand-held bayonets. He found himself thinking that he would not have been surprised to see them carrying crossbows.

General Savage waved to Page as the colonel and Hulser entered the shed. Colonel Page returned the gesture, stopped before a smooth-cheeked lieutenant near the tripod.

"Lieutenant," said Page, "have all explosives except the test stack been removed from the area?"

The lieutenant froze to ramrod attention, saluted, "Yes, sir, colonel."

Page took a cigarette from his pocket. "Let me have your cigarette lighter, please, lieutenant."

"Yes, sir." The lieutenant fumbled in a pocket, withdrew a chrome lighter, handed it to Page.

Colonel Page took the lighter in his hand, looked at it for a moment, hurled both lighter and cigarette out into the snow. The lighter landed about sixty feet away.

The lieutenant paled, then blushed.

The colonel said, "Every cigarette lighter, every match. And check with everyone to see that they took those special pills at least four hours ago. We don't want any *internal* combustion without a motor around it."

The lieutenant looked distraught, "Yes, sir."

"And, lieutenant, stop the last weasel and have the driver wait to cart the stuff you collect out of our area."

"Yes, sir." The lieutenant hurried away.

Page turned back to Hulser, who had mounted the projector on its tripod, and now stood beside it.

"All ready, sir," said Hulser. "Shall I connect the cable?"

"What do you think?" asked Page.

"We're as ready as we'll ever be."

"O.K. Connect it, then stand by with the switch in your hands."

Hulser turned to comply. And now, as the moment of the

critical test approached, he felt his legs begin to tremble. He felt sure that everyone could see his nervousness.

A tense stillness came over the people in the shed.

General Savage and his visitor approached. The general was explaining the theory of the projector.

His visitor nodded.

Seen close-up, the other man gave the same impression of hard competence that radiated from General Savage—only more competent, harder. His cheekbones were like two ridges of tan rock beneath cavernous sockets, brooding dark eyes.

General Savage pointed to the black mound of explosives in the distance. "We have instruments in there with the explosives, sir. The wires connect them with our recorders here in the shed. We have several types of explosives to be tested, including kerosene, gasoline, engine oil. Everything we could lay our hands on except atomics. But if these things blow, then we'll know the projector also will work on atomics."

The visitor spoke, and his voice came out with a quality like a stick dragged through gravel. "It was explained to me that—the theory being correct—this projector will work on any petroleum fuel, including coal."

"Yes, sir," said Savage. "It is supposed to ignite coal. We have a few lumps in a sack to one side. You can't see it because of the snow. But our instruments will tell us which of these things are effected—" he glanced at Hulser "—if any."

Colonel Page returned from checking the recording instruments.

Savage turned to the colonel. "Are we ready, Ed?"

"Yes, general." He glanced at Hulser, nodded. "Let's go, Larry. Give it power."

Hulser depressed the switch in his hand, involuntarily closed his eyes, then snapped them open and stared at the distant explosives.

A low humming arose from the projector.

Page spoke to the general. "It'll take a little time for the effect to build u—"

As he started to say "up" the mound of explosives went *up* in a giant roaring and rumbling. Colonel Page was left staring at the explosion, his mouth shaped to say "p."

Steam and dust hid the place where the explosives had been.

The gravel voice of the visitor spoke behind Hulser. "Well,

there goes the whole shooting match, general. And I *do* mean shooting!"

"It's what we were afraid of, sir," said Savage. "But there's no help for it now." He sounded bitter.

Hulser was struck by the bitterness in both voices. He turned, became conscious that the lieutenant whom Page had reprimanded was beating at a flaming breast pocket, face livid. The people around him were laughing, trying to help.

Page had hurried along the line of recorders, was checking each one.

The significance of the lieutenant's antics suddenly hit Hulser. *Matches! He forgot his spare matches after losing his cigarette lighter!* Hulser glanced to where the colonel had thrown the lighter, saw a black patch in the snow.

Page returned from checking the recorders. "We can't be sure about the coal, but as nearly as we can determine, it touched off everything else in the stack!" He put an arm on Hulser's shoulder. "This young genius has won the war for us."

Savage turned, scowled at Hulser.

The (civilian?) snorted.

But Hulser was staring out at the explosion crater, a look of euphoria on his face.

The technicians were moving out into the area now, probing cautiously for unexploded fragments.

The general and his visitor exchanged a glance that could have meant anything.

Savage signaled his radio operator to call for transportation.

Presently, a line of weasels came roaring up to the test site.

Savage took Hulser's arm in a firm grip. "You'd better come with us. You're a valuable piece of property now."

Hulser's mind came back to the curious conversation between Savage and the visitor after the explosion, and he was struck by the odd sadness in the general's voice. *Could he be an old war dog sorry to see it end?* Somehow, on looking at the general, that didn't fit.

They sped across the barrens to the base, Hulser uncomfortable between the general and his visitor. Apparently, no one wanted to discuss what had just happened. Hulser was made uncomfortable by the lack of elation around him. He looked at the back of the driver's neck, but that told him nothing.

They strode into the general's office, an oblong room without windows. Maps lined the walls. A low partition separated one space containing two barren tables from another space containing three desks, one set somewhat apart. They crossed to the separate desk.

Savage indicated his visitor. "This is Mr. Sladen." There was a slight hesitation on the "mister."

Hulser suppressed a desire to salute, shook hands. The other man had a hard grip in an uncalloused hand.

Sladen's gravelly baritone came out brusque and commanding. "Brief him, general. I'll go get my people and their gear together. We'll have to head right back."

Savage nodded. "Thank you, sir. I'll get right at it."

Sladen cast a speculative look at Hulser. "Make sure he understands clearly what has just happened. I don't believe he's considered it."

"Yes, sir."

Sladen departed.

Hulser felt an odd sinking sensation in his stomach.

Savage said, "I'm not rank happy, Hulser, and we haven't much time. We're going to forget about military formality for a few minutes."

Hulser nodded without speaking.

"Do you know what has just happened?" asked Savage.

"Yes, sir. But what puzzles me is that you people don't seem pleased about our gaining the whip hand so we can win this war. It's—"

"It's not certain that we have the whip hand." Savage sat down at his desk, picked up a book bound in red leather.

"You mean the enemy—"

"Bright ideas like yours just seem to float around in the air, Hulser. They may already have it, or they could be working on it. Otherwise, I'd have seen that your brainstorm was buried. It seems that once human beings realize something can be done, they're not satisfied until they've done it."

"Have there been any signs that the enemy—"

"No. But neither have *they* seen any signs of *our* new weapon ...I hope. The point is: we do have it and we're going to use it. We'll probably overwhelm them before they can do anything about it. And that'll be the end of *this* war."

"But, if explosives are made obsolete, that'll mean an end

to all wars," protested Hulser. "That's what I'm concerned about!"

The general sneered. "Nothing, my bright-eyed young friend, has thus far made war impossible! When this one's over, it'll be just a matter of time until there's another war, both sides using your projector."

"But, sir—"

"So the next war will be fought with horse cavalry, swords, crossbows and lances," said Savage. "And there'll be other little *improvements!*" He slammed the red book onto his desk, surged to his feet. "Elimination of explosives only makes espionage, poisons, poison gas, germ warfare—all of these—a necessity!"

"How can you—"

"Don't you understand, Hulser? You've made the military use of explosives impossible. That means gasoline. The internal combustion motor is out. That means jet fuels. Airplanes are out. That means gunpowder. Everything from the smallest sidearm to the biggest cannon is out!"

"Certainly, but—"

"But we have other alternatives, Hulser. We have the weapons King Arthur used. And we have some *modern* innovations: poison gases, curare-tipped crossbow bolts, bacterial—"

"But the Geneva Convention—"

"Geneva Convention be damned! And that's just what will happen to it as soon as a big enough group of people decide to ignore it!" General Savage hammered a fist on his desk. "Get this! Violence is a part of human life. The lust for power is a part of human life. As long as people want power badly enough, they'll use any means to get it—fair or foul! Peaceful or otherwise!"

"I think you're being a pessimist, sir."

"Maybe I am. I *hope* I am. But I come from a long line of military people. We've seen some things to make us pessimists."

"But the pressures for peace—"

"Have thus far not been strong enough to prevent wars, Hulser." The general shook his head. "I'll tell you something, my young friend: When I first saw the reference to your ideas in the charges against you, I had the sinking sensation one gets when going down for the third time. I hoped against hope that you were wrong, but I couldn't afford *not* to investigate. I hoped that Major Lipari and Sergeant Chamberlain had you pegged for—"

The general stopped, glared at Hulser. "There's another bone I have to pick with you! Your treatment of two fine soldiers was nothing short of juvenile! If it wasn't for the Liparis and the Chamberlains, you'd be getting thirty lashes every morning from your local slavekeeper!"

"But, sir—"

"Don't 'But, sir' me, Hulser! If there was time before you leave, I'd have you deliver personal apologies to both of them!"

Hulser blushed, shook his head. "I don't know. All I really know is that I was sure my idea would work, and that Lipari and Chamberlain didn't understand. And I knew if I was killed, or if my idea wasn't developed, the enemy might get it first."

Savage leaned back against his desk, passed a hand across his eyes. "You were right, of course. It's just that you were bucking the system, and you're not the right kind to buck the system. Your kind usually fails when you try."

Hulser sighed.

"You're now a valuable piece of property, my lad. So don't feel sorry for yourself. You'll be sent home where you can be around when your wife has that child."

Hulser looked surprised.

"Oh, yes, we found out about her," said Savage. "We thought at first you were just working a good dodge to get home to her." He shrugged. "You'll probably have it fairly soft now. You'll be guarded and coddled. You'll be expected to produce another act of *genius!* The Lord knows, maybe you *are* a genius."

"You wait and see, sir. I think this will mean an end to all wars."

The general suddenly looked thoughtful. "Hulser, a vastly underrated and greatly despised writer—in some circles—once said, 'There is nothing more difficult to take in hand, more perilous to conduct, or more uncertain in its success, than to take the lead in the introduction of a new order of things.' That's a very deep statement, Hulser. And there you are, way out in front with 'a new order of things.' I hope for the sake of that child you're going to have—for the sake of all children—that we don't have another war." He shrugged. "But I don't hold out too—"

Sladen popped back into the office. "Our air cover's coming up, general. We'll have to take him like he is. Send his gear along later, will you?"

"Certainly, sir." Savage straightened, stuck out his right hand, shook with Hulser. "Good luck, Hulser. You take what I said to heart. It's the bitter truth that men of war have to live with. You weren't attacking the source of the problem with your bright idea. You were attacking one of the symptoms."

Savage's left hand came up from his desk with the red book. "Here's a gift for that child you're going to have." He pressed the book into Hulser's hands. "The next generation will need to understand this book."

Hulser had time to say, "Thank you, sir." Then he was propelled out the door by Sladen.

It was not until he was on the plane winging south that Hulser had an opportunity to examine the book. Then he gripped it tightly in both hands, stared out the window at the sea of clouds. The book was a limited edition copy, unexpurgated, of the works of Niccolo Machiavelli, the master of deceit and treachery.

EPILOGUE

Many people labor under the misapprenhension that the discovery of the Hulser Detonator was made in a secret government laboratory. In actuality, the genius of Dr. Lawrence Hulser was first seen on the Arctic battlefields of 1972 where he conceived his idea and where that idea was immediately recognized.
Beecher Carson,
"The Coming of the Sword—A History of Ancient and Modern Wars"—Vol. 6, p. 112.

A
MATTER
OF
TRACES

The Special Subcommittee on Intergalactic Culture *(see page 33)* met, pursuant to call, at 1600 in the committee room, 8122 Senate Office Building, Wershteen City, Senator Jorj C. Zolam, chairman of the subcommittee, presiding.

Also present: Senator Arden G. Pingle of Proxistu I; Mergis W. Ledder, counsel to the subcommittee; Jorj X. McKie, saboteur extraordinary to the committee.

Senator Zolam: The subcommittee will be in order. Our first witness will be the Hon. Glibbis Hablar, Secretary of Fusion.

We are glad to see you, Mr. Secretary. We believe that you have some of the best cultural fusion experts in the universe working in your Department, and we are in the habit of leaning heavily upon them for our records of factual data.

As you know, our subcommittee is working under Senate Resolution 1443 of the 803rd Congress, First Session, to make a full and complete investigation of complaints received from economy groups that the Historical Preservation Teams of the Bureau of Cultural Affairs are excessively wasteful of their funds.

Now, Mr. Secretary, I understand that you are prepared to present a sample of the work being done by your Historical Preservation Teams.

Secretary Hablar: Yes, Senator. I have here a tri-di record of an interview with one of the early pioneers to Gomeisa III, also a transcription of the interview, and some explanatory matter necessary for a complete understanding of this exhibit.

Senator Zolam: Do you wish to project the tri-di at this time?

Secretary Hablar: Unfortunately, Senator, I am unable to do that. My projector has been officially sabotaged—presumably to save the time of the committee. I am embarrassed by my inability to...

Senator Zolam: Committee Saboteur McKie will enter an official explanation for the record.

Saboteur McKie: The Secretary may make the official excuse that his tri-di recording was faulty.

Secretary Hablar: Thank you, Mr. McKie. Your courtesy is deeply appreciated. May I add to my official excuse that the faulty recording is attributable to antiquated equipment which our appropriation for the last biennium was insufficient to renew or replace?

Senator Zolam: That request will be considered later by the full committee. Now, Mr. Secretary, you do have a written transcription of this interview?

Secretary Hablar: Yes, Senator.

Senator Zolam: What is the significance of this particular interview?

Secretary Hablar: The interview was recorded at Lauh Village on Gomeisa III. We consider this interview to be one of the best we've ever recorded. It is particularly interesting from the standpoint of the cultural tracings revealed in the vernacular used by the elderly gentleman interviewed.

Senator Zolam: Who did your men interview?

Secretary Hablar: His name is Hilmot Gustin. Students of intergalactic familial relationships recognize the name Gustin, or Gusten, or Gousting, or Gaustern—as stemming from the cultural milieu of Procyon out of the Mars Migration.

Senator Zolam: Will you identify this Gustin for the record, please?

Secretary Hablar: His parents took him to Gomeisa III in the pioneer days when he was nine-years-old. That was the year 6873, New Calendar, making him 238-years old now. Gustin's family was in the second migratory wave that arrived three standard years after the first settlement. He is now retired, living with a niece.

Senator Zolam: Do you have a likeness of Gustin?

Secretary Hablar: Only on the wire, Senator. However, he is described in one of the team reports as ... excuse me a moment, I believe I have the report right here. Yes ... as "... a crotchety old citizen who looks and acts about half his age. He is about two meters tall, narrow face, long gray hair worn in the ancient twin-braid style, watery blue eyes, a sharp chin and enormous ears and nose."

Senator Zolam: A very vivid description.

Secretary Hablar: Thank you, Senator. Some of our people take an artistic pride in their work.

Senator Zolam: That's quite apparent, Mr. Secretary. Now, are you prepared to submit the transcribed interview at this time?

Secretary Hablar: Yes, Senator. Do you want me to read it?

Senator Zolam: That will not be necessary. Submit it to the robo-sec here, and the interview will be printed at this point in the record.

INTERVIEW WITH HILMOT GUSTIN, PIONEER SETTLER ON GOMEISA III, TAKEN BY HISTORICAL PRESERVATION

PRESERVATION OF CULTURAL AND HISTORICAL TRACES
IN
THE GOMEISA PLANETS BY THE BUREAU OF
CULTURAL AFFAIRS
HEARINGS
before the
SPECIAL SUBCOMMITTEE ON INTERGALACTIC CULTURE
of the
COMMITTEE ON GALACTIC FUSION, DISPERSION,
MIGRATION
AND SETTLEMENT
INTERGALACTIC SENATE
803rd CONGRESS
First Session
pursuant to
S. Res. 1443
A resolution to investigate the activities of the Historical
Preservation Teams of the Bureau of Cultural Affairs

Part 1
Intergalactic Department of Fusion, Bureau of Cultural
Affairs
Domen 18, 19, 20, 21, 22, 23, 24, 25, 26: 7102
(New Calendar)
Printed for the use of the Committee on Galactic Fusion,
Dispersion, Migration and Settlement

*TEAM 579 OF THE BUREAU OF CULTURAL AFFAIRS,
DEPARTMENT OF FUSION.*

Interviewer Simsu Yaggata: Here we are in the home of Mr. and Mrs. Presby Kilkau in the village of Lauh, Gomeisa III. We are here to interview Hilmot Gustin, the gentleman seated across from me beside his niece, Mrs. Kilkau. Mr. Gustin is one of the few surviving pioneers to Gomeisa III, and he has kindly agreed to tell us some of the things he experienced first-hand in those early days. I want to thank you, Mrs. Kilkau, for your hospitality in inviting me here today.

Mrs. Kilkau: It is we who are honored, Mr. Yaggata.

Gustin: I still think this is a lot of frip-frap, Bessie. I was supposed to go bilker fishing today.

Mrs. Kilkau: But, Uncle Gus.

Gustin: How about you, Mr. Yaggata? Wouldn't you rather go fishing?

Yaggata: I'm sorry, sir. Our schedule doesn't permit me the time.

Gustin: Too bad. The bilker are biting like a flock of hungry fang-birds.

Yaggata: I wonder if we could begin by having you tell us when you first came to Gomeisa III?

Gustin: That was in '64.

Yaggata: That would be 6864?

Gustin: Yes. I was just a wicky boy then. My pap moved us from Procyon IV in the second wave.

Yaggata: I understand you come from a long line of pioneers, sir.

Gustin: My folks never did stay put after Mars. We spent five generations on Mars—then, just like boomer seeds: spang! all over creation!

Yaggata: You came out in the Mars Migration?

Gustin: That was my grandfather went to Procyon IV. My pap was born enroute. I was born on Procyon.

Yaggata: And what motivated your father to migrate here to Gomeisa III?

Gustin: He heard it was green. Procyon's nothing but one big sandstorm.

Yaggata: And what did he say when he found the vegetation was purple?

Gustin: He said anything was better than yellow dust.

Yaggata: And this is a very beautiful planet.

Gustin: One of the prettiest in the whole universe!

Yaggata: Now, sir, we're interested in the details of your life as it was in those early days. How did you find conditions when you arrived?

Gustin: Rougher than a chigger's ... Are you recording now, Mr. Yaggata?

Yaggata: Yes, I am.

Gustin: We found it pretty rough.

Yaggata: How soon after arrival did you take up your own claim?

Gustin: Ten or fifteen days we waited in the bracks with all the other chums. Then we came directly to Lauh. There were two other families in the district: the Pijuns and the Kilkaus. Bessie's husband is a grandson of old Effus Kilkau.

Yaggata: What did it look like around here in those days?

Gustin: Nothing but fritch brush and wally bugs, an occasional tiger snake and some duka-dukas, and, of course, those danged fangbirds.[1]

Yaggata: Most of the universe is familiar with the terrible fangbirds, sir. We can all be thankful they've been exterminated.

Gustin: They haven't been exterminated! They're just waiting in some hidden valley for the day when...

Mrs. Kilkau: Now, Uncle Gus!

Gustin: Well, they are!

Yaggata: The duka-dukas—those are the little fuzzy doglike creatures, aren't they?

Gustin: That's right. Their fuzz is stiff as wire and barbed. Scratch worse than a fritch thorn.

Yaggata: What was the first thing you did when you came here?

Gustin: We took sick with the toogies!

Yaggata: The toogies?

Gustin: The medics call it Fremont's boils after old Doc Fremont who was in the first wave. He's the one discovered they were caused by the micro-pollen of the fritch flowers.

Yaggata: I see. Did you build a house immediately?

Gustin: Well, sir, in between scratching the toogies we threw up a sod shelter with a shake roof, and piled fritch brush around for a compound to keep out the duka-dukas.

---

[1] Fangbirds, or pseudo-Pterodactylus, native to Gomeisa III. A flying reptile, now extinct, that grew to a wingspan of ten meters. Creature characterized by venomous fangs (formic acid) protruding from roof of nose hood.

Yaggata: That must have been exciting—listening to the weird screams of the fangbirds, the whistling calls of the duka-dukas.

Gustin: We all had too much work to do, and no time to feel excited.

Yaggata: Most of the early pioneers have their names attached to some element of this planet, sir. Was your family so honored?

Gustin: Heh, heh! Gustin swamp! That's what we've got! I'll tell you, Mr. Yaggata, Bessie wanted me to make out like our family was a pack of heroes, but the truth is we weren't anything but dirt farmers, and with a swamp making up about two-thirds of our dirt.

Yaggata: But you certainly must've had some interesting experiences while carving a ranch out of that wilderness.

Gustin: It's a funny thing, mister, but what some folks call *interesting experiences* aren't anything but labor and misery to those who're having them.

Yaggata: Wasn't there anything to lighten the load? Something amusing, perhaps?

Gustin: Well, sir, there was the time pap bought the rollit[2] and he...

Mrs. Kilkau: Oh, now, Uncle Gus! I'm sure Mr. Yaggata wouldn't be interested in a silly old commercial transaction like..."

Gustin: You see here, Bessie! I'm the one's being interviewed!

Mrs. Kilkau: Of course, Uncle Gus, but...

Gustin: And I think that story about the rollit has a real lesson for everyone!

Yaggata: It certainly wouldn't do any harm to hear the story, sir.

Gustin: You understand, mister, we weren't anything but lean chums[3] with the little kit[4]. Our power pack was busy all the time just producing bare essentials. So when old Effus Kilkau advertised that he had a draft animal for sale, pap was all for buying it.

Yaggata: Advertised? How was that done?

Gustin: On the checker net[5]. Old Effus advertised that he had one rollit for sale cheap, weight 2,500 kilos, trained to plow.

Yaggata: Some of those who will use this record will not be familiar with the genus rollitus sphericus, Mr. Gustin. Would you mind setting the record clear?

Gustin: In due time, son. Don't light a short fuse. The point is, my pap didn't know a rollit from a bowling ball, either, and he was too darned proud to admit it.

Yaggata: Ha, ha, ha. Wouldn't anyone enlighten him?

Gustin: Well, old Effus suspected pap was ignorant about rollits, and Effus thought it'd be a good joke just to let him have it cold.

Yaggata: I see. How was the transaction completed?

Gustin: All done on the checker net, and confirmed at base where they credited Effus with the seventy galars.

Yaggata: Your father bought it sight unseen?

Gustin: Oh, certainly! There was no question of hanky-panky in those days. People had to help each other...and they had to be honest because their lives depended on it. It's only after we get civilized that we feel free to cheat. Besides, we lived so far apart in those days that we'd have lost more going to look at the beast than just having it shipped over.

Yaggata: That certainly makes sense, sir. But didn't your father kind of feel around to find out specifically what it was that he was buying?

Gustin: Oh, he probed around some. But pap was afraid of appearing the sag[6]. I do remember he asked how the rollit was to feed. Old Effus just said that this rollit was trained to a whistle call, and could be turned loose to graze off the country. About then, somebody else chimed in on the net and said 70 galars was certainly cheap for a 2500-kilo rollit, and if pap didn't want the beast, then he'd take it. So pap closed the deal right then and there.

Yaggata: How did they deliver it?

Gustin: Well, the Kilkaus were some better off than we were. They had a freight platform null to 6000 kilos. They just put the rollit on that platform and flew it over.

Yaggata: What did your father say when he saw it?

---

[2]Rollit, genus Rollitus Sphericus, exterminated on Gomeisa III in the mutated mastitis epidemic of 6990. One herd may be seen in Galactic zoo, Aspidiske III, although this is the heavy planet adapted form. The original was an ovoid oviparous creature that grew to a size of some twenty meters diameter, moved by shifting balance.

[3]Lean chums—marginal pioneers, poor.

[4]Little Kit—minimum pioneer equipment permitted by settlement authorities—clothing suited to local climate (2 changes each); one Hellerite power pack; hand tools fitted for local resources and sufficient to build shelter, work the land.

[5]Checker net—daily radio check-in network required during pioneer period on all planets.

[6]Sag—a fool, stupid person, one easily sided.

Gustin: You mean about harness?

Yaggata: Yes.

Gustin: Well, sir, I don't think pap even thought about the harness problem. We'd had a ciget on Procyon, and pap'd made his own harness with good long traces so he could stay away from the stink of it. He just figured he'd have another set of harness to make.

Yaggata: Didn't he say *anything* about harness?

Gustin: No. He didn't have a chance to say anything. You see, the rollit was a little spooky from the flight. As soon as they let it down it rolled all over the landscape, and it made one pass and rolled right over me.

Yaggata: Galumpers! To someone who'd never seen a rollit before, I imagine that was quite frightening!

Gustin: It's a good thing Maw didn't see it. She'd have passed dead away. You know, a 2500-kilo rollit develops about 1500 kilos of forward thrust from a standing start, and once it gets moving it can really roll. They're deceptive, too. They look like a kind of giant amœba flowing over the landscape, and all of a sudden they're right on top of you—literally!

Yaggata: Weren't you frightened when it ran over you?

Gustin: Well, it knocked me down, there was a second of darkness and a kind of warm, firm pressure—then it was gone. You know, a rollit won't hurt you. In fact, they're really very friendly. There was a case of a fellow over in Mirmon County who was saved from a fangbird by his rollit. The rollit just sat on this fellow until the fangbird gave up.

Yaggata: I'll bet that was an experience!

Gustin: Sure was. You know, a rollit's ninety percent mobile fluid and pump muscles, and the rest a hide like flexible armor plate. An adult rollit's practically immune to physical attack— even from a fangbird—and there's nothing like being inde-structible to make you a friend of everyone.

Yaggata: What was your reaction to being run down by that big animated ball of flesh?

Gustin: After the first shock, I wanted to try it again. I thought it was fun. But pap was so shaken by it, that he rushed me indoors. It took old Effus a half hour to convince pap that a rollit wouldn't hurt anyone, that it distributed its weight over such a large area that it was just like a good massage.

Yaggata: Ha, ha, ha. So there was your father with a rollit and no idea how to harness it.

Gustin: That's right. He didn't even think about it until after lunch. Old Effus was gone by then. The rollit was outside just rolling around, browsing off the fritch brush, clearing quite an area of it, at that. Good brush buckers, rollits are.

Yaggata: How did your father approach the problem?

Gustin: He just walked up to the rollit, clucked at it and whistled like ole Effus had told him. He led the rollit over to the shed where we had our imperv plow. It was a three-gang plow with a two and a half foot bite.

Yaggata: How was it supposed to be towed?

Gustin: By a power pack rotor. But we only had the one pack, and we didn't want to go into three-ball for a rotor.

Yaggata: What did your father say?

Gustin: He said, "Well, let's figure out how to hook this beast to the front of that there..." And then it hit him. How do you put harness on a beast that rolls its whole body, and moves by shifting its center of gravity? That was a real stinker of a problem.

Yaggata: I've seen the diagrams. They appear quite obvious. Didn't it occur to your father right away how it had to be done?

Gustin: Sometimes the obvious isn't so obvious until someone's showed it to you, mister. Remember, pap had never seen anything even remotely like a rollit before. His whole concept of draft animals was tied up in something like a ciget—a creature with a specific number of legs and a body that would accommodate some kind of harness. The rollit was a different breed of beast entirely.

Yaggata: Certainly, but...

Gustin: And what you've been used to seeing can tie your mind up in little knots so tight you can't see anything else.

Yaggata: Why didn't your father just call up a neighbor and ask how to hitch a rollit to a plow?

Gustin: Pap was too proud. He wasn't going to ask and look foolish, and he wasn't going to give up. For about a week it was a regular ten-ring scrag fight around our compound. We learned later that old Effus and half his clan were up in the hills with binoculars laughing themselves silly. They ran bets on what we'd try next.

Yaggata: What'd you try *first*?

Gustin: Just a plain loop harness. Pap made a loop big enough to pass around the rollit. He clucked the beast into the loop, dropped the bight around near the top front—that is, around the end away from the plow. A rollit doesn't rightly have a front. Then he ordered the beast to pull. That rollit leaned into the line like it knew what it was doing. The plow moved forward about four feet, then the line was down where it slipped under the beast. Pap clucked it back into the harness and ordered it forward again. About three times that way and it was clear he'd never get his plowing done if he had to reharness every four feet.

Yaggata: Were your neighbors watching all this?

Gustin: Yes. By the second day the whole district was in on the joke. And we had a full flap in our compound and were really hupping it.

Yaggata: What'd he try next?

Gustin: A kind of web harness with rollers. It took us three days to make it. Meanwhile, we tried a vertical harness that went over the top and under the rollit. We greased the area that contacted the rollit, but the grease wouldn't last. As soon as it was gone, the harness would rub. Our rollit could rub through the toughest harness in about ten revolutions.

Yaggata: How'd the web harness work?

Gustin: It really wasn't a bad idea—better than what our neighbors were using right then if he'd perfected it.

Yaggata: What were your neighbors using?

Gustin: A kind of corral on wheels with rollers along the front to contact the front of the rollit. It had harness rings on the back. They opened one side to let the rollit in, hooked on the equipment, and the rollit pulled the whole rig.

Yaggata: I'm curious. Why didn't your father sneak over and watch his neighbors using their rollits?

Gustin: He tried. But they were all onto him. Our neighbors were just never using their beasts when pap came around. It was like a comic formal dance. They'd invite him in for a drink of chicker. Pap would remark about their plowing. He'd ask to look over their equipment, but there'd never be anything around that even remotely resembled rollit harness.

Yaggata: Uh...what was wrong with the web harness he tried?

Gustin: Pap hadn't made the web big enough to belly completely around the front of the rollit. And then the rollers kept fouling because he hadn't perfected a good sling system.

Yaggata: How did he finally solve the problem?

Gustin: He calmed down and started thinking straight. First, he put the plow out in the center of our compound. Then he stationed the rollit all around the plow, first one side then the other. And just like that—he had it.

Yaggata: I must be a little slow on obvious associations myself. Something has just occurred to me. Was your father the inventor of the standard rollitor?

Gustin: It was his idea.

Mrs. Kilkau: Uncle Gus! You never told us your father was an inventor! I never realized...

Gustin: He wasn't an inventor. He was just a darned good practical pioneer. As far as thinking up the original rollitor is concerned, that'd be obvious to anyone who'd given it a second's thought. What do you think the Gomeisa Historical Society has been trying to...

Mrs. Kilkau: Do you mean that musty old junk out in the number two warehouse?

Gustin: That *musty old junk* includes your mother's first swamp cream tritchet![7] And right spang in the middle of that *musty old junk* is the first rollitor!

Yaggata: Do you mean you have the original rollitor right here?

Gustin: Right out back in the warehouse.

Yaggata: Why...that thing's priceless! Could we go out and see it now?

Gustin: Don't see why not.

Mrs. Kilkau: Oh, Uncle Gus! It's so dirty out there and...

Gustin: A little dirt never hurt anyone, Bessie! Uhhhgh! That knee where the fangbird got me is giving me more trouble this week. Too bad we don't have any rollits around nowadays. There's nothing like a rollit massage to pep up the circulation.

Yaggata: Have *you* had an encounter with a fangbird?

Gustin: Oh, sure. A couple of times.

Yaggata: Could you tell us about it?

Gustin: Later, son, Let's go look at the rollitor.

(Editor: A raw splice break has been left on the wire at this point and should be repaired.)

Yaggata: Here we are in a corner of warehouse number two. Those stacked boxes you see in the background are cases of

---

[7]Swamp cream tritchet—the crude baffled incline first used to settle out the floating curds secreted by calophyllum gomeisum, the common swamp bush of Gomeisa III.

swamp cream so important to the cosmetic industry—and the chief output of the Gustin-Kilkau Ranch.

Gustin: This here's a trench climber used for mining the raw copper we discovered in the fumerole region.

Yaggata: And this must be the original rollitor attached to this plow.

Gustin: That's right. It's a simple thing rightly enough: just four wooden rollers set in two 'V's', one set of rollers above the other, and the whole rig attached directly to the plow at the rear.

Yaggata: They're quite large rollers.

Gustin: We had a big rollit. You see this ratchet thing in here?

Yaggata: Yes.

Gustin: That adjusted the height of the rollers and the distance between the two sets to fit the frontal curve of our rollit. The rollit just moved up against these rollers. One set of rollers rode high on the beast's frontal curve, and the other set of rollers rode low. The rollit kind of wedged in between them and pushed.

Yaggata: What are these wheels on the plow frame?

Gustin: They kept the plow riding level.

Yaggata: It's really such a simple device.

Gustin: Simple! We trained our rollit to plow all by itself!

Yaggata: What'd your neighbors think of that?

Gustin: I'll tell you they stopped laughing at pap! Inside of a forty-day, the old tow corrals were all discarded. They called the new rigs Gustin rollitors for awhile, but the name soon got shortened.

Mrs. Kilkau: I never realized! To think! Right here in our own warehouse! Why...the Historical Society...

Gustin: They can wait until I've passed on! I get a deal of satisfaction coming out here occasionally and just touching this *musty old junk*. It does you good to remember where you came from.

Mrs. Kilkau: But, Uncle Gus...

Gustin: And you came from dirt-farming pioneers, Bessie! Fine people! There wouldn't be any of this soft living you enjoy today if it weren't for them and this *musty old junk!*

Mrs. Kilkau: But I think it's selfish of you, keeping these *priceless*...

Gustin: Sure it's selfish! But that's a privilege of those who've done their jobs well, and lived long enough to look back awhile.

If you'll consider a minute, gal, I'm the one who saw what swamp cream did for the complexion. I've got a right to be selfish!

Mrs. Kilkau: Yes, Uncle Gus. I've heard that story.

Yaggata: But *we* haven't heard it, Mr. Gustin. Would you care to...

Gustin: Yes, I'd care to...but some other time, son. Right now I'm a wicky tired, and I'd better get some rest.

Yaggata: Certainly, sir! Shall we set the time for...

Gustin: I'll call you, son. Don't you call me. Uuuuugh! Damned fangbird wound! But I'll tell you one thing, son: I've changed my mind about this frip-frap of yours. It does us all good to see where we came from. If the people who see that record of yours have any brains, they'll think about where they came from. Do 'em good!

(Editor: Wire ends here. Attached note says Hilmot Gustin takes ill the following day. The second interview was delayed indefinitely.)

Senator Zolam: Do you have further records to introduce at this time, Mr. Secretary?

Secretary Hablar: I was hoping my Assistant Secretary for Cultural Affairs could make it here today. Unfortunately, he was called to an intercultural function with representatives of the Ring Planets.

Saboteur McKie: That was my doing, Mr. Secretary. The committee members are pressed for time today.

Secretary Hablar: I see.

Senator Zolam: There being no further business, the Special Subcommittee on Intergalactic Culture stands adjourned until 1600 tomorrow.

TRY
TO
REMEMBER

Every mind on earth capable of understanding the problem was focused on the spaceship with the ultimatum delivered by its occupants. *Talk or Die!* blared the newspaper headlines.

The suicide rate was up and still climbing. Religious cults were having a field day. A book by a science fiction author, *What the Deadly Inter-Galactic Spaceship Means to You!*, had smashed all previous best-seller records. And this had been going on for a frantic seven months.

The ship had *flapped* out of a gun-metal sky over Oregon, its shape that of a hideously magnified paramecium with edges that rippled like a mythological flying carpet. Its five green-skinned, froglike occupants had delivered the ultimatum, one copy printed on velvety paper to each major government, each copy couched faultlessly in the appropriate native tongue:

"You are requested to assemble your most gifted experts in human communication. We are about to submit a problem. We will open five identical rooms of our vessel to you. One of us will be available in each room.

"Your problem. To communicate with us.

"If you succeed, your rewards will be great.

"If you fail, that will result in destruction for all sentient life on your planet.

"We announce this threat with the deepest regret. You are urged to examine Eniwetok atoll for a small display of our power. Your artificial satellites have been removed from the skies.

"You must break away from this limited communication!"

Eniwetok had been cleared off flat as a table at one thousand feet depth ... with no trace of explosion! All Russian and United States artificial satellites had been combed from the skies.

All day long a damp wind poured up the Columbia Gorge from the ocean. It swept across the Eastern Oregon alkali flats with a false prediction of rain. Spiny desert scrub bent before the gusts, sheltering blur-footed coveys of quail and flop-eared jackrabbits. Heaps of tumbleweed tangled in the fence lines, and the air was filled with dry particles of grit that crept under everything and into everything and onto everything with the omnipresence of filterable virus.

On the flats south of the Hermiston Ordnance Depot the weird bulk of the spaceship caught pockets and eddies of sand. The thing looked like a monstrous oval of dun canvas draped across upright sticks. A cluster of quonsets and the Army's new desert prefabs dotted a rough half-circle around the north rim. They looked like dwarfed out-buildings for the most gigantic circus tent Earth had ever seen. Army Engineers said the ship was 6,218 feet long, 1,054 feet wide.

Some five miles east of the site the dust storm hazed across the monotonous structures of the cantonment that housed some thirty thousand people from every major nation: linguists, anthropologists, psychologists, doctors of every shape and description, watchers and watchers for the watchers, spies, espionage and counter-espionage agents.

For seven months the threat of Eniwetok, the threat of the unknown as well, had held them in check.

Towards evening of this day the wind slackened. The drifted sand began sifting off the ship and back into new shapes, trickling down for all the world like the figurative "sands of time" that here were most certainly running out.

Mrs. Francine Millar, clinical psychologist with the Indo-European Germanic-Root team, hurried across the bare patch of trampled sand outside the spaceship's entrance. She bent her head against what was left of the windstorm. Under her left arm she carried her briefcase tucked up like a football. Her other hand carried a rolled-up copy of that afternoon's *Oregon Journal*. The lead story said that Air Force jets had shot down a small private plane trying to sneak into the restricted area. Three unidentified men killed. The plane had been stolen.

Thoughts of a plane crash made her too aware of the circumstances in her own recent widowhood. Dr. Robert Millar had died in the crash of a transatlantic passenger plane ten days before the arrival of the spaceship. She let the newspaper fall out of her hands. It fluttered away on the wind.

Francine turned her head away from a sudden biting of the sandblast wind. She was a wiry slim figure of about five feet six inches, still trim and athletic at forty-one. Her auburn hair, mussed by the wind, still carried the look of youth. Heavy lids shielded her blue eyes. The lids drooped slightly, giving her a perpetual sleepy look even when she was wide awake and alert—a circumstance she found helpful in her profession.

She came into the lee of the conference quonset, and straightened. A layer of sand covered the doorstep. She opened the door, stepped across the sand only to find more of it on the floor inside, grinding underfoot. It was on tables, on chairs, mounded in corners—on every surface.

Hikonojo Ohashi, Francine's opposite number with the Japanese-Korean and Sino-Tibetan team, already sat at his place on the other side of the table. The Japanese psychologist was grasping, pen fashion, a thin-pointed brush, making notes in ideographic shorthand.

Francine closed the door.

Ohashi spoke without looking up: "We're early."

He was a trim, neat little man: flat features, smooth cheeks and even curve of chin, remote dark eyes behind the inevitable thick lenses of the Oriental scholar.

Francine tossed her briefcase onto the table and pulled out a chair opposite Ohashi. She wiped away the grit with a handkerchief before sitting down. The ever-present dirt, the monotonous landscape, her own frustration—all combined to hold her on the edge of anger. She recognized the feeling and its source, stifled a wry smile.

"No, Hiko," she said. "I think we're late. It's later than we think."

"Much later when you put it that way," said Ohashi. His Princeton accent came out low, modulated like a musical instrument under the control of a master.

"Now we're going to be banal," she said. Immediately, she regretted the sharpness of her tone, forced a smile to her lips.

"They gave us no deadline," said Ohashi. "That is one thing, anyway." He twirled his brush across an inkstone.

"Something's in the air," she said. "I can feel it."

"Very much sand in the air," he said.

"The wind has us all on edge," she said. "It feels like rain. A change in the weather." He made another note, put down the brush and began setting out papers for the conference. All at once, his head came up. He smiled at Francine. The smile made him look immature, and she suddenly saw back through the years to a serious little boy named Hiko Ohashi.

"It's been seven months," she said. "It stands to reason that they're not going to wait forever."

"The usual gestation period is two months longer," he said.

She frowned, ignoring the quip. "But we're no closer today than we were at the beginning!"

Ohashi leaned forward. His eyes appeared to swell behind the thick lenses. "Do you often wonder at their insistence that *we* communicate with *them?* I mean, rather than the other way around?"

"Of course I do. So does everybody else."

He sat back. "What do you think of the Islamic team's approach?"

"You know what I think, Hiko. It's a waste of time to compare all the Galactics' speech sounds to passages from the Koran." She shrugged. "But for all we know actually they could be closer to a solution than anyone else in..."

The door behind her banged open. Immediately, the room rumbled with the great basso voice of Theodore Zakheim, psychologist with the Ural-Altaic team.

"Hah-haaaaaaa!" he roared. "We're all here now!"

Light footsteps behind Zakheim told Francine that he was accompanied by Emile Goré of the Indo-European Latin-Root team.

Zakheim flopped onto a chair beside Francine. It creaked dangerously to his bulk.

Like a great uncouth bear! she thought.

"Do you always have to be so noisy?" she asked.

Goré slammed the door behind them.

"Naturally!" boomed Zakheim. "I am noisy! It's my nature, my little puchkin!"

Goré moved behind Francine, passing to the head of the table, but she kept her attention on Zakheim. He was a thick-bodied man, thick without fat, like the heaviness of a wrestler. His wide face and slanting pale blue eyes carried hints of Mongol ancestry. Rusty hair formed an uncombed brush atop his head.

Zakheim brought up his briefcase, flopped it onto the table, rested his hands on the dark leather. They were flat slab hands with thick fingers, pale wisps of hair growing down almost to the nails.

She tore her attention away from Zakheim's hands, looked down the table to where Goré sat. The Frenchman was a tall, gawk-necked man, entirely bald. Jet eyes behind steel-rimmed bifocals gave him a look of down-nose asperity like a comic bird. He wore one of his usual funereal black suits, every button secured. Knob wrists protruded from the sleeves. His long-fingered hands with their thick joints moved in constant restlessness.

"If I may differ with you, Zak," said Goré, "we are *not* all here. This is our same old group, and we were going to try to interest others in what we do here."

Ohashi spoke to Francine: "Have you had any luck inviting others to our conferences?"

"You can see that I'm alone," she said. "I chalked up five flat refusals today."

"Who?" asked Zakheim.

"The American Indian-Eskimo, the Hyperboreans, the Dravidians, the Malayo-Polynesians and the Caucasians."

"Hagglers!" barked Zakheim. "I, of course, can cover us with the Hamito-Semitic tongues, but..." He shook his head.

Goré turned to Ohashi. "The others?"

Ohashi said: "I must report the polite indifference of the Munda and Mon-Kmer, the Sudanese-Guinean and the Bantu."

"Those are big holes in our information exchange," said Goré. "What are they discovering?"

"No more than we are!" snapped Zakheim. "Depend on it!"

"What of the languages not even represented among the teams here on the international site?" asked Francine. "I mean the Hottentot-Bushmen, the Ainu, the Basque and the Australian-Papuan?"

Zakheim covered her left hand with his right hand. "You always have me, my little dove."

"We're building another Tower of Babel!" she snapped. She jerked her hand away.

"Spurned again," mourned Zakheim.

Ohashi said: *"Go to, let us go down, and there confound their language, that they may not understand one another's speech."* He smiled. "Genesis eleven-seven."

Francine scowled. "And we're missing about twenty per cent of Earth's twenty-eight hundred languages!"

"We have all the significant ones," said Zakheim.

"How do *you* know what's significant?" she demanded.

"Please!" Goré raised a hand. "We're here to exchange information, not to squabble!"

"I'm sorry," said Francine. "It's just that I feel so hopeless today."

"Well, what have we learned today?" asked Goré.

"Nothing new with us," said Zakheim.

Goré cleared his throat. "That goes double for me." He looked at Ohashi.

The Japanese shrugged. "We achieved no reaction from the Galactic, Kobai."

"Anthropomorphic nonsense," muttered Zakheim.

"You mean naming him Kobai?" asked Ohashi. "Not at all, Zak. That's the most frequent sound he makes, and the name helps with identification. We don't have to keep referring to him as 'The Galactic' or 'that creature in the spaceship.'"

Goré turned to Francine. "It was like talking to a green statue," she said.

"What of the lecture period?" asked Goré.

"Who knows?" she asked. "It stands there like a bow-legged professor in that black leotard. Those sounds spew out of it as though they'd never stop. It wriggles at us. It waves. It sways. Its face contorts, if you can call it a face. We recorded and filmed it all, naturally, but it sounded like the usual mishmash!"

"There's something in the gestures," said Ohashi. "If we only had more competent pasimologists."

"How many times have you seen the same total gesture repeated with the same sound?" demanded Zakheim.

"You've carefully studied our films," said Ohashi. "Not enough times to give us a solid base for comparison. But I do not despair—"

"It was a rhetorical question," said Zakheim.

"We really need more multilinguists," said Goré. "Now is when we most miss the loss of such great linguists as Mrs. Millar's husband."

Francine closed her eyes, took a short, painful breath. "Bob..." She shook her head. *No. That's the past. He's gone. The tears are ended.*

"I had the pleasure of meeting him in Paris shortly before the...end," continued Goré. "He was lecturing on the development of the similar sound schemes in Italian and Japanese."

Francine nodded. She felt suddenly empty.

Ohashi leaned forward. "I imagine this is...rather painful for Dr. Millar," he said.

"I am *very* sorry," said Goré. "Forgive me."

"Someone was going to check and see if there are any electronic listening devices in this room," said Ohashi.

"My nephew is with our recording section," said Goré. "He assures me there are no hidden microphones here."

Zakheim's brows drew down into a heavy frown. He fumbled with the clasp of his briefcase. "This is very dangerous," he grunted.

"Oh, Zak, you always say that!" said Francine. "Let's quit playing footsy!"

"I do not enjoy the thought of treason charges," muttered Zakheim.

"We all know our bosses are looking for an advantage," she said. "I'm tired of these sparring matches where we each try to get something from the others without giving anything away!"

"If your Dr. Langsmith or General Speidel found out what you were doing here, it would go hard for you, too," said Zakheim.

"I propose we take it from the beginning and re-examine everything," said Francine. "Openly this time."

"Why?" demanded Zakheim.

"Because I'm satisfied that the answer's right in front of us somewhere," she said.

"In the ultimatum, no doubt," said Goré. "What do you suppose is the *real* meaning of their statement that human languages are 'limited' communication? Perhaps they are telepathic?"

"I don't think so," said Ohashi.

"That's pretty well ruled out," said Francine. "Our Rhine people say no ESP. No. I'm banking on something else: By the very fact that they posed this question, they have indicated that we *can* answer it with our present faculties."

"*If* they are being honest," said Zakheim.

"I have no recourse but to assume that they're honest," she said. "They're turning us into linguistic detectives for a good reason."

"A good reason for *them*," said Goré.

"Note the phraseology of their ultimatum," said Ohashi. "They *submit* a problem. They *open* their rooms to us. They are *available* to us. They *regret* their threat. Even their display of power—admittedly awe-inspiring—has the significant characteristic of nonviolence. No explosion. They offer rewards for success, and this..."

"Rewards!" snorted Zakheim. "We lead the hog to its slaughter with a promise of food!"

"I suggest that they give evidence of being nonviolent," said Ohashi. "Either that, or they have cleverly arranged themselves to present the *face* of nonviolence."

Francine turned, and looked out of the hut's end window at the bulk of the spaceship. The low sun cast elongated shadows of the ship across the sand.

Zakheim, too, looked out of the window. "Why did they choose this place? If it had to be a desert, why not the Gobi? This is not even a good desert! This is a miserable desert!"

"Probably the easiest landing curve to a site near a large city," said Goré. "It is possible they chose a desert to avoid destroying arable land."

"Frogs!" snapped Zakheim. "I do not trust these frogs with their problem of communication!"

Francine turned back to the table, and took a pencil and scratch-pad from her briefcase. Briefly she sketched a rough outline of a Galactic, and wrote "frog?" beside it.

Ohashi said: "Are you drawing a picture of your Galactic?"

"We call it 'Uru' for the same reason you call yours 'Kobai,'" she said. "It makes the sound 'Uru' *ad nauseam.*"

She stared at her own sketch thoughtfully, calling up the memory image of the Galactic as she did so. Squat, about five feet ten inches in height, with the short bowed legs of a swimmer. Rippling muscles sent corded lines under the black leotard. The arms were articulated like a human's, but they were more graceful in movement. The skin was pale green, the neck thick and short. The wide mouth was almost lipless, the nose a mere blunt horn. The eyes were large and spaced wide with nictating lids. No hair, but a high-crowned ridge from the center of the forehead swept back across the head.

"I knew a Hawaiian distance swimmer once who looked much like these Galactics," said Ohashi. He wet his lips with his tongue. "You know, today we had a Buddhist monk from

Java at our meeting with Kobai."

"I fail to see the association between a distance swimmer and a monk," said Goré.

"You told us you drew a blank today," said Zakheim.

"The monk tried no conversing," said Ohashi. "He refused because that would be a form of earthly striving unthinkable for a Buddhist. He merely came and observed."

Francine leaned forward. "Yes?" She found an odd excitement in the way Ohashi was forcing himself to casualness.

"The monk's reaction was curious," said Ohashi. "He refused to speak for several hours afterwards. Then he said that these Galactics must be very holy people."

"Holy!" Zakheim's voice was edged with bitter irony.

"We are approaching this the wrong way," said Francine. She felt let down, spoke with a conscious effort. "Our access to these Galactics is limited by the space they've opened to us within their vessel."

"What is in the rest of the ship?" asked Zakheim.

"Rewards, perhaps," said Goré.

"Or weapons to demolish us!" snapped Zakheim.

"The pattern of the sessions is wrong, too," said Francine.

Ohashi nodded. "Twelve hours a day is not enough," he said. "We should have them under constant observation."

"I didn't mean that," said Francine. "They probably need rest just as we do. No. I meant the absolute control our team leaders—unimaginative men like Langsmith—have over the way we use our time in those rooms. For instance, what would happen if we tried to break down the force wall or whatever it is that keeps us from actually touching these creatures? What would happen if we brought in dogs to check how *animals* would react to them?" She reached in her briefcase, brought out a small flat recorder and adjusted it for playback. "Listen to this."

There was a fluid burst of sound: "Pau'timónsh' uego' iklo-prépre 'sauta' urusa'a'a..." and a long pause followed by "tu'kimóomo 'urulig 'lurulil 'oog 'shuquetoé..." pause, "sum 'a 'suma 'a 'uru 't 'shóap!"

Francine stopped the playback.

"Did you record that today?" asked Ohashi.

"Yes. It was using that odd illustration board with the moving pictures—weird flowers and weirder animals."

"We've seen them," muttered Zakheim.

"And those chopping movements of its hands," said Francine. "The swaying body, the undulations, the facial contortions." She shook her head. "It's almost like a bizarre dance."

"What are you driving at?" asked Ohashi.

"I've been wondering what would happen if we had a leading choreographer compose a dance to those sounds, and if we put it on for..."

"Faaa!" snorted Zakheim.

"All right," said Francine. "But we should be using some kind of random stimulation pattern on these Galactics. Why don't we bring in a nightclub singer? Or a circus barker? Or a magician? Or..."

"We tried a full-blown schizoid," said Goré.

Zakheim grunted. "And you got exactly what such tactics deserve: Your schizoid sat there and played with his fingers for an hour!"

"The idea of using artists from the entertainment world intrigues me," said Ohashi. "Some *Noh* dancers, perhaps." He nodded. "I'd never thought about it. But art is, after all, a form of communication."

"So is the croaking of a frog in a swamp," said Zakheim.

"Did you ever hear about the Paradox Frog?" asked Francine.

"Is this one of your strange jokes?" asked Zakheim.

"Of course not. The Paradox Frog is a very real creature. It lives on the island of Trinidad. It's a very small frog, but it has the opposable thumb on a five-fingered hand, and it..."

"Just like our visitors," said Zakheim.

"Yes. And it uses its hand just like we do—to grasp things, to pick up food, to stuff its mouth, to..."

"To make bombs?" asked Zakheim.

Francine shrugged, turned away. She felt hurt.

"My people believe these Galactics are putting on an elaborate sham," said Zakheim. "We think they are stalling while they secretly study us in preparation for invasion!"

Goré said: "So?" His narrow shoulders came up in a Gallic shrug that said as plainly as words: *"Even if this is true, what is there for us to do?"*

Francine turned to Ohashi. "What's the favorite theory current with your team?" Her voice sounded bitter, but she was unable to soften the tone.

"We are working on the assumption that this is a language

of one-syllable root, as in Chinese," said Ohashi.

"But what of the vowel harmony?" protested Goré. "Surely that must mean the harmonious vowels are all in the same words."

Ohashi adjusted the set of his glasses. "Who knows?" he asked. "Certainly, the back vowels and front vowels come together many times, but..." He shrugged, shook his head.

"What's happening with the group that's working on the historical analogy?" asked Goré. "You were going to find out, Ohashi."

"They are working on the assumption that all primitive sounds are consonants with nonfixed vowels...foot-stampers for dancing, you know. Their current guess is that the Galactics are missionaries, their language a religious language."

"What results?" asked Zakheim.

"None."

Zakheim nodded. "To be expected." He glanced at Francine. "I beg the forgiveness of the Mrs. Doctor Millar?"

She looked up, startled from a daydreaming speculation about the Galactic language and dancing. "Me? Good heavens, why?"

"I have been short-tempered today," said Zakheim. He glanced at his wristwatch. "I'm very sorry. I've been worried about another appointment."

He heaved his bulk out of the chair, took up his briefcase. "And it is time for me to be leaving. You forgive me?"

"Of course, Zak."

His wide face split into a grin. "Good!"

Goré got to his feet. "I will walk a little way with you, Zak."

Francine and Ohashi sat on for a moment after the others had gone.

"What good are we doing with these meetings?" she asked.

"Who knows how the important pieces of this puzzle will be fitted together?" asked Ohashi. "The point is: We are doing something different."

She sighed. "I guess so."

Ohashi took off his glasses, and it made him appear suddenly defenseless. "Did you know that Zak was recording our meeting?" he asked. He replaced the glasses.

Francine stared at him. "How do you know?"

Ohashi tapped his briefcase. "I have a device in here that reveals such things."

She swallowed a brief surge of anger. "Well, is it really important, Hiko?"

"Perhaps not." Ohashi took a deep, evenly controlled breath. "I did not tell you one other thing about the Buddhist monk."

"Oh? What did you omit?"

"He predicts that we will fail—that the human race will be destroyed. He is very old and very cynical for a monk. He thinks it is a good thing that all human striving must eventually come to an end."

Anger and a sudden resolve flamed in her. "I don't care! I don't care what anyone else thinks! I know that..." She allowed her voice to trail off, put her hands to her eyes.

"You have been very distracted today," said Ohashi. "Did the talk about your late husband disturb you?"

"I know. I'm..." She swallowed, whispered: "I had a dream about Bob last night. We were dancing, and he was trying to tell me something about this problem, only I couldn't hear him. Each time he started to speak the music got louder and drowned him out."

Silence fell over the room. Presently, Ohashi said: "The unconscious mind takes strange ways sometimes to tell us the right answers. Perhaps we should investigate this idea of dancing."

"Oh, Hiko! Would you help me?"

"I should consider it an honor to help you," he said.

It was quiet in the semi-darkness of the projection room. Francine leaned her head against the back-rest of her chair, looked across at the stand light where Ohashi had been working. He had gone for the films on Oriental ritual dances that had just arrived from Los Angeles by plane. His coat was still draped across the back of his chair, his pipe still smoldered in the ashtray on the worktable. All around their two chairs were stacked the residue of four days' almost continuous research: notebooks, film cans, boxes of photographs, reference books.

She thought about Hiko Ohashi: a strange man. He was fifty and didn't look a day over thirty. He had grown children. His wife had died of cholera eight years ago. Francine wondered what it would be like married to an Oriental, and she found herself thinking that he wasn't really Oriental with his Princeton education and Occidental ways. Then she realized that this attitude was a kind of white snobbery.

The door in the corner of the room opened softly. Ohashi came in, closed the door. "You awake?" he whispered.

She turned her head without lifting it from the chairback. "Yes."

"I'd hoped you might fall asleep for a bit," he said. "You looked so tired when I left."

Francine glanced at her wristwatch. "It's only three-thirty. What's the day like?"

"Hot and windy."

Ohashi busied himself inserting film into the projector at the rear of the room. Presently, he went to his chair, trailing the remote control cable for the projector.

"Ready?" he asked.

Francine reached for the low editing light beside her chair, and turned it on, focusing the narrow beam on a notebook in her lap. "Yes. Go ahead."

"I feel that we're making real progress," said Ohashi. "It's not clear yet, but the points of identity..."

"They're exciting," she said. "Let's see what this one has to offer."

Ohashi punched the button on the cable. A heavily robed Arab girl appeared on the screen, slapping a tambourine. Her hair looked stiff, black and oily. A sooty line of kohl shaded each eye. Her brown dress swayed slightly as she tinkled the tambourine, then slapped it.

The cultured voice of the commentator came through the speaker beside the screen: "This is a young girl of Jebel Tobeyk. She is going to dance some very ancient steps that tell a story of battle. The camera is hidden in a truck, and she is unaware that this dance is being photographed."

A reed flute joined the tambourine, and a twanging stringed instrument came in behind it. The girl turned slowly on one foot, the other raised with knee bent.

Francine watched in rapt silence. The dancing girl made short staccato hops, the tambourine jerking in front of her.

"It is reminiscent of some of the material on the Norse sagas," said Ohashi. "Battle with swords. Note the thrust and parry."

She nodded. "Yes." The dance stamped onward, then: "Wait! Rerun that last section."

Ohashi obeyed.

It started with a symbolic trek on camel-back: swaying, undulating. The dancing girl expressed longing for her warrior.

How suggestive the motions of her hands along her hips, thought Francine. With a feeling of abrupt shock, she recalled seeing almost the exact gesture from one of the films of the Galactics. "There's one!" she cried.

"The hands on the hips," said Ohashi. "I was just about to stop the reel." He shut off the film, searched through the notebooks around him until he found the correct reference.

"I think it was one of Zak's films," said Francine.

"Yes. Here it is." Ohashi brought up a reel, looked at the scene identifications. He placed the film can on a large stack behind him, restarted the film of Oriental dances.

Three hours and ten minutes later they put the film back in its can.

"How many new comparisons do you make it?" asked Ohashi.

"Five," she said. "That makes one hundred and six in all!" Francine leafed through her notes. "There was the motion of the hands on the hips. I call that one sensual pleasure."

Ohashi lighted a pipe, spoke through a cloud of smoke. "The others: How have you labeled them?"

"Well, I've just put a note on the motions of one of the Galactics and then the commentator's remarks from this dance film. Chopping motion of the hand ties to the end of Sobàya's first dream: *'Now, I awaken!'* Undulation of the body ties in with swaying of date palms in the desert wind. Stamping of the foot goes with Torak dismounting from his steed. Lifting hands, palms up—that goes with Ali offering his soul to God in prayer before battle."

"Do you want to see this latest film from the ship?" asked Ohashi. He glanced at his wristwatch. "Or shall we get a bite to eat first?"

She waved a hand distractedly. "The film. I'm not hungry. The film." She looked up. "I keep feeling that there's something I should remember...something..." She shook her head.

"Think about it a few minutes," said Ohashi. "I'm going to send out these other films to be cut and edited according to our selections. And I'll have some sandwiches sent in while I'm at it."

Francine rubbed at her forehead. "All right."

Ohashi gathered up a stack of film cans, left the room. He knocked out his pipe on a "No Smoking" sign beside the door as he left.

"Consonants," whispered Francine. "The ancient alphabets were almost exclusively made up of consonants. Vowels came later. They were the softeners, the swayers." She chewed at her lower lip. "Language constricts the *ways* you can think." She rubbed at her forehead. "Oh, if I only had Bob's ability with languages!"

She tapped her fingers on the chair arm. "It has something to do with our emphasis on *things* rather than on people and the things people do. Every Indo-European language is the same on that score. If only..."

"Talking to yourself?" It was a masculine voice, startling her because she had not heard the door open.

Francine jerked upright, turned towards the door. Dr. Irving Langsmith, chief of the American Division of the Germanic-Root team, stood just inside, closing the door.

"Haven't seen you for a couple of days," he said. "We got your note that you were indisposed." He looked around the room, then at the clutter on the floor beside the chairs.

Francine blushed.

Dr. Langsmith crossed to the chair Ohashi had occupied, sat down. He was a gray-haired runt of a man with a heavily seamed face, small features—a gnome figure with hard eyes. He had the reputation of an organizer and politician with more drive than genius. He pulled a stubby pipe from his pocket, lighted it.

"I probably should have cleared this through channels," she said. "But I had visions of it getting bogged down in red tape, especially with Hiko ... I mean, with another team represented in this project."

"Quite all right," said Langsmith. "We knew what you were up to within a couple of hours. Now, we want to know what you've discovered. Dr. Ohashi looked pretty excited when he left here a bit ago."

Her eyes brightened. "I think we're on to something," she said. "We've compared the Galactics' movements to known symbolism from primitive dances."

Dr. Langsmith chuckled. "That's very interesting, my dear, but surely you..."

"No, really!" she said. "We've found one hundred and six points of comparison, almost exact duplication of movements!"

"Dances? Are you trying to tell me that..."

"I know it sounds strange," she said, "but we..."

"Even if you *have* found exact points of comparison, that means nothing," said Langsmith. "These are *aliens* . . . from another world. You've no right to assume that their language development would follow the same pattern as ours has."

"But they're humanoid!" she said. "Don't you believe that language started as the unconscious shaping of the *speech* organs to imitate *bodily* gestures?"

"It's highly likely," said Langsmith.

"We can make quite a few pretty safe assumptions about them," she said. "For one thing, they apparently have a rather high standard of civilization to be able to construct—"

"Let's not labor the obvious," interrupted Langsmith, a little impatiently.

Francine studied the team chief a moment, said: "Did you ever hear how Marshal Foch planned his military campaigns?"

Langsmith puffed on his pipe, took it out of his mouth. "Uh . . . are you suggesting that a military . . ."

"He wrote out the elements of his problem on a sheet of paper," said Francine. "At the top of the paper went the lowest common denominator. There, he wrote: *'Problem—To beat the Germans.'* Quite simple. Quite obvious. But oddly enough *'beating the enemy'* has frequently been overlooked by commanders who got too involved in complicated maneuvers."

"Are you suggesting that the Galactics are enemies?"

She shook her head indignantly. "I am *not!* I'm suggesting that language is primarily an instinctive social reflex. The least common denominator of a social problem is a human being. One single human being. And here we are all involved with getting this thing into mathematical equations and neat word frequency primarily oral!"

"But you've been researching a visual . . ."

"Yes! But only as it modifies the sounds." She leaned towards Langsmith. "Dr. Langsmith, I believe that this language is a *flexional* language with the flexional endings and root changes contained entirely in the bodily movements."

"Hmmmmmmmm." Langsmith studied the smoke spiraling ceilingwards from his pipe. "Fascinating idea!"

"We can assume that this is a highly standardized language," said Francine. "Basing the assumption on their high standard of civilization. The two usually go hand in hand."

Langsmith nodded.

"Then the gestures, the sounds would tend to be ritual," she said.

"Mmmmm-hmmmm."

"Then ... may we have the help to go into this idea the way it deserves?" she asked.

"I'll take it up at the next top staff meeting," said Langsmith. He got to his feet. "Don't get your hopes up. This'll have to be submitted to the electronic computers. It probably has been cross-checked and rejected in some other problem."

She looked up at him, dismayed. "But ... Dr. Langsmith ... a computer's no better than what's put into it. I'm certain that we're stepping out into a region here where we'll have to build up a whole new approach to language."

"Now, don't you worry, said Langsmith. He frowned. "No ... don't worry about *this*."

"Shall we go ahead with what we're doing then?" she asked. "I mean—do we have permission to?"

"Yes, yes ... or course." Langsmith wiped his mouth with the back of his hand. "General Speidel has called a special meeting tomorrow morning. I'd like to have you attend. I'll send somebody to pick you up." He waved a hand at the litter around Francine. "Carry on, now." There was a pathetic emptiness to the way he put his pipe in his mouth and left the room. Francine stared at the closed door.

She felt herself trembling, and recognized that she was deathly afraid. *Why?* she asked herself. *What have I sensed to make me afraid?*

Presently, Ohashi came in carrying a paper bag.

"Saw Langsmith going out," he said. "What did he want?"

"He wanted to know what we're doing."

Ohashi paused before his chair. "Did you tell him?"

"Yes. I asked for help." She shook her head. "He wouldn't commit himself."

"I brought ham sandwiches," said Ohashi.

Francine's chin lifted abruptly. "Defeated!" she said. "That's it! He acted completed defeated!"

"What?"

"I've been trying to puzzle through the strange way Langsmith was acting. He just radiated defeat."

Ohashi handed her a sandwich. "Better brace yourself for a shock," he said. "I ran into Tsu Ong, liaison officer for our delegation...in the cafeteria." The Japanese raised the sandwich sack over his chair, dropped it into the seat with a curious air of preciseness. "The Russians are pressing for a combined attack on the Galactic ship to wrest their secret from them by force."

Francine buried her face in her hands. "The fools!" she whispered. "Oh, the fools!" Abruptly, sobs shook her. She found herself crying with the same uncontrollable racking that had possessed her when she'd learned of her husband's death.

Ohashi waited silently.

The tears subsided. Control returned. She swallowed, said: "I'm sorry."

"Do not be sorry." He put a hand on her shoulder. "Shall we knock off for the night?"

She put her hand over his, shook her head. "No. Let's look at the latest films from the ship."

"As you wish." Ohashi pulled away, threaded a new film into the projector.

Presently, the screen came alive to a blue-gray alcove filled with pale light: one of the "class" rooms in the spaceship. A squat, green-skinned figure stood in the center of the room. Beside the Galactic was the pedestal-footed projection board that all five used to illustrate their "lectures." The board displayed a scene of a wide blue lake, reeds along the shore stirring to a breeze.

The Galactic swayed. His face moved like a ripple of water. He said: "Ahon'atu'uklah'shoginai' eástruru." The green arms moved up and down, undulating. The webbed hands came out, palms facing and almost touching, began chopping from the wrists: up, down, up, down, up, down...

On the projection board the scene switched to an underwater view: myriad swimming shapes coming closer, closer—large-eyed fish creatures with long ridged tails.

"Five will get you ten," said Ohashi. "Those are the young of this Galactic race. Notice the ridge."

"Tadpoles," said Francine.

The swimming shapes darted through orange shadows and into a space of cold green—then up to splash on the surface, and again down into the cool green. It was a choreographic swinging, lifting, dipping, swaying—lovely in its synchronized symmetry.

"Chiruru'uklia'a'agudav'iaá," said the Galactic. His body

undulated like the movements of the swimming creatures. The green hands touched his thighs, slipped upward until elbows were level with shoulders.

"The maiden in the Oriental dance," said Francine.

Now, the hands came out, palms up, in a gesture curiously suggestive of giving. The Galactic said: "Pluainumiuri!" in a single burst of sound that fell on their ears like an explosion.

"It's like a distorted version of the ritual dances we've been watching," said Ohashi.

"I've a hunch," said Francine. "Feminine intuition. The repeated vowels: They could be an adverbial emphasis, like our word *very*. Where it says '*a-a-a*,' note the more intense gestures."

She followed another passage, nodding her head to the gestures. "Hiko, could this be a constructed language? Artificial?"

"The thought has occurred to me," said Ohashi.

Abruptly the projector light dimmed, the action slowed. All lights went out. They heard a dull, booming roar in the distance, a staccato rattling of shots. Feet pounded along the corridor outside the room.

Francine sat in stunned silence.

Ohashi said: "Stay here, please. I will have a look around to see what..."

The door banged open and a flashlight beam stabbed into the room, momentarily blinding them.

"Everything all right in here?" boomed a masculine voice.

They made out a white MP helmet visible behind the light.

"Yes," said Ohashi. "What is happening?"

"Somebody blew up a tower to the main transmission line from McNary Dam. Then there was an attempt to breach our security blockade on the south. Everything will be back to normal shortly." The light turned away.

"Who?" asked Francine.

"Some crazy civilians," said the MP. "We'll have the emergency power on in a minute. Just stay in this room until we give the all-clear." He left, closing the door.

They heard a rattle of machine-gun fire. Another explosion shook the building. Voices shouted.

"We are witnessing the end of a world," said Ohashi.

"Our world ended when that spaceship set down here," she said.

Abruptly the lights came on: dimly, then brighter. The projector resumed its whirring. Ohashi turned it off.

Somebody walked down the corridor outside, rapped on the door, said: "All clear." The footsteps receded down the hall, and they heard another rapping, a fainter "All clear."

"Civilians," she said. "What do you supposed they wanted so desperately to do a thing like that?"

"They are a symptom of the general sickness," said Ohashi. "One way to remove a threat is to destroy it—even if you destroy yourself in the process. These civilians are only a minor symptom."

"The Russians are the big symptom then," she said.

"Every major government is a *big* symptom right now," he said.

"I...I think I'll get back to my room," she said. "Let's take up again tomorrow morning. Eight o'clock all right?"

"Quite agreeable," said Ohashi. "If there is a tomorrow."

"Don't *you* get that way, too," she said, and she took a quavering breath. "I refuse to give up."

Ohashi bowed. He was suddenly very Oriental. "There is a primitive saying of the Ainu," he said: *The world ends every night ... and begins anew every morning."*

It was a room dug far underground beneath the Ordnance Depot, originally for storage of atomics. The walls were lead. It was an oblong space: about thirty by fifteen feet, with a very low ceiling. Two trestle tables had been butted end-to-end in the center of the room to form a single long surface. A series of green-shaded lights suspended above this table gave the scene an odd resemblance to a gambling room. The effect was heightened by the set look to the shoulders of the men sitting in spring-bottom chairs around the table. There was a scattering of uniforms: Air Force, Army, Marines; plus hard-faced civilians in expensive suits.

Dr. Langsmith occupied a space at the middle of one of the table's sides and directly across from the room's only door. His gnome features were locked in a frown of concentration. He puffed rhythmically at the stubby pipe like a witchman creating an oracle smoke.

A civilian across the table from Langsmith addressed a two-star general seated beside the team chief: "General Speidel, I think this is too delicate a spot to risk a woman."

Speidel grunted. He was a thin man with a high, narrow face: an aristocratic face that radiated granite convictions and stubborn pride. There was an air about him of spring steel under tension and vibrating to a chord that dominated the room.

"Our choice is limited," said Langsmith. "Very few of our personnel have consistently taken wheeled carts into the ship *and* consistently taken a position close to that force barrier or whatever it is."

Speidel glanced at his wristwatch. "What's keeping them?"

"She may already have gone to breakfast," said Langsmith.

"Be better if we got her in here hungry and jumpy," said the civilian.

"Are you sure you can handle her, Smitty?" asked Speidel.

Langsmith took his pipe from his mouth, peered into the stem as though the answer were to be found there. "We've got her pretty well analyzed," he said. "She's a recent widow, you know. Bound to still have a rather active deathwish structure."

There was a buzzing of whispered conversation from a group of officers at one end of the table. Speidel tapped his fingers on the arm of his chair.

Presently the door opened. Francine entered. A hand reached in from outside, closed the door behind her.

"Ah, there you are, Dr. Millar," said Langsmith. He got to his feet. There was a scuffling sound around the table as the others arose. Langsmith pointed to an empty chair diagonally across from him. "Sit down, please."

Francine advanced into the light. She felt intimidated, knew she showed it, and the realization filled her with a feeling of bitterness tinged with angry resentment. The ride down the elevator from the surface had been an experience she never wanted to repeat. It had seemed many times longer than it actually was—like a descent into Dante's Inferno.

She nodded to Langsmith, glanced covertly at the others, took the indicated chair. It was a relief to get the weight off her trembling knees, and she momentarily relaxed, only to tense up again as the others resumed their seats. She put her hands on the table, immediately withdrew them to hold them clasped tightly in her lap.

"Why was I brought here like a prisoner?" she demanded.

Langsmith appeared honestly startled. "But I told you last night that I'd send somebody for you."

Speidel chuckled easily. "Some of our Security boys are a little grim-faced," he said. "I hope they didn't frighten you."

She took a deep breath, began to relax. "Is this about the request I made last night?" she asked. "I mean, for help in this new line of research?"

"In a way," said Langsmith. "But first I'd like to have you answer a question for me." He pursed his lips. "Uh... I've never asked one of my people for just a wild guess before, but I'm going to break that rule with you. What's your guess as to why these Galactics are here?"

"Guess?"

"Logical assumption, then," he said.

She looked down at her hands. "We've all speculated, of course. They might be scientists investigating us for reasons of their own."

"Damnation!" barked the civilian beside her. Then: "Sorry, ma'am. But that's the pap we keep using to pacify the public."

"And we aren't keeping them very well pacified," said Langsmith. "That group that stormed us last night called themselves the *Sons of Truth!* They had thermite bombs, and were going to attack the spaceship."

"How foolish," she whispered. "How pitiful."

"Go on with your guessing, Dr. Millar," said Speidel.

She glanced at the general, again looked at her hands. "There's the military's idea—that they want Earth for a strategic base in some kind of space war."

"It could be," said Speidel.

"They could be looking for more living space for their own kind," she said.

"In which case, what happens to the native population?" asked Langsmith.

"They would either be exterminated or enslaved, I'm afraid. But the Galactics could be commercial traders of some sort, interested in our art forms, our animals for their zoos, our archaeology, our spices, our..." She broke off, shrugged. "How do we know what they may be doing on the side... secretly?"

"Exactly!" said Speidel. He glanced sidelong at Langsmith. "She talks pretty level-headed, Smitty."

"But I don't believe any of these things," she said.

"What is it you believe?" asked Speidel.

"I believe they're just what they represent themselves to be—

representatives of a powerful Galactic culture that is immeasurably superior to our own."

"Powerful, all right!" It was a marine officer at the far end of the table. "The way they cleaned off Eniwetok and swept our satellites out of the skies!"

"Do you think there's a possibility they could be concealing their true motives?" asked Langsmith.

"A possibility, certainly."

"Have you ever watched a confidence man in action?" asked Langsmith.

"I don't believe so. But you're not seriously suggesting that these..." She shook her head. "Impossible."

"The *mark* seldom gets wise until it's too late," said Langsmith.

She looked puzzled. "Mark?"

"The fellow the confidence men choose for a victim." Langsmith relighted his pipe, extinguished the match by shaking it. "Dr. Millar, we have a very painful disclosure to make to you."

She straightened, feeling a sudden icy chill in her veins at the stillness in the room.

"Your husband's death was not an accident," said Langsmith.

She gasped, and turned deathly pale.

"In the six months before this spaceship landed, there were some twenty-eight mysterious deaths," said Langsmith. "More than that, really, because innocent bystanders died, too. These accidents had a curious similarity: In each instance there was a fatality of a foremost expert in the field of language, cryptoanalysis, semantics..."

"The people who might have solved this problem died before the problem was even presented," said Speidel. "Don't you think that's a curious coincidence?"

She was unable to speak.

"In one instance there was a survivor," said Langsmith. "A British jet transport crashed off Ceylon, killing Dr. Ramphit U. The lone survivor, the co-pilot, said a brilliant beam of light came from the sky overhead and sliced off the port wing. Then it cut the cabin in half!"

Francine put a hand to her throat. Langsmith's cautious hand movements suddenly fascinated her.

"Twenty-eight air crashes?" she whispered.

"No. Two were auto crashes." Langsmith puffed a cloud of

smoke before his face.

Her throat felt sore. She swallowed, said: "But how can you be sure of that?"

"It's circumstantial evidence, yes," said Speidel. He spoke with thin-lipped precision. "But there's more. For the past four months all astronomical activity of our nation has been focused on the near heavens, including the moon. Our attention was drawn to evidence of activity near the moon crater Theophilus. We have been able to make out the landing rockets of more than five hundred spacecraft!"

"What do you think of that?" asked Langsmith. He nodded behind his smokescreen.

She could only stare at him; her lips ashen.

"These *frogs* have massed an invasion fleet on the moon!" snapped Speidel. "It's obvious!"

They're lying to me! she thought. *Why this elaborate pretense?* She shook her head, and something her husband had once said leapt unbidden into her mind: *"Language clutches at us with unseen fingers. It conditions us to the way others are thinking. Through language, we impose upon each other our ways of looking at things."*

Speidel leaned forward. "We have more than a hundred atomic warheads aimed at that moon-base! One of those warheads will do the job if it gets through!" He hammered a fist on the table. "But first we have to capture this ship here!"

Why are they telling me all this? she asked herself. She drew in a ragged breath, said: "Are you sure you're right?"

"Of course we're sure!" Speidel leaned back, lowered his voice. "Why else would they insist we learn their language? The first thing a conqueror does is impose his language on his new slaves!"

"No ... no, wait," she said. "That only applies to recent history. You're getting language mixed up with patriotism because of our own imperial history. Bob always said that such misconceptions are a serious hindrance to sound historical scholarship."

"We know what we're talking about, Dr. Millar," said Speidel.

"You're suspicious of language because our imperialism went hand in hand with our language," she said.

Speidel looked at Langsmith. "You talk to her."

"If there actually were communication in the sounds these Galactics make, you know we'd have found it by now," said Langsmith. "You know it!"

She spoke in sudden anger: "I don't know it! In fact, I feel that we're on the verge of solving their language with this new approach we've been working on."

"Oh, come now!" said Speidel. "Do you mean that after our finest cryptographers have worked over this thing for seven months, you disagree with them entirely?"

"No, no, let her say her piece," said Langsmith.

"We've tapped a new source of information in attacking this problem," she said. "Primitive dances."

"Dances?" Speidel looked shocked.

"Yes. I think the Galactics' gestures may be their adjectives and adverbs—the full emotional content of their language."

"Emotion!" snapped Speidel. "Emotion isn't language!"

She repressed a surge of anger, said: "We're dealing with something completely outside our previous experience. We have to discard old ideas. We know that the habits of a native tongue set up a person's speaking responses. In fact you can define language as the system of habits you reveal when you speak."

Speidel tapped his fingers on the table, stared at the door behind Francine.

She ignored his nervous distraction, said: "The Galactics use almost the full range of implosive and glottal stops with a wide selection of vowel sounds: fricatives, plosives, voiced and unvoiced. And we note an apparent lack of the usual interfering habits you find in normal speech."

"This isn't normal speech!" blurted Speidel. "Those are nonsense sounds!" He shook his head. "Emotions!"

"All right," she said. "Emotions! We're pretty certain that language begins with emotions—pure emotional actions. The baby pushes away the plate of unwanted food."

"You're wasting our time!" barked Speidel.

"I didn't ask to come down here," she said.

"Please." Langsmith put a hand on Speidel's arm. "Let Dr. Millar have her say."

"Emotion," muttered Speidel.

"Every spoken language of earth has migrated away from emotion," said Francine.

"Can you write an emotion on paper?" demanded Speidel.

"That does it," she said. "That really tears it! You're blind! You say language has to be written down. That's part of the magic! Your mind is tied in little knots by academic tradition! Language, general, is primarily oral! People like you, though, want to make it into ritual noise!"

"I didn't come down here for an egg-head argument!" snapped Speidel.

"Let me handle this, please," said Langsmith. He made a mollifying gesture toward Francine. "Please continue."

She took a deep breath. "I'm sorry I snapped," she said. She smiled. "I think we let emotion get the best of us."

Speidel frowned.

"I was talking about language moving away from emotion," she said. "Take Japanese, for example. Instead of saying, 'Thank you' they say 'Katajikenai'—'I am insulted.' Or they say, 'Kino doku' which means 'This poisonous feeling!'" She held up her hands. "This is ritual exclusion of showing emotion. Our Indo-European languages—especially Anglo-Saxon tongues—are moving the same way. We seem to think that emotion isn't quite nice, that..."

"It tells you nothing!" barked Speidel.

She forced down the anger that threatened to overwhelm her. "If you can read the emotional signs," she said, "they reveal if a speaker is telling the truth. That's all, general. They just tell you if you're getting at the truth. Any good psychologist knows this, general. Freud said it: 'If you try to conceal your feelings, every pore oozes betrayal.' You seem to think that the opposite is true."

"Emotions! Dancing!" Speidel pushed his chair back. "Smitty, I've had as much of this as I can take."

"Just a minute," said Langsmith. "Now, Dr. Millar, I wanted you to have your say because we've already considered these points. Long ago. You're interested in the gestures. You say this is a dance of emotions. Other experts say with equal emphasis that these gestures are ritual combat! Freud, indeed! They ooze betrayal. This chopping gesture they make with the right hand"—he chopped the air in illustration—"is identical to the karate or judo chop for breaking the human neck!"

Francine shook her head, put a hand to her throat. She was momentarily overcome by a feeling of uncertainty.

Langsmith said: "That outward thrust they make with one

hand: That's the motion of a sword being shoved into an opponent! They ooze betrayal all right!"

She looked from Langsmith to Speidel, back to Langsmith. A man to her right cleared his throat.

Langsmith said: "I've just given you two examples. We have hundreds more. Every analysis we've made has come up with the same answer: treachery! The pattern's as old as time: Offer a reward; pretend friendship; get the innocent lamb's attention on your empty hand while you poise the axe in your other hand!"

Could I be wrong? she wondered. *Have we been duped by these Galactics?* Her lips trembled. She fought to control them, whispered: "Why are you telling me these things?"

"Aren't you at all interested in revenge against the creatures who murdered your husband?" asked Speidel.

"I don't know that they murdered him!" She blinked back tears. "You're trying to confuse me!" And a favorite saying of her husband's came into her mind: *"A conference is a group of people making a difficult job out of what one person could do easily."* The room suddenly seemed too close and oppressive.

"Why have I been dragged into this conference?" she demanded. "Why?"

"We were hoping you'd assist us in capturing that spaceship," said Langsmith.

"Me? Assist you in..."

"Someone has to get a bomb past the force screens at the door—the ones that keep sand and dirt out of the ship. We've got to have a bomb inside."

"But why me?"

"They're used to seeing you wheel in the master recorder on that cart," said Langsmith. "We thought of putting a bomb in..."

"No!"

"This has gone far enough," said Speidel. He took a deep breath, started to rise.

"Wait," said Langsmith.

"She obviously has no feelings of patriotic responsibility," said Speidel. "We're wasting our time."

Langsmith said: "The Galactics are used to seeing her with that cart. If we change now, they're liable to become suspicious."

"We'll set up some other plan, then," said Speidel. "As far as I'm concerned, we can write off any possibility of further cooperation from her."

"You're little boys playing a game," said Francine. "This isn't an exclusive American problem. This is a human problem that involves every nation on Earth."

"That ship is on United States soil," said Speidel.

"Which happens to be on the only planet controlled by the human species," she said. "We ought to be sharing everything with the other teams, pooling information and ideas to get at every scrap of knowledge."

"We'd all like to be idealists," said Speidel. "But there's no room for idealism where our survival is concerned. These *frogs* have full space travel, apparently between the stars—not just satellites and moon rockets. If we get their ship we can enforce peace on our own terms."

"National survival," she said. "But it's our survival as a species that's at stake!"

Speidel turned to Langsmith. "This is one of our more spectacular failures, Smitty. We'll have to put her under close surveillance."

Langsmith puffed furiously on his pipe. A cloud of pale blue smoke screened his head. "I'm ashamed of you, Dr. Millar," he said.

She jumped to her feet, allowing her anger full scope at last. "You must think I'm a rotten psychologist!" she snapped. "You've been lying to me since I set foot in here!" She shot a bitter glance at Speidel. "Your gestures gave you away! The noncommunicative emotional gestures, general!"

"What's she talking about?" demanded Speidel.

"You said different things with your mouths than you said with your bodies," she explained. "That means you were lying to me—concealing something vital you didn't want me to know about."

"She's insane!" barked Speidel.

"There wasn't any survivor of a plane crash in Ceylon," she said. "There probably wasn't even the plane crash you described."

Speidel froze to sudden stillness, spoke through thin lips: "Has there been a security leak? Good Lord!"

"Look at Dr. Langsmith there!" she said. "Hiding behind that pipe! And you, general: moving your mouth no more than absolutely necessary to speak—trying to hide your real feelings! Oozing betrayal!"

"Get her out of here!" barked Speidel.

"You're all logic and no intuition!" she shouted. "No understanding of feeling and art! Well, general: Go back to your computers, but remember this—you can't build a machine that thinks like a man! You can't feed emotion into an electronic computer and get back anything except numbers! Logic, to you, general!"

"I said get her out of here!" shouted Speidel. He rose half out of his chair, turned to Langsmith who sat in pale silence. "And I want a thorough investigation! I want to know where the security leak was that put her wise to our plans."

"Watch yourself!" snapped Langsmith.

Speidel took two deep breaths, sank back.

They're insane, thought Francine. *Insane and pushed into a corner. With that kind of fragmentation they could slip into catatonia or violence.* She felt weak and afraid.

Others around the table had arisen. Two civilians moved up beside Francine. "Shall we lock her up, general?" asked one.

Speidel hesitated.

Langsmith spoke first: "No. Just keep her under very close surveillance. If we locked her up, it would arouse questions that we don't want to answer."

Speidel glowered at Francine. "If you give us away, I'll have you shot!" He motioned to have her taken out of the room.

When she emerged from the headquarters building, Francine's mind still whirled. *Lies!* she thought. *All lies!*

She felt the omnipresent sand grate under her feet. Dust hazed the concourse between her position on the steps and the spaceship a hundred yards away. The morning sun already had burned off the night chill of the desert. Heat devils danced over the dun surface of the ship.

Francine ignored the security agent loitering a few steps behind her, glanced at her wristwatch: nine-twenty. *Hiko will be wondering what's happened to me*, she thought. *We were supposed to get started by eight.* Hopelessness gripped her mind. The spaceship looming over the end of the concourse appeared like a malignant growth—an evil thing crouched ready to envelope and smother her.

Could that fool general be right? The thought came to her mind unbidden. She shook her head. *No! He was lying! But why did he want me to* ... Delayed realization broke off the thought. *They wanted me to take a small bomb inside the ship, but there was no mention of my escaping! I'd have had to stay with the cart and the bomb to allay suspicions. My God! Those beasts expected me to commit suicide for them! They wanted me to blame the Galactics for Bob's death! They tried to build a lie in my mind until I'd fall in with their plan. It's hard enough to die for an ideal, but to give up your life for a lie* ...

Anger coursed through her. She stopped on the steps, stood there shivering. A new feeling of futility replaced the anger. Tears blurred her vision. *What can one lone woman do against such ruthless schemers?*

Through her tears, she saw movement on the concourse: a man in civilian clothes crossing from right to left. Her mind registered the movement with only partial awareness: *Man stops, points.* She was suddenly alert, tears gone, following the direction of the civilian's extended right arm, hearing his voice shout: "Hey! Look at that!"

A thin needle of an aircraft stitched a hurtling line across the watery desert sky. It banked, arrowed toward the spaceship. Behind it roared an airforce jet—delta wings vibrating, sun flashing off polished metal. Tracers laced out towards the airship.

Someone's attacking the spaceship! she thought. *It's a Russian ICBM!*

But the needle braked abruptly, impossibly, over the spaceship. Behind it, the air force jet's engine died, and there was only the eerie whistling of air burning across its wings.

Gently, the needle lowered itself into a fold of the spaceship. *It's one of theirs—the Galactics',* she realized. *Why is it coming here now? Do they suspect attack? Is that some kind of reinforcement?*

Deprived of its power, the jet staggered, skimmed out to a dust-geyser, belly-landing in the alkali flats. Sirens screamed as emergency vehicles raced toward it.

The confused sounds gave Francine a sudden feeling of nausea. She took a deep breath and stepped down to the concourse, moving without conscious determination, her thoughts in a turmoil. The grating sand beneath her feet was like an emery surface rubbing her nerves. She was acutely conscious of an acrid, burning odor, and she realized with a sudden stab of alarm that her security guard still waited behind her on the steps of the administration building.

Vaguely, she heard voices babbling in the building doorways on both sides of the concourse—people coming out to stare at the spaceship and off across the flats where red trucks clustered around the jet.

A pebble had worked its way into her right shoe. Her mind registered it, rejected an urge to stop and remove the irritant. An idea was trying to surface in her mind. Momentarily she was distracted by a bee humming across her path. Quite inanely her mind dwelt on the thought that the insect was too commonplace for this moment. A mental drunkenness made her giddy. She felt both elated and terrified. *Danger! Yes: terrible danger,* she thought. *Obliteration for the entire human race. But something had to be done. She started to run....*

An explosion rocked the concourse, threw her stumbling to her hands and knees. Sand burned against her palms. Dumb instinct brought her back to her feet. Another explosion— farther away to the right, behind the buildings. Bitter smoke swept across the concourse. Abruptly men lurched from behind the buildings on the right, slogging through the sand toward the spaceship.

Civilians! Possibly—and yet they moved with the purposeful unity of soldiers.

It was like a dream scene to Francine. The men carried weapons. She stopped, saw the gleam of sunlight on metal, heard the peculiar crunch-crunch of men running in sand. Through a dreamy haze she recognized one of the runners: Zakheim. He carried a large black box on his shoulders. His red hair flamed out in the group like a target.

The Russians! she thought. *They've started their attack! If our people join them now, it's the end!*

A machine-gun stuttered somewhere to her right. Dust puffs walked across the concourse, swept into the running figures. Men collapsed, but others still slogged toward the spaceship. An explosion lifted the leaders, sent them sprawling. Again, the machine-gun chattered. Dark figures lay on the sand like thrown dominoes. But still a few continued their mad charge.

MPs in American uniforms ran out from between the buildings on the right. The leaders carried submachine-guns.

We're stopping the attack, thought Francine. But she knew the change of tactics did not mean a rejection of violence by Speidel and the others. It was only a move to keep the Russians from taking the lead. She clenched her fists, ignored the fact that she stood exposed—a lone figure in the middle of the concourse. Her senses registered an eerie feeling of unreality.

Machine-guns renewed their chatter and then—abrupt silence. But now the last of the Russians had fallen. Pursuing MPs staggered. Several stopped, wrenched at their guns.

Francine's shock gave way to cold rage. She moved forward, slowly at first and then striding. Off to the left someone shouted: "Hey! Lady! Get down!" She ignored the voice.

There on the sand ahead was Zakheim's pitiful crumpled figure. A gritty redness spread around his chest.

Someone ran from between the buildings on her left, waved at her to go back. *Hiko!* But she continued her purposeful stride, compelled beyond any conscious willing to stop. She saw the red-headed figure on the sand as though she peered down a tunnel.

Part of her mind registered the fact that Hiko stumbled, slowing his running charge to intercept her. He looked like a man clawing his way through water.

Dear Hiko, she thought. *I have to get to Zak. Poor foolish Zak. That's what was wrong with him the other day at the conference. He knew about this attack and was afraid.*

Something congealed around her feet, spread upward over her ankles, quickly surged over her knees. She could see nothing unusual, but it was as though she had ploughed into a pool of molasses. Every step took terrible effort. The molasses pool moved above her hips, her waist.

So that's why Hiko and the MPs are moving so slowly, she thought. *It's a defensive weapon from the ship. Must be.*

Zakheim's sprawled figure was only three steps away from her now. She wrenched her way through the congealed air, panting with the exertion. Her muscles ached from the effort. She knelt beside Zakheim. Ignoring the blood that stained her skirt she took up one of his outstretched hands, felt for a pulse. Nothing. Now, she recognized the marks on his jacket. They were bullet holes. A machine-gun burst had caught him across the chest. He was dead. She thought of the big garrulous red-head, so full of blooming life only minutes before. *Poor foolish*

Zak. She put his hand down gently, shook the tears from her eyes. A terrible rage swelled in her.

She sensed Ohashi nearby, struggling toward her, heard him gasp: "Is Zak dead?"

Tears dripped unheeded from her eyes. She nodded. "Yes, he is." And she thought: *I'm not crying for Zak. I'm crying for myself . . . for all of us . . . so foolish, so determined, so blind . . .*

"EARTH PEOPLE!" The voice roared from the spaceship, cutting across all thought, stilling all emotion into a waiting fear. "WE HAD HOPED YOU COULD LEARN TO COMMUNICATE!" roared the voice. "YOU HAVE FAILED!"

Vibrant silence.

Thoughts that had been struggling for recognition began surging to the surface of Francine's mind. She felt herself caught in the throes of a mental earthquake, her soul brought to a crisis as sharp as that of giving birth. The crashing words had broken through a last barrier in her mind. "*COMMUNICATE!*" At last she understood the meaning of the ultimatum.

But was it too late?

"No!" she screamed. She surged to her feet, shook a fist at the ship. "Here's one who didn't fail! I know what you meant!" She shook both fists at the ship. "See my hate!"

Against the almost tangible congealing of air she forced her way toward the now silent ship, thrust out her left hand toward the dead figures on the sand all around her. "You killed these poor fools! What did you expect from them? You did this! You forced them into a corner!"

The doors of the spaceship opened. Five green-skinned figures emerged. They stopped, stood staring at her, their shoulders slumped. Simultaneously, Francine felt the thickened air relax its hold upon her. She strode forward, tears coursing down her cheeks.

"You made them afraid!" she shouted. "What else could they do? The fearful can't think."

Sobs overcame her. She felt violence shivering in her muscles. There was a terrible desire in her—a need to get her hands on those green figures, to shake them, hurt them. "I hope you're proud of what you've done."

"QUIET!" boomed the voice from the ship.

"I will not!" she screamed. She shook her head, feeling the wildness that smothered her inhibitions. "Oh, I know you were right about communicating...but you were wrong, too. You didn't have to resort to violence."

The voice from the ship intruded on a softer tone, all the more compelling for the change: "Please?" There was a delicate sense of pleading to the word.

Francine broke off. She felt that she had just awakened from a lifelong daze, but that this clarity of thought-cum-action was a delicate thing she could lose in the wink of an eye.

"We did what we had to do," said the voice. "You see our five representatives there?"

Francine focused on the slump-shouldered Galactics. They looked defeated, radiating sadness. The gaping door of the ship a few paces behind was like a mouth ready to swallow them.

"Those five are among the eight hundred survivors of a race that once numbered six billion," said the voice.

Francine felt Ohashi move up beside her, glanced sidelong at him, then back to the Galactics. Behind her, she heard a low mumbling murmur of many voices. The slow beginning of reaction to her emotional outburst made her sway. A sob caught in her throat.

The voice from the ship rolled on: "This once great race did not realize the importance of unmistakable communication. They entered space in that sick condition—hating, fearing, fighting. There was appalling bloodshed on their side and—ours—before we could subdue them."

A scuffing sound intruded as the five green-skinned figures shuffled forward. They were trembling, and Francine saw glistening drops of wetness below their crests. Their eyes blinked. She sensed the aura of sadness about them, and new tears welled in her eyes.

"The eight hundred survivors—to atone for the errors of their race and to earn the right of further survival—developed a new language," said the voice from the ship. "It is, perhaps, the ultimate language. They have made themselves the masters of all languages to serve as our interpreters." There was a long pause, then: "Think very carefully, Mrs. Millar. Do you know why they are our interpreters?"

The held breath of silence hung over them. Francine swallowed past the thick tightness in her throat. This was the moment that could spell the end of the human race, or could open new doors for them—and she knew it.

"Because they cannot lie," she husked.

"Then you have truly learned," said the voice. "My original purpose in coming down here just now was to direct the sterilization of your planet. We thought that your military preparations were a final evidence of your failure. We see now that this was merely the abortive desperation of a minority. We have acted in haste. Our apologies."

The green-skinned Galactics shuffled forward, stopped two paces from Francine. Their ridged crests drooped, shoulders sagged.

"Slay us," croaked one. His eyes turned toward the dead men on the sand around them.

Francine took a deep, shuddering breath, wiped at her damp eyes. Again she felt the bottomless sense of futility. "Did it have to be this way?" she whispered.

The voice from the ship answered: "Better this than a sterile planet—the complete destruction of your race. Do not blame our interpreters. If a race can learn to communicate, it can be saved. Your race can be saved. First we had to make certain you held the potential. There will be pain in the new ways, no doubt. Many still will try to fight us, but you have not yet erupted fully into space where it would be more difficult to control your course."

"Why couldn't you have just picked some of us, tested a few of us?" she demanded. "Why did you put this terrible pressure on the entire world?"

"What if we had picked the wrong ones?" asked the voice. "How could we be certain with a strange race such as yours that we had a fair sampling of your highest potential? No. All of you had to have the opportunity to learn of our problem. The pressure was to be certain that your own people chose their best representatives."

Francine thought of the unimaginative rule-book followers who had led the teams. She felt hysteria close to the surface.

So close. So hellishly close!

Ohashi spoke softly beside her: "Francine?"

It was a calming voice that subdued the hysteria. She nodded. A feeling of relief struggled for recognition within her, but it had not penetrated all nerve channels. She felt her hands twitching.

Ohashi said: "They are speaking English with you. What of

their language that we were supposed to solve?"

"We leaped to a wrong conclusion, Hiko," she said. "We were asked to communicate. We were supposed to remember our own language—the language we knew in childhood, and that was slowly lost to us through the elevation of reason."

"Ahhhhh," sighed Ohashi.

All anger drained from her now, and she spoke with sadness. "We raised the power of reason, the power of manipulating words, above all other faculties. The written word became our god. We forgot that before words there were actions—that there have always been things beyond words. We forgot that the spoken word preceded the written one. We forgot that the written forms of our letters came from ideographic pictures—that standing behind every letter is an image like an ancient ghost. The image stands for natural movements of the body or of other living things."

"The dances," whispered Ohashi.

"Yes, the dances," she said. "The primitive dances did not forget. And the body did not forget—not really." She lifted her hands, looked at them. "I am my own past. Every incident that ever happened to every ancestor of mine is accumulated within me." She turned, faced Ohashi.

He frowned. "Memory stops at the beginning of your..."

"And the body remembers beyond," she said. "It's a different kind of memory: encysted in an overlay of trained responses like the thing we call language. We have to look back to our childhood because all children are primitives. Every cell of a child knows the language of emotional movements—the clutching reflexes, the wails and contortions, the sensuous twistings, the gentle reassurances."

"And you say these people cannot lie," murmured Ohashi.

Francine felt the upsurge of happiness. It was still tainted by the death around her and the pain she knew was yet to come for her people, but the glow was there expanding. "The body," she said, and shook her head at the scowl of puzzlement on Ohashi's face. "The intellect..." She broke off, aware that Ohashi had not yet made the complete transition to the new way of communicating, that she was still most likely the only member of her race even aware of the vision of this high plateau of being.

Ohashi shook his head, and sunlight flashed on his glasses.

"I'm trying to understand," he said.

"I know you are," she said. "Hiko, all of our Earth languages have a bias toward insanity because they split off the concept of intellect from the concept of body. That's an oversimplification, but it will do for now. You get fragmentation this way, you see? Schizophrenia. These people now—" She gestured toward the silent Galactics. "—they have reunited body and intellect in their communication. A gestalten thing that requires the total being's participation. They cannot lie because that would be to lie to themselves—and this would completely inhibit speech." She shook her head. "Speech is not the word, but it is the only word we have now."

"A paradox," said Ohashi.

She nodded. "The self that is one cannot lie to the self. When body and intellect say the same thing...that is truth. When words and wordlessness agree...that is truth. You see?"

Ohashi stood frozen before her, eyes glistening behind the thick lenses. He opened his mouth, closed it, then bowed his head. In that moment he was the complete Oriental and Francine felt that she could look through him at all of his ancestry, seeing and understanding every culture and every person that had built to the point of the pyramid here in one person: Hiko Ohashi.

"I see it," he murmured. "It was example they showed. Not words to decipher. Only example for recognition, to touch our memories and call them forth. What great teachers! What great masters of being!"

One of the Galactics stepped closer, gestured toward the area behind Francine. His movements and the intent were clear to her, interpreted through her new understanding.

The Galactic's wide lips moved. "You are being recorded," he said. "It would be an opportune moment to begin the education of your people—since all new things must have a point of birth."

She nodded, steeling herself before turning. *Even with the pain of birth*, she thought. This was the moment that would precipitate the avalanche of change. Without knowing precisely how she would set off this chain reaction, she had no doubt that she would do it. Slowly, she turned, saw the movie cameras, the television lenses, the cone microphones all directed at her. People were pressed up against an invisible wall that drew an arc around the ship's entrance and this charmed circle where she stood. *Part of the ship's defenses,* she thought. *A force field to stop intruders.*

A muted murmuring came from the wall of people.

Francine stepped toward them, saw the lenses and microphones adjust. She focused on angry faces beyond the force field—and faces with fear—and faces with nothing but a terrible awe. In the foreground, well within the field, lay Zakheim's body, one hand outstretched and almost pointing at her. Silently, she dedicated this moment to him.

"Listen to me very carefully," she said. "But more important, see beyond my words to the place where words cannot penetrate." She felt her body begin to tingle with a sudden release of energy. Briefly, she raised herself onto her toes. "If you see the truth of my message, if you see through to this place that I show you, then you will enter a higher order of existence: happier, sadder. Everything will take on more depth. You will feel more of all the things there are in this universe for us to feel."

Her new-found knowledge was like a shoring up within, a bottomless well of strength.

"All the window widows of all the lonely homes of Earth am I," she said. And she bent forward. It was suddenly not Dr. Francine Millar, psychologist, there on the sand. By the power of mimesis, she projected the figure of a woman in a housedress leaning on a windowsill, staring hopelessly into an empty future.

"And all the happy innocence seeking pain."

Again, she moved: the years peeled away from her. And now, she picked up a subtle rhythm of words and movements that made experienced actors cry with envy when they saw the films.

"Nature building Nature's thunder am I," she chanted, her body swaying.

"Red roses budding
"And the trout thudding water
"And the moon pounding out stars
"On an ocean wake—
"All these am I!
"A fast hurling motion am I!
"What you think I am—that I am not!

"Dreams tell your senses all my names:
"Not harshly loud or suddenly neglectful, sarcastic, preoccupied or rebukeful—
"But murmuring.
"You abandoned a twelve-hour day for a twelve-hour night
"To meddle carefully with eternity!
"Then you realize the cutting hesitancy
"That prepares a star for wishing...
"When you see my proper image—
"A candle flickering am I.
"Then you will feel the lonely intercourse of the stars.
"Remember! Remember! Remember!"

THE
TACTFUL
SABOTEUR

Better men than you have tried!" snarled Clinton Watt.

"I quote paragraph four, section ninety-one of the Semantic Revision to the Constitution," said saboteur extraordinary Jorj X. McKie. "'The need for obstructive processes in government having been established as one of the chief safeguards for human rights, the question of immunities must be defined with extreme precision.'"

McKie sat across a glistening desk from the Intergalactic Government's Secretary of Sabotage, Clinton Watt. An air of tension filled the green-walled office, carrying over into the screenview behind Watt, which showed an expanse of the System Government's compound and people scurrying about their morning business with a sense of urgency.

Watt, a small man who appeared to crackle with suppressed energy, passed a hand across his shaven head. "All right," he said in a suddenly tired voice. "This is the only Secretariat of government that's never immune from sabotage. You've satisfied the legalities by quoting the law. Now, do your damnedest!"

McKie, whose bulk and fat features usually gave him the appearance of a grandfatherly toad, glowered like a gnome-dragon. His mane of red hair appeared to dance with inner flame.

"Damnedest!" he snapped. "You think I came in here to try to unseat you? You think that?"

And McKie thought: *Let's hope he thinks that!*

"Stop the act, McKie!" Watt said. "We both know you're eligible for this chair." He patted the arm of his chair. "And we both know the only way you can eliminate me and qualify yourself for the appointment is to overcome me with a masterful sabotage. Well, McKie, I've sat here more than eighteen years. Another five months and it'll be a new record. Do your damnedest. I'm waiting."

"I came in here for only one reason," McKie said. "I want to report on the search for saboteur extraordinary Napoleon Bildoon."

McKie sat back wondering: *If Watt knew my real purpose here, would he act just this way? Perhaps.* The man had been behaving oddly since the start of this interview, but it was difficult to determine real motive when dealing with a fellow member of the Bureau of Sabotage.

Cautious interest quickened Watt's bony face. He wet his lips with his tongue and it was obvious he was asking himself if this were more of an elaborate ruse. But McKie had been assigned the task of searching for the missing agent, Bildoon, and it was just possible...

"Have you found him?" Watt asked.

"I'm not sure," McKie said. He ran his fingers through his red hair. "Bildoon's a Pan-Spechi, you know."

"For disruption's sake!" Watt exploded. "I know who and what my own agents are! But we take care of our own. And when one of our best people just drops from sight... What's this about not being sure?"

"The Pan-Spechi are a curious race of creatures," McKie said. "Just because they've taken on humanoid shape we tend to forget their five-phase life cycle."

"Bildoon told me himself he'd hold his group's ego at least another ten years," Watt said. "I think he was being truthful, but..." Watt shrugged and some of the bursting energy seemed to leave him. "Well, the group ego's the only place where the Pan-Spechi show vanity so..." Again he shrugged.

"My questioning of the other Pan-Spechi in the Bureau has had to be circumspect, of course," McKie said. "But I did follow one lead clear to Achus."

"And?"

McKie brought a white vial from his copious jacket, scattered metallic powder on the desktop.

Watt pushed himself back from the desk, eyeing the powder with suspicion. He took a cautious sniff, smelled chalf, the quick-scribe powder. Still...

"It's just chalf," McKie said. And he thought: *If he buys that, I may get away with this.*

"So scribe it," Watt said.

Concealing his elation, McKie held a chalf-memory stick over the dusted surface. A broken circle with arrows pointing to a right-hand flow appeared in the chalf. At each break in the circle stood a symbol—in one place the Pan-Spechi character for ego, then the delta for fifth gender and, finally, the three lines that signified the dormant creche-triplets.

McKie pointed to the fifth gender delta. "I've seen a Pan-Spechi in this position who looks a bit like Bildoon and *appears* to have some of his mannerisms. There's no identity response from the creature, of course. Well, you know how the quasi-feminine fifth gender reacts."

"Don't ever let that amorous attitude fool you," Watt warned. "In spite of your nasty disposition I wouldn't want to lose you into a Pan-Spechi creche."

"Bildoon wouldn't rob a fellow agent's identity," McKie said. He pulled at his lower lip, feeling an abrupt uncertainty. Here, of course, was the most touchy part of the whole scheme. "If it was Bildoon."

"Did you meet this group's ego holder?" Watt asked and his voice betrayed real interest.

"No," McKie said. "But I think the ego-single of this Pan-Spechi is involved with the Tax Watchers."

McKie waited, wondering if Watt would rise to the bait.

"I've never heard of an ego change being forced onto a Pan-Spechi," Watt said in a musing tone, "but that doesn't mean it's impossible. If those Tax Watcher do-gooders found Bildoon sabotaging their efforts and ... hmmm."

"Then Bildoon *was* after the Tax Watchers," McKie said.

Watt scowled. McKie's question was in extreme bad taste. Senior agents, unless joined on a project or where the information was volunteered, didn't snoop openly into the work of their fellows. Left hand and right hand remained mutually ignorant in the Bureau of Sabotage and for good reason. Unless ... Watt stared speculatively at his saboteur extraordinary.

McKie shrugged as Watt remained silent. "I can't operate on inadequate information," he said. "I must, therefore, resign the assignment to search for Bildoon. Instead, I will now look into the Tax Watchers."

"You will not!" Watt snapped.

McKie forced himself not to look at the design he had drawn on the desktop. The next few moments were the critical ones.

"You'd better have a legal reason for that refusal," McKie said.

Watt swiveled sideways in his chair, glanced at the screenview, then addressed himself to the side wall. "The situation has become one of extreme delicacy, Jorj. It's well known that you're one of our finest saboteurs."

"Save your oil for someone who needs it," McKie growled.

"Then I'll put it this way," Watt said, returning his gaze to McKie. "The Tax Watchers in the last few days have posed a real threat to the Bureau. They've managed to convince a High Court magistrate they deserve the same immunity from our ministrations that a...well, public water works or...ah... food processing plant might enjoy. The magistrate, Judge Edwin Dooley, invoked the Public Safety amendment. Our hands are tied. The slightest suspicion that we've disobeyed the injunction and..."

Watt drew a finger across his throat.

"Then I quit," McKie said.

"You'll do nothing of the kind!"

"This TW outfit is trying to eliminate the Bureau, isn't it?" McKie asked. "I remember the oath I took just as well as you do."

"Jorj, you couldn't be that much of a simpleton," Watt said. "You quit, thinking that absolves the Bureau from responsibility for you! That trick's as old as time!"

"Then fire me!" McKie said.

"I've no legal reason to fire you, Jorj."

"Refusal to obey orders of a superior," McKie said.

"It wouldn't fool anybody, you dolt!"

McKie appeared to hesitate, said: "Well, the public doesn't know the inner machinery of how we change the Bureau's command. Perhaps it's time we opened up."

"Jorj, before I could fire you there'd have to be a reason so convincing that...Just forget it."

The fat pouches beneath McKie's eyes lifted until the eyes were mere slits. The crucial few moments had arrived. He had managed to smuggle a Jicuzzi stim into this office past all of Watt's detectors, concealing the thing's detectable radiation core within an imitation of the lapel badge that Bureau agents wore.

"In Lieu of Red Tape," McKie said and touched the badge with a finger, feeling the raised letters there—"ILRT." The touch focused the radiation core onto the metallic dust scattered over the desktop.

Watt gripped the arms of the chair, studying McKie with a new look of wary tension.

"We are under legal injunction to keep hands off the Tax Watchers," Watt said. "Anything that happens to those people or to their project for scuttling us—even legitimate accidents—will be laid at our door. We must be able to defend ourselves. No one who has ever been connected with us dares fall under the slightest suspicion of complicity."

"How about a floor waxed to dangerous slickness in the path of one of their messengers? How about a doorlock changed to delay—"

"Nothing."

McKie stared at his chief. Everything depended now on the man holding very still. He knew Watt wore detectors to warn him of concentrated beams of radiation. But this Jicuzzi stim had been rigged to diffuse its charge off the metallic dust on the desk and that required several seconds of relative quiet.

The men held themselves rigid in the staredown until Watt began to wonder at the extreme stillness of McKie's body. The man was even holding his breath!

McKie took a deep breath, stood up.

"I warn you, Jorj," Watt said.

"Warn me?"

"I can restrain you by physical means if necessary."

"Clint, old enemy, save your breath. What's done is done."

A smile touched McKie's wide mouth. He turned, crossed to the room's only door, paused there, hand on knob.

"What have you done?" Watt exploded.

McKie continued to look at him.

Watt's scalp began itching madly. He put a hand there, felt a long tangle of...tendrils! They were lengthening under his fingers, growing out of scalp, waving and writhing.

"A Jicuzzi stim," Watt breathed.

McKie let himself out, closed the door.

Watt leaped out of his chair, raced to the door.

Locked!

He knew McKie and didn't try unlocking it. Frantically, Watt slapped a molecular dispersion wad against the door, dived through as the wad blasted. He landed in the outer hall, stared first in one direction, then the other.

The hall was empty.

Watt sighed. The tendrils had stopped growing, but they were long enough now that he could see them writhing past his eyes—a rainbow mass of wrigglers, part of himself. And McKie with the original stim was the only one who could reverse the process—unless Watt were willing to spend an interminable time with the Jicuzzi themselves. No. That was out of the question.

Watt began assessing his position.

The stim tendrils couldn't be removed surgically, couldn't be tied down or contained in any kind of disguise without endangering the person afflicted with them. Their presence would hamper him, too, during the critical time of trouble with the Tax Watchers. How could he appear in conferences and interviews with these things writhing in their Medusa dance on his head? It would be laughable! He'd be an object of comedy.

And if McKie could stay out of the way until a Case of Exchangement was brought before the full Cabinet . . . But, no! Watt shook his head. This wasn't the kind of sabotage that required a change of command in the Bureau. This was a gross thing. No subtlety to it. This was like a practical joke.Clownish.

But McKie was noted for his clownish attitude, his irreverence for all the blundering self-importance of government.

Have I been self-important? Watt wondered.

In all honesty, he had to admit it.

I'll have to submit my resignation today, he thought. *Right after I fire McKie. One look at me and there'll be no doubt of why I did it. This is about as convincing a reason as you could find.*

Watt turned to his right, headed for the lab to see if they could help him bring this wriggling mass under control.

The President will want me to stay at the helm until McKie makes his next move, Watt thought. *I have to be able to function somehow.*

McKie waited in the living room of the Achusian mansion with ill-concealed unease. Achus was the administrative planet for the Vulpecula region, an area of great wealth, and this room high on a mountaintop commanded a natural view to the southwest across lesser peaks and foothills misted in purple by a westering G3 sun.

But McKie ignored the view, trying to watch all corners of the room at once. He had seen a fifth-gender Pan-Spechi here in company with the fourth-gender ego-holder. That could only mean the creche with its three dormants was nearby. By all accounts, this was a dangerous place for someone not protected by bonds of friendship and community of interest.

The value of the Pan-Spechi to the universal human society in which they participated was beyond question. What other species had such refined finesse in deciding when to hinder and when to help? Who else could send a key member of its group into circumstances of extreme peril without fear that the endangered one's knowledge would be lost?

There was always a dormant to take up where the lost one had left off.

Still, the Pan-Spechi did have their idiosyncrasies. And their hungers were at times bizarre.

"Ahhh, McKie."

The voice, deep and masculine, came from his left. McKie whirled to study the figure that came through a door carved from a single artificial emerald of glittering creme de menthe colors.

The speaker was humanoid but with Pan-Spechi multifaceted eyes. He appeared to be a terranic man (except for the blue-green eyes) of an indeterminate, well-preserved middle age. The body suggested a certain daintiness in its yellow tights and singlet. The head was squared in outline with close-cropped blond hair, a fleshy chunk of nose and thick splash of mouth.

"Panthor Bolin here," the Pan-Spechi said. "You are welcome in my home, Jorj McKie."

McKie relaxed slightly. Pan-Spechi were noted for honoring hospitality once it was extended ... provided the guest didn't violate their mores.

"I'm honored that you've agreed to see me," McKie said.

"The honor is mine," Bolin said. "We've long recognized you as a person whose understanding of the Pan-Spechi is most subtle and penetrating. I've longed for the chance to have uninhibited conversation with you. And here you are." He indicated a chairdog against the wall to his right, snapped his fingers. The semi-sentient artifact glided to a position behind McKie. "Please be seated."

McKie, his caution realerted by Bolin's reference to "uninhibited conversation," sank into the chairdog, patting it until it assumed the contours he wanted.

Bolin took a chairdog facing him, leaving only about a meter separating their knees.

"Have our egos shared nearness before?" McKie asked. "You appeared to recognize me."

"Recognition goes deeper than ego," Bolin said. "Do you wish to join identities and explore this question?"

McKie wet his lips with his tongue. This was delicate ground with the Pan-Spechi, whose one ego moved somehow from member to member of the unit group as they traversed their *circle of being*.

"I . . . ah . . . not at this time," McKie said.

"Well spoken," Bolin said. "Should you ever change your mind, my ego-group would consider it a most signal honor. Yours is a strong identity, one we respect."

"I'm . . . most honored," McKie said. He rubbed nervously at his jaw, recognizing the dangers in this conversation. Each Pan-Spechi group maintained a supremely jealous attitude of and about its wandering ego. The ego imbued the holder of it with a touchy sense of honor. Inquiries about it could be carried out only through such formula questions as McKie already had asked.

Still, if this were a member of the pent-archal life circle containing the missing saboteur extraordinary Napoleon Bildoon . . . if it were, much would be explained.

"You're wondering if we really can communicate," Bolin said. McKie nodded.

"The concept of *humanity*," Bolin said, "—our term for it would translate approximately as *consentiency*—has been extended to encompass many differing shapes, life systems and methods of mentation. And yet we have never been sure about this question. It's one of the major reasons many of us have adopted your life-shape and much of your metabolism. We wished to experience your strengths and your weaknesses. This helps . . . but is not an absolute solution."

"Weaknesses?" McKie, suddenly wary.

"Ahhh-hummm," Bolin said. "I see. To allay your suspicions I will have translated for you soon one of our major works. Its title would be, approximately, *The Developmental Influence of Weaknesses*. One of the strongest sympathetic bonds we have with your species, for example, is the fact that we both originated as extremely vulnerable surface-bound creatures, whose most sophisticated defense came to be the social structure."

"I'll be most interested to see the translation," McKie said.

"Do you wish more amenities or do you care to state your business now?" Bolin asked.

"I was...ah...assigned to seek out a missing agent of our Bureau," McKie said, "to be certain no harm has befallen this ...ah...agent."

"Your avoidance of gender is most refined," Bolin said. "I appreciate the delicacy of your position and your good taste. I will say this for now: the Pan-Spechi you seek is not at this time in need of your assistance. Your concern, however, is appreciated. It will be communicated to those upon whom it will have the most influence."

"That's a great relief to me," McKie said. And he wondered: *What did he really mean by that?* This thought elicited another, and McKie said: "Whenever I run into this problem of communication between species I'm reminded of an old culture/teaching story."

"Oh?" Bolin registered polite curiosity.

"Two practitioners of the art of mental healing, so the story goes, passed each other every morning on their way to their respective offices. They knew each other, but weren't on intimate terms. One morning as they approached each other, one of them turned to the other and said, 'Good morning.' The one greeted failed to respond, but continued toward his office. Presently, though, he stopped, turned and stared at the retreating back of the man who'd spoken, musing to himself: 'Now what did he really mean by that?'"

Bolin began to chuckle, then laugh. His laughter grew louder and louder until he was holding his sides.

It wasn't that funny, McKie thought.

Bolin's laughter subsided. "A very educational story," he said. "I'm deeply indebted to you. This story shows your awareness of how important it is in communication that we be aware of the other's identity."

Does it? McKie wondered. *How's that?*

And McKie found himself caught up by his knowledge of how the Pan-Spechi could pass a single ego-identity from individual to individual within the life circle group of five distinct protoplasmic units. He wondered how it felt when the ego-holder gave up the identity to become the fifth gender, passing the ego spark to a newly matured unit from the creche. Did the fifth gender willingly become the creche nurse and give itself up as a mysterious identity-food for the three dormants in the creche? he wondered.

"I heard about what you did to Secretary of Sabotage Clinton Watt," Bolin said. "The story of your dismissal from the service preceded you here."

"Yes," McKie said. "That's why I'm here, too."

"You've penetrated to the fact that our Pan-Spechi community here on Achus is the heart of the Tax Watchers' organization," Bolin said. "It was very brave of you to walk right into our hands. I understand how much more courage it takes for your kind to face unit extinction than it does for our kind. Admirable! You are indeed a prize."

McKie fought down a sensation of panic, reminding himself that the records he had left in his private locker at Bureau headquarters could be deciphered in time even if he did not return.

"Yes," Bolin said, "you wish to satisfy yourself that the ascension of a Pan-Spechi to the head of your Bureau will pose no threat to other human species. This is understandable."

McKie shook his head to clear it. "Do you read minds?" he demanded.

"Telepathy is not one of our accomplishments," Bolin said, his voice heavy with menace. "I do hope that was a generalized question and in no way directed at the intimacies of my ego-group."

"I felt that you were reading my mind," McKie said, tensing himself for defense.

"That was how I interpreted the question," Bolin said. "Forgive my question. I should not have doubted your delicacy or your tact."

"You do hope to place a member in the job of Bureau Secretary, though?" McKie said.

"Remarkable that you should've suspected it," Bolin said. "How can you be sure our intention is not merely to destroy the Bureau?"

"I'm not," McKie glanced around the room, regretting that he had been forced to act alone.

"Where did we give ourselves away?" Bolin mused.

"Let me remind you," McKie said, "that I have accepted the hospitality you offered and that I've not offended your mores."

"Most remarkable," Bolin said. "In spite of all the temptations I offered, you have not offended our mores. This is true. You are an embarrassment, indeed you are. But perhaps you have a weapon. Yes?"

McKie lifted a wavering *shape* from an inner pocket.

"Ahhh, the Jicuzzi stim," Bolin said. "Now, let me see, is that a weapon?"

McKie held the *shape* on his palm. It appeared flat at first, like a palm-sized sheet of pink paper. Gradually, the flatness grew a superimposed image of a tube laid on its surface, then another image of an S-curved spring that coiled and wound around the tube.

"Our species can control its shape to some extent," Bolin said. "There's some question on whether I can consider this a weapon."

McKie curled his fingers around the *shape*, squeezed. There came a pop, and fumeroles of purple light emerged between his fingers accompanied by an odor of burnt sugar.

"Exit stim," McKie said. "Now I'm completely defenseless, entirely dependent upon your hospitality."

"Ah, you are a tricky one," Bolin said. "But have you no regard for Ser Clinton Watt? To him, the change you forced upon him is an affliction. You've destroyed the instrument that might have reversed the process."

"He can apply to the Jicuzzi," McKie said, wondering why Bolin should concern himself over Watt.

"Ah, but they will ask your permission to intervene," Bolin said. "They are so formal. Drafting their request should take at least three standard years. They will not take the slightest chance of offending you. And you, of course, cannot volunteer your permission without offending them. You know, they may even build a nerve-image of you upon which to test their petition. You are not a callous person, McKie, in spite of your clownish poses. I'd not realized how important this confrontation was to you."

"Since I'm completely at your mercy," McKie said, "would you try to stop me from leaving here?"

"An interesting question," Bolin said. "You have information I don't want revealed at this time. You're aware of this, naturally?"

"Naturally."

"I find the Constitution a most wonderful document," Bolin said. "The profound awareness of the individual's identity and its relationship to society as a whole. Of particular interest is the portion dealing with the Bureau of Sabotage, those amendments recognizing that the Bureau itself might at times need ...ah...adjustment."

Now what's he driving at? McKie wondered. And he noted how Bolin squinted his eyes in thought, leaving only a thin line of faceted glitter.

"I shall speak now as chief officer of the Tax Watchers," Bolin said, "reminding you that we are legally immune from sabotage."

I've found out what I wanted to know, McKie thought. Now if I can only get out of here with *it!*

"Let us consider the training of saboteurs extraordinary," Bolin said. "What do the trainees learn about the make-work and featherbedding elements in Bureau activity?"

He's not going to trap me in a lie, McKie thought. "We come right out and tell our trainees that one of our chief functions is to create jobs for the politicians to fill," he said. "The more hands in the pie, the slower the mixing."

"You've heard that telling a falsehood to your host is a great breach of Pan-Spechi mores, I see," Bolin said. "You understand, of course, that refusal to answer certain questions is interpreted as a falsehood?"

"So I've been told," McKie said.

"Wonderful! And what are your trainees told about the foot dragging and the monkeywrenches you throw into the path of legislation?"

"I quote from the pertinent training brochure," McKie said. "A major function of the Bureau is to slow passage of legislation."

"Magnificent! And what about the disputes and outright battles Bureau agents have been known to incite?"

"Strictly routine," McKie said. "We're duty-bound to encourage the growth of anger in government wherever we can. It exposes the temperamental types, the ones who can't control themselves, who can't think on their feet."

"Ah," Bolin said. "How entertaining."

"We keep entertainment value in mind," McKie admitted. "We use drama and flamboyance wherever possible to keep our activities fascinating to the public."

"Flamboyant obstructionism," Bolin mused.

"Obstruction is a factor in strength," McKie said. "Only the strongest surmount the obstructions to succeed in government. The strongest... or the most devious, which is more or less the same thing when it comes to government."

"How illuminating," Bolin said. He rubbed the backs of his hands, a Pan-Spechi mannerism denoting satisfaction. "Do you have special instructions regarding political parties?"

"We stir up dissent between them," McKie said. "Opposition tends to expose reality, that's one of our axioms."

"Would you characterize Bureau agents as troublemakers?"

"Of course! My parents were happy as the devil when I showed troublemaking tendencies at an early age. They knew there'd be a lucrative outlet for this when I grew up. They saw to it that I was channeled in the right directions all through school—special classes in Applied Destruction, Advanced Irritation, Anger I and II... only the best teachers."

"You're suggesting the Bureau's an outlet for society's regular crop of troublemakers?"

"Isn't that obvious? And troublemakers naturally call for the services of troubleshooters. That's an outlet for do-gooders. You've a check and balance system serving society."

McKie waited, watching the Pan-Spechi, wondering if his answers had gone far enough.

"I speak as a Tax Watcher, you understand?" Bolin asked.

"I understand."

"The public pays for this Bureau. In essence, the public is paying people to cause trouble."

"Isn't that what we do when we hire police, tax investigators and the like?" McKie asked.

A look of gloating satisfaction came over Bolin's face. "But these agencies operate for the greater good of humanity!" he said.

"Before he begins training," McKie said, and his voice took on a solemn, lecturing tone, "the potential saboteur is shown the entire sordid record of history. The do-gooders succeeded once... long ago. They eliminated virtually all red tape from government. This great machine with its power over human lives slipped into high speed. It moved faster and faster." McKie's voice grew louder. "Laws were conceived and passed in the same hour! Appropriations came and were gone in a fortnight. New bureaus flashed into existence for the most insubstantial reasons."

McKie took a deep breath, realizing he'd put sincere emotional weight behind his words.

"Fascinating," Bolin said. "Efficient government, eh?"

"Efficient?" McKie's voice was filled with outrage. "It was like a great wheel thrown suddenly out of balance! The whole structure of government was in imminent danger of fragmenting before a handful of people, wise with hindsight, used measures of desperation and started what was called the Sabotage Corps."

"Ahhh, yes, I've heard about the Corps' violence."

He's needling me, McKie thought, but found that honest anger helped now. "All right, there was bloodshed and terrible destruction at the beginning," he said. "But the big wheels were slowed. Government developed a controllable speed."

"Sabotage," Bolin sneered. "In lieu of red tape."

I needed that reminder, McKie thought.

"No task too small for Sabotage, no task too large," McKie said. "We keep the wheel turning slowly and smoothly. Some anonymous Corpsman put it into words a long time ago: 'When in doubt, delay the big ones and speed the little ones.'"

"Would you say the Tax Watchers were a 'big one' or a 'little one'?" Bolin asked, his voice mild.

"Big one," McKie said and waited for Bolin to pounce.

But the Pan-Spechi appeared amused. "An unhappy answer."

"As it says in the Constitution," McKie said, "'The pursuit of unhappiness is an inalienable right of all humans.'"

"Trouble is as trouble does," Bolin said and clapped his hands.

Two Pan-Spechi in the uniforms of system police came through the crème de menthe emerald door.

"You heard?" Bolin asked.

"We heard," one of the police said.

"Was he defending his bureau?" Bolin asked.

"He was," the policeman said.

"You've seen the court order," Bolin said. "It pains me because Ser McKie accepted the hospitality of my house, but he must be held incommunicado until he's needed in court. He's to be treated kindly, you understand?"

Is he really bent on destroying the Bureau? McKie asked himself in sudden consternation. *Do I have it figured wrong?*

"You contend my words were sabotage?" McKie asked.

"Clearly an attempt to sway the chief officer of the Tax Watchers from his avowed duties," Bolin said. He stood, bowed.

McKie lifted himself out of the chairdog, assumed an air of confidence he did not feel. He clasped his thick-fingered hands together and bowed low, a grandfather toad rising from the deep to give his benediction. "In the words of the ancient proverb," he said, "'The righteous man lives deep within a cavern and the sky appears to him as nothing but a small round hole.'"

Wrapping himself in dignity, McKie allowed the police to escort him from the room.

Behind him, Bolin gave voice to puzzlement: "Now, what did he mean by that?"

"Hear ye! Hear ye! System High Court, First Bench, Central Sector, is now in session!"

The robo-clerk darted back and forth across the cleared lift dais of the courtarena, its metal curves glittering in the morning light that poured down through the domed weather cover. Its voice, designed to fit precisely into the great circular room, penetrated to the farthest walls: "All persons having petitions before this court draw near!"

The silvery half-globe carrying First Magistrate Edwin Dooley glided through an aperture behind the lift dais and was raised to an appropriate height. His white sword of justice lay diagonally across the bench in front of him. Dooley himself sat in dignified silence while the robo-clerk finished its stentorian announcement and rolled to a stop just beyond the lift field.

Judge Dooley was a tall, black-browed man who affected the ancient look with ebon robes over white linen. He was noted for decisions of classic penetration.

He sat now with his face held in rigid immobility to conceal his anger and disquiet. Why had they put him in this hot spot? Because he'd granted the Tax Watchers' injunction? No matter how he ruled now, the result likely would be uproar. Even President Hindley was watching this one through one of the hotline projectors.

The President had called shortly before this session. It had been Phil and Ed all through the conversation, but the intent remained clear. The Administration was concerned about this case. Vital legislation pended; votes were needed. Neither the budget nor the Bureau of Sabotage had entered their conversation, but the President had made his point—*don't compromise the Bureau but save that Tax Watcher support for the Administration!*

"Clerk, the roster," Judge Dooley said.

And he thought: *They'll get judgment according to strict interpretation of the law! Let them argue with that!*

The robo-clerk's reelslate buzzed. Words appeared on the repeater in front of the judge as the clerk's voice announced: "The People versus Clinton Watt, Jorj X. McKie and the Bureau of Sabotage."

Dooley looked down into the courtarena, noting the group seated at the black oblong table in the Defense ring on his left: a sour-faced Watt with his rainbow horror of Medusa head, McKie's fat features composed in a look of someone trying not to snicker at a sly joke—the two defendants flanking their attorney, Pander Oulson, the Bureau of Sabotage's chief counsel. Oulson was a great thug of a figure in defense white with glistening eyes under beetle brows and a face fashioned mostly of scars.

At the Prosecution table on the right sat Prosecutor Holjance Vohnbrook, a tall scarecrow of a man dressed in conviction red. Gray hair topped a stern face as grim and forbidding as a latter-day Cotton Mather. Beside him sat a frightened appearing young aide and Panthor Bolin, the Pan-Spechi complainant, his multifaceted eyes hidden beneath veined lids.

"Are we joined for trial?" Dooley asked.

Both Oulson and Vohnbrook arose, nodded.

"If the court pleases," Vohnbrook rumbled, "I would like to remind the Bureau of Sabotage personnel present that this court is exempt from their ministrations."

"If the prosecutor trips over his own feet," Oulson said, "I assure him it will be his own clumsiness and no act of mine nor of my colleagues."

Vohnbrook's face darkened with a rush of blood. "It's well known how you..."

A great drumming boomed through the courtarena as Dooley touched the handle of his sword of office. The sound drowned the prosecutor's words. When silence was restored, Dooley said: "This court will tolerate no displays of personality. I wish that understood at the outset."

Oulson smiled, a look like a grimace in his scarred face. "I apologize, Your Honor," he said.

Dooley sank back into his chair, noting the gleam in Oulson's eyes. It occurred to Dooley then that the defense attorney, sabotage-trained, could have brought on the prosecutor's attack to gain the court's sympathy.

"The charge is outlaw sabotage in violation of this court's injunction," Dooley said. "I understand that opening statements have been waived by both sides, the public having been admitted to causae in this matter by appropriate postings?"

"So recorded," intoned the robo-clerk.

Oulson leaned forward against the defense table, said: "Your Honor, defendant Jorj X. McKie has not accepted me as counsel and wishes to argue for separate trial. I am here now representing only the Bureau and Clinton Watt."

"Who is appearing for defendant McKie?" the judge asked.

McKie, feeling like a man leaping over a precipice, got to his feet, said: "I wish to represent myself, Your Honor."

"You should be cautioned against this course," Dooley said.

"Ser Oulson has advised me I have a fool for a client," McKie said. "But in common with most Bureau agents, I have legal training. I've been admitted to the System Bar and have practiced under such codes as the Gowachin where the double-negative innocence requirement must be satisfied before bringing criminal accusation against the prosecutor and proceeding backward the premise that..."

"This is not Gowachin," Judge Dooley said.

"May I remind the Court," Vohnbrook said, "that defendant McKie is a saboteur extraordinary. This goes beyond questions of champerty. Every utterance this man..."

"The law's the same for official saboteurs as it is for others in respect to the issue at hand," Oulson said.

"Gentlemen!" the judge said. "If you please? I will decide the law in this court." He waited through a long moment of silence. "The behavior of all parties in this matter is receiving my most careful attention."

McKie forced himself to radiate calm good humor.

Watt, whose profound knowledge of the saboteur extraordinary made this pose a danger signal, tugged violently at the sleeve of defense attorney Oulson. Oulson waved him away. Watt glowered at McKie.

"If the court permits," McKie said, "a joint defense on the present charge would appear to violate..."

"The court is well aware that this case was bound over on

the basis of deposa summation through a ruling by a robo-legum," Dooley said. "I warn both defense and prosecution, however, that I make my own decisions in such matters. Law and robo-legum are both human constructions and require human interpretation. And I will add that, as far as I'm concerned, in all conflicts between human agencies and machine agencies, the human agencies are paramount."

"Is this a hearing or a trial?" McKie asked.

"We will proceed as in trial, subject to the evidence as presented."

McKie rested his palms on the edge of the defense table, studying the judge. The saboteur felt a surge of misgiving. Dooley was a no-nonsense customer. He had left himself a wide avenue within the indictment. And this was a case that went far beyond immediate danger to the Bureau of Sabotage. Far-reaching precedents could be set here this day—or disaster could strike. Ignoring instincts of self-preservation, McKie wondered if he dared try sabotage within the confines of the court.

"The robo-legum indictment requires joint defense," McKie said. "I admit sabotage against Ser Clinton Watt, but remind the court of Paragraph Four, section ninety-one, of the Semantic Revision to the Constitution, wherein the Secretary of Sabotage is exempted from all immunities. I move to quash the indictment as it regards myself. I was at the time a legal officer of the Bureau required by my duties to test the abilities of my superior."

Vohnbrook scowled at McKie.

"Mmmm," Dooley said. He saw that the prosecutor had detected where McKie's logic must lead. If McKie were legally dismissed from the Bureau at the time of his conversation with the Pan-Spechi, the prosecution's case might fall through.

"Does the prosecutor wish to seek a conspiracy indictment?" Dooley asked.

For the first time since entering the courtarena, defense attorney Oulson appeared agitated. He bent his scarred features close to Watt's gorgon head, conferred in whispers with the defendant. Oulson's face grew darker and darker as he whispered. Watt's gorgon tendrils writhed in agitation.

"We don't seek a conspiracy indictment at this time," Vohnbrook said. "However, we would be willing to separate..."

"Your Honor!" Oulson said, surging to his feet. "Defense must protest separation of indictments at this time. It's our contention that..."

"Court cautions both counsel in this matter that this is not a Gowachin jurisdiction," Dooley said in an angry voice. "We don't have to convict the defender and exonerate the prosecutor before trying a case! However, if either of you would wish a change of venue..."

Vohnbrook, a smug expression on his lean face, bowed to the judge. "Your Honor," he said, "we wish at this time to request removal of defendant McKie from the indictment and ask that he be held as a prosecution witness."

"Objection!" Oulson shouted.

"Prosecution well knows it cannot hold a key witness under trumped up..."

"Overruled," Dooley said.

"Exception!"

"Noted."

Dooley waited as Oulson sank into his chair. *This is a day to remember*, the judge thought. *Sabotage itself outfoxed!* Then he noted the glint of sly humor in the eyes of saboteur extraordinary McKie, realizing with an abrupt sense of caution that McKie, too, had maneuvered for this position.

"Prosecution may call its first witness," the judge said, and he punched a code signal that sent a robo-aide to escort McKie away from the defense table and into a holding box.

A look of almost-pleasure came over prosecutor Vohnbrook's cadaverous face. He rubbed one of his downdrooping eyelids, said: "Call Panthor Bolin."

The Achusian capitalist got to his feet, strode to the witness ring. The robo-clerk's screen flashed for the record: "Panthor Bolin of Achus IV, certified witness in case A011-5BD$_4$gGY74R$_6$ of System High Court ZRZ[1]."

"The oath of sincerity having been administered, Panthor Bolin is prepared for testifying," the robo-clerk recited.

"Panthor Bolin, are you chief officer of the civil organization known as the Tax Watchers?" Vohnbrook asked.

"I...ah...y-yes," Bolin faltered. He passed a large blue handkerchief across his forehead, staring sharply at McKie.

He just now realizes what it is I must do, McKie thought.

"I show you this recording from the robo-legum indictment

proceedings," Vohnbrook said. "It is certified by System police as being a conversation between yourself and Jorj X. McKie in which..."

"Your Honor!" Oulson objected. "Both witnesses to this alleged conversation are present in this courtarena. There are more direct ways to bring out any pertinent information from this matter. Further, since the clear threat of a conspiracy charge remains in this case, I object to introducing this recording as forcing a man to testify against himself."

"Ser McKie is no longer on trial here and Ser Oulson is not McKie's attorney of record," Vohnbrook gloated.

"The objection does, however, have some merit," Dooley said. He looked at McKie seated in the holding box.

"There's nothing shameful about that conversation with Ser Bolin," McKie said. "I've no objection to introducing this record of the conversation."

Bolin rose up on his toes, made as though to speak, sank back.

Now he is certain, McKie thought.

"Then I will admit this record subject to judicial deletions," Dooley said.

Clinton Watt, seated at the defense table, buried his gorgon head in his arms.

Vohnbrook, a death's-head grin on his long face, said: "Ser Bolin, I show you this recording. Now, in this conversation, was Sabotage Agent McKie subjected to any form of coercion?"

"Objection!" Oulson roared, surging to his feet. His scarred face was a scowling mask. "At the time of this alleged recording, Ser McKie was not an agent of the Bureau!" He looked at Vohnbrook. "Defense objects to the prosecutor's obvious effort to link Ser McKie with..."

"*Alleged* conversation!" Vohnbrook snarled. "Ser McKie himself admits the exchange!"

In a weary voice, Dooley said: "Objection sustained. Unless tangible evidence of conspiracy is introduced here, references to Ser McKie as an agent of Sabotage will not be admitted here."

"But Your Honor," Vohnbrook protested, "Ser McKie's own actions preclude any other interpretation!"

"I've ruled on this point," Dooley said. "Proceed."

McKie got to his feet in the holding box, said: "Would Your

Honor permit me to act as a friend of the Court here?"

Dooley leaned back, hand on chin, turning the question over in his mind. A general feeling of uneasiness about the case was increasing in him and he couldn't pinpoint it. McKie's every action appeared suspect. Dooley reminded himself that the saboteur extraordinary was notorious for sly plots, for devious and convoluted schemes of the wildest and most improbable inversions—like onion layers in a five dimensional klein-shape. The man's success in practicing under the Gowachin legal code could be understood.

"You may explain what you have in mind," Dooley said, "but I'm not yet ready to admit your statements into the record."

"The Bureau of Sabotage's own Code would clarify matters," McKie said, realizing that these words burned his bridges behind him. "My action in successfully sabotaging *acting* Secretary Watt is a matter of record."

McKie pointed to the gorgon mass visible as Watt lifted his head and glared across the room.

"*Acting* Secretary?" the judge asked.

"So it must be presumed," McKie said. "Under the Bureau's Code, once the Secretary is sabotaged he..."

"Your Honor!" Oulson shouted. "We are in danger of breach of security here! I understand these proceedings are being broadcast!"

"As Director-in-Limbo of the Bureau of Sabotage, I will decide what is a breach of security and what isn't!" McKie snapped.

Watt returned his head to his arms, groaned.

Oulson sputtered.

Dooley stared at McKie in shock.

Vohnbrook broke the spell. The prosecutor said: "Your Honor, this man has not been sworn to sincerity. I suggest we excuse Ser Bolin for the time being and have Ser McKie continue his *explanation* under oath."

Dooley took a deep breath, said: "Does defense have any questions of Ser Bolin at this time?"

"Not at this time," Oulson muttered. "I presume he's subject to recall?"

"He is," Dooley said, turning to McKie. "Take the witness ring, Ser McKie."

Bolin, moving like a sleepwalker, stepped out of the ring,

returned to the prosecution table. The Pan-Spechi's multi-faceted eyes reflected an odd glitter, moving with a trapped sense of evasiveness.

McKie entered the ring, took the oath and faced Vohnbrook, composing his features in a look of purposeful decisiveness that he knew his actions must reflect.

"You called yourself Director-in-Limbo of the Bureau of Sabotage," Vohnbrook said. "Would you explain that, please?"

Before McKie could answer, Watt lifted his head from his arms, growled: "You traitor, McKie!"

Dooley grabbed the pommel of his sword of justice to indicate an absolute position and barked: "I will tolerate no outbursts in my court!"

Oulson put a hand on Watt's shoulder. Both of them glared at McKie. The Medusa tendrils of Watt's head writhed as they ranged through the rainbow spectrum.

"I caution the witness," Dooley said, "that his remarks would appear to admit a conspiracy. Anything he says now may be used against him."

"No conspiracy, Your Honor," McKie said. He faced Vohnbrook, but appeared to be addressing Watt. "Over the centuries, the function of Sabotage in the government has grown more and more open, but certain aspects of changing the guard, so to speak, have been held as a highly placed secret. The rule is that if a man can protect himself from sabotage he's fit to boss Sabotage. Once sabotaged, however, the Bureau's Secretary must resign and submit his position to the President and the full Cabinet."

"He's out?" Dooley asked.

"Not necessarily," McKie said. "If the act of sabotage against the Secretary is profound enough, subtle enough, carries enough far-reaching effects, the Secretary is replaced by the successful saboteur. He is, indeed, out."

"Then it's now up to the President and the Cabinet to decide between Ser Watt and yourself, is that what you're saying?" Dooley asked.

"Me?" McKie asked. "No, I'm Director-in-Limbo because I accomplished a successful *act* of sabotage against Ser Watt and because I happen to be senior saboteur extraordinary on duty."

"But it's alleged that you were fired," Vohnbrook objected.

"A formality," McKie said. "It's customary to fire the saboteur who's successful in such an effort. This makes him eligible for appointment as Secretary if he so aspires. However, I have no such ambition at this time."

Watt jerked upright, staring at McKie.

McKie ran a finger around his collar, realizing the physical peril he was about to face. A glance at the Pan-Spechi confirmed the feeling. Panthor Bolin was holding himself in check by a visible effort.

"This is all very interesting," Vohnbrook sneered, "but how can it possibly have any bearing on the present action? The charge here is outlaw sabotage against the Tax Watchers represented by the person of Ser Panthor Bolin. If Ser McKie..."

"If the distinguished Prosecutor will permit me," McKie said, "I believe I can set his fears at rest. It should be obvious to—"

"There's conspiracy here!" Vohnbrook shouted. "What about the..."

A loud pounding interrupted him as Judge Dooley lifted his sword, its theremin effect filling the room. When silence had been restored, the judge lowered his sword, replaced it firmly on the ledge in front of him.

Dooley took a moment to calm himself. He sensed now the delicate political edge he walked and thanked his stars that he had left the door open to rule that the present session was a hearing.

"We will now proceed in an orderly fashion," Dooley said. "That's one of the things courts are for, you know." He took a deep breath. "Now, there are several people present whose dedication to the maintenance of law and order should be beyond question. I'd think that among those we should number Ser Prosecutor Vohnbrook; the distinguished defense counsel, Ser Oulson; Ser Bolin, whose race is noted for its reasonableness and humanity; and the distinguished representatives of the Bureau of Sabotage, whose actions may at times annoy and anger us, but who are, we know, consecrated to the principle of strengthening us and exposing our inner resources."

This judge missed his calling, McKie thought. *With speeches like that, he could get into the Legislative branch.*

Abashed, Vohnbrook sank back into his chair.

"Now," the judge said, "unless I'm mistaken, Ser McKie has referred to two acts of sabotage." Dooley glanced down at McKie. "Ser McKie?"

"So it would appear, Your Honor," McKie said, hoping he

read the judge's present attitude correctly. "However, this court may be in a unique position to rule on that very question. You see, Your Honor, the alleged act of sabotage to which I refer was initiated by a Pan-Spechi agent of the Bureau. Now, though, the secondary benefits of that action appear to be sought after by a creche mate of that agent, whose..."

"You dare suggest that I'm not the holder of my cell's ego?" Bolin demanded.

Without knowing quite where it was or what it was, McKie was aware that a weapon had been trained on him by the Pan-Spechi. References in their culture to the weapon for defense of the ego were clear enough.

"I make no such suggestion," McKie said, speaking hastily and with as much sincerity as he could put into his voice. "But surely you cannot have misinterpreted the terranic-human culture so much that you do not know what will happen now."

Warned by some instinct, the judge and other spectators to this interchange remained silent.

Bolin appeared to be trembling in every cell of his body. "I am distressed," he muttered.

"If there were a way to achieve the necessary rapport and avoid that distress I would have taken it," McKie said. "Can you see another way?"

Still trembling, Bolin said: "I must do what I must do."

In a low voice, Dooley said: "Ser McKie, just what is going on here?"

"Two cultures are, at last, attempting to understand each other," McKie said. "We've lived together in apparent understanding for centuries, but appearances can be deceptive."

Oulson started to rise, was pulled back by Watt.

And McKie noted that his former Bureau chief had assessed the peril here. It was a point in Watt's favor.

"You understand, Ser Bolin," McKie said, watching the Pan-Spechi carefully, "that these things must be brought into the open and discussed carefully before a decision can be reached in this court. It's a rule of law to which you've submitted. I'm inclined to favor your bid for the Secretariat, but my own decision awaits the outcome of this hearing."

"What things must be discussed?" Dooley demanded. "And what gives you the right, Ser McKie, to call this a hearing?"

"A figure of speech," McKie said, but he kept his attention on the Pan-Spechi, wondering what the terrible weapon was that the race used in defense of its egos. "What do you say, Ser Bolin?"

"You protect the sanctity of your home life," Bolin said. "Do you deny me the same right?"

"Sanctity, not secrecy," McKie said.

Dooley looked from McKie to Bolin, noted the compressed-spring look of the Pan-Spechi, the way he kept a hand hidden in a jacket pocket. It occurred to the judge then that the Pan-Spechi might have a weapon ready to use against others in this court. Bolin had that look about him. Dooley hesitated on the point of calling guards, reviewed what he knew of the Pan-Spechi. He decided not to cause a crisis. The Pan-Spechi were admitted to the concourse of humanity, good friends but terrible enemies, and there were always those allusions to their hidden powers, to their ego jealousies, to the fierceness with which they defended the secrecy of their creches.

Slowly, Bolin overcame the trembling. "Say what you feel you must," he growled.

McKie said a silent prayer of hope that the Pan-Spechi could control his reflexes, addressed himself to the nexus of pickups on the far wall that was recording this courtarena scene for broadcast to the entire universe.

"A Pan-Spechi who took the name of Napoleon Bildoon was one of the leading agents in the Bureau of Sabotage," McKie said. "Agent Bildoon dropped from sight at the time Panthor Bolin took over as chief of the Tax Watchers. It's highly probable that the Tax Watcher organization is an elaborate and subtle sabotage of the Bureau of Sabotage itself, a move originated by Bildoon."

"There is no such person as Bildoon!" Bolin cried.

"Ser McKie," Judge Dooley said, "would you care to continue this interchange in the privacy of my chambers?" The judge stared down at the saboteur, trying to appear kindly but firm.

"Your Honor," McKie said, "may we, out of respect for a fellow human, leave that decision to Ser Bolin?"

Bolin turned his multifaceted eyes toward the bench, spoke in a low voice: "If the court please, it were best this were done openly." He jerked his hand from his pocket. It came out empty. He leaned across the table, gripped the far edge. "Continue, if you please, Ser."

McKie swallowed, momentarily overcome with admiration

for the Pan-Spechi. "It will be a distinct pleasure to serve under you, Ser Bolin," McKie said.

"Do what you must!" Bolin rasped.

McKie looked from the wonderment in the faces of Watt and the attorneys up to the questioning eyes of Judge Dooley. "In Pan-Spechi parlance, there is no person called Bildoon. But there was such a person, a group mate of Ser Bolin. I hope you notice the similarity in the names they chose for themselves?"

"Ah...yes," Dooley said.

"I'm afraid I've been somewhat of a nosy Parker, a peeping Tom and several other categories of snoop where the Pan-Spechi are concerned," McKie said. "But it was because I suspected the act of sabotage to which I've referred here. The Tax Watchers revealed too much inside knowledge of the Bureau of Sabotage."

"I...ah...am not quite sure I understand you," Dooley said.

"The best kept secret in the universe, the Pan-Spechi cyclic change of gender and identity, is no longer a secret where I'm concerned," McKie said. He swallowed as he saw Bolin's fingers go white where they tightly gripped the prosecution table.

"It relates to the issue at hand?" Dooley asked.

"Most definitely, Your Honor," McKie said. "You see, the Pan-Spechi have a unique gland that controls mentation, dominance, the relationship between reason and instinct. The five group mates are, in reality, one person. I wish to make that clear for reasons of legal necessity."

"Legal necessity?" Dooley asked. He glanced down at the obviously distressed Bolin, back to McKie.

"The gland, when it's functioning, confers ego dominance on the Pan-Spechi in whom it functions. But it functions for a time that's definitely limited—twenty-five to thirty years." McKie looked at Bolin. Again, the Pan-Spechi was trembling. "Please understand, Ser Bolin," he said, "that I do this out of necessity and that this is not an act of sabotage."

Bolin lifted his face toward McKie. The Pan-Spechi's features appeared contorted in grief. "Get it over with, man!" he rasped.

"Yes," McKie said, turning back to the judge's puzzled face. "Ego transfer in the Pan-Spechi, Your Honor, involves a transfer of what may be termed basic-experience-learning. It's accomplished through physical contractor when the ego holder dies;

no matter how far he may be separated from the creche, this seems to fire up the eldest of the creche triplets. The ego-single also bequeaths a verbal legacy to his mate whenever possible—and that's most of the time. Specifically, it's this time."

Dooley leaned back. He was beginning to see the legal question McKie's account had posed.

"The act of sabotage which might make a Pan-Spechi eligible for appointment as Secretary of the Bureau of Sabotage was initiated by a...ah...cell mate of the Ser Bolin in court today, is that it?" Dooley asked.

McKie wiped his brow. "Correct, Your Honor."

"But that cell mate is no longer the ego dominant, eh?"

"Quite right, Your Honor."

"The...ah...former ego holder, this...ah...Bildoon, is no longer eligible?"

"Bildoon, or what was once Bildoon, is a creature operating solely on instinct now, Your Honor," McKie said. "Capable of acting as creche nurse for a time and, eventually, fulfilling another destiny I'd rather not explain."

"I see." Dooley looked at the weather cover of the court-arena. He was beginning to see what McKie had risked here. "And you favor this, ah, Ser Bolin's bid for the Secretariat?" Dooley asked.

"If President Hindley and the Cabinet follow the recommendation of the Bureau's senior agents, the procedure always followed in the past, Ser Bolin will be the new Secretary," McKie said. "I favor this."

"Why?" Dooley asked.

"Because of this unique roving ego, the Pan-Spechi have a more communal attitude toward fellow sentients than do most other species admitted to the concourse of humanity," McKie said. "This translates as a sense of responsibility toward all life. They're not necessarily maudlin about it. They oppose where it's necessary to build strength. Their creche life demonstrates several clear examples of this which I'd prefer not to describe."

"I see," Dooley said, but he had to admit to himself that he did not. McKie's allusions to unspeakable practices were beginning to annoy him. "And you feel that this Bildoon-Bolin act of sabotage qualifies him, provided this court rules they are one and the same person?"

"We are not the same person!" Bolin cried. "You don't dare

say I'm that...that shambling, clinging..."

"Easy," McKie said. "Ser Bolin, I'm sure you see the need for this legal fiction."

"Legal fiction," Bolin said as though clinging to the words. The multifaceted eyes glared across the courtarena at McKie. "Thank you for the verbal nicety, McKie."

"You've not answered my question, Ser McKie," Dooley said, ignoring the exchange with Bolin.

"Sabotaging Ser Watt through an attack on the entire Bureau contains subtlety and finesse never before achieved in such an effort," McKie said. "The entire Bureau will be strengthened by it."

McKie glanced at Watt. The acting Secretary's Medusa tangle had ceased its writhing. He was staring at Bolin with a speculative look in his eyes. Sensing the quiet in the courtarena, he glanced up at McKie.

"Don't you agree, Ser Watt?" McKie asked.

"Oh, yes. Quite." Watt said.

The note of sincerity in Watt's voice startled the judge. For the first time, he wondered at the dedication which these men brought to their jobs.

"Sabotage is a very sensitive Bureau," Dooley said. "I've some serious reservations—"

"If Your Honor please," McKie said, "forbearance is one of the chief attributes a saboteur can bring to his duties. Now, I wish you to understand what our Pan-Spechi friend has done here this day. Let us suppose that I have spied upon the most intimate moments between you, Judge, and your wife, and that I reported them in detail here in open court with half the universe looking on. Let us suppose further that you had the strictest moral code against such discussions with outsiders. Let us suppose that I made these disclosures in the basest terms with every four-letter word at my command. Let us suppose that you were armed, traditionally, with a deadly weapon to strike at such blasphemers, such—"

"Filth!" Bolin grated.

"Yes," McKie said. "Filth. Do you suppose, Your Honor, that you could have stood by without killing me?"

"Good heavens!" Dooley said.

"Ser Bolin," McKie said, "I offer you and all your race my most humble apologies."

"I'd hoped once to undergo the ordeal in the privacy of a judge's chambers with as few outsiders as possible," Bolin said. "But once you were started in open court..."

"It had to be this way," McKie said. "If we'd done it in private, people would've come to be suspicious about a Pan-Spechi in control of..."

"People?" Bolin asked.

"Non Pan-Spechi," McKie said. "It'd have been a barrier between our species.

"And we've been strengthened by all this," McKie said. "Those provisions of the Constitution that provide the people with a slowly moving government have been demonstrated anew. We've admitted the public to the inner workings of Sabotage, shown them the valuable character of the man who'll be the new Secretary."

"I've not yet ruled on the critical issue here," Dooley said.

"But Your Honor!" McKie said.

"With all due respect to you as a saboteur extraordinary, Ser McKie," Dooley said, "I'll make my decision on evidence gathered under my direction." He looked at Bolin. "Ser Bolin, would you permit an agent of this court to gather such evidence as will allow me to render verdict without fear of harming my own species?"

"We're humans together," Bolin growled.

"But terranic humans hold the balance of power," Dooley said. "I owe allegiance to law, yes, but my terranic fellows depend on me, too. I have a..."

"You wish your own agents to determine if Ser McKie has told the truth about us?"

"Ah...yes," Dooley said.

Bolin looked at McKie. "Ser McKie, it is I who apologize to you. I had not realized how deeply xenophobia penetrated your fellows."

"Because," McKie said, "outside of your natural modesty, you have no such fear. I suspect you know the phenomenon only through reading of us."

"But all strangers are potential sharers of identity," Bolin said. "Ah, well."

"If you're through with your little chat," Dooley said, "would you care to answer my question, Ser Bolin? This is still, I hope, a court of law."

"Tell me, Your Honor," Bolin said, "would you permit me to witness the tenderest intimacies between you and your wife?"

Dooley's face darkened, but he saw suddenly in all of its stark detail the extent of McKie's analogy and it was to the judge's credit that he rose to the occasion. "If it were necessary to promote understanding," he rasped, "yes!"

"I believe you would," Bolin murmured. He took a deep breath. "After what I've been through here today one more sacrifice can be borne, I guess. I grant your investigators the privilege requested, but advise that they be discreet."

"It will strengthen you for the trials ahead as Secretary of the Bureau," McKie said. "The Secretary, you must bear in mind, has no immunities from sabotage whatsoever."

"But," Bolin said, "the Secretary's legal orders carrying out his Constitutional functions must be obeyed by all agents."

McKie nodded, seeing in the glitter of Bolin's eyes a vista of peeping Tom assignments with endless detailed reports to the Secretary of Sabotage—at least until the fellow's curiosity had been satisfied and his need for revenge satiated.

But the others in the courtarena, not having McKie's insight, merely wondered at the question: *What did he really mean by that?*

THE
ROAD
TO
DUNE

You have arrived on the planet Arrakis. You will embark on a walking tour of epic proportions. Rarely does a visitor on the road to Dune make his or her way without an Imperium guide. Here is a sampling from such a guide, complete with illustrations.

Your walking tour of Arrakis must include this approach across the dunes to the Grand Palace at Arrakeen (background). From a distance, the dimensions of this construction are deceptive, especially when hazed by wind-blown dust. The largest man-made structure ever built, the Grand Palace could cover more than ten of the Imperium's most populous cities under the one roof, a fact that becomes more apparent when you learn Atreides attendants and their families, housed spaciously in the Palace Annex (foreground), number some thirty-five million souls.

(Following pages) When you walk into the Grand Reception Hall of the Palace at Arrakeen, be prepared to feel dwarfed before an immensity never before conceived. A statue of St. Alia Atreides (foreground), shown as "The Soother of Pains," stands twenty-two meters tall but is one of the smallest adornments in the hall. Two hundred such statues could be stacked one atop the other against the entrance pillars (background) and still fall short of the doorway's capitol arch, which itself is almost a thousand meters below the first beams upholding the lower roof.

If you are numbered among "the heartfelt pilgrims," you will cross the last thousand meters of this approach to the Temple of Alia on your knees. Those thousand meters fall well within the sweeping curves (background) leading your eyes up to the transcendant symbols dedicating this Temple to St. Alia of the Knife. The famed "Sun-Sweep Window" (left face of the Temple) incorporates every solar calendar known to human history in the one translucent display whose brilliant colors, driven by the sun of Dune, thread through the interior on prismatic pathways.

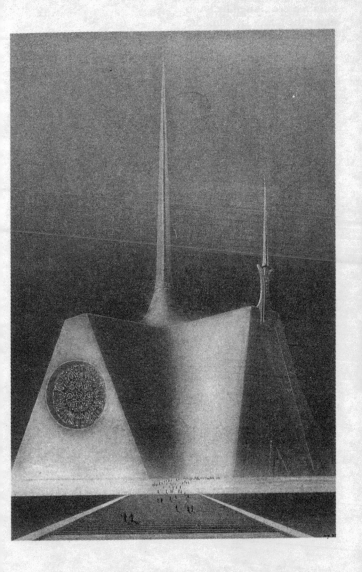

On each pilgrimage, one
hundred are chosen by lot to
make the three-day climb up
secret passages of the Grand
Palace and, half-way up, may
look down from this vantage
on Muad'Dib's personal ornithopter. It sits on His private
landing platform against an
inner wall of the Palace. A
narrow strip of windows in
Atreides family quarters glisten
on the high wall (left). An attendant has just made the regular inspection of the 'thopter,
returning to the Palace with a
traditional Fremen cry heard
clearly from the observation
stop: "His water is secure!"

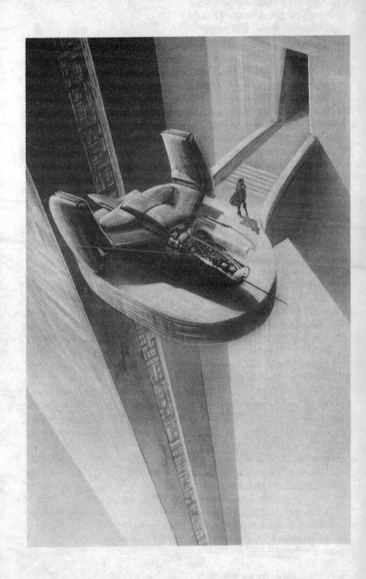

This Ixian heating device, set like a giant pearl in an ornate stand, greets you in a smaller passage of the Grand Palace. The ring-bound queue of the attendant servicing the device marks him as a city Fremen. On your walking tour of Arrakis, you will see many such Ixian artifacts, some set with rare gems, all worked in precious metals by dedicated artisans, some of whom devote years to the completion of a single decorative line. Attention to detail can be seen on this space heater. It incorporates twenty precious metals in each lapped scale.

(Following pages) Rarely, in a private passage of the Grand Palace, the walking pilgrim will encounter the Reverend Mother Gaius Helen Mohiam. The famed Bene Gesserit graciously paused here to be recorded in the light of a glowglobe. Note her wedding bands. They signify her eternal bond to the Sisterhood. The glowglobe is of an ancient design and may have come from Caladan in the original Atreides migration. The cracked vascule rim on the lower left side of the globe could indicate rough treatment in the Harkonnen attack. Many artifacts from those troubled times survived and were restored on orders of Muad'Dib himself.

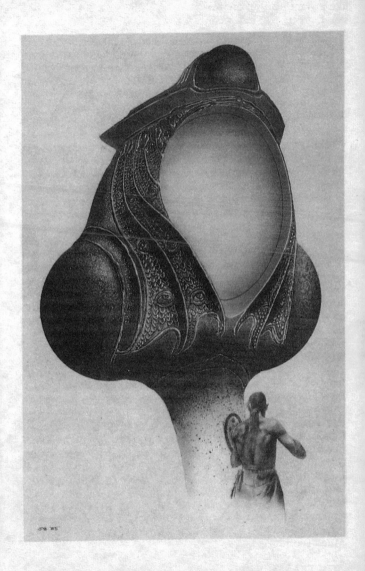

This authentic visage of the Princess Irulan, Muad'Dib's virgin consort, should be committed to memory before your walking tour of Arrakis. The pilgrim should beware of false images. You will be beset by tradesmen hawking such mementoes. Irulan authorized only this portrait for official sale to pilgrims.

The face of Duncan Idaho,
ghola warrior, teacher, friend
and advisor of Muad'Dib stares
out at you from this official
portrait. It is sold to pilgrims on
the walking tour of Arrakis
only in Palace shops. All pro-
ceeds go to support retired
Fremen and provide for the
education of Fremen orphans.

BY
THE
BOOK

You will take your work seriously. Infinite numbers of yet-unborn humankind depend upon you who keep open the communications lines through negative space. Let the angle-transmission networks fail and Man will fail.

"You and the Haigh Company"
(Employees Handbook)

He was too old for this kind of work even if his name was Ivar Norris Gump, admittedly the best troubleshooter in the company's 900-year history. If it'd been anyone but his old friend Poss Washington calling for help, there'd have been a polite refusal signed "Ing." Semi-retirement gave a troubleshooter the right to turn down dangerous assignments.

Now, after three hours on duty in a full vac suit within a Skoarnoff tube's blank darkness, Ing ached with tiredness. It impaired his mental clarity and his ability to survive and he knew it.

You will take your work seriously at all times, he thought. *Axiom: A troubleshooter shall not get into trouble.*

Ing shook his head at the handbook's educated ignorance, took a deep breath and tried to relax. Right now he should be back home on Mars, his only concerns the routine maintenance of the Phobos Relay and an occasional lecture to new 'shooters.

Damn that Poss, he thought.

The big trouble was in here, though—in the tube, and six good men had died trying to find it. They were six men he had helped train—and that was another reason he had come. They were all caught up in the same dream.

Around Ing stretched an airless tubular cave twelve kilometers long, two kilometers diameter. It was a lightless hole carved through lava rock beneath the moon's Mare Nectaris. Here was the home of the "Beam"—the beautiful, deadly, vitally *serious* beam, a tamed violence which suddenly had become balky.

Ing thought of all the history which had gone into this tube. Some nine hundred years ago the Seedling Compact had been signed. In addition to its Solar System Communications duties, the Haigh Company had taken over then the sending out of small containers, their size severely limited by the mass an angtrans pulse could push. Each container held twenty female rabbits. In the rabbit uteri, dormant, their metabolism almost at a standstill, lay two hundred human embryos nestled with embryos of cattle, all the domestic stock needed to start a new human economy. With the rabbits went plant seeds, insect eggs and design tapes for tools.

The containers were rigged to fold out on a planet's surface to provide a shielded living area. There the embryos would be machine-transferred into inflatable gestation vats, brought to full term, cared for and educated by mechanicals until the human *seed* could fend for itself.

Each container had been pushed to trans-light speed by ang-trans pulses—"like pumping a common garden swing," said the popular literature. The life mechanism was controlled by signals transmitted through the "Beam" whose tiny impulses went "around the corner" to bridge in milliseconds distances which took matter centuries to traverse.

Ing glanced up at the miniature beam sealed behind its quartz window in his suit. There was the hope and the frustration. If they could only put a little beam such as that in each container, the big beam could home on it. But under that harsh bombardment, beam anodes lasted no longer than a month. They made-do with reflection plates on the containers, then, with beam-bounce and programmed approximations. And somewhere the programmed approximations were breaking down.

Now, with the first Seedling Compact vessel about to land on Theta Apus IV, with mankind's interest raised to fever pitch—beam contact had turned unreliable. The farther out the container, the worse the contact.

Ing could feel himself being drawn toward that frail cargo out there. His instincts were in communion with those containers which would drift into limbo unless the beam was brought under control. The embyros would surely die eventually and the dream would die with them.

Much of humanity feared the containers had fallen into the hands of alien life, that the human embyros were being taken over by something *out there*. Panic ruled in some quarters and there were shouts that the SC containers betrayed enough human secrets to make the entire race vulnerable.

To Ing and the six before him, the locus of the problem seemed obvious. It lay in here and in the anomaly math newly derived to explain how the beam might be deflected from the containers. What to do about that appeared equally obvious.

But six men had died following that obvious course. They had died here in this utter blackness.

Sometimes it helped to quote the book.

Often you didn't know what you hunted here—a bit of stray radiation perhaps, a few cosmic rays that had penetrated a weak spot in the force-baffle shielding, a dust leak caused by a moon-quake, or a touch of heat, a hot spot coming up from the depths. The big beam wouldn't tolerate much interference. Put a pin-head flake of dust in its path at the wrong moment, let a tiny flicker of light intersect it, and it went whiplash wild. It writhed like a giant snake, tore whole sections off the tube walls. Beam auroras danced in the sky above the moon then and the human attendants scurried.

A troubleshooter at the wrong spot in the tube died.

Ing pulled his hands into his suit's barrel top, adjusted his own tiny beam scope, the unit that linked him through a short reach of angspace to beam control. He checked his instruments, read his position from the modulated contact ripple through the soles of his shielded suit.

He wondered what his daughter, Lisa, was doing about now. Probably getting the boys, his grandsons, ready for the slotride to school. It made Ing feel suddenly old to think that one of his grandsons already was in Mars Polytechnic aiming for a Haigh Company career in the footsteps of his famous grand-father.

The vac suit was hot and smelly around Ing after a three-hour tour. He noted from a dial that his canned-cold temperature balance system still had an hour and ten minutes before red-line.

It's the cleaners, Ing told himself. *It has to be the vacuum clean-ers. It's the old familiar cussedness of inanimate objects.*

What did the handbook say? *"Frequently it pays to look first for the characteristics of devices in use which may be such that an essential pragmatic approach offers the best chance for success. It often is possible to solve an accident or malfunction problem with straightforward and uncomplicated approaches, deliberately ignoring their more subtle aspects."*

He slipped his hands back into his suit's arms, shielded his particle counter with an armored hand, cracked open the cover, peered in at the luminous dial. Immediately, an angry voice crackled in the speakers:

"Douse that light! We're beaming!"

Ing snapped the lid closed by reflex, said: "I'm in the backboard shadow. Can't see the beam." Then: "Why wasn't I told you're beaming?"

Another voice rumbled from the speakers: "It's Poss here, Ing. I'm monitoring your position by sono, told them to go ahead without disturbing you."

"What's the Supetrans doing monitoring a troubleshooter?" Ing asked.

"All right, Ing."

Ing chuckled, then: "What're you doing, testing?"

"Yes. We've an inner-space transport to beam down on Titan, thought we'd run it from here."

"Did I foul the beam?"

"We're still tracking clean."

Inner-space transmission open and reliable, Ing thought, *but the long reach out to the stars was muddied.* Maybe the scare mongers were right. Maybe it was outside interference, an alien intelligence.

"We've lost two cleaners on this transmission," Washington said. "Any sign of them?"

"Negative."

They'd lost two cleaners on the transmission, Ing thought. That was getting to be routine. The flitting vacuum cleaners—supported by the beam's field, patrolling its length for the slightest trace of interference, had to be replaced at the rate of about a hundred a year normally, but the rate had been going up. As the beam grew bigger, unleashed more power for the long reach, the cleaners proved less and less effective at dodging the angtrans throw, the controlled whiplash. No part of a cleaner survived contact with the beam. They were energy-charged in phase with the beam, keyed for instant dissolution to add their energy to the transmission.

"It's the damned cleaners," Ing said.

"That's what you all keep saying," Washington said.

Ing began prowling to his right. Somewhere off there the glassite floor curved gradually upward and became a wall—and then a ceiling. But the opposite side was always two kilometers away, and the moon's gravity, light as that was, imposed limits on how far he could walk up the wall. It wasn't like the little Phobos beam where they could use a low-power magnafield outside and walk right around the tube.

He wondered then if he was going to insist on riding one of the cleaners...the way the six others had done.

Ing's shuffling, cautious footsteps brought him out of the anode backboard's shadow. He turned, saw a pencil line of glowing purple stretching away from him to the cathode twelve kilometers distant. He knew there actually was no purple glow, that what he saw was a visual simulation created on the one-way surface of his faceplate, a reaction to the beam's presence displayed there for his benefit alone.

Washington's voice in his speaker said: "Sono has you in Zone Yellow. Take it easy, Ing."

Ing altered course to the right, studied the beam.

Intermittent breaks in the purple line betrayed the presence between himself and that lambent energy of the robot vacuum cleaners policing the perimeter, hanging on the sine lines of the beam field like porpoises gamboling on a bow wave.

"Transport's down," Washington said. "We're phasing into a long-throw test. Ten-minute program."

Ing nodded to himself, imagined Washington sitting there in the armored bubble of the control room, a giant, with a brooding face, eyes alert and glittering. Old Poss didn't want to believe it was the cleaners, that was sure. If it was the cleaners, someone was going to have to ride the wild goose. There'd be more deaths...more rides...until they tested out the new theory. It certainly was a helluva time for someone to come up with an anomaly *hole* in the angtrans math. But that's what someone back at one of the trans-time computers on Earth had done... and if he was right—then the problem had to be the cleaners.

Ing studied the shadow breaks in the beam—robotic torpedoes, sensor-trained to collect the tiniest debris. One of the shadows suddenly reached away from him in both directions until the entire beam was hidden. A cleaner was approaching him. Ing waited for it to identify the Authorized Intruder markings which he could *see* the same way he saw the beam.

The beam reappeared.

"Cleaner just looked you over," Washington said. "You're getting in pretty close."

Ing heard the worry in his friend's voice, said: "I'm all right long's I stay up here close to the board."

He tried to picture in his mind then the cleaner lifting over him and returning to its station along the beam.

"I'm plotting you against the beam," Washington said. "Your shadow width says you're approaching Zone Red. Don't crowd it, Ing. I'd rather not have to clean a fried troubleshooter out of there."

"Hate to put you to all that extra work," Ing said.

"Give yourself plenty of 'lash room."

"I'm milking the beam thickness against my helmet crosshairs, Poss. Relax."

Ing advanced another two steps, sent his gaze traversing the beam's length, seeking the beginnings of the controlled whiplash which would *throw* the test message into angspace. The chained energy of the purple rope began to bend near its center far down the tube. It was an action visible only as a gentle flickering outward against the cross-hairs of his faceplate.

He backed off four steps. The throw was a chancy thing when you were this close—and if interfering radiation ever touched that beam...

Ing crouched, sighted along the beam, waited for the throw. An experienced troubleshooter could tell more from the way the beam whipped than banks of instruments could reveal. Did it push out a double bow? Look for faulty field focus. Did it waver up and down? Possible misalignment of vertical hold. Did it split or spread into two loops? Synchronization problem.

But you had to be in here close and alert to that fractional margin between good seeing and *good night!* forever.

Cleaners began paying more attention to him in this close, but he planted himself with his AI markings visible to them, allowing them to fix his position and go on about their business.

To Ing's trained eye, the cleaner action appeared more intense, faster than normal. That agreed with all the previous reports—unless a perimeter gap had admitted stray foreign particles, or perhaps tiny shades dislodged from the tube's walls by the pulse of the moon's own life.

Ing wondered then if there could be an overlooked hole in the fanatic quadruple-lock controls giving access to the tube. But they'd been sniffing along that line since the first sign of trouble. Not likely a hole would've escaped the inspectors. No—it was in here. And cleaner action *was* increased, a definite lift in tempo.

"Program condition?" Ing asked.

"Transmission's still Whorf positive, but we haven't found an angspace opening yet."

"Time?"

"Eight minutes to program termination."

"Cleaner action's way up," Ing said. "What's the dirt count?"

A pause, then: "Normal."

Ing shook his head. The monitor that kept constant count of the quantity of debris picked up by the cleaners shouldn't show normal in the face of this much activity.

"What's the word from Mare Nubium transmitter?" Ing asked.

"Still shut down and full of inspection equipment. Nothing to show for it at last report."

"Imbrium?"

"Inspection teams are out and they expect to be back into test phase by 0900. You're not thinking of ordering *us* to shut down for a complete clean-out?"

"Not yet."

"We've got a budget to consider, too, Ing. Remember that."

Huh! Ing thought. *Not like Poss to worry about budget in this kind of an emergency. He trying to tell me something?*

What did the handbook say? *"The good troubleshooter is cost conscious, aware that down time and equipment replacement are factors of serious concern to the Haigh Company."*

Ing wondered then if he should order the tube opened for thorough inspection. But the Imbrium and Nubium tubes had revealed nothing and the decontamination time *was* costly. They were the older tubes, though—Nubium the first to be built. They were smaller than Nectaris, simpler locks. But their beams weren't getting through any better than the Nectaris tube with its behemoth size, greater safeguards.

"Stand by," Washington said. "We're beginning to get whip-count on the program."

In the abrupt silence, Ing saw the beam curl. The whiplash came down the twelve kilometers of tube curling like a purple wave, traveling the entire length in about two thousandths of a second. It was a thing so fast that the visual effect was of seeing it *after* it had happened.

Ing stood up, began analyzing what he had seen. The beam had appeared clean, pure—a perfect throw... except for one little flare near the far end and another about midway. Little flares. The afterimage was needle shaped, right... pointed.

"How'd it look?" Washington asked.

"Clean," Ing said. "Did we get through?"

"We're checking," Washington said, then: "Limited contact.

Very muddy. About thirty percent...just about enough to tell us the container's still there and its contents seem to be alive."

"Is it in orbit?"

"Seems to be. Can't be sure."

"Give me the cleaner count," Ing said.

A pause, then: "Damnation! We're down another two."

"Exactly two?"

"Yes. Why?"

"Dunno yet. Do your instruments show beam deflections from hitting two cleaners? What's the energy sum?"

"Everyone thinks the cleaners are causing this," Washington muttered. "I tell you they couldn't. They're fully phased *with* the beam, just add energy to it if they hit. They're *not* debris!"

"But does the beam really eat them?" Ing asked. "You saw the anomaly report."

"Oh, Ing, let's not go into that again." Washington's voice sounded tired, irritated.

The stubbornness of Washington's response confused Ing. This wasn't like the man at all. "Sure," Ing said, "but what if they're going somewhere we can't see?"

"Come off that, Ing! You're as bad as all the others. If there's one place we know they're *not* going, that's into angspace. There isn't enough energy in the universe to put cleaner mass around the corner."

"Unless that hole in our theories really exists," Ing said. And he thought: *Poss is trying to tell me something. What? Why can't he come right out and say it?* He waited, wondering at an idea that nibbled at the edge of his mind—a concept...What was it? Some half-forgotten association...

"Here's the beam report," Washington said. "Deflection shows only one being taken, but the energy sum's doubled all right. One balanced out the other. That happens."

Ing studied the purple line, nodding to himself. The beam was almost the color of a scarf his wife had worn on their honeymoon. She'd been a good wife, Jennie—raising Lisa in Mars camps and blister pods, sticking with her man until the canned air and hard life had taken her.

The beam lay quiescent now with only the faintest auroral bleed off. Cleaner tempo was down. The test program still had a few minutes to go, but Ing doubted it'd produce another throw into angspace. You acquired an instinct for the transmission pulse after a while. You could sense when the beam was going to open its tiny signal window across the light-years.

"I saw both of those cleaners go," Ing said. "They didn't seem to be torn apart or anything—just flared out."

"Energy consumed," Washington said.

"Maybe."

Ing thought for a moment. A hunch was beginning to grow in him. He knew a way to test it. The question was: Would Poss go along with it? Hard to tell in his present mood. Ing wondered about his friend. Darkness, the isolation of this position within the tube gave voices from outside a disembodied quality.

"Poss, do me a favor," Ing said. "Give me a straight 'lashgram. No fancy stuff, just a demonstration throw. I want a clean ripple the length of the beam. Don't try for angspace, just 'lash it."

"Have you popped your skull? Any 'lash can hit angspace. And you get one fleck of dust in that beam path..."

"We'd rip the sides off the tube; I know. But this is a clean beam, Poss. I can see it. I just want a little ripple."

"Why?"

Can I tell him? Ing wondered.

Ing decided to tell only part of the truth, said: "I want to check the cleaner tempo during the program. Give me a debris monitor and a crossing count for each observation post. Have them focus on the cleaners, not on the beam."

"Why?"

"You can see for yourself cleaner activity doesn't agree with the beam condition," Ing said. "Something's wrong there—accumulated programming error or...I dunno. But I want some actual facts to go on—a physical count during the 'lash."

"You're not going to get new data running a test that could be repeated in the laboratory."

"This isn't a laboratory."

Washington absorbed this, then: "Where would you be during the 'lash?"

He's going to do it, Ing thought. He said: "I'll be close to the anode end here. 'Lash can't swing too wide here."

"And if we damage the tube?"

Ing hesitated remembering that it was a friend out there, a friend with responsibilities. No telling who might be monitoring the conversation, though...and this test was vital to the idea nibbling at Ing's awareness.

"Humor me, Poss," Ing said.

"Humor him," Washington muttered. "All right, but this'd better not be humorous."

"Wait till I'm in position," Ing said. "A straight 'lash."

He began working up the tube slope out of Zone Yellow into the Gray and then the White. Here, he turned, studied the beam. It was a thin purple ribbon stretching off left and right—shorter on the left toward the anode. The long reach of it going off toward the cathode some twelve kilometers to his right was a thin wisp of color broken by the flickering passage of cleaners.

"Any time," Ing said.

He adjusted the suit rests against the tube's curve, pulled his arms into the barrel top, started the viewplate counter recording movement of the cleaners. Now came the hard part—waiting and watching. He had a sudden feeling of isolation then, wondering if he'd done the right thing. There was an element of burning bridges in this action.

What did the handbook say? *"There is no point in planning sophisticated research on a specific factor's role unless that factor is known to be present."*

If it isn't there, you can't study it, Ing thought.

"You will take your work seriously," he muttered. Ing smiled then, thinking of the tragicomic faces, the jowly board chairman he visualized behind the handbook's pronouncements. Nothing was left to chance—no task, no item of personal tidiness, no physical exercise. Ing considered himself an expert on handbooks. He owned one of the finest collections of them dating from ancient times down to the present. In moments of boredom he amused himself with choice quotes.

"Program going in," Washington said. "I wish I knew what you hope to find by this."

"I quote," Ing said. "The objective worker makes as large a collection of data as possible and analyzes these in their entirety in relation to selected factors whose relationship to a questioned phenomenon is to be investigated."

"What the devil's that supposed to mean?" Washington demanded.

"Damned if I know," Ing said, "but it's right out of the Haigh Handbook." He cleared his throat. "What's the cleaner tempo from your stations?"

"Up a bit."

"Give me a countdown on the 'lash."

"No sign yet. There's...wait a minute! Here's some action—twenty-five...twenty seconds."

Ing began counting under his breath.

Zero.

A progression of tiny flares began far off to his right, flickered past him with increasing brightness. They were a blur that left a glimmering afterimage. Senson in his suit soles began reporting the fall of debris.

"Holy O'Golden!" Washington muttered.

"How many'd we lose?" Ing asked. He knew it was going to be bad—worse than he'd expected.

There was a long wait, then Washington's shocked voice: "A hundred and eighteen cleaners down. It isn't possible!"

"Yeah," Ing said. "They're all over the floor. Shut off the beam before that dust drifts up into it."

The beam disappeared from Ing's faceplate responders.

"Is that what you thought would happen, Ing?"

"Kind of."

"Why didn't you warn me?"

"You wouldn't have given me that 'lash."

"Well, how the devil're we going to explain a hundred and eighteen cleaners? Accounting'll be down on my neck like a..."

"Forget Accounting," Ing said. "You're a beam engineer; open your eyes. Those cleaners weren't absorbed by the beam. They were cut down and scattered over the floor."

"But the..."

"Cleaners are designed to respond to the beam's needs," Ing said. "As the beam moves they move. As the debris count goes up, the cleaners work harder. If one works a little too hard and doesn't get out of the way fast enough, it's supposed to be absorbed—its energy converted by the beam. Now, a false 'lash catches a hundred and eighteen of them off balance. Those cleaners weren't eaten; they were scattered over the floor."

There was silence while Washington absorbed this.

"Did that 'lash touch angspace?" Ing asked.

"I'm checking," Washington said. Then: "No...wait a minute: there's a whole ripple of angspace...contacts, very low energy—a series lasting about an eighty-millionth of a second.

I had the responders set to the last decimal or we'd have never caught it."

"To all intents and purposes we didn't touch," Ing said.

"Practically not." Then: "Could somebody in cleaner programming have flubbed the dub?"

"On a hundred and eighteen units?"

"Yeah. I see what you mean. Well, what're we going to say when they come around for an explanation?"

"We quote the book. 'Each problem should be approached in two stages: one, locate those areas which contribute most to the malfunction, and two, take remedial action designed to reduce hazards which have been positively identified.' We tell 'em, Poss, that we were positively identifying hazards."

Ing stepped over the lock sill into the executive salon, saw that Washington already was seated at the corner table which convention reserved for the senior beam engineer on duty, the Supervisor of Transmission.

It was too late for day lunch and too early for the second-shift coffee break. The salon was almost empty. Three junior executives at a table across the room to the right were sharing a private joke, but keeping it low in Washington's presence. A security officer sat nursing a teabulb beside the passage to the kitchen tram on the left. His shoulders bore a touch of dampness from a perspiration reclaimer to show that he had recently come down from the surface. Security had a lot of officers on the station, Ing noted . . . and there always seemed to be one around Washington.

The vidwall at the back was tuned to an Earthside news broadcast: There were hints of political upsets because of the beam failure, demands for explanations of the money spent. Washington was quoted as saying a solution would be forthcoming.

Ing began making his way toward the corner, moving around the empty tables.

Washington had a coffeebulb in front of him, steam drifting upward. Ing studied the man—Possible Washington (Impossible, according to his junior engineers) was a six-foot eight-inch powerhouse of a man with wide shoulders, sensitive hands, a sharply Moorish-Semitic face of café au lait skin and startlingly blue eyes under a dark crewcut. (The company's senior medic referred to him as "a most amazing throw of the genetic dice.")

Washington's size said a great deal about his abilities. It took a considerable expenditure to lift his extra kilos moonside. He had to be worth just that much more.

Ing sat down across from Washington, gestured to the waiter-eye on the table surface, ordered Marslichen tea.

"You just come from Assembly?" Washington asked.

"They said you were up here," Ing said. "You look tired. Earthside give you any trouble about your report?"

"Until I used your trick and quoted the book: 'Every test under field conditions shall approximate as closely as possible the conditions set down by laboratory precedent.'"

"Hey, that's a good one," Ing said. "Why didn't you tell them you were following a hunch—you had a hunch I had a hunch."

Washington smiled.

Ing took a deep breath. It felt good to sit down. He realized he'd worked straight through two shifts without a break.

"You look tired yourself," Washington said.

Ing nodded. Yes, he was tired. He was too old to push this hard. Ing had few illusions about himself. He'd always been a runt, a little on the weak side—skinny and with an almost weaselish face that was saved from ugliness by widely set green eyes and a thick crewcut mop of golden hair. The hair was turning gray now, but the brain behind the wide brow still functioned smoothly.

The teabulb came up through the table slot. Ing pulled the bulb to him, cupped his hands around its warmth. He had counted on Washington to keep the worst of the official pressure off him, but now that it had been done, Ing felt guilty.

"No matter how much I quote the book," Washington said, "they don't like that explanation."

"Heads will roll and all that?"

"To put it mildly."

"Well, we have a position chart on where every cleaner went down," Ing said. "Every piece of wreckage has been reassembled as well as possible. The undamaged cleaners have been gone over with the proverbial comb of fine teeth."

"How long until we have a clean tube?" Washington asked.

"About eight hours."

Ing moved his shoulders against the chair. His thigh muscles still ached from the long session in the Skoarnoff tube and there was a pain across his shoulders.

"Then it's time for some turkey talk," Washington said.

Ing had been dreading this moment. He knew the stand Washington was going to take.

The Security officer across the room looked up, met Ing's eyes, looked away. *Is he listening to us?* Ing wondered.

"You're thinking what the others thought," Washington said. "That those cleaners were kicked around the corner into angspace."

"One way to find out," Ing said.

There was a definite lift to the Security officer's chin at that remark. He *was* listening.

"You're not taking that suicide ride," Washington said.

"Are the other beams getting through to the Seed Ships?" Ing asked.

"You know they aren't!"

Across the room, the junior executives stopped their own conversation, peered toward the corner table. The Security officer hitched his chair around to watch both the executives and the corner table.

Ing took a sip of his tea, said: "Damn tea here's always too bitter. They don't know how to serve it anywhere except on Mars." He pushed the bulb away from him. "Join the Haigh Company and save the Universe for Man."

"All right, Ing," Washington said. "We've known each other a long time and can speak straight out. What're you hiding from me?"

Ing sighed.

"I guess I owe it to you," he said. "Well, I guess it begins with the fact that every transmitter's a unique individual, which you know as well as I do. We map what it does and operate by prediction statistics. We play it by ear, as they say. Now, let's consider something out of the book. A tube is, after all, just a big cave in the rock, a controlled environment for the beam to do its work. The book says: *'By anglespace transmissions, any place in the universe is just around the corner from any other place.'* This is a damned loose way to describe something we don't really understand. It makes it sound as though we know what we're talking about."

"And you say we're putting matter around that corner," Washington said, "but you haven't told me what you're—"

"I know," Ing said. "We place a modulation of energy where it can be *seen* by the Seed Ship's instruments. But that's a transfer of energy, Poss. And energy's interchangeable with matter."

"You're twisting definitions. We put a highly unstable, highly transitory reflection phenomenon in such a position that time/ space limitations are changed. That's by the book, too. But you're still not telling me..."

"Poss, I have a crew rigging a cleaner for me to ride. We've analyzed the destruction pattern—which is what I wanted from that test 'lash—and I think we can kick me into angspace aboard one of these wild geese."

"You fool! I'm still Supetrans here and I say you're not going in there on..."

"Now, take it easy, Poss. You haven't even..."

"Granting you get kicked around that stupid corner, how do you expect to get back? And what's the purpose, anyway? What can you do if you..."

"I can go there and look, Poss. And the cleaner we're rigging will be more in the nature of a lifeboat. I can get down on TA-IV, maybe take the container with me, give our *seeds* a better chance. And if we learn how to kick me around there, we can do it again with..."

"This is stupidity!"

"Look," Ing said. "What're we risking? One old man long past his prime."

Ing faced the angry glare in Washington's eyes and realized an odd thing about himself. He wanted to get through there, wanted to give that container of embryos its chance. He was drunk with the same dream that had spawned the Seeding Compact. And he saw now that the other troubleshooters, the six who'd gone before him, must have been caught in the same web. They'd all seen where the trouble had to be. One of them would get through. There were tools in the container; another beam could be rigged on the other side. There was a chance of getting back...afterward...

"I let them talk me into sending for you," Washington growled. "The understanding was you'd examine the setup, confirm or deny what the others saw—but I didn't have to send you into that..."

"I want to go, Poss," Ing said. He saw what was eating on his friend now. The man had sent six troubleshooters in there to die—or disappear into an untraceable void, which was worse. Guilt had him.

"And I'm refusing permission," Washington said.

The Security officer arose from his table, crossed to stand over Washington. "Mr. Washington," he said, "I've been listening and it seems to me if Mr. Gump wants to go you can't..."

Washington got to his feet, all six feet eight inches of him, caught the Security man by the jacket. "So they told you to interfere if I tried to stop him!" He shook the man with an odd gentleness. "If you are on my station after the next shuttle leaves, I will see to it personally that you have an unexplained accident." He released his grip.

The Security agent paled, but stood his ground. "One call from me and this no longer will be *your* station."

"Poss," Ing said, "you can't fight city hall. And if you try they'll take you out of here. Then I'll have to make do with second best at this end. I need you as beam jockey here when I ride that wild goose."

Washington glared at him. "Ing, it won't work!"

Ing studied his friend, seeing the pressures which had been brought to bear, understanding how Earthside had maneuvered to get that request sent from a friend to Ivar Norris Gump. It all said something about Earthside's desperation. The patterns of secrecy, the Security watch, the hints in the newscasts—Ing felt something of the same urgency himself which these things betrayed. And he knew if Washington could overcome this guilt block the man would share mankind's need to help those drifting containers.

"No matter how many people get hurt—or killed," Ing said, "we have to give the embryos in those containers their chance. You know I'm right—this is the main chance. And we need you, Poss. I want everything going for me I can get. And no matter what happens, we'll know you did your best for me..."

Washington took two short breaths. His shoulders slumped. "And nothing I say..."

"Nothing you say."

"You're going?"

"I'm going where the wild goose goes."

"And who faces the family afterward?"

"A friend, Poss. A friend faces the family and makes the blow as soft as possible."

"If you'll excuse me," the Security officer said.

They ignored him as the man returned to his table.

Washington allowed himself a deep, sighing breath. Some of the fire returned to his eyes. "All right," he growled. "But I'm going to be on this end every step of the way. And I'm telling you now you get no Go signal until everything's rigged to my satisfaction."

"Of course, Poss. That's why I can't afford to have you get into a fracas and be booted out of here."

Ing's left ankle itched.

It was maddening. His hand could reach only to the calf inside the webbing of his shieldsuit. The ankle and its itch could not be lifted from the area of the sole contact controls.

The suit itself lay suspended in an oil bath within a shocktank. Around the shocktank was something that resembled a standard cleaner in shape but not in size. It was at least twice the length of a cleaner and it was fatter. The fatness allowed for phased shells—Washington's idea. It had grown out of analysis of the debris left by the test 'lash.

The faint hissing of his oxygen regenerators came to Ing through his suit sensors. His viewplate had been replaced by a set of screens linked to exterior pickups. The largest screen, at top center, reported the view from a scanner on the belly. It showed a rope of fluorescing purple surrounded by blackness.

The beam.

It was a full five centimeters across, larger than Ing had ever before seen it. The nearness of that potential violence filled him with a conditioned dread. He'd milked too many beams in too many tubes, wary of the slightest growth in size to keep him at a safe distance.

This was a monster beam. All his training and experience cried out against its size.

Ing reminded himself of the analysis which had produced the false cleaner around him now.

Eighty-nine of the cleaners recovered from the tube floor had taken their primary damage at the pickup orifice. They'd been oriented to the beam itself, disregarding the local particle count. But the most important discovery was that the cleaners had fallen through the beam without being sliced in two. They had passed completely through the blade of that purple knife without being severed. There'd been no break in the beam. The explanation had to rest in that topological anomaly—angspace. Part of the beam and/or the cleaners had gone into angspace.

He was gambling his life now that the angspace bounce coincided with the energy phasing which kept the cleaners from deflecting the beam. The outside carrier, Ing's false cleaner, was phased with the beam. It would be demolished. The next inner shell was 180 degrees out of phase. The next shell was back in place. And so on for ten shells.

In the center lay Ing, his hands and feet on the controls of a suit that was in effect a miniature lifeboat.

As the moment of final commitment approached Ing began to feel a prickly sensation in his stomach. And the ankle continued to itch. But there was no way he could turn back and still live with himself. He was a troubleshooter, the best in the Haigh Company. There was no doubt that the company—and those lonely drifting human embryos—had never needed him more desperately.

"Report your condition, Ing."

The voice coming from the speaker beside Ing's facemask wàs Washington's with an unmistakable edge of fear in it.

"All systems clear," Ing said.

"Program entering its second section," Washington said. "Can you see any of the other cleaners?"

"Forty contacts so far," Ing said. "All normal." He gasped as his cleaner dodged a transient 'lash.

"You all right?"

"All right," Ing said.

The ride continued to be a rough one, though. Each time the beam 'lashed, his cleaner dodged. There was no way to anticipate the direction. Ing could only trust his suit webbing and the oil-bath shocktank to keep him from being smashed against a side of the compartment.

"We're getting an abnormal number of transients," Washington said.

That called for no comment and Ing remained silent. He looked up at his receiver above the speaker. A quartz window gave him a view of the tiny beam which kept him in contact with Washington. The tiny beam, less than a centimeter long, glowed sharply purple through its inspection window. It, too, was crackling and jumping. The little beam could stand more interference than a big one, but it clearly was disturbed.

Ing turned his attention to the big beam in the viewscreen, glanced back at the little beam. The difference was a matter of degree. It often seemed to Ing that the beams should illuminate the area around them, and he had to remind himself that the parallel quanta couldn't deviate that much.

"Getting 'lash count," Washington said. "Ing! Condition critical! Stand by."

Ing concentrated on the big beam now. His stomach was a hard knot. He wondered how the other troubleshooters had felt in this moment. The same, no doubt. But they'd been flying without the protection Ing had. They'd paved the way, died to give information.

The view of the beam was so close and restricted that Ing knew that he'd get no warning of the whip—just a sudden shift in size or position.

His heart leaped as the beam flared in the screen. The cleaner rolled sideways as it dodged, letting the beam pass to one side, but there was an ominous bump. Momentarily, the screen went black, but the purple rope flickered back into view as his cleaner's sensors lined up and brought him back into position.

Ing checked his instruments. That bump—what had that been?

"Ing!" Washington's voice came sharply urgent from the speaker.

"What's the word?"

"We have one of the other cleaners on grav-track," Washington said. "It's in your shadow. Hold on."

There came a murmur of voices, hushed words, indistinguishable, then: "The beam touched you, Ing. You're got a phase arc between two of your shells on the side opposite the beam. One of the other cleaners has locked onto that arc with one of its sensors. Its other sensors are still on the beam and it's riding parallel with you, in your shadow. We're getting you out of there."

Ing tried to swallow in a dry throat. He knew the danger without having it explained. There was an arc light in the tube. His cleaner was between the arc and the beam, but the other cleaner was up there behind him, too. If they had to dodge a 'lash, the other cleaner would be confused because its sensor contacts were now split. It'd be momentarily delayed. The two cleaners would collide and release light in the tube. The big beam would go wild. The protective shells would be struck from all sides.

Washington was working to get him out, but that would take time. You couldn't just yank a primary program out. That created its own 'lash conditions. And if you damped the beam, the other cleaners would home on the arc. There'd be carnage in the tube.

"Starting phase out," Washington said. "Estimating three minutes to control the second phase. We'll just..."

"'Lash!"

The word rang in Ing's ears even as he felt his cleaner lift at the beginning of a dodge maneuver. He had time to think that the warning must've come from one of the engineers on the monitor board, then a giant gong rang out.

A startled: "What the hell!" blasted from his speaker to be replaced by a strident hissing, the ravening of a billion snakes.

Ing felt his cleaner still lifting, pressing him down against the webbing, his face hard against the protective mask. There was no view of the big beam in his screen and the small beam which should've shown the line of his own beam revealed a wavering, crackling worm of red-purple.

It was like being squeezed flat into a one-molecule puddle and stretched out to infinity. He *saw* around the outside of an inner-viewed universe with light extended to hard rods of brilliance that poked through from one end to the other. He realized he wasn't seeing with his eyes, but was absorbing a sensation compounded from every sense organ he possessed. Beyond this inner view everything was chaos, undefined madness.

The beam got me, he thought. *I'm dying.*

One of the light rods resolved itself into a finite row of spinning objects—over, under, around... over, under, around. ...The movement was hypnotic. With a feeling of wonder, Ing recognized that the object was his own suit and a few shattered pieces of the protective shells. The tiny beam of his own transmitter had been opened and was spitting shards of purple.

With the recognition came a sensation of being compressed. Ing felt himself being pushed down into the blackness that jerked at him, twisting, pounding. It was like going over a series of rapids. He felt the web harness bite into his skin.

Abruptly, the faceplate viewscreens showed jewel brilliance against velvet black—spots of light: sharp blue, red, green, gold. A glaring white light spun into view surrounded by whipping purple ribbons. The ribbons looked like beam auroras.

Ing's body ached. His mind felt as though immersed in fog, every thought laboring against deadly slowness.

Jewel brilliance—spots of light.

Again, glaring white.

Purple ribbons.

The speaker above him crackled with static. Through its window, he saw his tiny beam spattering and jumping. It seemed important to do something about that. Ing slipped a hand into one of his suit arms, encountered a shattered piece of protective shell drifting close.

The idea of drifting seemed vital, but he couldn't decide why.

Gently, he nudged the piece of shell up until it formed a rough shield over his receiver beam.

Immediately, a tinny little voice came from his speaker: "Ing! Come in, Ing! Can you hear me, Ing?" Then, more distant: "You there! To hell with the locks! Suit up and get in there. He must be down..."

"Poss?" Ing said.

"Ing! Is that you, Ing?"

"Yeah, Poss. I'm...I seem to be all in one piece."

"Are you down on the floor some place? We're coming in after you. Hold on."

"I dunno where I am. I can see beam auroras."

"Don't try to move. The tube's all smashed to hell. I'm patched through the Imbrium tube to talk to you. Just stay put. We'll be right with you."

"Poss, I don't think I'm in the tube."

From some place that Ing felt existed on a very tenuous basis, he felt his thoughts stirring, recognition patterns forming.

Some of the jewel brilliance he saw was stars. He saw that now. Some of it was...debris, bits and pieces of cleaners, odd chunks of matter. There was light somewhere toward his feet, but the sensors there appeared to've been destroyed or something was covering them.

Debris.

Beam auroras.

The glaring white spun once more into view. Ing adjusted his spin with a short burst from a finger jet. He saw the thing clearly now, recognized it: the ball and sensor tubes of a Seeding Compact container.

He grew conscious that the makeshift shield for his little beam had slipped. Static filled his speakers. Ing replaced the bit of shell.

"...Do you mean you're not in the tube?" Washington's voice asked. "Ing, come in. What's wrong?"

"There's an SC container about a hundred meters or so directly in front of me," Ing said. "It's surrounded by cleaner debris. And there're auroras, angspace ribbons, all over the sky here. I...think I've come through."

"You couldn't have. I'm receiving you too strong. What's this about auroras?"

"That's why you're receiving me," Ing said. "You're stitching a few pieces of beam through here. Light all over the place; there's a sun down beneath my feet somewhere. You're getting through to me, but the container's almost surrounded by junk. The reflection and beam spatter in there must be enormous. I'm going in now and clean a path for the beam contact."

"Are you sure you're..." *Hiss, crackle.*

The little piece of shell had slipped again.

Ing eased it back into position as he maneuvered with his belt jets.

"I'm all right, Poss."

The turn brought the primary into view—a great golden ball that went dim immediately as his scanner filters adjusted. To his right beyond the sun lay a great ball of blue with chunks of cottony clouds drifting over it. Ing stared, transfixed by the beauty of it.

A virgin planet.

A check of the lifeboat instruments installed in his suit showed what the SC container had revealed before contact had gone intermittent—Theta Apus IV, almost Earth normal except for larger oceans, smaller land masses.

Ing took a deep breath, smelled the canned air of his suit.

To work, he thought.

His suit jets brought him in close to the debris and he began nudging it aside, moving in closer and closer to the container. He lost his beam shield, ignored it, cut down receiver volume to reduce the static.

Presently, he drifted beside the container.

With an armored hand, he shielded his beam.

"Poss? Come in, Poss."

"Are you really there, Ing?"

"Try a beam contact with the container, Poss."

"We'll have to break contact with you."

"Do it."

Ing waited.

Auroral activity increased—great looping ribbons over the sky all around him.

So that's what it looks like at the receiving end, Ing thought. He looked up at the window revealing his own beam—clean and sharp under the shadow of his upraised hand. The armored fingers were black outlines against the blue world beyond. He began calculating then how long his own beam would last without replacement of anode and cathode. Hard bombardment, sharp tiny beam—its useful life would only be a fraction of what a big beam could expect.

Have to find a way to rig a beam once we get down, he thought.

"Ing? Come in, Ing?"

Ing heard the excitement in Washington's voice.

"You got through, eh, Poss, old hoss?"

"Loud and clear. Now, look—if you can weld yourself fast to the tail curve of that container we can get you down with it. It's over-engineered to handle twice your mass on landing sequence."

Ing nodded to himself. Riding the soft, safe balloon, which the container would presently become, offered a much more attractive prospect than maneuvering his suit down, burning it out above a watery world where a landing on solid ground would take some doing.

"We're maneuvering to give re-entry for contact with a major land mass," Washington said. "Tell us when you're fast to the container."

Ing maneuvered in close, put an armored hand on the container's surface, feeling an odd sensation of communion with the metal and life that had spent nine hundred years in the void.

Old papa Ing's going to look after you, he thought.

As he worked, welding himself solidly to the tail curve of the container, Ing recalled the chaos he had glimpsed in his spewing, jerking ride through angspace. He shuddered.

"Ing, when you feel up to it, we want a detailed report," Washington said. "We're planning now to put people through for every one of the containers that's giving trouble."

"You figured out how to get us back?" Ing asked.

"Earthside says it has the answer if you can assemble enough mass at your end to anchor a full-sized beam."

Again, Ing thought of that ride through chaos. He wasn't sure he wanted another such trip. Time to solve that problem when it arose, though. There'd be something in the book about it.

Ing smiled at himself then, sensing an instinctive reason for all the handbooks of history. Against chaos, man had to raise a precise and orderly alignment of actions, a system within which he could sense his own existence.

A watery world down there, he thought. *Have to find some way to make paper for these kids before they come out of their vats. Plenty of things to teach them.*

Watery world.

He recalled then a sentence of swimming instructions from the "Blue Jackets Manual," one of the ancient handbooks in his collection: "Breathing may be accomplished by swimming with the head out of water."

Have to remember that one, he thought. *The kids'll need a secure and orderly world.*

SEED
STOCK

**W**hen the sun had sunk almost to the edge of the purple ocean, hanging there like a giant orange ball—much larger than the sun of Mother Earth which he remembered with such nostalgia—Kroudar brought his fishermen back to the harbor.

A short man, Kroudar gave the impression of heaviness, but under his shipcloth motley he was as scrawny as any of the others, all bone and stringy muscle. It was the sickness of this planet, the doctors told him. They called it "body burdens," a subtle thing of differences in chemistry, gravity, diurnal periods and even the lack of a tidal moon.

Kroudar's yellow hair, his one good feature, was uncut and contained in a protective square of red cloth. Beneath this was a wide, low forehead, deeply sunken large eyes of a washed-out blue, a crooked nose that was splayed and pushed in, thick lips over large and unevenly spaced yellow teeth, and a melon chin receding into a short, ridged neck.

Dividing his attention between sails and shore, Kroudar steered with one bare foot on the tiller.

They had been all day out in the up-coast current netting the shrimplike *trodi* which formed the colony's main source of edible protein. There were nine boats and the men in all of them were limp with fatigue, silent, eyes closed or open and staring at nothing.

The evening breeze rippled its dark lines across the harbor, moved the sweat-matted yellow hair on Kroudar's neck. It bellied the shipcloth sails and gave the heavily loaded boats that last necessary surge to carry them up into the strand.

Men moved then. Sails dropped with a slatting and rasping. Each thing was done with sparse motion in the weighted slowness of their fatigue.

Trodi had been thick in the current out there, and Kroudar pushed his people to their limit. It had not taken much push.

241

They all understood the need. The swarmings and runnings of useful creatures on this planet had not been clocked with any reliable precision. Things here exhibited strange gaps and breaks in seeming regularity. The *trodi* might vanish at any moment into some unknown place—as they had been known to do before.

The colony had experienced hunger and children crying for food that must be rationed. Men seldom spoke of this anymore, but they moved with the certain knowledge of it.

More than three years now, Kroudar thought, as he shouldered a dripping bag of *trodi* and pushed his weary feet through the sand, climbing the beach toward the storage huts and racks where the sea creatures were dried for processing. It had been more than three years since their ship had come down from space.

The colony ship had been constructed as a multiple tool, filled with select human stock, their domestic animals and basic necessities, and it had been sent to plant humans in this far place. It had been designed to land once, then be broken down into useful things.

Somehow, the basic necessities had fallen short, and the colony had been forced to improvise its own tools. They had not really settled here yet, Kroudar realized. More than three years—and three years here were five years of Mother Earth—and they still lived on the edge of extinction. They were trapped here. Yes, that was true. The ship could never be reconstructed. And even if that miracle were accomplished, the fuel did not exist.

The colony was *here*.

And every member knew the predatory truth of their predicament: Survival had not been assured. It was known in subtle things to Kroudar's unlettered mind, especially in a fact he observed without being able to explain.

Not one of their number had yet accepted a name for this planet. It was "here" or "this place."

Or even more bitter terms.

Kroudar dumped his sack of *trodi* onto a storage hut porch, mopped his forehead. The joints of his arms and legs ached. His back ached. He could feel the sickness of *this place* in his bowels. Again, he wiped perspiration from his forehead, removed the red cloth he wore to protect his head from that brutal sun.

Yellow hair fell down as he loosed the cloth, and he swung the hair back over his shoulders.

It would be dark very soon.

The red cloth was dirty, he saw. It would require another gentle washing. Kroudar thought it odd, this cloth: Grown and woven on Mother Earth, it would end its days on *this place*.

Even as he and the others.

He stared at the cloth for a moment before placing it carefully in a pocket.

All around him, his fishermen were going through the familiar ritual. Brown sacks woven of coarse native roots were dumped dripping onto the storage hut porches. Some of his men leaned then against the porch uprights, some sprawled in the sand.

Kroudar lifted his gaze. Fires behind the bluff above them sent smoke spirals into the darkening sky. Kroudar was suddenly hungry. He thought of Technician Honida up there at the cookfire, their twin sons—two years old next week—nearby at the door of the shipmetal longhouse.

It stirred him to think of Honida. She had chosen *him*. With men from the Scientist class and the Technicians available to her, Honida had reached down into the Labor pool to tap the one they all called "Old Ugly." He wasn't old, Kroudar reminded himself. But he knew the source of the name. *This place* had worked its changes on him with more visible evidence than upon any of the others.

Kroudar held no illusions about why he had been brought on this human migration. It was his muscles and his minimal education. The reason was embodied in that label written down in the ship manifest—laborer. The planners back on Mother Earth had realized there were tasks which required human muscles not inhibited by too much thinking. The *kroudars* landed *here* were not numerous, but they knew each other and they knew themselves for what they were.

There'd even been talk among the higher echelons of not allowing Honida to choose him as mate. Kroudar knew this. He did not resent it particularly. It didn't even bother him that the vote among the biologists—they'd discussed his ugliness at great length, so it was reported—favored Honida's choice on philosophical rather than physical grounds.

Kroudar knew he was ugly.

He knew also that his present hunger was a good sign. A strong desire to see his family grew in him, beginning to ignite his muscles for the climb from the beach. Particularly, he wanted to see his twins, the one yellow-haired like himself, and the other dark as Honida. The other women favored with children looked down upon his twins as stunted and sickly, Kroudar knew. The women fussed over diets and went running to the medics almost every day. But as long as Honida did not worry, Kroudar remained calm. Honida, after all, was a technician, a worker in the hydroponics gardens.

Kroudar moved his bare feet softly in the sand. Once more, he looked up at the bluff. Along the edge grew scattered native trees. Their thick trunks hugged the ground, gnarled and twisted, supports for bulbous, yellow-green leaves that exuded poisonous milky sap in the heat of the day. A few of the surviving Earth-falcons perched in the trees, silent, watchful.

The birds gave Kroudar an odd confidence in his own decisions. For what do the falcons watch, he wondered. It was a question the most exalted of the colony's thinkers had not been able to answer. Search 'copters had been sent out following the falcons. The birds flew offshore in the night, rested occasionally on barren islands, and returned at dawn. The colony command had been unwilling to risk its precious boats in the search, and the mystery of the falcons remained unsolved.

It was doubly a mystery because the other birds had perished or flown off to some unfound place. The doves, the quail— the gamebirds and songbirds—all had vanished. And the domestic chickens had all died, their eggs infertile. Kroudar knew this as a comment by *this place*, a warning for the life that came from Mother Earth.

A few scrawny cattle survived, and several calves had been born *here*. But they moved with a listless gait and there was distressed lowing in the pastures. Looking into their eyes was like looking into open wounds. A few pigs still lived, as listless and sickly as the cattle, and all the wild creatures had strayed off or died.

Except the falcons.

How odd it was, because the people who planned and conceived profound thoughts had held such hopes for *this place*.

The survey reports had been exciting. This was a planet without native land animals. It was a planet whose native plants appeared not too different from those of Mother Earth—in some respects. And the sea creatures were primitive by sophisticated evolutionary standards.

Without being able to put it into those beautifully polished phrases which others admired, Kroudar knew where the mistake had been made. Sometimes, you had to search out a problem with your flesh and not with your mind.

He stared around now at the motley rags of his men. They were *his* men. He was the master fisherman, the one who had found the *trodi* and conceived these squat, ugly boats built within the limitations of native woods. The colony was alive now because of his skills with boat and net.

There would be more gaps in the *trodi* runs, though. Kroudar felt this as an awareness on the edges of his fatigue. There would be unpopular and dangerous things to do then, all necessary because *thinking* had failed. The salmon they had introduced, according to plan, had gone off into the ocean vastness. The flatfish in the colony's holding ponds suffered mysterious attrition. Insects flew away and were never seen again.

There's food here, the biologists argued. Why do they die?

The colony's maize was a sometime thing with strange ears. Wheat came up in scabrous patches. There were no familiar patterns of growth or migration. The colony lived on the thin edge of existence, maintained by protein bulk from the processed *trodi* and vitamins from vegetables grown hydroponically with arduous filtering and adjustment of their water. Breakdown of a single system in the chain could bring disaster.

The giant orange sun showed only a small arc above the sea horizon now, and Kroudar's men were stirring themselves, lifting their tired bodies off the sand, pushing away from the places where they had leaned.

"All right now," Kroudar ordered. "Let's get this food inside on the racks."

"Why?" someone asked from the dusk. "You think the falcons will eat it?"

They all knew the falcons would not eat the *trodi*. Kroudar recognized the objection: It was tiredness of the mind speaking. The shrimp creatures fed only humans—after careful processing to remove dangerous irritants. A falcon might take up a frond-legged *trodi*, but would drop it at the first taste.

What did they eat, those waiting birds?

Falcons knew a thing about *this place* that humans did not know. The birds knew it in their flesh in the way Kroudar sought the knowledge.

Darkness fell, and with a furious clatter, the falcons flew off toward the sea. One of Kroudar's men kindled a torch and, having rested, anxious now to climb the bluff and join their families, the fishermen pitched into the work that must be done. Boats were hauled up on the rollers. *Trodi* were spread out in thin layers along racks within the storage huts. Nets were draped on racks to dry.

As he worked Kroudar wondered about the scientists up there in the shining laboratories. He had the working man's awe of knowledge, a servility in the face of titles and things clearly superior, but he had also the simple man's sure awareness of when superior things failed.

Kroudar was not privy to the high-level conferences in the colony command, but he knew the physical substance of the ideas discussed there. His awareness of failure and hovering disaster had no sophisticated words or erudition to hold itself dancingly before men's minds, but his knowledge carried its own elegance. He drew on ancient knowledge adjusted subtly to the differences of *this place*. Kroudar had found the *trodi*. Kroudar had organized the methods of capturing them and preserving them. He had no refined labels to explain it, but Kroudar knew himself for what he could do and what he was.

He was the first sea peasant *here*.

Without wasting energy on talk, Kroudar's band finished the work, turned away from the storage huts and plodded up the cliff trail, their course marked by, here and there, men with flaming torches. There were fuzzy orange lights, heavy shadows, inching their way upward in a black world, and they gave heart to Kroudar.

Lingering to the last, he checked the doors of the huts, then followed, hurrying to catch up. The man directly ahead of him on the path carried a torch, native wood soaked in *trodi* oil. It flickered and smoked and gave off poisonous fumes. The light revealed a troglodyte figure, a human clad in patched shipcloth, body too thin, muscles moving on the edge of collapse.

Kroudar sighed.

It was not like this on Mother Earth, he knew. There, the women waited on the strand for their men to return from the sea. Children played among the pebbles. Eager hands helped with the work onshore, spreading the nets, carrying the catch, pulling the boats.

Not *here*.

And the perils *here* were not the perils of Home. Kroudar's boats never strayed out of sight of these cliffs. One boat always carried a technician with a radio for contact with shore. Before its final descent, the colony ship had seeded space with orbiting devices—watchers, guardians against surprises from the weather. The laboriously built fishing fleet always had ample warning of storms. No monster sea creatures had ever been seen in that ocean.

This place lacked the cruel savagery and variety of seas Kroudar had known, but it was nonetheless deadly. He *knew* this.

The women should wait for us on the shore, he thought.

But colony command said the women—and even some of the children—were needed for too many other tasks. Individual plants from home required personal attention. Single wheat stalks were nurtured with tender care. Each orchard tree existed with its own handmaiden, its guardian dryad.

Atop the cliff, the fishermen came in sight of the longhouses, shipmetal *quonsets* named for some far distant place and time in human affairs. Scattered electric lights ringed the town. Many of the unpaved streets wandered off unlit. There were mechanical sounds here and murmurous voices.

The men scattered to their own affairs now, no longer a band. Kroudar plodded down his street toward the open cook-fires in the central plaza. The open fires were a necessity to conserve the more sophisticated energies of the colony. Some looked upon those flames as admission of defeat. Kroudar saw them as victory. It was *native* wood being burned.

Off in the hills beyond the town, he knew, stood the ruins of the wind machines they had built. The storm which had wreaked that destruction had achieved no surprise in its coming, but had left enormous surprise at its power.

For Kroudar, the *thinkers* had begun to diminish in stature then. When native chemistry and water life had wrecked the turbines in the river which emptied into the harbor, those men of knowledge had shrunk even more. Then it was that Kroudar had begun his own search for native foods.

Now, Kroudar heard, native plant life threatened the cooling systems for their atomic generators, defying radiation in a way no life should. Some among the technicians already were fashioning steam engines of materials not intended for such use. Soon, they would have native metals, though—materials to resist the wild etchings and rusts of *this place*.

They might succeed—provided the dragging sickness did not sap them further.

If they survived.

Honida awaited him at the door to their quarters, smiling, graceful. Her dark hair was plaited and wound in rings around her forehead. The brown eyes were alive with welcome. Firelight from the plaza cast a familiar glow across her olive skin. The high cheekbones of her Amerind ancestry, the full lips and proudly hooked nose—all filled him with remembered excitement.

Kroudar wondered if the *planners* had known this thing about her which gave him such warmth—her strength and fecundity. She had chosen *him*, and now she carried more of their children—twins again.

"Ahhh, my fisherman is home," she said, embracing him in the doorway for anybody to see.

They went inside then, closed the door, and she held him with more ardor, stared up into his face which, reflected in her eyes, lost some of its ugliness.

"Honida," he said, unable to find other words.

Presently, he asked about the boys.

"They're asleep," she said, leading him to the crude trestle table he had built for their kitchen.

He nodded. Later, he would go in and stare at his sons. It did not bother him that they slept so much. He could feel the reasons for this somewhere within himself.

Honida had hot *trodi* soup waiting for him on the table. It was spiced with hydroponic tomatoes and peas and contained other things which he knew she gathered from the land without telling the scientists.

Whatever she put in front of him, Kroudar ate. There was bread tonight with an odd musty flavor which he found pleasant. In the light of the single lamp they were permitted for this room, he stared at a piece of the bread. It was almost purple—like the sea. He chewed it, swallowed.

Honida, watchfully eating across from him, finished her bread and soup, asked: "Do you like the bread?"

"I like it."

"I made it myself in the coals," she said.

He nodded, took another slice.

Honida refilled his soup bowl.

They were privileged, Kroudar realized, to have this privacy for their meals. Many of the others had opted for communal cooking and eating—even among the technicians and higher echelons who possessed more freedom of choice. Honida had seen something about *this place*, though, which required secrecy and going private ways.

Kroudar, hunger satisfied, stared across the table at her. He adored her with a devotion that went far deeper than the excitement of her flesh. He could not say the thing she was, but he knew it. If they were to have a future here, that future was in Honida and the things he might learn, form and construct of himself with his own flesh.

Under the pressure of his eyes, Honida arose, came around the table and began massaging the muscles of his back—the very muscles he used to haul the nets.

"You're tired," she said. "Was it difficult out there today?"

"Hard work," Kroudar said.

He admired the way she spoke. She had many words at her disposal. He had heard her use some of them during colony meetings and during the time of their application for mating choice. She had words for things he did not know, and she knew also when to speak with her body rather than with her mouth. She knew about the muscles of his back.

Kroudar felt such a love for her then that he wondered if it went up through her fingers into her body.

"We filled the boats," he said.

"I was told today that we'll soon need more storage huts," she said. "They're worried about sparing the labor for the building."

"Ten more huts," he said.

She would pass that word along, he knew. Somehow, it would be done. The other technicians listened to Honida. Many among the scientists scoffed at her; it could be heard beneath the blandness of their voices. Perhaps it was because she had chosen Kroudar for mate. But technicians listened. The huts would be built.

And they would be filled before the *trodi* run stopped.

Kroudar realized then that he knew when the run would stop, not as a date, but almost as a physical thing which he could reach out and touch. He longed for the words to explain this to Honida.

She gave his back a final kneading, sat down beside him and leaned her dark head against his chest. "If you're not too tired," she said, "I have something to show you."

With a feeling of surprise, Kroudar became aware of unspoken excitement in Honida. Was it something about the hydroponic gardens where she worked? His thoughts went immediately to that place upon which the scientists pinned their hopes, the place where they chose the tall plants, the beautiful, engorged with richness from Mother Earth. Had they achieved something important at last? Was there, after all, a clear way to make *this place* arable?

Kroudar was a primitive then, wanting his gods redeemed. He found himself full of peasant hopes for the land. Even a sea peasant knew the value of land.

He and Honida had responsibilities, though. He nodded questioningly toward the twins' bedroom.

"I arranged..." She gestured toward their neighbor's cubicle. "They will listen."

She had planned this, then. Kroudar stood up, held out his hand for her. "Show me."

They went out into the night. Their town was quieter now; he could hear the distant roistering of the river. For a moment, he thought he heard a cricket, but reason told him it could only be one of the huts cooling in the night. He longed wordlessly for a moon.

Honida had brought one of the rechargeable electric torches, the kind issued to technicians against emergency calls in the night. Seeing that torch, Kroudar sensed a deeper importance in this mysterious thing she wanted to show him. Honida had the peasant's hoarding instinct. She would not waste such a torch.

Instead of leading him toward the green lights and glass roofs of the hydroponic gardens, though, she guided their steps in the opposite direction toward the deep gorge where the river plunged into the harbor.

There were no guards along the footpath, only an occasional stone marker and grotesqueries of native growth. Swiftly, without speaking, she led him to the gorge and the narrow path which he knew went only down to a ledge which jutted into the damp air of the river's spray.

Kroudar found himself trembling with excitement as he followed Honida's shadowy figure, the firefly darting of her light. It was cold on the ledge and the alien outline of native trees revealed by the torch filled Kroudar with disquiet.

What had Honida discovered—or created?

Condensation dripped from the plants here. The river noise was loud. It was marsh air he breathed, dank and filled with bizarre odors.

Honida stopped, and Kroudar held his breath. He listened. There was only the river.

For a moment, he didn't realize that Honida was directing the orange light of the torch at her discovery. It looked like one of the native plants—a thing with a thick stem crouched low to the land, gnarled and twisted, bulbous yellow-green protrusions set with odd spacing along its length.

Slowly, realization came over him. He recognized a darker tone in the green, the way the leaf structures were joined to the stalk, a bunching of brown-yellow silk drooping from the bulbous protrusions.

"Maize," he whispered.

In a low voice, pitching her explanation to Kroudar's vocabulary, Honida explained what she had done. He saw it in her words, understood why she had done this thing stealthily, here away from the scientists. He took the light from her, crouched, stared with rapt attention. This meant the death of those things the scientists held beautiful. It ended their plan for *this place*.

Kroudar could see his own descendants in this plant. They might develop bulbous heads, hairless, wide thick-lipped mouths. Their skins might become purple. They would be short statured; he knew that.

Honida had assured this—right here on the river-drenched ledge. Instead of selecting seed from the tallest, the straightest stalks, the ones with the longest and most perfect ears—the ones most like those from Mother Earth—she had tested her maize almost to destruction. She had chosen sickly, scrawny plants, ones barely able to produce seed. She had taken only those plants which *this place* influenced most deeply. From these, she had selected finally a strain which lived *here* as native plants lived.

This was *native* maize.

She broke off an ear, peeled back the husk.

There were gaps in the seed rows and, when she squeezed a kernel, the juice ran purple. He recognized the smell of the bread.

Here was the thing the scientists would not admit. They were trying to make *this place* into another Earth. But it was not and it could never be. The falcons had been the first among their creatures to discover this, he suspected.

The statement Honida made here was that she and Kroudar would be short-lived. Their children would be sickly by Mother Earth's standards. Their descendants would change in ways that defied the hopes of those who had planned this migration. The scientists would hate this and try to stop it.

This gnarled stalk of maize said the scientists would fail.

For a long while, Kroudar crouched there, staring into the future until the torch began to dim, losing its charge. He aroused himself then, led the way back out of the gorge.

At the top, with the lights of their dying civilization visible across the plain, he stopped, said: "The *trodi* run will stop ... soon. I will take one boat and ... friends. We will go out where the falcons go."

It was one of the longest speeches he had ever made.

She took the light from his hand, extinguished it, pressed herself against him.

"What do you think the falcons have found?"

"The seed," he said.

He shook his head. He could not explain it, but the thing was there in his awareness. Everything here exuded poisonous vapors, or juices in which only its own seed could live. Why should the *trodi* or any other sea creature be different? And, with the falcons as evidence, the seed must be slightly less poisonous to the intruders from Mother Earth.

"The boats are slow," she said.

He agreed silently. A storm could trap them too far out for a run to safety. It would be dangerous. But he heard also in her voice that she was not trying to stop him or dissuade him.

"I will take good men," he said.

"How long will you be gone?" Honida asked.

He thought about this for a moment. The rhythms of *this place* were beginning to make themselves known to him. His awareness shaped the journey, the days out, the night search over the water where the falcons were known to sweep in their low guiding runs—then the return.

"Eight days," he said.

"You'll need fine mesh nets," she said. "I'll see to having them made. Perhaps a few technicians, too. I know some who will go with you."

"Eight days," he said, telling her to choose strong men.

"Yes," she said. "Eight days. I'll be waiting on the shore when you return."

He took her hand then and led the way back across the plain. As they walked he said: "We must name *this place.*"

"When you come back," she said.

MURDER WILL IN

As the body died, the Tegas/Bacit awoke. Unconsciousness had lasted its usual flickering instant for the Tegas element. He came out of it with his Bacit negative identity chanting: "... not William Bailey—I'm not William Bailey—I'm not William Bailey..."

It was a painful, monotonous refrain—schismatic, important. The Tegas had to separate its identity from this fading flesh. Behind the chant lay a sense of many voices clamoring.

Awareness began to divide, a splitting seam that separated him from the compressed contact which controlled the host. There came a sensation of tearing fabric and he rode free, still immersed in the dying neural system because he had no other place to go, but capable of the identity leap.

Bacit and Tegas now functioning together, sticking him to each instant. He searched his surroundings: twenty meters... twenty meters...

Flickering, pale emotions registered on his awareness. Another attendant. The man passed out of range. Cold-cold-cold.

Nothing else.

What a rare joke this was, he thought. What a mischievous thing for fate to do. A Tegas to be caught like this! Mischievous. Mischievous. It wasn't fair. Hadn't he always treated the captive flesh with gentle care? Hadn't he made fun-lovers out of killers? Fate's mischief was cruel, not kindly in the manner of the Tegas.

The Bacit negative identity projected terror, accusation, embarrassment. He had lived too long in the William Bailey flesh. Too long. He had lived down where men were, where things were made—in the thick of being. He'd loved the flesh too much. He should've stopped occasionally and looked around him. The great Tegas curiosity which masqueraded as diffidence to hide itself had failed to protect him.

Failed... failed...

Within the dying neural system, frantic messages began darting back and forth. His mind was a torrent, a flare of being. Thoughts flew off like sparks from a grinding wheel.

"It's decided," the Tegas transmitted, seeking to quiet his negative self. The communicative contact returned a sharp feeling of shame and loss.

The Bacit shifted from terror to fifth-order displeasure, which was almost as bad as the terror. All the lost experiences. Lost . . . lost . . . lost . . .

"I had no idea the Euthanasia Center would be that simple and swift," the Tegas transmitted. "The incident is past changing. What can we do?"

He thought of the one vid-call he'd permitted himself, to check on the center's hours and routine. A gray-haired, polished contact-with-the-public type had appeared on the screen.

"We're fast, clean, neat, efficient, sanitary, and reverent," the man had said.

"Fast?"

"Who would want a slow death?"

The Tegas wished in this instant for nothing more than a slow death. If only he'd checked further. He'd expected this place to be seething with emotions. But it was emotionally dead—silent as a tomb. The joke-thought fell on inner silence.

The Bacit transfixed their composite self with a projection of urgent measurement—the twenty meters limit across which the Tegas could launch them into a new host.

But there'd been no way of knowing this place was an emotional vacuum until the Tegas element had entered here, probed the place. And these chambers where he now found himself were much farther from the street than twenty meters.

Momentarily, the Tegas was submerged in accusatory terror. *This death isn't like murder at all!*

Yet, he'd thought it would be *like* murder. And it was murder that'd been the saving device of the Tegas/Bacit for centuries. A murderer could be depended upon for total emotional involvement. A murderer could be lured close . . . close . . . close, much closer than twenty meters. It'd been so easy to goad the human creatures into that violent act, to set up the ideal circumstances for the identity leap. The Tegas absolutely required profound emotions in a prospective host. One couldn't focus on the neural totality without it. Bits of the creature's awareness center tended to escape. That could be fatal—as fatal as the trap in which he now found himself.

Murder.

The swift outflow of life from the discarded host, the emotional concentration of the new host—and before he knew it, the murderer was captive of the Tegas, captive in his own body. The captive awareness cried out silently, darting inward with ever tightening frenzy until it was swallowed.

And the Tegas could get on about its business of enjoying life.

This world had changed, though, in the past hundred years of the William Bailey period. Murder had been virtually eliminated by the new predictive techniques and computers of the Data Center. The android law-niks were everywhere, anticipating violence, preventing it. This was an elliptical development of society and the Tegas realized he should've taken it into account long ago. But life tended to be so pleasant when it held the illusion of never ending. For the Tegas, migrating across the universe with its hosts, moving as a predator in the dark of life, the illusion could be a fact.

Unless it ended here.

It didn't help matters that decisions had been forced upon him. Despite a fairly youthful appearance, the host flesh of William Bailey had been failing. The Tegas could keep its host going far beyond the normal span, but when the creature began to fail, collapse could be massive and abrupt.

I should've tried to attack someone in circumstances where I'd have been killed, he thought. But he'd seen the flaw there. The emotionless law-niks would have been on him almost instantly. Death might've escaped him. He could've been trapped in a crippled, dying host surrounded by android blankness or, even worse, surrounded by humans rendered almost emotionless by that damnable "Middle Way" and "Eight-fold Karma."

And the hounds were on his trail. He knew they were. He'd seen plenty of evidence, sensed the snoopers. He'd lived too long as William Bailey. The ones who thrived on suspicion had become suspicious. And they couldn't be allowed to examine a Tegas host too closely. He knew what'd put them on his trail: that diabolical "total profile of motives." The Tegas in William Bailey was technically a murderer thousands of times over. Not that he went on killing and killing; once in a human lifetime was quite enough. Murder could take the fun out of life.

Thoughts were useless now, he realized. He had, after all, been trapped. Thinking about it led only to Bacit accusations.

And while he jumped from thought to thought, the William Bailey body moved nearer and nearer to dissolution. The body now held only the faintest contact with life, and that only because of desperate Tegas efforts. A human medic would've declared Bailey dead. Breathing had stopped. Abruptly, the heart fibrillated, ceased function.

Less than five minutes remained for the Tegas. He had to find a new host in five minutes with this one.

"Murder-murder-murder," the Bacit intruded. "You said euthanasia would be murder."

The Tegas felt William Bailey-shame. He cursed inwardly. The Bacit, normally such a useful function for a Tegas (driving away intellectual loneliness, providing companionship and caution) had become a distracting liability. The intrusion of terrifying urgency stopped thought.

Why couldn't the Bacit be silent and let him think?

Momentarily, the Tegas realized he'd never before considered the premises of his own actions.

What was the Bacit?

He'd never hungered after his own kind, for he had the Bacit. But what, after all, was the Bacit? Why, for example, would it let him captivate only males? Female thinking might be a help in this emergency. Why couldn't he mix the sexes?

The Bacit used the inner shout: "Now we have time for philosophy?"

It was too much.

"Silence!" the Tegas commanded.

An immediate sense of loneliness rocked him. He defied it, probed his surroundings. Any host would do in this situation— even a lower animal, although he hadn't risked one of those in aeons. Surely there must be some emotional upset in this terrible place ... something ... anything ...

He remembered a long-ago incident when he'd allowed himself to be slain by a type who'd turned out to be completely emotionless. He'd barely managed to shift in time to an eyewitness to the crime. The moment had been like this one in its sudden emergency, but who was eye-witness to this killing? Where was an alternative host?

He searched fruitlessly.

Synapses began snapping in the William Bailey neural system. The Tegas withdrew to the longest-lived centers, probed with increasing frenzy.

A seething emotional mass lifted itself on his awareness horizon. Fear, self-pity, revenge, anger: a lovely prospect, like a rescue steamer bearing down on a drowning mariner.

"I'm not William Bailey," he reminded himself and launched outwards, homing on that boiling tangle of paradox, that emotional beacon...

There came the usual bouncing shock as he grabbed for the new host's identity centers. He poured out through a sensorium, discovered his own movements, felt something cold against a wrist. It was not yet completely his wrist, but the eyes were sufficiently under control for him to force them towards the source of sensation.

A flat, gray metallic object swam into focus. It was pressed against *his* wrist. Simultaneously, there occurred a swarming sense of awareness within the host. It was a sighing-out—not submission, but negative exaltation. The Tegas felt an old heart begin to falter, looked at an attendant: unfamiliar face—owlish features around a sharp nose.

But no emotional intensity, no central hook of being to be grabbed and captivated.

The room was a twin to the one in which he'd been captured by this system. The ceiling's time read-out said only eight minutes had passed since that other wrist had been touched by death.

"If you'll be so kind as to go through the door behind you," the owl-faced attendant said. "I do hope you can make it. Had to drag three of you in there already this shift; I'm rather weary. Let's get moving, eh?"

Weary? Yes—the attendant radiated only emotional weariness. It was nothing a Tegas could grasp.

The new host responded to the idea of urgency, pushed up out of a chair, shambled towards an oval door. The attendant hurried him along with an arm across the old shoulders.

The Tegas moved within the host, consolidated neural capacity, swept in an unresisting awareness. It wasn't an awareness he'd have taken out of choice—defeated, submissive. There was something strange about it. The Tegas detected a foreign object pressed against the host's spine. A capsule of some kind—neural transmitter/receiver. It radiated an emotional-damper effect, commands of obedience.

The Tegas blocked it off swiftly, terrified by the implications of such an instrument.

He had the host's identity now: James Daggett; that was the name. Age seventy-one. The body was a poor, used-up relic, weaker, more debilitated than William Bailey had been at 236. The host's birdlike awareness, giving itself up to the Tegas as it gave up to death, radiated oddly mystical thoughts, confusions, assumptions, filterings.

The Tegas was an angel "come to escort me."

Still trailing wisps of William Bailey, the Tegas avoided too close a linkage with this new host. The name and self-recognition centers were enough.

He realized with a twisted sense of defeat that the old body was being strapped on to a hard surface. The ceiling loomed over him a featureless gray. Dulled nostrils sniffed at an antiseptic breeze.

"Sleep well, paisano," the attendant said.

Not again! the Tegas thought.

His Bacit half reasserted itself: "We can jump from body to body—dying a little each time. What fun!"

The Tegas transmitted a remote obscenity from another world and another aeon, describing what the Bacit half could do with its bitterness.

Vacuity replaced the intrusion.

Defeat . . . defeat . . .

Part of this doomed mood, he realized, came out of the James Daggett personality. The Tegas took the moment to probe that host's memories, found the time when the transmitter had been attached to his spine.

Defeat-obedience-defeat . . .

It stemmed from that surgical instant.

He restored the blocks, quested outwards for a new host. Questing, he searched his Tegas memory. There must be a clue somewhere, a hint, a thought—some way of escape. He missed the Bacit contribution, parts of his memory felt cut off. The neural linkage with the dying James Daggett clung like dirty mud to his thoughts.

Ancient, dying James Daggett remained filled with mystical confusions until he was swallowed by the Tegas. It was a poor neural connection. The host was supposed to resist. That strengthened the Tegas grip. Instead, the Tegas ran into softly dying walls of other-memory. Linkages slipped. He felt his awareness range contracting.

Something swam into the questing field—anger, outrage of the kind frequently directed against stupidities. The Tegas waited, wondering if this could be another *client* of the center.

Now, trailing the angry one came another identity. Fear dominated this one. The Tegas went into a mental crouch, focused its awareness hungrily. An object of anger, a fearful one—there was a one a Tegas could grab.

Voices came to him from the hallway outside the alcove—rasping, attacking and (delayed) fearful.

James Daggett's old and misused ears cut off overtones, reduced volume. There wasn't time to strengthen the host's hearing circuits, but the Tegas grasped the sense of the argument.

"...told to notify...immediately if...Bailey! William Bailey!...saw the...your desk..."

And the fearful one: "....busy...you've no idea how... and understaffed and...teen an hour...only...this shift..."

The voices receded, but the emotional auras remained within Tegas range.

"Dead!" It was the angry one, a voice-blast accompanied by a neural overload that rolled across the Tegas like a giant wave.

At the instant of rage, the fearful one hit a momentary fear peak: abject retreat.

The Tegas pounced, quitting James Daggett in the blink-out as life went under. It was like stepping off a sinking boat into a storm-racked cockleshell. He was momentarily lost in the tracery of material spacetime which was the chosen host. Abruptly, he realized the fearful one had husbanded a reserve of supercilious hate, an ego corner fortified by resentments against authority accumulated over many years. The bouncing shock of the contact was accompanied by an escape of the host's awareness into the fortified corner.

The Tegas knew then he was in for a fight such as he'd never before experienced. The realization was accompanied by a blurred glimpse through host-eyes of a darkly suspicious face staring at him across a strapped-down body. The death-locked features of the body shook him—William Bailey! He almost lost the battle right there.

The host took control of the cheeks, contorted them. The eyes behaved independently: one looking up, the other down. He experienced direct perception, seeing with the fingertips (pale glowing), hearing with the lips (an itch of sound). Skin trembled and flushed. He staggered, heard a voice shout: "Who're you? What you doing to me?"

It was the host's voice, and the Tegas, snatching at the vocal centers, could only burr the edges of sound, not blank out intelligibility. He glimpsed the dark face across from him in an eye-swirling flash. The other had recoiled, staring.

It was one of the suspicious ones, the hated ones, the ones-who-rule. No time to worry about that now. The Tegas was fighting for survival. He summoned every trick he'd ever learned—cajolery, mystical subterfuges, a flailing of religious illusion, love, hate, word play. Men were an instrument of language and could be snared by it. He went in snake-striking dashes along the neural channels.

The name! He had to get the name!

"Carmy . . . Carmichael!"

He had half the name then, a toehold on survival. Silently, roaring inward along synaptic channels, he screamed the name—

"I'm Carmichael! I'm Carmichael!"

"No!"

"Yes! I'm Carmichael!"

"You're not! You're not!"

"I'm Carmichael!"

The host was bludgeoned into puzzlement: "Who're you? You can't be me. I'm . . . Joe—Joe Carmichael!"

The Tegas exulted, snapping up the whole name: "I'm Joe Carmichael!"

The host's awareness spiraled inward, darting, frenzied. Eyes rolled. Legs trembled. Arms moved with a disjointed flapping. Teeth gnashed. Tears rolled down the cheeks.

The Tegas smashed at him now: "I'm Joe Carmichael!"

"No . . . no . . . no . . ." It was a fading inner scream, winking out . . . back . . . out . . .

Silence.

"I'm Joe Carmichael," the Tegas thought.

It was a Joe Carmichael thought faintly touched by Tegas inflections and Bacit's reproving: "That was too close."

The Tegas realized he lay flat on his back on the floor. He looked up into dark features identified by host-memories: "Chadrick Vicentelli, Commissioner of Crime Prevention."

"Mr. Carmichael," Vicentelli said. "I've summoned help. Rest quietly. Don't try to move just yet."

What a harsh, unmoving face, the Tegas thought. Vicentelli
was a Noh mask face. And the voice: wary, cold, suspiciou
This violent incident wasn't on any computer's predictives...
Or was it? No matter—a suspicious man had seen too much
Something had to be done—immediately. Feet already coul
be heard pounding along the corridor.

"Don't know what's wrong with me," the Tegas said, man
aging the Carmichael voice with memory help from the Baile
period. "Dizzy...whole world seemed to go red...."

"You look alert enough now," Vicentelli said.

There was no *give* in that voice, no love. Violence there
suspicious hate contained in sharp edges.

"You look alert enough now."

A Tegas shudder went through the Carmichael body. H
studied the probing, suspicious eyes. This was the breed Tega
avoided. Rulers possessed terrible resources for the inner battle
That was one of the reasons they ruled. Tegas had been swa
lowed by rulers—dissolved, lost. Mistakes had been made i
the dim beginnings before Tegas learned to avoid ones such a
this. Even on this world, the Tegas recalled early fights, nea
things that had resulted in rumors and customs, myths, raci.
fears. All primitives knew the code: *"Never reveal your tr*
name!"

And here was a ruler who had seen too much in times whe
that carried supreme danger. Suspicion was aroused. A sha
intelligence weighed data it should never have received.

Two red-coated android law-niks, as alike in their blan
featured intensity as obedient dogs, swept through the alcov
hangings, came to a stop waiting for Vicentelli's orders. It wa
unnerving: even with androids, the ones-who-submitted nev
hesitated in looking first to a ruler for their orders.

The Tegas thought of the control capsule that had been o
James Daggett's spine. A new fear trembled through him. Th
host's mouth was dry with a purely Carmichael emotion.

"This is Joseph Carmichael," Vicentelli said, pointing. "I wa
him taken to IC for a complete examination and motivation.
profile. I'll meet you there. Notify the appropriate cadres."

The law-niks helped the Tegas to his new feet.

IC—Investigation Central, he thought.

"Why're you taking me to IC?" he demanded. "I should g

to a hospital for—"

"We've medical facilities," Vicentelli said. He made it sound ominous.

Medical facilities for what?

"But why—"

"Be quiet and obey," Vicentelli said. He glanced at William Bailey's body, back to Carmichael. It was a look full of weighted suspicions, half knowledge, educated assumptions.

The Tegas glanced at William Bailey's body, was caught by an inward-memory touch that wrenched at his new awareness. It had been a superior host, flesh deserving of love. The nostalgia passed. He looked back at Vicentelli, formed a vacant stare of confusion. It was not a completely feigned reaction. The Carmichael takeover had occurred in the presence of the suspected William Bailey—no matter that William Bailey was a corpse; that merely fed the suspicions. Vicentelli, assuming an unknown presence in William Bailey, would think it had leaped from the corpse to Carmichael.

"We're interested in you," Vicentelli said. "Very interested. Much more interested than we were before your recent... ahhh, seizure." He nodded to the androids.

Seizure! the Tegas thought.

Firm, insistent hands propelled him through the alcove curtains into the hallway, down the hall, through the antiseptic white of the employees' dressing room and out of the back door.

The day he'd left such a short time before as William Bailey appeared oddly transformed to the Carmichael eyes. There was a slight change in the height of the eyes, of course—a matter of perhaps three centimeters taller for Carmichael. He had to break his visual reactions out of perspective habits formed by more than two centuries at Bailey's height. But the change was more than that. He felt that he was seeing the day through many eyes—many more than the host's two.

The sensation of multi-ocular vision confused him, but he hadn't time to examine it before the law-niks pushed him into the one-way glass cage of an aircar. The door hissed closed, thumping on its seals, and he was alone, peering out through the blue-gray filtering of the windows. He leaned back on padded plastic.

The aircar leaped upward out of the plastrete canyon, sped

across the great tableland roof of the Euthanasia Center toward the distant man-made peaks of IC. The central complex of government was an area the Tegas always had avoided. He wished nothing more now than to continue avoiding it.

A feeling came over him that his universe had shattered. He was trapped here—not just trapped in the aircar flitting towards the plastrete citadel of IC, but trapped in the ecosystem of the planet. It was a sensation he'd never before experienced—not even on that aeons-distant day when he'd landed here in a conditioned host at the end of a trip which had taxed the limits of the host's viability. It was the way of the Tegas, though, to reach out for new planets, new hosts. It had become second nature to choose the right kind of planet, the right kind of developing life forms. The right kind always developed star travel, releasing the Tegas for a new journey, new explorations, new experiences. That way, boredom never intervened. The creatures of this planet were headed towards the stellar leap, too—given time.

But the Tegas, experiencing a new fear for him, realized he might not be around to take advantage of that stellar leap. It was a realization that left him feeling exhausted, time-scalded, injured in his responses like a mistreated instrument.

Where did I go wrong? he wondered. *Was it in the original choice of the planet?*

His Bacit half, usually so explicit in reaction to inner searching, spread across their mutual awareness a projected sense of the fuzzy unknowns ahead.

This angered the Tegas. The future always was unknown. He began exploring his host-self, assessing what he could use in the coming showdown. It was a good host—healthy, strong, its musculature and neural system capable of excellent Tegas reinforcement and intensification. It was a host that could give good service, perhaps even longer than William Bailey. The Tegas began doing what he could in the time available, removing inhibitory blocks for quicker and smoother neural responses, setting up a heart and vascular system buffer. He took a certain pride in the work; he'd never misused a host as long as it remained viable.

The natural Tegas resilience, the thing that kept him going, kept him alive and interested—the endless curiosity—reasserted itself. Whatever was about to happen, it would be new.

He seated himself firmly in the host, harnessed the Carmichael memory system to his Tegas responses, and readied himself to meet the immediate future.

A thought crept into his mind:

In the delicate immensity that was his own past there lay nonhuman experiences. How subtle was this "Total Profile of Personality"? Could it detect the nonhuman? Could it cast a template which would compare too closely with William Bailey ... or any of the others they might have on their Data Center lists?

He sensed the dance of the intellects within him, pounding out their patterns on the floor of his awareness. In a way, he knew he was all the captive stalks bound up like a sheaf of grain.

The city-scape passing beneath the aircar became something sensed rather than seen. Tiny frenzies of fear began to dart about in him. What tools of psychometry would his interrogators use? How discreet? How subtle? Beneath their probes, he must be nothing other than Joe Carmichael. Yet... he was far more. He felt the current of *now* sweeping his existence toward peril.

Danger-danger-danger. He could see it intellectually as Tegas. He responded to it as Joe Carmichael.

Sweat drenched his body.

The aircar began to descend. He stared at the backs of the androids' heads visible through the glass of the control cab. They were two emotionless blobs; no help there. The car left the daylight, rocked once in a recognition-field, slid down a tube filled with cold aluminium light into the yellow glowing of a gigantic plastrete parking enclosure—tawny walls and ceiling, a sense of cavernous distance humming with activity.

It made the Tegas think of a hive society he'd once experienced; not one of his better memories. He shuddered.

The aircar found its parking niche, stopped. Presently, the doors hissed open. The androids flanked the opening. One gestured for him to emerge.

The Tegas swallowed in a dry Carmichael throat, climbed out, stared around at the impersonal comings and goings of androids. Neither by eye or emotional aura could he detect a human in the region around him. Intense loneliness came over him.

Still without speaking, the androids took his arms, propell
him across an open space into the half-cup of a ring lift. T
field grabbed them, shot them upward past blurred walls a
flickers of openings. The lift angled abruptly, holding the
softly with their faces tipped downward at something ne
forty-five degrees. The androids remained locked beside hi
like two fish swimming in the air. The lift grip returned
vertical, shot them upward into the center of an amphithea
room.

The lift hole became floor beneath his feet.

The Tegas stared up and around at a reaching space, immen
blue skylight, people-people-people, tiers of them peering do
at him, tiers of them all around.

He probed for emotions, met the terrifying aura of the pla
an icy neural stare, a psychic *chutzpah*. The watchers—rule
all, their minds disconnected from any religion except the se
no nervous coughs, no impatient stirrings.

They were an iceberg of silent waiting.

He had never imagined such a place even in a nightmal
But he knew this place, recognized it immediately. If a Teg
must end, he thought, then it must be in some such place
this. All the lost experiences that might come to an end he
began wailing through him.

Someone emerged from an opening on his left, strode towa
him across the floor of the amphitheater: Vicentelli.

The Tegas stared at the approaching man, noted the ey
favored by deep shadows: dense black eyes cut into a fa
where lay a verseless record—hard glyphs of cheeks, ston
cut mouth. Everything was labor in that face: work-wor
work. It held no notion of fun. It was a contrivance for asserti
violence, both spectator and participant. It rode the flesh, che
ishing no soft thing at all.

A vat of liquid as blue as glowing steel arose from the flo
beside the Tegas. Android hands gripped him tightly as he jerk
with surprise.

Vicentelli stopped in front of him, glanced once at the su
rounding banks of faces, back to his victim.

"Perhaps you're ready to save us the trouble of an interr
gation in depth," he said.

The Tegas felt his body tremble, shook his head.

Vicentelli nodded.

With impersonal swiftness, the androids stripped the clothing from the Tegas host, lifted him into the vat. The liquid felt warm and tingling. A harness was adjusted to hold his arms and keep his face just above the surface. An inverted dome came down to rest just above his head. The day became a blue stick of light and he wondered inanely what time it was. It'd been early when he'd entered the Euthanasia Center, now, it was very late. Yet, he knew the day had hardly advanced past mid-morning.

Again, he probed the emotional aura, recoiled from it.

What if they kill me coldly? he wondered.

Where he could single out individuals, he was reminded of the play of lightning on a far horizon. The emotional beacons were thin, yet filled with potency.

A room full of rulers. The Tegas could imagine no more hideous place.

Something moved across his stick of light: Vicentelli.

"Who are you?" Vicentelli asked.

I'm Joe Carmichael, he thought. *I must be only Joe Carmichael.*

But Carmichael's emotions threatened to overwhelm him. Outrage and submissive terror flickered through the neural exchanges. The host body twitched. Its legs made faint running motions.

Vicentelli turned away, spoke to the surrounding watchers:

"The problem with Joseph Carmichael is this violent incident which you're now seeing on your recorders. Let me impress upon you that this incident was not predicted. It was outside our scope. We must assume, therefore, that it was not a product of Joseph Carmichael. During this examination, each of you will study the exposed profile. I want each of you to record your reactions and suggestions. Somewhere here there will be a clue to the unknowns we observed in William Bailey and before that in Almiro Hsing. Be alert, observant."

God of Eternity! the Tegas thought. *They've traced me from Hsing to Bailey!*

This change in human society went back farther than he'd suspected. How far back?

"You will note, please," Vicentelli said, "that Bailey was in the immediate vicinity when Hsing fell from the Peace Tower at Canton and died. Pay particular attention to the material which points to a previous association between Hsing and Bailey. There is a possibility Bailey was at that particular place on

Hsing's invitation. This could be important."

The Tegas tried to withdraw his being, to encyst his emotions. The ruling humans had gone down a developmental side path he'd never expected. They had left him somewhere.

He knew why: Tegas-like, he had immersed himself in the concealing presence of the mob, retreated into daily drudgery, lived like the living. Yet, he had never loved the flesh more than in this moment when he knew he could lose it forever. He loved the flesh the way a man might love a house. This intricate structure was a house that breathed and felt.

Abruptly, he underwent a sense of union with the flesh more intimate than anything of his previous experience. He knew for certain in this instant how a man would feel here. Time had never been an enemy of the Tegas. But Time was man's enemy. He was a man now and he prepared his flesh for maximum reactions, for high-energy discharge.

Control: That was what this society was up to—super control.

Vicentelli's face returned to the stick of light.

"For the sake of convenience," he said, "I'll continue to call you Carmichael."

The statement told him baldly that he was in a corner and Vicentelli knew it. If the Tegas had any doubts, Vicentelli now removed them.

"Don't try to kill yourself," Vicentelli said. "The mechanism in which you now find yourself can sustain your life even when you least wish that life to continue."

Abruptly, the Tegas realized his Carmichael self should be panic-stricken. There could be no Tegas watchfulness or remoteness here.

He was panic-stricken.

The host body threshed in the liquid, surged against the bonds. The liquid was heavy—oily, but not oily. It held him as an elastic suit might, dampening his movements, always returning him to the quiescent, fishlike floating.

"Now," Vicentelli said.

There was a loud click.

Light dazzled the Carmichael eyes. Color rhythms appeared within the light. The rhythms held an epileptic beat. They jangled his mind, shook the Tegas awareness like something loosed in a violent cage.

Out of the voice which his universe had become there appeared questions. He knew they were spoken questions, but he saw them: word shapes tumbling in a torrent.

"Who are you?"

"What are you?"

"We see you for what you are. Why don't you admit what you are? We know you."

The aura of the surrounding watchers drummed at him with accusing vibrations: "We know you—know you—know you—know you..."

The Tegas felt the words rocking him, subduing him.

No Tegas can by hypnotized, he told himself. But he could feel his being coming out in shreds. Something was separating. Carmichael! The Tegas was losing his grip on the host! But the flesh was being reduced to a mesmerized idiot. The sense of separation intensified.

Abruptly, there was an inner sensation of stirring, awakening. He felt the host ego awakening, was powerless to counter it.

Thoughts crept along the dancing, shimmering neural paths—

"Who...what are...where do..."

The Tegas punched frantically at the questings: "I'm Joe Carmichael...I'm Joe Carmichael...I'm Joe Carmichael..."

He found vocal control, mouthed the words in dumb rhythm, making this the one answer to all questions. Slowly, the host fell silent, smothered in a Tegas envelope.

The blundering, bludgeoning interrogation continued.

Shake-rattle-question.

He felt himself losing all sense of distinction between Tegas and Carmichael. The Bacit half, whipped and terrorized by the unexpected sophistication of this attack, strewed itself in tangles through the identity net.

Voices of old hosts came alive in his mind: "...you can't... mustn't...I'm Joe Carmichael...stop them...why can't we..."

"You're murdering me!" he screamed.

The ranked watchers in the amphitheater united in an aura of pouncing glee.

"They're monsters!" Carmichael thought.

It was a pure Carmichael thought, unmodified by Tegas awareness, an unfettered human expression surging upwards from within.

"You hear me, Tegas?" Carmichael demanded. "They're monsters!"

The Tegas crouched in the flesh not knowing how to counter this. Never before had he experienced direct communication from a host after that final entrapment. He tried to locate the source of communication, failed.

"Look at 'em staring down at us like a pack of ghouls!" Carmichael thought.

The Tegas knew he should react, but before he could bring himself to it, the interrogation assumed a new intensity: shake-rattle-question.

"Where do you come from? Where do you come from? Where do you come from?"

The question tore at him with letters tall as giant buildings—faceless eyes, thundering voices, shimmering words.

Carmichael anger surged across the Tegas.

Still, the watchers radiated their chill amusement.

"Let's die and take one of 'em!" Carmichael insisted.

"Who speaks?" the Bacit demanded. "How did you get away? Where are you?"

"God! How cold they are." That had been a Bailey thought.

"Where do you come from?" the Bacit demanded, seeking the host awareness. "You are here, but we cannot find you."

"I come from Zimbue," Carmichael projected.

"You cannot come from Zimbue," the Tegas countered. "I come from Zimbue."

"But Zimbue is nowhere," the Bacit insisted.

And all the while—shake-rattle-question—Vicentelli's interrogation continued to jam circuits.

The Tegas felt he was being bombarded from all sides and from within. How could Carmichael talk of Zimbue?

"Then whence comest thou?" Carmichael asked.

How could Carmichael know of this matter? the Tegas asked himself. Whence had all Tegas come? The answer was a rote memory at the bottom of all his experiences: At the instant time began, the Tegas intruded upon the blackness where no star—not even a primal dust fleck—had tracked the dimensions with its being. They had been where senses had not been. How could Carmichael's ego still exist and know to ask of such things?

"And why shouldn't I ask?" Carmichael insisted. "It's what Vicentelli asks."

But where had the trapped ego of the host flesh hidden? Whence took it an existence to speak now?

The Bacit half had experienced enough. "Say him down!" the Bacit commanded. "Say him down! We are Joe Carmichael! You are Joe Carmichael! I am Joe Carmichael!"

"Don't panic," Carmichael soothed. "You are Tegas/Bacit, one being. I am Joe Carmichael."

And from the outer world, Vicentelli roared: "Who are you? I command you to tell me who you are! You must obey me! Are you William Bailey?"

Silence—inward and outward.

In the silence, the Tegas probed the abused flesh, understood part of the nature behind Vicentelli's attack. The liquid in which the host lay immersed: It was an anesthetic. The flesh was being robbed of sensation until only inner nerve tangles remained. Even more—the anesthetized flesh had been invaded by a control device. A throbbing capsule lay against the Carmichael spine—signalling, commanding, interfering.

"The capsule has been attached," Vicentelli said. "I will take him now to the lower chamber where the interrogation can proceed along normal channels. He's completely under our control now."

In the trapped flesh, the Bacit half searched out neural connections of the control capsule, tried to block them, succeeded only partly. Anesthetized flesh resisted Bacit probes. The Tegas, poised like a frightened spider in the host awareness, studied the softly throbbing neural currents for a solution. Should he attack, resume complete control? What could he attack? Vicentelli's interrogation had tangled identities in the host in a way that might never be unravelled.

The control capsule pulsed.

Carmichael's flesh obeyed a new command. Restraining bands slid aside. The Tegas stood up in the tank on unfeeling feet. Where his chest was exposed, sensation began to return. The inverted hemisphere was lifted from his head.

"You see," Vicentelli said, addressing the watchers above them. "He obeys perfectly."

Inwardly, Carmichael asked: "Tegas, can you reach out and see how they feel about all this? There might be a clue in their emotions."

"Do it!" the Bacit commanded.

The Tegas probed surrounding space, felt boredom, undertones of suspicion, a cat-licking sense of power. Yes, the mouse lay trapped between claws. The mouse could not escape.

Android hands helped the Tegas out of the tank, stood him on the floor, steadied him.

"Perfect control," Vicentelli said.

As the control capsule commanded, the Carmichael eyes stared straight ahead with a blank emptiness.

The Tegas sent a questing probe along the nearest channels, met Bacit, Carmichael, uncounted bits of others.

"How can you be here, Joe Carmichael?" he asked.

The host flesh responded to a capsule command, walked straight ahead across the floor of the amphitheater.

"Why aren't you fleeing or fighting me?" the Tegas insisted.

"No need," Carmichael responded. "We're all mixed up together, as you can see."

"Why aren't you afraid?"

"I was...am...hope not to be."

"How do you know about the Tegas?"

"How not? We're each other."

The Tegas experienced a shock-blink of awareness at this, felt an uneasy Bacit-projection. Nothing in all Tegas experience recalled such an inner encounter. The host fought and lost or the Tegas ended there. And the lost host went...where? A fearful questing came from the Bacit, a sense of broken continuity.

That damnable interrogation!

The host flesh, responding to the capsule's commands, had walked through a doorway into a blue hallway. As sensation returned, Tegas/Carmichael/Bacit grew aware of Vicentelli following...and other footsteps—android law-niks.

"What do you want, Joe Carmichael?" the Tegas demanded.

"I want to share."

"Why?"

"You're...more than I was. You can give me...longer life. You're curious...interesting. Half the creeps we got at the E-Center were worn down by boredom, and I was almost at that stage myself. Now...living is interesting once more."

"How can we live together—in here?"

"We're doing it."

"But I'm Tegas! I must rule in here!"

"So rule."

And the Tegas realized he had been restored to almost complete contact with the host's neural system. Still, the intrusive Carmichael ego remained. And the Bacit was doing nothing about this situation, appeared to have withdrawn to wherever the Bacit went. Carmichael remained—a slithering, mercuric thing: right there! No! Over here! No...no...not there, not here. Still, he remained.

"The host must submit without reservation," the Tegas commanded.

"I submit," Carmichael agreed.

"Then where are you?"

"We're all in here together. You're in command of the flesh, aren't you?"

The Tegas had to admit he was in command.

"What do you want, Joe Carmichael?" he insisted.

"I've told you."

"You haven't."

"I want to...watch...to share."

"Why should I let you do that?"

Vicentelli and his control capsule had brought the host flesh now to a drop chute. The chute's field gripped the Carmichael flesh, sent it whispering downward...downward...downward.

"Maybe you have no choice in whether I stay and watch," Joe Carmichael responded.

"I took you once," the Tegas countered. "I can take you again."

"What happens when they resume the interrogation?" Carmichael asked.

"What do you mean?"

"He means," the Bacit intruded, "that the true Joe Carmichael can respond with absolute verisimilitude to their search for a profile comparison."

The drop chute disgorged him into a long icy-white laboratory space. Through the fixated eyes came a sensation of metal shapes, of instruments, of glitterings and flashings, of movement.

The Tegas stood in capsule-induced paralysis. It was a condition any Tegas could override, but he dared not. No human could surmount this neural assault. The merest movement of a finger now amounted to exposure.

In the shared arena of their awareness, Carmichael said:

"Okay, let me have the con for a while. Watch. Don't intrude at all."

The Tegas hesitated.

"Do it!" the Bacit commanded.

The Tegas withdrew. He found himself in emptiness, a no-where of the mind, an unseen place, constrained vacuity... nothing...never...an unspoken, unspeaking pill of absence ...uncontained. This was a place where senses had not been, could not be. He feared it, but felt protected by it—hidden.

A sense of friendship and reassurance came to him from Carmichael. The Tegas felt a hopeless sense of gratitude for the first other-creature friendship he'd ever experienced. But why should Carmichael-ego be friendly? Doubt worried at him, nipped and nibbled. Why?

No answer came, unless an unmeasured simplicity radiating from the Bacit could be interpreted as answer. The Tegas found he had an economy of reservations about his position. This astonished him. He recognized he was making something new with all the dangers inherent in newness. It wasn't logical, but he knew thought might be the least careless when it was the least logical.

Time is the enemy of the flesh, he reminded himself. *Time is not my enemy.*

Reflections of meaning, actions, and intentions began coming to him from the outer-being-place where Carmichael sat. Vicentelli had returned to the attack with induced colors, shapes, flarings and dazzles. Words leaped across a Tegas mind-sky: "Who are you? Answer! I know you're there! Answer! Who are you?"

Joe Carmichael mumbled half-stupefied protests: "Why're you torturing me? What're y'doing?"

Shake-rattle-question: "STOP HIDING FROM ME!"

Carmichael's response wiggled outwards: "Wha' y' doing?"

Silence enveloped the flesh.

The Tegas began receiving muted filterings of a debate: "I tell you, his profile matches the Carmichael identity with exactness."..."Saw him change."..."...perhaps chemical poisoning...Euthanasia Center...consistent with ingestion of picrotoxin...coincidence..."

Creeping out into the necessary neural channels, the Tegas probed his surroundings for the emotional aura, found only

Vicentelli and two androids. The androids were frigid, emotionless shells. Vicentelli was a blazing core of frustrated anger.

Voices rained from a communications screen in the lab ceiling: "Have an end to it!" "Eliminate him and have done with it!" "This is a waste of time!" "You're mistaken, Vic!" "Stop wasting our time!"

They were commanding death for the Carmichael flesh, the Tegas realized. He thought of an arena, its rim dripping with thumbs: death. Those had been the days—short-lived hosts and easy transfers. But now: Would he dare tackle Vicentelli? It was almost certain failure, and the Tegas knew it. The hard shell of a ruler's ego could resist any assault.

A sharp "snap!" echoed in the lab. The communications screen went blank.

What now? the Tegas wondered.

"If Bailey's death didn't eliminate it," Vicentelli muttered, "why should the death of Carmichael be any different? What can stop it? The thing survived Hsing, and lord knows how many before that."

The Tegas felt his Bacit half flexing unseen membranes.

"If I'm right," Vicentelli muttered, "the thing lives on forever in host bodies. It lives—enjoys.... What if life were not... enjoyable?"

"The death of this human has been commanded," one of the androids said. "Do you wish us to leave?"

"Leave ... yes," Vicenteilli said.

The frigid android radiations receded, were gone.

The other rulers who'd been watching through the screen were convinced Vicentelli was wrong, the Tegas realized. But they'd commanded death for Carmichael. The androids had been sent away, of course: they could have no part in a human death.

The Tegas felt Carmichael cringing, demanding: "What'll we do?"

The Bacit tested a muscle in the host's left arm, a muscle the Tegas host had never before consciously sensed. Flesh rippled, relaxed.

"Exposure means final dissolution," the Tegas warned. It was his most basic inhibition. "We must remain cryptic in color and behavior, impossible to separate from any background."

"We're already exposed!" It was a pure Joe Carmichael thought. "What'll we do?"

A sensation of flowing wetness radiated from the control capsule on the host's spine.

"All right," Vicentelli said. "They don't believe me. But we're alone now." He stared into Carmichael eyes. "And I can try whatever I want. What if your life isn't enjoyable, eh?"

The sensation of wetness reached the brain.

Immediate blackness!

The Tegas recoiled upward, fighting past the neural shock, regaining some awareness. Carmichael's neurosystem quivered and rolled, filtered out some sounds, let others through with a booming roar. The Tegas felt outraged by scraping tactility— harsh movements, rollings.

Vicentelli was doing something at a glittering console directly in front of him.

The rolling sensation went on and on and on—swaying, dipping, gliding . . . and pain.

Tegas, measuring out his attention, felt the shuttlecock entanglements of his being with that of Carmichael. Blank spots were Carmichael . . . fuzzy grayness . . . and tightly stretched threads that linked bulbs of ego-reserve. There! There! And there! Pieces of Carmichael, all quiescent.

The Bacit nudged his awareness, an inner touch like the prickling of cactus spines. Whisper-thoughts came: "Got to get out of here. Trapped. Got to get out of here. Trapped-trapped."

He was forming verbal concepts in thousands of languages simultaneously.

What was Vicentelli doing?

The Tegas felt a pulse from the control capsule. A leg twitched. He snapped a reflex block on to that neural region to resume control. One eye opened, rolled. The Tegas fought for control of the visual centers, saw a multi-faceted creation of wires and crystals directly above him, blurs of green movement. All focused on the control capsule. The host's flesh felt as though it had been encased in a tight skin.

Vicentelli swam into his range of vision.

"Now, let us see how long you can hide," Vicentelli said. "We call this the torture skin." He moved something on the control console.

Tegas felt alertness return. He moved a left foot. Pain slashed at knee and ankle.

He gasped. Pain raked his back and chest.

"Very good," Vicentelli said. "It's the movements you make,

do you understand? Remain unmoving, no pain. Move—pain."

Tegas permitted his host to take a deep, quivering breath. Knives played with his chest and spine.

"To breathe, to flex a wrist, to walk—all equal pain," Vicentelli said. "The beauty of it is there's no bodily harm. But you'll pray for something simple as injury unless you give up."

"You're an animal!" the Tegas managed. Agony licked along his jaw and lips, flayed his temples.

"Give up," Vicentelli said.

"Animal," the Tegas whispered. He felt his Bacit half throwing pain blocks into the neural system, tried a shallow breath. Faint irritation rewarded the movement, but he simulated a pain reaction—closed his eyes. Fire crept along his brows. A swift block eased the pain.

"Why prolong it?" Vicentelli asked. "What are you?"

"You're insane," Tegas whispered. He waited, feeling the pain blocks click into place.

Darting lights glittered in Vicentelli's eyes. "Do you really feel the pain?" he asked. He moved a handle on the console.

The host was hurled to the floor by a flashing command from the control capsule.

Under Bacit guidance, he writhed with the proper pain reactions, allowed them to subside slowly.

"You feel it," Vicentelli said. "Good." He reached down, jerked his victim upright, steadied him.

The Bacit had almost all the pain under control, signalling proper concealment reactions. The host flesh grimaced, resisted movement, stood awkwardly.

"I have all the time I need," Vicentelli said. "You cannot outlast me. Surrender. Perhaps I may even find a use for you. I know you're there, whatever you are. You must realize this by now. You can speak candidly with me. Confess. Explain yourself. What are you? What use can I make of you?"

Moving his lips stiffly as though against great pain, Tegas said: "If I were what you suggest, what would I fear from such as you?"

"Very good!" Vicentelli crowed. "We progress. What should you fear from me? Hah! And what should I fear from you?"

"Madman," Tegas whispered.

"Ahh, now," Vicentelli said. "Hear if this is mad: My profile on you says I should fear you only if you die. Therefore, I will not kill you. You may wish to die, but I will not permit you to die. I can keep the body alive indefinitely. It will not be an enjoyable life, but it will be life. I can make you breathe. I can make your heart work. Do you wish a full demonstration?"

The inner whispers resumed and the Tegas fought against them. "We can't escape. Trapped."

The Bacit radiated hesitant uncertainty.

A Bailey thought: "It's a nightmare! That's what!"

Tegas stood in wonder: a Bailey thought!

Bacit admonitions intruded: "Be still. We must work together. Serenity...serenity...serenity..."

The Tegas felt himself drifting off on waves of tranquility, was shocked by a Bacit thought-scream: "NOT YOU!"

Vicentelli moved one of his console controls.

Tegas let out a muffled scream as both his arms jerked upward.

Another Vicentelli adjustment and Tegas bent double, whipped upright.

Bacit-prompted whimpering sounds escaped his lips.

"What are you?" Vicentelli asked in his softest voice.

Tegas sensed the frantic inner probings as the Bacit searched out the neural linkages, blocked them. Perspiration bathed the host flesh.

"Very well," Vicentelli said. "Let us go for a long hike."

The host's legs began pumping up and down in a stationary march. Tegas stared straight ahead, pop-eyed with simulation of agony.

"This will end when you answer my questions," Vicentelli said. "What are you? Hup-two-three-four. Who are you? Hup-two-three-four..."

The host flesh jerked with obedience to the commands.

Tegas again felt the thousands of old languages taking place within him—a babble. With an odd detachment, he realized he must be a museum of beings and remembered energies.

"Ask yourself how long you can stand this," Vicentelli said.

"I'm Joe Carmichael," he gasped.

Vicentelli stepped close, studied the evidences of agony. "Hup-two-three-four..."

Still, the babble persisted. He was a flow of energy, Tegas realized. Energy...energy...energy. Energy was the only *solid* in the universe. He was wisdom seated in a bed of languages.

But wisdom chastised the wise and spit upon those who came to pay homage. Wisdom was for copyists and clerks.

Power, then, he thought.

But power, when exercised, fragmented.

How simple to attack Vicentelli now, Tegas thought. *We're alone. No one is watching. I could strike him down in an instant.*

The habits of all that aeons-long history inhibited action. Inevitably, he had picked up some of the desires, hopes and fears—especially the fears—of his uncounted hosts. Their symbols sucked at him now.

A pure Bailey thought: "We can't keep this up forever."

The Tegas felt Bailey's sharings, then Carmichael's, the mysterious coupling of selves, the never-before engagement with the captive.

"One clean punch," Carmichael insisted.

"Hup-two-three-four," Vicentelli said, peering closely at his victim.

Abruptly, the Tegas felt himself looking inward from the far end of his being. He saw all his habits of thought contained in the shapes of every action he'd ever contemplated. The thoughts took form to control flesh, a blaze of energy, a *solid.* In that flaring instant, he became pure performance. All the violent killers the Tegas had overwhelmed rose up in him, struck outward, and he *was* the experience—overpoweringly single with it, not limited by any description . . . without symbols.

Vicentelli lay unconscious on the floor.

Tegas stared at his own right hand. The thing had taken on a life of its own. Its movement had been unique to the moment, a flashing jab with fingers extended, a crushing impact against a nerve bundle in Vicentelli's neck.

Have I killed him? he wondered.

Vicentelli stirred, groaned.

So there'd been Tegas inhibitions on the blow, an exquisite control that could overpower but not kill, the Tegas thought.

Tegas moved to Vicentelli's head, stooped to examine him. Moving, he felt the torture skin relax, glanced up at the green-glowing construction, realized the thing's field was limited.

Again, Vicentelli groaned.

Tegas pressed the nerve bundle in the man's neck. Vicentelli subsided, went limp.

Pure Tegas thoughts rose up in the Carmichael neural system.

He realized he'd been living for more than a century immersed in a culture which had regressed. They had invented a new thing—almost absolute control—but it held an old pattern. The Egyptians had tried it, and many before them, and a few since. The Tegas thought of the phenomenon as the man-machine. Pain controlled it—and food...pleasure, ritual.

The control capsule irritated his senses. He felt the aborted action message, a faint echo, Bacit-repressed: "Hup-two-three-four..." With the action message went the emotional inhibitions deadly to Tegas survival.

The Tegas felt sensually subdued. He thought of a world where no concentrated emotions remained, no beacons upon which he could home his short-burst transfer of identity.

The Carmichael flesh shuddered to a Tegas response. The Bacit stirred, transmitting sensations of urgency.

Yes, there was urgency. Androids might return. Vicentelli's fellow rulers might take it upon themselves to check the activity of this room.

He reached around to his back, felt the control capsule: a flat, tapered package...cold, faintly pulsing. He tried to insert a finger beneath it, felt the flesh rebel. Ahhh, the linkage was mortal. The diabolic thing joined the spine. He explored the connections internally, realized the thing could be removed, given time and the proper facilities.

But he had not the time.

Vicentelli's lips made feeble writhings—a baby's mouth searching for the nipple.

Tegas concentrated on Vicentelli. A ruler. Tegas rightly avoided such as this. Vicentelli's kind knew how to resist the mind-swarm. They had ego power.

Perhaps the Vicentellis had provided the key to their own destruction, though. Whatever happened, the Tegas knew he could never return into the human mass. The new man-machine provided no hiding place. In this day of new things, another new thing had to be tried.

Tegas reached for the control capsule on his back, inserted three fingers beneath it. With the Bacit blocking off the pain, he wrenched the capsule free.

All sensation left his lower limbs. He collapsed across Vicentelli, brought the capsule around to study it. The removal had dealt a mortal blow to the Carmichael host, but there were no protests in their shared awareness, only a deep curiosity about the capsule.

Simple, deadly thing—operation obvious. Barbed needles protruded along its inner surface. He cleaned shreds of flesh from them, working fast. The host was dying rapidly, blood pumping onto the floor—and spinal fluid. He levered himself onto one elbow, rolled Vicentelli onto one side, pulled away the man's jacket and shirt. A bit of fleshly geography, a ridge of spine lay exposed.

Tegas knew this landscape from the inward examination of the capsule. He gauged the position required, slapped the capsule home.

Vicentelli screamed.

He jerked away, scrabbled across the floor, leaped upright. "Hup-two-three-four..."

His legs jerked up and down in terrible rhythm. Sounds of agony escaped his lips. His eyes rolled.

The Carmichael body slumped to the floor, and Tegas waited for the host to die. Too bad about this host—a promising one—but he was committed now. No turning back.

Death came as always, a wink-out, and after the flicker of blankness, he centered on the emotional scream which was Vicentelli. The Tegas divided from dead flesh, bore away with that always-new sensation of supreme discovery—a particular thing, relevant to nothing else in the universe except himself.

He was pain.

But it was pain he had known, analyzed, understood and could isolate. The pain contained all there was of Vicentelli's identity. Encapsulated that way, it could be absorbed piecemeal, shredded off at will. And the new host's flesh was grateful. With the Tegas came surcease from pain.

Slowly, the marching subsided.

The Tegas blocked off control circuits, adjusted Vicentelli's tunic to conceal the capsule on his back, paused to contemplate how easy this capture had been. It required a dangerous change of pattern, yes: a Tegas must dominate, risk notice—not blend with his surroundings.

With an abrupt sense of panic, William Bailey came alive in his awareness. "We made it!"

In that instant, the Tegas was hanging by the hook of his being, momentarily lost in the host he'd just captured. The intermittency of mingled egos terrified and enthralled. As he had inhabited others, now he was inhabited.

Even the new host—silent, captivated—became part of a changed universe, one that threatened in a different way: all maw. He realized he'd lost contact with the intellectual centers. His path touched only nerve ends. He had no home for his breath, couldn't find the flesh to wear it.

Bacit signals darted around him: a frantic, searching clamor. The flesh—the flesh—the flesh...

He'd worn the flesh too gently, he realized. He'd been lulled by its natural laws and his own. He'd put aside all reaching questions about the organism, had peered out of the flesh unconcerned, leaving all worries to the Bacit.

One axiom had soothed him: *The Bacit knows.*

But the Bacit was loosed around him and he no longer held the flesh. The flesh held him, a grip so close it threatened to choke him.

The flesh cannot choke me, he thought. *It cannot. I love the flesh.*

Love—there was a toehold, a germ of contact. The flesh remembered how he had eased its agony. Memories of other flesh intruded. Tendrils of association accumulated. He thought of all the flesh he'd loved on this world: the creatures with their big eyes, their ears flat against their heads, smooth caps of hair, beautiful mouths and cheeks. The Tegas always noticed mouths. The mouth betrayed an infinite variety of things about the flesh around it.

A Vicentelli self-image came into his awareness, swimming like a ghost in a mirror. The Tegas thought about the verseless record, the stone-cut mouth. No notion of fun—that was the thing about Vicentelli's mouth.

He'll have to learn fun now, the Tegas thought.

He felt the feet then, hard against the floor, and the Bacit was with him. But the Bacit had a voice that touched the auditory centers from within. It was the voice of William Bailey and countless others.

"Remove the signs of struggle before the androids return," the voice said.

He obeyed, looked down at the empty flesh which had been Joe Carmichael. But Joe Carmichael was with him in this flesh, Vicentelli's flesh, which still twitched faintly to the broadcast commands transmitted through the capsule on his spine.

"Have to remove the capsule as soon as possible," the Bacit voice reminded. "You know the way to do it."

The Tegas marveled at the Vicentelli overtones suddenly noticeable in the voice. Abruptly, he glimpsed the dark side of his being through Vicentelli, and he saw an aspect of the Bacit he'd never suspected. He realized he was a net of beings who enjoyed their captivity, were strong in their captivity, would not exchange it for any other existence.

They *were* Tegas in a real sense, moving him by habits of thought, shaping actions out of uncounted mediations. The Bacit half had accumulated more than forty centuries of mediations on this one world. And there were uncounted worlds before this one.

Language and thought.

Language was the instrument of the sentient being—yet, the being was the instrument of language as Tegas was the instrument of the Bacit. He searched for significant content in this new awareness, was chided by the Bacit's sneer. To search for content was to search for limits where there were no limits. Content was logic and classification. It was a word sieve through which to judge experience. It was nothing in itself, could never satisfy.

Experience, that was the thing. Action. The infinite reenactment of life accompanied by its endless procession of images.

There are things to be done, the Tegas thought.

The control capsule pulsed on his spine.

The capsule, yes—and many more things.

They have bugged the soul, he thought. *They've mechanized the soul and are forever damned. Well, I must join them for a while.*

He passed a hand through a call beam, summoned the androids to clear away the discarded host that had been Carmichael.

A door opened at the far end of the lab. Three androids entered, marching in line towards him. They were suddenly an amusing six-armed figure, their arms moving that way in obedient cadence.

The Vicentelli mouth formed an unfamiliar smile.

Briefly he set the androids to the task of cleaning up the mess in the lab. Then, the Tegas began the quiet exploration of his new host, a task he found remarkably easy with his new understanding. The host cooperated. He explored Vicentelli slowly—strong, lovely, healthy flesh—explored as one might explore a strange land, swimming across coasts of awareness that loomed and receded.

A host had behavior that must be learned. It was not well to dramatize the Tegas difference. There would be changes, of course—but slow ones; nothing dramatic in its immediacy.

While he explored he thought of the mischief he could do in this new role. There were so many ways to disrupt the man-machine, to revive individualism, to have fun. Lovely mischief.

Intermittently, he wondered what had become of the Bailey ego and the Joe Carmichael ego. Only the Bacit remained in the host with him, and the Bacit transmitted a sensation of laughter.

PASSAGE
FOR
PIANO

**H**ad some cosmic crystal gazer suggested to Margaret Hatchell that she would try to smuggle a concert grand piano onto the colony spaceship, she would have been shocked. Here she was at home in her kitchen on a hot summer afternoon, worried about how to squeeze *ounces* into her family's meager weight allowance for the trip—and the piano weighed more than half a *ton*.

Before she had married Walter Hatchell, she had been a working nurse-dietician, which made her of some use to the colony group destined for Planet C. But Walter, as the expedition's chief ecologist, was one of the most important cogs in the effort. His field was bionomics; the science of setting up the delicate balance of growing things to support human life on an alien world.

Walter was tied to his work at the White Sands base, hadn't been home to Seattle for a month during this crucial preparation period. This left Margaret with two children and several problems—the chief problem being that one of their children was a blind piano prodigy subject to black moods.

Margaret glanced at the clock on her kitchen wall: three-thirty, time to start dinner. She wheeled the micro-filming cabinet out of her kitchen and down the hall to the music room to get it out of her way. Coming into the familiar music room, she suddenly felt herself a hesitant stranger here—almost afraid to look too closely at her favorite wing-back chair, or at her son's concert grand piano, or at the rose pattern rug with afternoon sun streaming dappled gold across it.

It was a sensation of unreality—something like the feeling that had caught her the day the colonization board had notified them that the Hatchells had been chosen.

"We're going to be pioneers on Planet C," she whispered. But that made it no more real. She wondered if others among the 308 chosen colonists felt the same way about moving to a virgin world.

In the first days after the selection, when they all had been assembled at White Sands for preliminary instructions, a young astronomer had given a brief lecture.

"Your sun will be the star Giansar," he had said, and his voice had echoed in the barnlike hall as he pointed to the star on the chart. "In the tail of constellation Dragon. Your ship will travel sixteen years on sub-macro drive to make the passage from Earth. You already know, of course, that you will pass this time in sleep-freeze, and it'll feel just like one night to you. Giansar has a more orange light than our sun, and it's somewhat cooler. However, Planet C is closer to its sun, and this means your climate will average out warmer than we experience here."

Margaret had tried to follow the astronomer's words closely, just as she had done in the other lectures, but only the high points remained from all of them: orange light, warmer climate, less moisture, conserve weight in what you take along, seventy-five pounds of private luggage allowed for each adult, forty pounds for children to age fourteen...

Now, standing in her music room, Margaret felt that it must have been some other person who had listened to those lectures. *I should be excited and happy,* she thought. *Why do I feel so sad?*

At thirty-five Margaret Hatchell looked an indeterminate mid-twenties with a good figure, a graceful walk. Her brown hair carried reddish lights. The dark eyes, full mouth and firm chin combined to give an impression of hidden fire.

She rubbed a hand along the curved edge of the piano lid, felt the dent where the instrument had hit the door when they'd moved here to Seattle from Denver. *How long ago?* she asked herself. *Eight years? Yes ... it was the year after Grandfather Maurice Hatchell died ... after playing his final concert with this very piano.*

Through the open back windows she could hear her nine-year-old; Rita, filling the summer afternoon with a *discussion* of the strange insects to be discovered on Planet C. Rita's audience consisted of noncolonist playmates overawed by the fame of their companion. Rita was referring to their colony world as "Ritelle," the name she had submitted to the Survey and Exploration Service.

Margaret thought: *If they choose Rita's name we'll never hear the end of it ... literally!*

Realization that an entire planet could be named for her daughter sent Margaret's thoughts reeling off on a new tangent. She stood silently in the golden shadows of the music room, one hand on the piano that had belonged to her husband's father, Maurice Hatchell—*the* Maurice Hatchell of concert fame. For the first time, Margaret saw something of what the news service people had been telling her just that morning—that her family and all the other colonists were "chosen people," and for this reason their lives were of tremendous interest to everyone on Earth.

She noted her son's bat-eye radar box and its shoulder harness atop the piano. That meant David was somewhere around the house. He never used the box in the familiarity of his home where memory served in place of the sight he had lost. Seeing the box there prompted Margaret to move the microfilming cabinet aside where David would not trip over it if he came to the music room to practice. She listened, wondering if David was upstairs trying the lightweight electronic piano that had been built for him to take on the spaceship. There was no hint of his music in the soft sounds of the afternoon, but then he could have turned the sound low.

Thinking of David brought to her mind the boy's tantrum that had ended the newsfilm session just before lunch. The chief reporter—*What was his name? Bonaudi?*—had asked how they intended to dispose of the concert grand piano. She could still hear the awful discord as David had crashed his fists onto the keyboard. He had leaped up, dashed from the room—a dark little figure full of impotent fury.

Twelve is such an emotional age, she told herself.

Margaret decided that her sadness was the same as David's. *It's the parting with beloved possessions . . . it's the certain knowledge that we'll never see these things again . . . that all we'll have will be films and lightweight substitutes.* A sensation of terrible longing filled her. *Never again to feel the homely comfort of so many things that spell family tradition: the wing-back chair Walter and I bought when we furnished our first house, the sewing cabinet that great-great grandmother Chrisman brought from Ohio, the oversize double bed built specially to accommodate Walter's long frame . . .*

Abruptly, she turned away from the piano, went back to the kitchen. It was a white tile room with black fixtures, a laboratory kitchen cluttered now with debris of packing. Margaret pushed aside her recipe files on the counter beside the sink, being careful not to disturb the yellow scrap paper that marked where she'd stopped microfilming them. The sink was still piled with her mother's Spode china that was being readied for the space journey. Cups and saucers would weigh three and a half pounds in their special packing. Margaret resumed washing the dishes, seating them in the delicate webs of the lightweight box.

The wall phone beside her came alive to the operator's face. "Hatchell residence?"

Margaret lifted her dripping hands from the sink, nudged the call switch with her elbow. "Yes?"

"On your call to Walter Hatchell at White Sands: He is still not available. Shall I try again in twenty minutes?"

"Please do."

The operator's face faded from the screen. Margaret nudged off the switch, resumed washing. The newsfilm group had shot several pictures of her working at the sink that morning. She wondered how she and her family would appear on the film. The reporter had called Rita a "budding entomologist" and had referred to David as "the blind piano prodigy—one of the few victims of the *drum* virus brought back from the uninhabitable Planet A-4."

Rita came in from the yard. She was a lanky nine-year-old, a precocious extrovert with large blue eyes that looked on the world as her own private problem waiting to be solved.

"I am desperately ravenous," she announced. "When do we eat?"

"When it's ready," Margaret said. She noted with a twinge of exasperation that Rita had acquired a torn cobweb on her blonde hair and a smudge of dirt across her left cheek.

Why should a little girl be fascinated by bugs? Margaret asked herself. *It's not natural.* She said: "How'd you get the cobweb in your hair?"

"Oh, succotash!" Rita put a hand to her hair, rubbed away the offending web.

"How?" repeated Margaret.

"Mother! If one is to acquire knowledge of the insect world, one inevitably encounters such things! I am just dismayed that I tore the web."

"Well, I'm dismayed that you're filthy dirty. Go upstairs and wash so you'll look presentable when we get the call through to your father."

Rita turned away.

"And weigh yourself," called Margaret. "I have to turn in our family's weekly weight aggregate tomorrow."

Rita skipped out of the room.

Margaret felt certain she had heard a muttered "parents!" The sound of the child's footsteps diminished up the stairs. A door slammed on the second floor. Presently, Rita clattered back down the stairs. She ran into the kitchen. "Mother, you..."

"You haven't had time to get clean." Margaret spoke without turning.

"It's David," said Rita. "He looks peculiar and he says he doesn't want any supper."

Margaret turned from the sink, her features set to hide the gripping of fear. She knew from experience that Rita's "peculiar" could be anything... literally anything.

"How do you mean *peculiar*, dear?"

"He's so pale. He looks like he doesn't have any blood."

For some reason, this brought to Margaret's mind a memory picture of David at the age of three—a still figure in a hospital bed, flesh-colored feeding tube protruding from his nose, and his skin as pale as death with his breathing so quiet it was difficult to detect the chest movements.

She dried her hands on a dishtowel. "Let's go have a look. He's probably just tired."

David was stretched out on his bed, one arm thrown across his eyes. The shades were drawn and the room was in semi-darkness. It took a moment for Margaret's eyes to adjust to the gloom, and she thought: *Do the blind seek darkness because it gives them the advantage over those with sight?* She crossed to the bedside. The boy was a small, dark-haired figure—his father's coloring. The chin was narrow and the mouth a firm line like his grandfather Hatchell's. Right now he looked thin and defenseless... and Rita was right: terribly pale.

Margaret adopted her best hospital manner, lifted David's arm from his face, took his pulse.

"Don't you feel well, Davey?" she asked.

"I wish you wouldn't call me that," he said. "That's a baby name." His narrow features were set, sullen.

She took a short, quick breath. "Sorry. I forgot. Rita says you don't want any supper."

Rita came in from the hallway. "He looks positively infirm, mother."

"Does she have to keep pestering me?" demanded David.

"I thought I heard the phone chime," said Margaret. "Will you go check, Rita?"

"You're being offensively obvious," said Rita. "If you don't want me in here, just say so." She turned, walked slowly out of the room.

"Do you hurt someplace, David?" asked Margaret.

"I just feel tired," he muttered. "Why can't you leave me alone?"

Margaret stared down at him—caught as she had been so many times by his resemblance to his grandfather Hatchell. It was a resemblance made uncanny when the boy sat down at the piano: that same intense vibrancy . . . the same musical genius that had made Hatchell a name to fill concert halls. And she thought: *Perhaps it's because the Steinway belonged to his grandfather that he feels so badly about parting with it. The piano's a symbol of the talent he inherited.*

She patted her son's hand, sat down beside him on the bed. "Is something troubling you, David?"

His features contorted, and he whirled away from her. "Go away!" He muttered, "Just leave me alone!"

Margaret sighed, felt inadequate. She wished desperately that Walter were not tied to the work at the launching site. She felt a deep need of her husband at this moment. Another sigh escaped her. She knew what she had to do. The rules for colonists were explicit: any symptoms at all—even superficial ones—were to get a doctor's attention. She gave David's hand a final pat, went downstairs to the hall phone, called Dr. Mowery, the medic cleared for colonists in the Seattle area. He said he'd be out in about an hour.

Rita came in as Margaret was completing the call, asked: "Is David going to die?"

All the tenseness and aggravation of the day came out in Margaret's reply: "Don't be such a beastly little fool!"

Immediately, she was sorry. She stopped, gathered Rita to her, crooned apologies.

"It's all right, mother," Rita said. "I realize you're overwrought."

Filled with contriteness, Margaret went into the kitchen, prepared her daughter's favorite food: tuna-fish sandwiches and chocolate milkshakes.

I'm getting too jumpy, thought Margaret. *David's not really sick. It's the hot weather we've had lately and all this tension of getting ready to go.* She took a sandwich and milkshake up to the boy, but he still refused to eat. And there was such a pallid sense of defeat about him. A story about someone who had died merely because he gave up the will to live entered her mind and refused to be shaken.

She made her way back down to the kitchen, dabbled at the work there until the call to Walter went through. Her husband's craggy features and deep voice brought the calmness she had been seeking all day.

"I miss you so much, darling," she said.

"It won't be much longer," he said. He smiled, leaned to one side, exposing the impersonal wall of a pay booth behind him. He looked tired. "How's my family?"

She told him about David, saw the worry creep into his eyes. "Is the doctor there yet?" he asked.

"He's late. He should've been here by six and it's half past."

"Probably busy as a bird dog," he said. "It doesn't really sound as though David's actually sick. Just upset more likely ... the excitement of leaving. Call me as soon as the doctor tells you what's wrong."

"I will. I think he's just upset over leaving your father's piano behind."

"David knows it's not that we want to leave these things." A grin brightened his features. "Lord! Imagine taking that thing on the ship! Dr. Charlesworthy would flip!"

She smiled. "Why don't you suggest it?"

"You're trying to get me in trouble with the old man!"

"How're things going, dear?" she asked.

His face sobered. He sighed. "I had to talk to poor Smythe's widow today. She came out to pick up his things. It was rather trying. The old man was afraid she might still want to come along ... but no..." He shook his head.

"Do you have his replacement yet?"

"Yes. Young fellow from Lebanon. Name's Teryk. His wife's a cute little thing." Walter looked past her at the kitchen. "Looks like you're getting things in order. Decided yet what you're taking?"

"Some of the things. I wish I could make decisions like you do. I've definitely decided to take mother's Spode china cups and saucers and the sterling silver... for Rita when she gets married... and the Utrillo your father bought in Lisbon... and I've weeded my jewelry down to about two pounds of basics ... and I'm not going to worry about cosmetics since you say we can make our own when we..."

Rita ran into the kitchen, pushed in beside Margaret. "Hello, father."

"Hi, punkin head. What've you been up to?"

"I've been cataloging my insect collection and filling it out. Mother's going to help me film the glassed-in specimens as soon as I'm ready. They're so *heavy!*"

"How'd you wangle her agreement to get that close to your bugs?"

"Father! They're not bugs; they're entomological specimens."

"They're bugs to your mother, honey. Now, if..."

"Father! There's one other thing. I told Raul—he's the new boy down the block—I told him today about those hawklike insects on Ritelle that..."

"They're not insects, honey; they're adapted amphibians."

She frowned. "But Spencer's report distinctly says that they're chitinous and they..."

"Whoa down! You should've read the technical report, the one I showed you when I was home last month. These critters have a copper-base metabolism, and they're closely allied to a common fish on the planet."

"Oh... Do you think I'd better branch out into marine biology?"

"One thing at a time, honey. Now..."

"Have we set the departure date yet, father? I can hardly wait to get to work there."

"It's not definite yet, honey. But we should know any day. Now, let me talk to your mother."

Rita pulled back.

Walter smiled at his wife. "What're we raising there?"

"I wish I knew."

"Look... don't worry about David. It's been nine years since ... since he recovered from that virus. All the tests show that he was completely cured."

And she thought: *Yes... cured—except for the little detail of no optic nerves.* She forced a smile. "I know you're probably right.

It'll turn out to be something simple... and we'll laugh about this when..." The front doorbell chimed. "That's probably the doctor now."

"Call me when you find out," said Walter.

Margaret heard Rita's footsteps running toward the door.

"I'll sign off, sweet," she said. She blew a kiss to her husband. "I love you."

Walter held up two fingers in a victory sign, winked. "Same here. Chin up."

They broke the connection.

Dr. Mowery was a gray-haired, flint-faced bustler—addicted to the nodding head and the knowing (but unintelligible) murmur. One big hand held a gray instrument bag. He had a pat on the head for Rita, a firm handshake for Margaret, and he insisted on seeing David alone.

"Mothers just clutter up the atmosphere for a doctor," he said, and he winked to take the sting from his words.

Margaret sent Rita to her room, waited in the upstairs hall. There were 106 flower panels on the wallpaper between the door to David's room and the corner of the hall. She was moving on to count the rungs in the balustrade when the doctor emerged from David's room. He closed the door softly behind him, nodding to himself.

She waited.

"Mmmmmm-hmmmmm," said Dr. Mowery. He cleared his throat.

"Is it anything serious?" asked Margaret.

"Not sure." He walked to the head of the stairs. "How long's the boy been acting like that... listless and upset?"

Margaret swallowed a lump in her throat. "He's been acting differently ever since they delivered the electronic piano... the one that's going to substitute for his grandfather's Steinway. Is that what you mean?"

"Differently?"

"Rebellious, short-tempered... wanting to be alone."

"I suppose there's not the remotest possibility of his taking the big piano," said the doctor.

"Oh, my goodness... it must weigh all of a thousand pounds," said Margaret. "The electronic instrument is only twenty-one pounds." She cleared her throat. "Is it worry about the piano, doctor?"

"Possibly." Dr. Mowery nodded, took the first step down the stairs. "It doesn't appear to be anything organic that my instruments can find. I'm going to have Dr. Linquist and some others look in on David tonight. Dr. Linquist is our chief psychiatrist. Meanwhile, I'd try to get the boy to eat something."

She crossed to Dr. Mowery's side at the head of the stairs. "I'm a nurse," she said. "You can tell me if it's something serious that..."

He shifted his bag to his right hand, patted her arm. "Now don't you worry, my dear. The colonization group is fortunate to have a musical genius in its roster. We're not going to let anything happen to him."

Dr. Linquist had the round face and cynical eyes of a fallen cherub. His voice surged out of him in waves that flowed over the listener and towed him under. The psychiatrist and colleagues were with David until almost ten P.M.. Then Dr. Linquist dismissed the others, came down to the music room where Margaret was waiting. He sat on the piano bench, hands gripping the lip of wood beside him.

Margaret occupied her wing-back chair—the one piece of furniture she knew she would miss more than any other thing in the house. Long usage had worn contours in the chair that exactly complemented her, and its rough fabric upholstery held the soothing texture of familiarity.

The night outside the screened windows carried a sonorous sawing of crickets.

"We can say definitely that it's a fixation about this piano," said Linquist. He slapped his palms onto his knees. "Have you ever thought of leaving the boy behind?"

"Doctor!"

"Thought I'd ask."

"Is it *that* serious with Davey?" she asked. "I mean, after all ...we're all of us going to miss things." She rubbed the chair arm. "But good heavens, we..."

"I'm not much of a musician," said Linquist. "I'm told by the critics, though, that your boy already has concert stature ...that he's being deliberately held back now to avoid piling confusion on confusion...I mean with your leaving so soon and all." The psychiatrist tugged at his lower lip. "You realize, of course, that your boy worships the memory of his grandfather?"

"He's seen all the old stereos, listened to all the tapes," said Margaret. "He was only four when grandfather died, but David remembers everything they ever did together. It was..." She shrugged.

"David has identified his inherited talent with his inherited piano," said Linquist. "He..."

"But pianos can be replaced," said Margaret. "Couldn't one of our colony carpenters or cabinetmakers duplicate..."

"Ah, no," said Linquist. "Not duplicate. It would not be the piano of Maurice Hatchell. You see, your boy is overly conscious that he inherited musical genius from his grandfather...just as he inherited the piano. He's tied the two together. He believes that if—not consciously, you understand? But he believes, nonetheless, that if he loses the piano he loses the talent. And there you have a problem more critical than you might suspect."

She shook her head. "But children get over these..."

"He's not a child, Mrs. Hatchell. Perhaps I should say he's not *just* a child. He is that sensitive thing we call *genius*. This is a delicate state that goes sour all too easily."

She felt her mouth go dry. "What are you trying to tell me?"

"I don't want to alarm you without cause, Mrs. Hatchell. But the truth is—and this is the opinion of all of us—that if your boy is deprived of his musical outlet...well, he could die."

She paled. "Oh, no! He..."

"Such things happen, Mrs. Hatchell. There are therapeutic procedures we could use, of course, but I'm not sure we have the time. They're expecting to set your departure date momentarily. Therapy *could* take years."

"But David's..."

"David is precocious and overemotional," said Linquist. "He's invested much more than is healthy in his music. His blindness accounts for part of that, but over and above the fact of blindness there's his need for musical expression. In a genius such as David this is akin to one of the basic drives of life itself."

"We just couldn't. You don't understand. We're such a close family that we..."

"Then perhaps you should step aside, let some other family have your..."

"It would kill Walter...my husband," she said. "He's lived

for this chance." She shook her head. "Anyway, I'm not sure we could back out now. Walter's assistant, Dr. Smythe, was killed in a copter crash near Phoenix last week. They already have a replacement, but I'm sure you know how important Walter's function is to the colony's success."

Linquist nodded. "I read about Smythe, but I failed to make the obvious association here."

"I'm not important to the colony," she said. "Nor the children, really. But the ecologists—the success of our entire effort hangs on them. Without Walter..."

"We'll just have to solve it then," he said. He got to his feet. "We'll be back tomorrow for another look at David, Mrs. Hatchell. Dr. Mowery made him take some amino pills and then gave him a sedative. He should sleep right through the night. If there're any complications—although there shouldn't be—you can reach me at this number." He pulled a card from his wallet, gave it to her. "It is too bad about the weight problem. I'm sure it would solve everything if he could just take this monster with him." Linquist patted the piano lid. "Well...good night."

When Linquist had gone, Margaret leaned against the front door, pressed her forehead against the cool wood. "No," she whispered. "No...no...no..." Presently, she went to the living room phone, placed a call to Walter. It was ten-twenty P.M. The call went right through, proving that he had been waiting for it. Margaret noted the deep worry creases in her husband's forehead, longed to reach out, touch them, smooth them.

"What is it, Margaret?" he asked. "Is David all right?"

"Dear, it's..." she swallowed. "It's about the piano. Your father's Steinway."

"The *piano?*"

"The doctors have been here all evening up to a few minutes ago examining David. The psychiatrist says if David loses the piano he may lose his...his music...his...and if he loses that he could die."

Walter blinked. "Over a piano? Oh, now, surely there must be some..."

She told him everything Dr. Linquist had said.

"The boy's so much like dad," said Walter. "Dad once threw the philharmonic into an uproar because his piano bench was a half inch too low. Good Lord! I...What'd Linquist say we could do?"

"He said if we could take the piano it'd solve..."

"That concert grand? The damn thing must weigh over a thousand pounds. That's more than three times what our whole family is allowed in private luggage."

"I know. I'm almost at my wits' end. All this turmoil of deciding what's to go and now...David."

"To go!" barked Walter. "Good Lord! What with worrying about David I almost forgot: Our departure date was set just tonight." He glanced at his watch. "Blastoff is fourteen days and six hours away—give or take a few minutes. The old man said..."

"Fourteen days!"

"Yes, but *you* have only eight days. That's the colony assembly date. The pickup crews will be around to get your luggage on the afternoon of..."

"Walter! I haven't even decided what to..." She broke off. "I was sure we had at least another month. You told me yourself that we..."

"I know. But fuel production came out ahead of schedule, and the long-range weather forecast is favorable. And it's part of the psychology not to drag out leavetaking. This way the shock of abruptness cuts everything clean."

"But what're we going to do about David?" She chewed her lower lip.

"Is he awake?"

"I don't think so. They gave him a sedative."

Walter frowned. "I want to talk to David first thing in the morning. I've been neglecting him lately because of all the work here, but..."

"He understands, Walter."

"I'm sure he does, but I want to see him for myself. I only wish I had the time to come home, but things are pretty frantic here right now." He shook his head. "I just don't see how that diagnosis could be right. All this fuss over a piano!"

"Walter...you're not attached to things. With you it's people and ideas." She lowered her eyes, fought back tears. "But some people can grow to love inanimate objects, too...things that mean comfort and security." She swallowed.

He shook his head. "I guess I just don't understand. We'll work out something, though. Depend on it."

Margaret forced a smile. "I know you will, dear."

"Now that we have the departure date it may blow the whole thing right out of his mind," Walter said.

"Perhaps you're right."

He glanced at his wristwatch. "I have to sign off now. Got some experiments running." He winked. "I miss my family."

"So do I," she whispered.

In the morning there was a call from Prester Charlesworthy, colony director. His face came onto the phone screen in Margaret's kitchen just as she finished dishing up breakfast for Rita. David was still in bed. And Margaret had told neither of them about the departure date.

Charlesworthy was a man of skinny features, nervous mannerisms. There was a bumpkin look about him until you saw the incisive stare of the pale blue eyes.

"Forgive me for bothering you like this, Mrs. Hatchell," he said.

She forced herself to calmness. "No bother. We were expecting a call from Walter this morning. I thought this was it."

"I've just been talking to Walter," said Charlesworthy. "He's been telling me about David. We had a report first thing this morning from Dr. Linquist."

After a sleepless night with periodic cat-footed trips to look in on David, Margaret felt her nerves jangling out to frayed helplessness. She was primed to leap at the worst interpretations that entered her mind. "You're putting us out of the colony group!" she blurted. "You're getting another ecologist to . . ."

"Oh, no, Mrs. Hatchell!" Dr. Charlesworthy took a deep breath. "I know it must seem odd—my calling you like this—but our little group will be alone on a very alien world, very dependent upon each other for almost ten years—until the next ship gets there. We've got to work together on everything. I sincerely want to help you."

"I'm sorry," she said. "But I didn't get much sleep last night."

"I quite understand. Believe me, I'd like nothing better than to be able to send Walter home to you right now." Charlesworthy shrugged. "But that's out of the question. With poor Smythe dead there's a terribly heavy load on Walter's shoulders. Without him, we might even have to abort this attempt."

Margaret wet her lips with her tongue. "Dr. Charlesworthy, is there any possibility at all that we could . . . I mean . . . the piano—take it on the ship?"

"Mrs. Hatchell!" Charlesworthy pulled back from his screen. "It must weigh half a ton!"

She sighed. "I called the moving company first thing this morning—the company that moved the piano here into this house. They checked their records. It weighs fourteen hundred and eight pounds."

"Out of the question! Why...we've had to eliminate high priority technical equipment that doesn't weigh half that much!"

"I guess I'm desperate," she said. "I keep thinking over what Dr. Linquist said about David dying if..."

"Of course," said Charleworthy. "That's why I called you. I want you to know what we've done. We dispatched Hector Torres to the Steinway factory this morning. Hector is one of the cabinetmakers we'll have in the colony. The Steinway people have generously consented to show him all of their construction secrets so Hector can build an exact duplicate of this piano—correct in all details. Philip Jackson, one of our metallurgists, will be following Hector this afternoon for the same reason. I'm sure that when you tell David this it'll completely resolve all his fears."

Margaret blinked back tears. "Dr. Charlesworthy...I don't know how to thank you."

"Don't thank me at all, my dear. We're a team...we pull together." He nodded. "Now, one other thing: a favor you can do for me."

"Certainly."

"Try not to worry Walter too much this week if you can. He's discovered a mutation that may permit us to cross earth plants with ones already growing on Planet C. He's running final tests this week with dirt samples from C. These are crucial tests, Mrs. Hatchell. They could cut several years off the initial stage of setting up a new life-cycle balance."

"Of course," she said. "I'm sorry that I..."

"Don't you be sorry. And don't you worry. The boy's only twelve. Time heals all things."

"I'm sure it'll work out," she said.

"Excellent," said Charlesworthy. "That's the spirit. Now, you call on me for any help you may need...day or night. We're a team. We have to pull together."

They broke the connection. Margaret stood in front of the phone, facing the blank screen.

Rita spoke from the kitchen table behind her. "What'd he say about the departure date?"

"It's been set, dear." Margaret turned. "We have to be with Daddy at White Sands in eight days."

"Whooopeee!" Rita leaped to her feet, upsetting her breakfast dishes. "We're going! We're going!"

"Rita!"

But Rita was already dashing out of the room, out of the house. Her "Eight days!" echoed back from the front hall.

Margaret stepped to the kitchen door. "Rita!"

Her daughter ran back down the hall. "I'm going to tell the kids!"

"You will calm down right now. You're making enough noise to..."

"I heard her." It was David at the head of the stairs. He came down slowly, guiding himself by the bannister. His face looked white as eggshell, and there was a dragging hesitancy to his steps.

Margaret took a deep breath, told him about Dr. Charlesworthy's plan to replace the piano.

David stopped two steps above her, head down. When she had finished, he said: "It won't be the same." He stepped around her, went into the music room. There was a slumped finality to his figure.

Margaret whirled back into the kitchen. Angry determination flared in her. She heard Rita's slow footsteps following, spoke without turning: "Rita, how much weight can you cut from your luggage?"

"Mother!"

"We're going to take that piano!" snapped Margaret.

Rita came up beside her. "But our whole family gets to take only two hundred thirty pounds! We couldn't possibly..."

"There are 308 of us in this colonization group," said Margaret. "Every adult is allowed seventy-five pounds, every child under fourteen years gets forty pounds." She found her kitchen scratch pad, scribbled figures on it. "If each person donates only four pounds and twelve ounces we can take that piano!" Before she could change her mind, she whirled to the drainboard, swept the package with her mother's Spode china cups and saucers into the discard box. "There! A gift for the people who bought our house! And that's three and a half pounds of it!"

Then she began to cry.

Rita sobered. "I'll leave my insect specimens," she whispered. Then she buried her head in her mother's dress, and she too was sobbing.

"What're you two crying about?" David spoke from the kitchen doorway, his bat-eye box strapped to his shoulders. His small features were drawn into a pinched look of misery.

Margaret dried her eyes. "Davey...David, we're going to try to take your piano with us."

His chin lifted, his features momentarily relaxed, then the tight unhappiness returned. "Sure. They'll just dump out some of dad's seeds and a few tools and scientific instruments for my..."

"There's another way," she said.

"What other way?" His voice was fighting against a hope that might be smashed.

Margaret explained her plan.

"Go begging?" he asked. "Asking people to give up their own..."

"David, this will be a barren and cold new world we're going to colonize—very few comforts, drab issue clothing—almost no refinements or the things we think of as belonging to a civilized culture. A real honest-to-goodness earth piano and the...man to play it would help. It'd help our morale, and keep down the homesickness that's sure to come."

His sightless eyes appeared to stare at her for a long moment of silence; then he said: "That would be a terrible responsibility for me."

She felt pride in her son flow all through her, said: "I'm glad you see it that way."

The small booklet of regulations and advice handed out at the first assembly in White Sands carried names and addresses of all the colonists. Margaret started at the top of the list, called Selma Atkins of Little Rock, wife of the expedition's head zoologist.

Mrs. Atkins was a dark little button of a woman with flaming hair and a fizzing personality. She turned out to be a born conspirator. Before Margaret had finished explaining the problem, Selma Atkins was volunteering to head a phone committee. She jotted down names of prospects, said: "Even if we get the weight allowance, how'll we get the thing aboard?"

Margaret looked puzzled. "What's wrong with just showing

that we have the weight allowance, and handing the piano over to the people who pack things on the ship?"

"Charlesworthy'd never go for it, honey. He's livid at the amount of equipment that's had to be passed over because of the weight problem. He'd take one look at one thousand four hundred and eight pounds of piano and say: 'That'll be a spare atomic generation kit!' My husband says he's had to drill holes in packing boxes to save ounces!"

"But how could we smuggle..."

Selma snapped her fingers. "I know! Ozzy Lucan!"

"Lucan?"

"The ship's steward," said Selma. "You know: the big horse of a man with red hair. He spoke at one of the meetings on— you know—all about how to conserve weight in packing and how to use the special containers."

"Oh, yes," said Margaret. "What about him?"

"He's married to my third cousin Betty's oldest daughter. Nothing like a little family pressure. I'll work on it."

"Wouldn't he be likely to go directly to Charlesworthy with it?" asked Margaret.

"Hah!" barked Selma. "You don't know Betty's side of our family!"

Dr. Linquist arrived in the middle of the morning, two consultant psychiatrists in tow. They spent an hour with David, came down to the kitchen where Margaret and Rita were finishing the microfilming of the recipe files. David followed them, stood in the doorway.

"The boy's apparently tougher than I realized," said Linquist. "Are you sure he hasn't been told he can take that piano? I hope you haven't been misleading him to make him feel better."

David frowned.

Margaret said: "Dr. Charlesworthy refused to take the piano when I asked him. However, he's sent two experts to the Steinway factory so we'll be sure of an exact duplicate."

Linquist turned to David. "And that's all right with you, David?"

David hesitated, then: "I understand about the weight."

"Well, I guess you're growing up," said Linquist.

When the psychiatrists had gone, Rita turned on Margaret. "Mother! You lied to them!"

"No she didn't," said David. "She told the exact truth."

"But not all of it," said Margaret.

"That's just the same as lying," said Rita.

"Oh, stop it!" snapped Margaret. Then: "David, are you sure you want to leave your braille texts?"

"Yes. That's sixteen pounds. We've got the braille punch kit and the braille typewriter; I can type new copies of everything I'll need if Rita will read to me."

By three o'clock that afternoon they had Chief Steward Oswald Lucan's reluctant agreement to smuggle the piano aboard if they could get the weight allowance precise to the ounce. But Lucan's parting words were: "Don't let the old man get wind of this. He's boiling about the equipment we've had to cut out."

At seven-thirty, Margaret added the first day's weight donations: sixty-one commitments for a total of two hundred and seven pounds and seven ounces. *Not enough from each person, she told herself. But I can't blame them. We're all tied to our possessions. It's so hard to part with all the little things that link us with the past and with Earth. We've got to find more weight somewhere.* She cast about in her own mind for things to discard, knew a sense of futility at the few pounds she had at her disposal.

By ten o'clock on the morning of the third day they had 554 pounds and 8 ounces from 160 of their fellow colonists. They also had an even twenty violent rejections. The tension of fear that one of these twenty might give away their conspiracy was beginning to tell on Margaret.

David, too, was sinking back into gloom. He sat on the piano bench in the music room, Margaret behind him in her favorite chair. One of David's hands gently caressed the keys that Maurice Hatchell had brought to such crashing life.

"We're getting less than four pounds per person, aren't we?" asked David.

Margaret rubbed her cheek. "Yes."

A gentle chord came from the piano. "We aren't going to make it," said David. A fluid rippling of music lifted in the room. "I'm not sure we have the right to ask this of people anyway. They're giving up so much already, and then we..."

"Hush, Davey."

He let the baby name pass, coaxed a floating passage of Debussy from the keys.

Margaret put her hands to her eyes, cried silently with fatigue and frustration. But the tears coming from David's fingers on the piano went deeper.

Presently, he stood up, walked slowly out of the room, up the stairs. She heard his bedroom door close softly. The lack of violence in his actions cut her like a knife.

The phone chime broke Margaret from her blue reverie. She took the call on the portable in the hall. Selma Atkins's features came onto the screen, wide-eyed, subdued.

"Ozzy just called me," she blurted. "Somebody snitched to Charlesworthy this morning."

Margaret put a hand over her mouth.

"Did you tell your husband what we were doing?" asked Selma.

"No." Margaret shook her head. "I was going to and then I got afraid of what he'd say. He and Charlesworthy are very close friends, you know."

"You mean he'd peach on his own wife?"

"Oh, no, but he might..."

"Well, he's on the carpet now," said Selma. "Ozzy says the whole base is jumping. He was shouting and banging his hands on the desk at Walter and..."

"Charlesworthy?"

"Who else? I called to warn you. He..."

"But what'll we do?" asked Margaret.

"We run for cover, honey. We fall back and regroup. Call me as soon as you've talked to him. Maybe we can think of a new plan."

"We've contributions from more than half the colonists," said Margaret. "That means we've more than half of them on our side to begin..."

"Right now the colony organization is a dictatorship, not a democracy," said Selma. "But I'll be thinking about it. Bye now."

David came up behind her as she was breaking the connection. "I heard," he said. "That finishes us, doesn't it?"

The phone chimed before she could answer him. She flipped the switch. Walter's face came onto the screen. He looked haggard, the craggy lines more pronounced.

"Margaret," he said. "I'm calling from Dr. Charlesworthy's office." He took a deep breath. "Why didn't you come to me about this? I could've told you how foolish it was!"

"That's why!" she said.

"But smuggling a piano onto the ship! Of all the..."

"I was thinking of Davey!" she snapped.

"Good Lord, I know it! But..."

"When the doctors said he might die if he lost his..."

"But Margaret, a thousand-pound piano!"

"Fourteen hundred and eight pounds," she corrected him.

"Let's not argue, darling," he said. "I admire your guts... and I love you, but I can't let you endanger the social solidarity of the colony group. . ." he shook his head, "not even for David."

"Even if it kills your own son?" she demanded.

"I'm not about to kill my son," he said. "I'm an ecologist, remember? It's my job to keep us alive... as a group *and* singly! And I..."

"Dad's right," said David. He moved up beside Margaret.

"I didn't know you were there, son," said Walter.

"It's all right, Dad."

"Just a moment, please." It was Charlesworthy, pushing in beside Walter. "I want to know how much weight allowance you've been promised."

"Why?" asked Margaret. "So you can figure how many more scientific *toys* to take along?"

"I want to know how close you are to success in your little project," he said.

"Five hundred and fifty-four pounds and eight ounces," she said. "Contributions from one hundred and sixty people!"

Charlesworthy pursed his lips. "Just about one-third of what you need," he said. "And at this rate you wouldn't get enough. If you had any chance of success I'd almost be inclined to say go ahead, but you can see for yourself that..."

"I have an idea," said David.

Charlesworthy looked at him. "You're David?"

"Yes, sir."

"What's your idea?"

"How much would the harp and keyboard from my piano weigh? You have people at the factory..."

"You mean take just that much of your piano?" asked Charlesworthy.

"Yes, sir. It wouldn't be the same... it'd be better. It would have roots in both worlds—part of the piano from Earth and part from Planet C."

"Darned if I don't like the idea," said Charlesworthy. He

turned. "Walter, call Phil Jackson at the Steinway plant. Find out how much that portion of the piano would weigh."

Walter left the field of the screen. The others waited. Presently, Walter returned, said: "Five hundred and sixty-two pounds, more or less. Hector Torres was on the line, too. He said he's sure he can duplicate the rest of the piano exactly."

Charlesworthy smiled. "That's it, then! I'm out of my mind . . . we need so many other things with us so desperately. But maybe we need this too: for morale."

"With the right morale we can make anything else we may need," said Walter.

Margaret found a scratch pad in the phone drawer, scribbled figures on it. She looked up: "I'll get busy right now and find a way to meet the extra few pounds we'll need to . . ."

"How much more?" asked Charlesworthy.

Margaret looked down at her scratch pad. "Seven pounds and eight ounces."

Charlesworthy took a deep breath. "While I'm still out of my mind, let me make another gesture: Mrs. Charlesworthy and I will contribute seven pounds and eight ounces to the cultural future of our new home."

DEATH
OF
A
CITY

t was such a beautiful city, Bjska thought. An observer's eyes could not avoid the overwhelming beauty. As the City Doctor called to treat the city, Bjska found the beauty heartbreaking. He found his thoughts drawn again and again to the individuals who called this place *home*, two hundred and forty-one thousand humans who now faced the prospect of homeless lives.

Bjska stared across open water at the city from the wooded peninsula that protected the inner harbor. The low light of late afternoon cast a ruddy glow on the scene. His eyes probed for flaws, but from this distance not even the tastefully applied patches could be seen.

Why was I chosen for this? he asked himself. Then: *If the damn fools had only built an ugly city!*

Immediately, he rejected this thought. It made as much sense as to ask why Mieri, the intern who stood near the ornithopter behind him, personified such feminine beauty. Such things happened. It was the task of a City Doctor to recognize inescapable facts and put them in their proper context.

Bjska continued to study the city, striving for the objective/subjective synthesis that his calling demanded. The city's builders had grafted their ideas onto the hills below the mountains with such a profound emotional sense of harmony that no trick of the eye could reject their creation. Against a backdrop of snow peaks and forests, the builders had rightly said: "The vertical threatens a man; it puts danger above him. A man cannot relax and achieve human balance in a vertical setting."

Thus, they had built a city whose very *rightness* might condemn it. Had they even suspected what they had created? Bjska thought it unlikely.

How could the builders have missed it? he asked himself.

Even as the question appeared in his mind, he put it down. It served no purpose for him to cry out against the circumstances that said *he* must make this decision. The City Doctor was here on behalf of the species, a representative of all humans together. He must act for *them*.

The city presented an appearance of awesome solidity that Bjska knew to be false. It could be destroyed quite easily. He had but to give the order, certifying his decision with his official seal. People would rage against fate, but they would obey. Families would be broken and scattered. The name of this place would be erased from all but the City Doctors' records. The natural landscape would be restored and there would remain no visible sign that a city such as this one had stood here. In time, only the builders of cities would remember this place, and that as a warning.

Behind him, Mieri cleared her throat. She would speak out soon, Bjska realized. She had been patient, but they were past the boundaries of patience. He resisted an impulse to turn and feast his eyes upon her beauty as a change from the cityscape. That was the problem. There would be so little change in trading one prospect of beauty for another.

While Mieri fidgeted he continued to delay. Was there no alternative? Mieri had left her own pleadings unvoiced, but Bjska had heard them in every word she uttered. This was Mieri's own city. She had been born here—beauty born in beauty. Where was the medical *point of entry* in this city?

Bjska allowed his frustration to escape in a sigh.

The city played its horizontal lines across the hills with an architecture that opened outward, that expanded, that condemned no human within its limits to a containerized existence. The choice of where every element should stand had been made with masterful awareness of the human psyche. Where things that grew without man's interference should grow, there they were. Where structures would amplify existing forms, there stood the required structures . . . precisely! Every expectation of the human senses had been met. And it was in this very conformity to human demands that the cancerous flaw arose.

Bjska shook his head sadly. *If conformity were the definition of artistic survival . . .*

As he had anticipated, Mieri moved closer behind him, said, "Sometimes when I see it from out here I think my city is too beautiful. Words choke in my throat. I long for words to describe it and there are none." Her voice rang with musical softness in the quiet evening air.

Bjska thought: *My city!* She had said it and not heard herself saying it. A City Doctor could have no city.

He said, "Many have tried and failed. Even photographs fall short of the reality. A supreme holopaint artist might capture it, but only for a fleeting moment."

"I wish every human in the universe could see my city," Mieri said.

"I do not share that wish," Bjska said. And he wondered if this bald statement was enough to shock her into the required state of awareness. She wanted to be a City Doctor? Let her stretch into the inner world as well as the outer.

He sensed her weighing his words. Beauty could play such a vitalizing role in human life that the intellect tended to overlook its devitalizing possibilities. If beauty could not be ignored, was that not indiscreet? The fault was blatancy. There was something demandingly immodest about the way this city gilded its hills, adding dimension to the peaks behind it. One saw the city and did *not* see it.

Mieri knew this! Bjska told himself. She knew it as she knew that Bjska loved her. Why not? Most men who saw her loved her and desired her. Why had she no lovers then? And why had *her* city no immigrants? Had she ever put both of these questions to herself, setting them in tension against each other? It was the sort of thing a City Doctor must do. The species knew the source of its creative energy. The Second Law made the source plain.

He said, "Mieri, why does a City Doctor have such awesome powers? I can have the memories of whole populations obliterated, selectively erased, or have individuals thus treated. I can even cause death. You aspire to such powers. Why do we have them?"

She said, "To make sure that the species faces up to Infinity."

He shook his head sadly. A rote answer! She gave him a rote answer when he'd demanded personal insight!

The awareness that had made Bjska a City Doctor pervaded him. Knowledge out of his most ancient past told him the builders of this city had succeeded too well. Call it *chance* or *fate*. It was akin to the genetic *moment* that had produced Mieri's compelling beauty—the red-gold hair, the green eyes, the female proportions applied with such exactitude that a male might feast his senses, but never invest his flesh. There existed a creative peak that alarmed the flesh. Bjska stood securely in his own stolid, round-faced ugliness, knowing this thing. Mieri must find that inner warmth that spoke with chemical insistence of latent wrinkles and aging.

What would Mieri do if her city died before its time?

If she was ever to be a City Doctor, she must be made to understand this lesson of the flesh *and* the spirit.

He said, "Do you imagine there's a city more beautiful in the entire world?"

She thought she heard bantering in his voice and wondered: *Is he teasing?* It was a shocking thought. City Doctors might joke to keep their own sanity in balance, but at such a time as this ... with so much at stake ...

"There must be a city more beautiful somewhere," she said. "Where?"

She took a deep breath to put down profound disquiet. "Are you making fun of my city?" she demanded. "How can you? It's a sick city and you know it!" She felt her lips quiver, moisture at the corners of her eyes. She experienced both fear and shame. She loved her city, but it was sick. The outbreaks of vandalism, the lack of creativity here, the departure of the best people, the blind violence from random elements of its citizenry when they moved to other settings. All had been traced back here. The sickness had its focus in her city. That was why a City Doctor had come. She had worked hard to have that doctor be Bjska, her old teacher, and more than the honor of working with him once more had been involved. She had felt a personal need.

"I'm sorry," Bjska said. "This is the city where you were born and I understand your concern. I am the teacher now. I wish to share my thought processes with you. What is it we must do most carefully as we diagnose?"

She looked across the water at the city, feeling the coolness of onrushing nightfall, seeing the lights begin to wink on, the softness of low structures and blended greenery, the pastel colors and harmony. Her senses demanded more than this, however. You did not diagnose a city just by its appearance. Why had Bjska brought her here? The condition of a city's inhabitants represented a major concern. Transient individuals, always tenants on the land, were the single moving cells. Only the species owned land, owned cities. A City Doctor was hired by the species. In effect, he diagnosed the species. They told him the imprint of the setting. It had been a gigantic step toward Infinity when the species had recognized that settings might contribute to its illnesses.

"Are you diagnosing me to diagnose the city?" she asked.

"I diagnose my own reactions," he said. "I find myself loving your city with a fierce protectiveness that at the same time repels me and insists that I scar this place. Having seen this city, I will try to find pieces of it in every other city, but I will not know what I seek because I have not really experienced this city. Every other city will be found wanting and I will not know what it wants."

Mieri felt suddenly threatened and wondered: *What is he trying to tell me?* There was threat in Bjska's words. It was as though he had been transformed abruptly into a dirty old man who demanded obscene things of her, who affronted her. He was dangerous! Her city was too good for him! He was a square, ugly little man who offended her city whenever he entered it.

Even as these reactions pulsed through her awareness, she sensed her training taking its dominant place. She had been educated to become a City Doctor. The species relied on her. Humans had given her a matrix by which to keep them on the track through Infinity.

"This is the most beautiful city man has ever conceived," she whispered, and she felt the betrayal in every word coming from her lips. Surely there were more beautiful places in their world? Surely there were!

"If it were only that," Bjska said. "If it were only the conception of beauty in itself."

She nodded to herself, the awareness unfolding. The Second Law told humans that absolutes were lethal. They provided no potential, no *differences in tension* that the species could employ as energy sources. Change and growth represented necessities for things that lived. A species lived. Humans dared conceive of beauty only in the presence of change. Humans prevented wars, but not *absolutely*. Humans defined crimes and judgments, but only in that fluid context of change.

"I love the city," she said.

No longer *my* city, Bjska thought. Good. He said, "It's right to love the place where you were born. That's the way it is with humans. I love a little community on a muddy river, a place called Eeltown. Sometimes when the filters aren't working properly, it smells of pulpwood and the digesters. The river is muddy because we farm its watershed for trees. Recapturing all of that muddy silt and replacing it on the hill terraces is hard work and costly in human energy, but it gives human beings places where they fit into the order that we share with the rest of the world. We have points of entry. We have things we can change. Someday, we'll even change the way we exchange the silt energy. There's an essential relationship between change and exchange that we have learned to appreciate and use."

Mieri felt like crying. She had spent fifteen years in the single-minded pursuit of her profession and all for what purpose? She said, "Other cities have been cured of worse than this."

Bjska stared meditatively at the darkening city. The sun had moved onto the horizon while he and Mieri talked. Now, its light painted orange streamers on the clouds in the west. There would be good weather on the morrow, provided the old mariners' saying was correct. The city had become a maze of lights in a bowl of darkness, with the snow peaks behind it reflecting the sunset. Even in this transition moment, the place blended with its environment in such a way that the human resisted any disturbance, even with his own words. Silence choked him—dangerous silence.

Mieri felt a breaking tension within her, a product of her training and not of her city. The city had been her flesh, but was no longer.

"Humans have always been restless animals," Bjska said. "A good thing, too. We both know what's wrong here. There's such a thing as too much comfort, too much beauty. Life requires the continuing struggle. That may be the only basic law in the *living* universe."

Again, she sensed personal threat in his words. Bjska had become a dark shadow against the city's lights. *Too much beauty!* That spoke of the context in which the beauty existed, against which the beauty stood out. It was not the beauty itself, but the lack of tensions in this context. She said, "Don't offer me any false hopes."

"I offer you no hopes at all," he said. "That's not the function of a City Doctor. We just make sure the generative tensions continue. If there are walls, we break them down. But walls happen. To try to prevent them can lead us into absolutes. How long have outsiders learned to love your city only to hate it?"

She tried to swallow in a throat suddenly dry.

"How long?" he insisted.

She forced herself to answer. "At first, when I saw hate, I asked why, but people denied it."

"Of course they did!"

"I doubted my own senses at times," she said. "Then I noted that the most talented among us moved away. Always, it was for good reasons. It was so noticeable, though, that our Council Chairman said it was cause for celebration when I returned here for my internship. I hadn't the heart to tell him it wasn't my doing, that you had sent me."

"How did they react when you told them I was coming?"

She cleared her throat. "You understand I had made some suggestions for *adjustments* within the city, changes in flow patterns and such."

"Which were not taken seriously," he said.

"No. They wonder at my discontent." She stared across at the lights. It was full dark now. Night birds hummed after insects above them. "The hate has been going on for many years. I know that's why you sent me here."

"We need all of the City Doctors we can generate," he said. "We need you."

She recognized the "we" in his statement with mounting terror. That was the species talking through a City Doctor whose powers had been tempered in action. The individual could be transformed or shattered by that "we."

"The Councilmen only wanted to be comforted," she protested, but a voice within her pleaded: *Comfort me, comfort me, comfort me.* She knew Bjska heard that other voice.

"How naive of them," he said, "to want to be told that truth is untruth, that what the senses report must not be believed." He inhaled a deep breath. "Truth changes so rapidly that it's dangerous to look only in one direction. This is an infinite universe."

Mieri heard her teeth chattering, tried to still them. Fear drove her now and not the sudden cold of nightfall. She felt a trembling all through her body. Something Bjska had once said came back to her now: *"It requires a certain kind of abandoned courage even to* want *to be a City Doctor."*

Do I have that courage? she asked herself. *Humanity help me! Will I fail now?*

Bjska, turning to face her in the darkness, detected a faint odor of burning. Someone from the city had a forbidden fire somewhere along the beaches. The tension of protest rode on that odor and he wondered if that tension carried the kind of hope that could be converted into life. Mieri no longer was visible in the darkness. Night covered the perfection of her beauty and the clothing that was like armor in its subtle harmonizing with her flesh. Could she ask *how* rather than *why*? Would she make the required transition?

He waited, tense and listening.

"Some of them will always hate," she whispered.

She knows, he thought. He said, "The sickness of a city reaches far beyond its boundaries."

Mieri clenched her fists, trembling. *"The arm is not sick without the body being sick."* Bjska had said that once. And: *"A single human unloved can set the universe afire."*

"Life is in the business of constructing dichotomies," she told herself. "And all dichotomies lead to contradictions. Logic that is sound for a finite system is not necessarily sound for an infinite system."

The words from the City Doctors' creed restored a measure of her calm. She said, "It'll take more than a few adjustments."

"It's like a backfire with which our ancestors stopped a runaway grass fire," he said. "You give them a bad case of discontent. No comfort whatsoever except that you love the human in each of them. Some contradictions *do* lead to ugliness."

He heard her moving in the darkness. Cloth ripped. Again. He wondered: *Which of the infinite alternatives has she chosen?* Would she scar the brittle armor of her beauty?

"I will begin by relocating the most contented half of the city's population," she said.

I will . . . he thought. It was always thus the City Doctor began his creation.

"There's no profit in adjusting their memories," she said. "They're more valuable just as they are. Their present content will be the measure of their future energies."

Again, he heard her clothing rip. What was she doing?

She said, "I will, of course, move in with you during this period and present at least the appearance of being your mistress. They will hate that."

He sensed the energy she had required to overcome personal barriers and he willed himself to remain silent. She must win this on her own, decide on her own.

"If you love me, it will be more than appearance," she said. "We have no guarantee that we will create only beauty, but if we create with love and if our creation generates new life, then we can love... and we will go on living."

He felt the warmth of her breath on his face. She had moved closer without his hearing! He willed himself to remain immobile.

"If the people of the city must hate, and some of them always will," she said, "better they hate us than one another."

He felt a bare arm go around his neck; her lips found his cheek. "I will save *our* city," she said, "and I don't believe you will hate me for it."

Bjska relaxed, enfolded her unarmored flesh in his arms. He said, "We begin with unquestioning love for each other. That is a very good prescription, Doctor, my love, as long as there remains sufficient energy to support the next generation. Beauty be damned! Life requires a point of entry."

FROGS
AND
SCIENTISTS

Two frogs were counting the minnows in a hydroponics trough one morning when a young maiden came down to the water to bathe. "What's that?" one frog (who was called Lavu) asked the other. "That's a human female," said Lapat, for that was the other frog's name.

"What is she doing?" Lavu asked.

"She is taking off her garments," Lapat said.

"What are garments?" Lavu asked.

"An extra skin humans wear to conceal themselves from the gaze of strangers," said Lapat.

"Then why is she taking off her extra skin?" Lavu asked.

"She wants to bathe her primary skin," Lapat said. "See how she piles her garments beside the trough and steps daintily into the water.

"She is oddly shaped," Lavu said.

"Not for a human female," Lapat said. "All of them are shaped that way."

"What are those two bumps on her front?" Lavu asked.

"I have often pondered that question," Lapat said. "As we both know, function follows form and vice versa. I have seen human males clasp their females in a crushing embrace. It is my observation that the two bumps are a protective cushion."

"Have you noticed," Lavu asked, "that there is a young male human watching her from the concealment of the control station?"

"That is a common occurrence," Lapat said. "I have seen it many times."

"But can you explain it?" Lavu asked.

"Oh, yes. The maiden seeks a mate; that is the real reason she comes here to display her primary skin. The male is a possible mate, but he watches from concealment because if he were to show himself, she would have to scream, and that would prevent the mating."

"How is it you know so many things about humans?" Lavu asked.

"Because I pattern my life after the most admirable of all humans, the scientist."

"What's a scientist?" Lavu asked.

"A scientist is one who observes without interfering. By observation alone all things are made clear to the scientist. Come, let us continue counting the minnows."

About the Author

Journalist, ecologist, conservationist and bestselling novelist Frank Herbert has captured the imagination of an entire generation. Novels like THE DOSADI EXPERIMENT and THE WHITE PLAGUE have explored science's effect on society. THE GREEN BRAIN and THE DRAGON IN THE SEA introduced Herbert's main theme: how societies and individuals respond to changing or threatening environments. In DUNE, winner of both the Hugo and Nebula awards, Herbert expanded this theme to create a landscape so complex that even six books have not exhausted its richness. The DUNE series has fascinated more readers than any other contemporary work of the imagination and it continues to delight in the latest volume, CHAPTER-HOUSE: DUNE.

Among Frank Herbert's other works are THE EYES OF HEISENBERG; SANTAROGA BARRIER; WHIPPING STAR: PROJECT 40; THRESHOLD, and two anthologies of his short fiction. The fifth DUNE novel, HERETICS OF DUNE was published in 1984. WITHOUT ME, YOU'RE NOTHING, a collaboration with Max Barnard, expressed Herbert's thoughts about the potential dangers of government use of computers in the context of a computer primer.

About the Artist

Jim Burns in his own words

I must print up a definitive biography! I'm continually being asked to jot down the unimaginably tedious details of my life so far! I was born unspectacularly in Cardiff, South Wales on April 10th, 1948. My undramatic entry into life was followed by a number of equally undramatic years (Nobody was drowned as the picture postcard says.) until 1966 when, at the age of 18, I left Basseleg Grammar School and entered the Royal Air Force as a trainee pilot. During the next 18 months I managed to solo fly piston-engined De Havilland Chipmunks and Hunting Jet Provosts, but despite all my attempts at hoodwinking flying instructors into believing that I was the reincarnation of Von Richtofen, there was ultimately no disguising the fact that I was a lousy pilot. Given the option to switch to some other non-flying training or get the hell out, I got the hell out. God I was miserable! All I'd wanted to do as a kid was hurl iron-mongery around the sky. Somebody had given me the toys and now had snatched them away again with the absolute promise that there was *no way* I'd be given them back!

But I don't think I ever made a wiser decision really. The idea in the back of my head when I opted to leave the RAF was that I should get myself into art college and follow my other love in life—painting pictures. At school they had all said I should have been doing that anyway. They were right.

Having the best part of a year to fill before commencing the course I'd successfully applied for on the basis of a few wretched scribbles retrieved from a dusty drawer in my old school art department and one or two pretentious new efforts, I earned a bit of cash at a U.S. Army depot in Caerwent, South Wales. This was in 1968. The scintillating work offered me was as an "Inventory Clerk" to locate and count up on the various "pads" around the depot all the different rounds of ammunition. After 30,000 rounds or so, 155mm howitzer shells get *very* boring indeed!

Then, in September 1968, I enrolled for one year at Newport College of Art, South Wales, and completed the Foundation Course there. Fancying a move away from the Land of my Fathers to the Big Smoke, I applied successfully to St. Martins

School of Art in London and commenced a three year course in graphic design there in 1969.

I don't want to be too hard on the place as I had a *good* time and met my future wife, Sue. She was a "proper" painter — canvas, oil paints and all that mystical sort of stuff — whilst I was a singularly mediocre would-be illustrator who worked in coloured pencils much as my own small children do now.

Round about May or June, 1972, John Spencer of the Young Artists agency paid a visit to the college and looked at the various "Diploma Shows" on exhibit. Well blow me down, if he didn't offer me the chance of some work! At the same time the college gave me almost the lowest pass possible. But I was one of the lucky ones. I took up John Spencer's offer and I think I learned more about the business of professional illustration in the first month than in the whole previous three years. I've been with the same agency ever since. Since 1980 more and more of my work has been for U.S. clients. Being a very slow worker, that's pretty fortunate as they pay substantially more than their British counterparts. The work has evolved through periods of painting in gouache, oils and currently, acrylics. It's only very recently that I've taken on any black-and-white work. In fact, EYE represents my first large scale project in that medium.

Most of my work is still for the book jacket market; "cover art" as it is called in the States. Occasionally different projects pop up. I spent ten weeks in Los Angeles in 1980 working on the film BLADE RUNNER. The inappropriateness of oil paint prompted my switch to acrylics. I've also done a variety of interesting projects with Sir Clive Sinclair, the British computer boffin, in particular some design work on his various electric vehicle projects. Currently I'm working on an anthology of my collected efforts to be published by Dragon's World in the spring of 1986.

I presently live in southeast London with my wife Sue and our three daughters, Elinor, Megan and Gwendolen, but we anticipate a move to a more rural backdrop "real soon."

About the Illustrations

by Jim Burns

'The Touaregs, who are the Berber lords, were haughty beyond words ... If they deigned to look down on you, it was with a stare in which fearless hostility and fearless curiosity seemed at a hairtrigger balance ... Since they swathe their heads in a turban and veil the lower parts of their faces, all you see of them is their eyes, which are the most remarkable in both colour and setting I have ever seen.'

I came across this quotation from TIMBUCTOO (Leland Hall, 1934) about the time I was pondering the alternatives open to me in tackling the illustrated part of the project you now hold in your hands in the form of the book EYE. In the epic of perverted theocracy that is DUNE, I have been struck time and again by the parallels between the real-life Touaregs of North Africa and the fictional Dune Fremen. Of course, this is not a novel discovery. Repeated allusions through words like 'Jihad', 'Mahdi', 'Zensunni', etc., are evidence enough of Herbert's hints at the possible directions of the near future and the role perhaps to be played in it by the followers of Islam. The equation between melange, the Fremen and a Universal dependency, and oil, the oil-rich Arab states and a Global dependency has always struck me as a pretty shrewd observation, particularly given that DUNE was written a good half-dozen years or more before we buried our noses in A BLUEPRINT FOR SURVIVAL!

Anyway, to come more to the point; I've always relished the prospect of painting in a straightforward but dramatic manner a portrait of a Fremen. The opportunity arose with this commission. It wasn't what was being asked for but I couldn't resist making at least a tentative, later to be accepted, suggestion. The title suggested it as much as anything, the coming together of the words *Frank Herbert* and *Eye* immediately conjured up in *my* mind's eye the 'blue in blue' of melange addiction. (By the way, did you know that wealthy Touareg men wear veils stained with an indigo dye, which is *beaten* into the cloth due to the lack of water? This dye rubs off easily on to their skin and permeates it, earning the Touareg the name, "blue men of the desert.")

Just about this time I saw the film version of DUNE, which Frank Herbert discusses earlier in this book. Well, to me it's a curate's egg of a movie, but I enjoyed it a lot. Like many films, it had a lot going for it and a few things which rankled. A major rankle was the thoroughly un-Touareg–like Fremen! It's just my personal interpretation, but I reckon Frank Herbert's Fremen are more like the desert-evolved being on the cover of this book than the G-suited characters of the big screen!

In more than a decade of illustrating science fiction, I must have read hundreds of science fiction novels, novellas, short story collections etc. (I always try to read the stuff I illustrate — one owes that much to any writer I think — to convey on the cover at least a semblance of some aspect of the world contained within.) Amongst these are quite a few Frank Herberts, but I have to admit to a gap in my reading vis-a-vis his short stories. So I came to know all the material contained in this volume. Suffice it to say that each one presented a novel challenge so far as an appropriate image was concerned. Each was quite distinct from the other and all were a joy to read. I think in the end there is enough variation in the images to do some small justice to the richness that is Frank Herbert's imagination and I for one am glad to have caught up with a glaring omission in my science fiction reading.

Then there is "THE ROAD TO DUNE." Byron Preiss, the editor of EYE, suggested a collaboration between myself and Frank Herbert that would be in the tradition of Hiroshige's 52 STATIONS OF THE TOKAIDO, that is, an artist's view of a progression of places. I was put in mind of a pub down the Old Kent Road called THE WORLD TURNED UPSIDE-DOWN and its painted sign with the image of a huge fish standing on a river bank with a rod in its fin/hand. Dangling at the end of the line is a freshly hooked angler. I was reminded of this as I tried to tackle THE ROAD TO DUNE. The opportunity was sort of a privilege, but good grief! So difficult! Embarras de richesses! I would have to extract from DUNE's dense potpourri some singular aspect, and convey in a short series of black-and-white illustrations some hint of an integrated story line, all the while regarding myself as some kind of itinerant artist sketching madly through some yet-to-be Frank Herbert, DUNE-related scenario!

Well, a project like that could take months. The bywaters merely hinted at in the series of novels each conveyed rich tapestries of their own. What about the Sardaukar and their ghastly home planet, Salusa Secundus? Perhaps we should know a little more about the Harkonnens and life on old Giedi Prime. The Bene Gesserit, yes, far too mysterious a bunch. We could investigate them a little and uncover a few more of their plots and intrigues. Surely there are half a dozen books waiting to be written about the Butlerian Jihad alone! No, too broad a brush required for all those possibilities.

But I couldn't resist the Tleilaxu. Here was a weird crew if ever there were one. The enigmatic technocrats who steered a barely tolerated line past the dictates of the Butlerian creed. Yes, let's go ahead, thought I — and then I met someone who had read the recently released HERETICS OF DUNE and who suggested to me that all my embryonic ideas were way off beam and that the Tleilaxu weren't in the tiniest bit anything like the beings I was about the depict!

So that's how I came to the subject I eventually tackled. I would be an artist in residence in the Palace at Arrakeen, single most colossal structure in all of human history. As I write this, the pictures are nearing completion and I don't envy Frank Herbert one bit the job of weaving something new around them. But I must say that in working through the various sketches, reading extracts from the different DUNE books, I have begun to appreciate the scale of this edifice.—"Designed to reduce a pilgrim's soul to motedom!"—ultimately though, big as it is, it's only a building. Frank Herbert's DUNE myth is far, far bigger. I look forward to one day tackling some other neglected corner of his great yarn!